Herbert Maxwell

**The Life of Wellington**

Vol. 2

Herbert Maxwell

**The Life of Wellington**
*Vol. 2*

ISBN/EAN: 9783337813604

Printed in Europe, USA, Canada, Australia, Japan

Cover: Foto ©Raphael Reischuk / pixelio.de

More available books at **www.hansebooks.com**

# The Life of Wellington

# CONTENTS OF VOL. II.

## CHAPTER I.

### LIGNY AND QUATRE-BRAS. 1815.

## CHAPTER II.

### THE SEVENTEENTH OF JUNE. 1815.

## CHAPTER III.

### WATERLOO. 18th June, 1815.

## CHAPTER IV.

### THE ARMY OF OCCUPATION. 1815–1818.

## CHAPTER V.

### WELLINGTON AS CABINET MINISTER. 1818–1822.

## CHAPTER VI.

### The Feud with Canning. 1822–1827.

## CHAPTER VII.

### The Duke as Prime Minister. 1828–1829.

## CHAPTER VIII.

### THE EVE OF REFORM. 1830–1831.

## CHAPTER IX.

### THE BATTLE OF REFORM. 1831–1834.

## CHAPTER X.

### AFTER THE STORM. 1834–1839.

## CHAPTER XI.

### THE CORN LAWS. 1840–1846.

## CHAPTER XII.

### LAST DAYS. 1848–1852.

# LIST OF ILLUSTRATIONS.

——◦◦◦——

# LIST OF MAPS AND BATTLE PLANS.

———◦———

*₊* *Such of the Maps and Plans in this work as are printed by Messrs. W. & A. K. Johnston, of Edinburgh, are given by permission of Messrs. Wm. Blackwood & Sons, of Edinburgh and London. The Map of Belgium (vol. ii. p. 2) is taken from M. Houssaye's " Waterloo," by permission of MM. Perrin et Cie, Paris, and Messrs. A. and C. Black, London, and the Plan of Waterloo (vol. ii. p. 64) has been altered and adapted from one in the same work.*

# THE LIFE OF WELLINGTON.

## CHAPTER I.

### LIGNY AND QUATRE-BRAS.

### 1815.

THE Duke of Wellington had an interview with Prince Blücher on 3rd May at Tirlemont, and came to a good understanding with him.* It had become evident by this

The Allies assume defensive positions.

* *Despatches*, xii. 345.

time that the Allies would have to receive the attack. Although the forces of both Wellington and Blücher were much scattered, covering about one hundred miles of frontier, they were more capable of concentration than is apparent at first sight. Each of Blücher's four corps could assemble at its own headquarters within twelve hours; little more would have sufficed to concentrate his whole army at Namur; while in thirty hours it could form line of battle at any point threatened with attack. Wellington's cantonments were more distantly extended, but they formed a segment of a circle round Brussels, whence his reserve could be moved along excellent roads to strengthen any part of the line, upon which two-thirds of his whole force might be concentrated within twenty-four hours. Orders could be conveyed within six hours from his headquarters in Brussels to any part of his army. As early as 30th April, when it first became apparent that the position of the Russian and Austrian armies made it necessary to yield the initiative to Napoleon, Wellington drew up a secret memorandum for the guidance of the Prince of Orange, Lord Hill, Lord Uxbridge,* commanding the cavalry, and Sir W. de Lancey, the Quartermaster-General.† There were three main routes leading from France to Belgium along which Napoleon might direct his attack—the paved roads of Charleroi, Mons, and Tournay. On the first route there were no fortifications, the defences designed for Charleroi not being in an advanced state; but those at Mons, Tournay, and Ath, formerly destroyed by the revolutionary armies, had been repaired, and must have been taken or masked by an enemy invading on either of these routes—a serious consideration for Napoleon, whose army was so greatly inferior in numbers to the Allies. Nevertheless Wellington so confidently expected that he would choose one or both of the more northern roads, that he placed his best troops on the right, massing his

---

\* Afterwards Marquis of Anglesey.

† Killed at Waterloo. His rank was that of Deputy-Quartermaster-General, but he was the senior in his department.

# GENERAL MAP

reproduced from HENRY HOUSSAYE'S

## "CAMPAGNE DE 1815"

BY PERMISSION OF M.M. PERRIN ET CIᵉ PARIS,
AND MESSʳˢ A.& C.BLACK,LONDON

Scale.

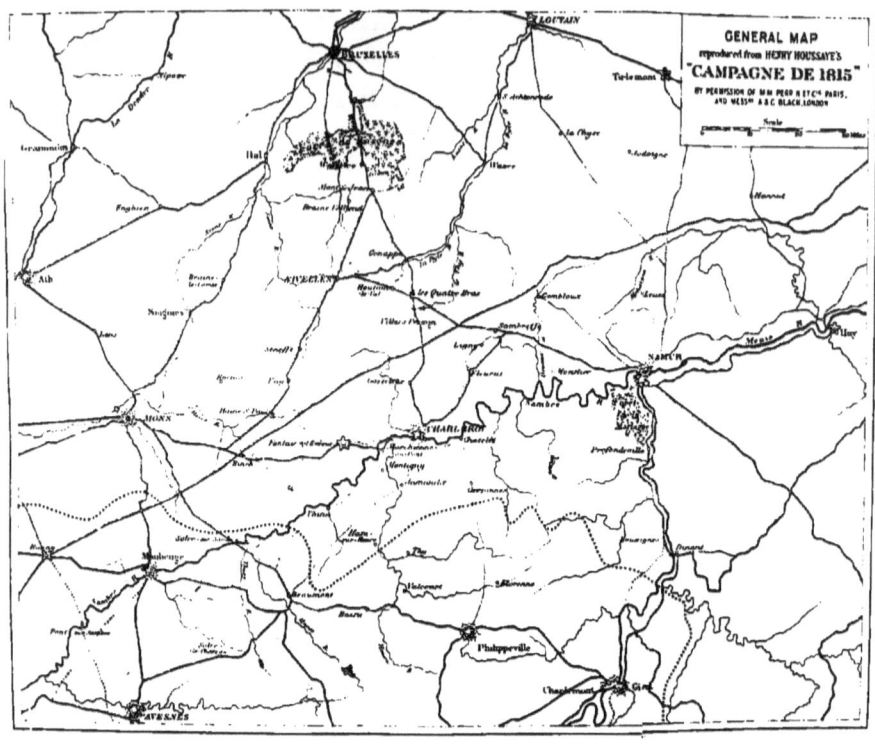

cavalry in that direction also, at Grammont, and moving the A$_{NN.}$ 1815. Dutch and Belgian divisions to the left of his position next the Prussian right. He was convinced that the attack should have been made by way of Mons rather than by the Meuse and the Sambre, and he maintained that opinion all his life.[*]

Up to the latest moment before his final advance Napoleon Skilful masked his real intention, by maintaining detachments along manœuvres by Napothe whole Franco-Belgian frontier. The regular troops gar- leon. risoning the fortresses were secretly withdrawn and replaced by National Guards, and it was not till 13th June that Major-General Sir Hussey Vivian discovered that he had opposite to him at Tournay, not a French cavalry picket, but a handful of custom-house officials, who made no secret that the army was concentrating at Maubeuge. Napoleon left Paris at daybreak on 12th June; on the 14th his head-quarters were at Beaumont, about sixteen miles south of Charleroi, the whole of his forces being well within reach of his personal command. The corps of Gérard, 16,000 strong, bivouacked before Philippeville, forming the right wing. The centre, composed of two corps of the Imperial Guard under Vandamme and Lobau, 66,000 men, lay at Beaumont; and the left wing, composed of 44,000 men of the two corps of d'Erlon and Reille, was posted on the Sambre at Solre-sur-Sambre. On arriving to take command of the army, the Emperor—Emperor not only *de facto* but *de jure*, for his titles had been secured to him when he was interned in Elba—issued one of those stirring proclamations by which he knew so well how to exalt the spirit of his soldiers. Herein Salamanca and Vitoria were but named to recall what evils might happen when he placed the command on lieutenants; on the anniversary of Marengo and Friedland he summoned Frenchmen to revive the glories of Austerlitz and Wagram, of Jena and Montmirail. "To every Frenchman who has a heart," he cried, "the moment is arrived to conquer or to die!"

---

[*] See the Duke's memorandum on Waterloo, written in 1846 (*Suppl. Despatches*, x. 513).

ÆT. 46.

In spite of this demonstration on his left, Wellington, believing it to be a feint, still expected the attack to come by way of Mons.

**Napoleon's plan of campaign.** A great deal has been written about Napoleon's intentions and choice of a route in advancing upon his objective—Brussels; and it does not encourage one to find that the two able writers who have most lately applied themselves to the study of this campaign have arrived at opposite conclusions. On the one hand, M. Houssaye is filled with just admiration of *la belle opération stratégique* conceived by the Emperor before he left Paris, by which he should steer his attack upon the point of contact between the armies of Wellington and Blücher and wedge them asunder, to be dealt with thereafter in detail.* On the other hand, Mr. Ropes has collected evidence to prove that Napoleon never entertained the idea of thrusting himself between the two armies, but marched against the Prussian left because he believed that Wellington's divisions could not concentrate so rapidly as Blücher's corps, and that he would have time to defeat the Prussians before the Allies could be on the ground in force.† In support of this view, which is opposed to that taken by almost every other historian, Mr. Ropes claims the support of the German critic Clausewitz; of Wellington, as interpreted by Lord Ellesmere; and of Napoleon himself. Clausewitz may be dismissed as balanced by Alison, Jomini, Charras, and a host of other writers; the reveries of Napoleon at St. Helena, where he had access to no sources of information outside his own memory, are well known to have led him beyond the limits of fact; and as for Wellington, one cannot but call to mind a conversation repeated by Croker. Mr. Gleig said something about "Buonaparte's plans of campaign." "Pooh!" interjected the Duke, "he *had* no general preconceived idea of a campaign. In one of his campaigns, that of 1809, General Wrede, the Bavarian, commanded the army until the arrival of Buonaparte. When

---

* *Houssaye*, 99, 131.        † *Ropes*, 3-15.

the Emperor came, Wrede expressed a hope that the measures
he had taken might be found to fall in with his Imperial
Majesty's plan of campaign. Buonaparte immediately said
that he never had a general plan of campaign; that he
collected his forces together as well as he could, and then
acted *pro re nata*, as he thought best, adding that Wrede had
done exactly what he could have wished by concentrating
the army as much as possible, and handing it over to him to
be employed according to the circumstances of the moment.
This," added the Duke, "I had from Wrede himself." *
There is also a passage in the Duke's conversations with
Lady Salisbury which shows that Mr. Ropes has put too
implicit faith on Lord Ellesmere's interpretation, and that the
Duke fully believed that Napoleon deliberately tried to force
the English and Prussians asunder. "Napoleon," said he,
"committed a great mistake in endeavouring to cut in
between the Prussians and the English. He ought to have
gone along the direct road by Mons." †

Having, then, determined before leaving Paris to possess
himself of Brussels, it seems rather fruitless to pursue
inquiry as to the exact moment when Napoleon decided on
the best means of accomplishing this. From the moment
when he arrived at Beaumont, his mark was where his
adversaries were weakest and least able to concentrate
rapidly—the point of junction between the Prussian and
Anglo-Belgian lines, through which lay what seemed to him
the easiest way to Brussels. Curiosity about the exact
sequence of his intentions is merged in admiration of the

---

* *Croker*, ii. 123. Lady Salisbury also repeats this anecdote from the Duke's
conversation. "When General Wrede," said the Duke, "asked Napoleon before
the battles of Eylau and Friedland what was his plan of campaign, 'Je n'en
ai pas,' answered the Emperor; 'je n'ai point de plan de campagne.' And it was
true: he had no plan: all he required was that his troops should be assembled
and posted as he directed, and then he marched, and struck a great blow,
defeated the enemy, and acted afterwards as circumstances would allow "
(*Salisbury MSS.*, 1838).

† *Salisbury MSS.*, 1838.

Æt. 46.

The French cross the Sambre.

faultlessness of their execution. By the evening of the day after his arrival at Beaumont, Napoleon had led his army across the Sambre, captured Charleroi, advanced twenty miles into Belgian territory, and bivouacked with 124,000 men disposed in a triangle between the points of Campinaire, Gosselies, and Charleroi. Whether such had been Napoleon's deliberate purpose or not, the wedge had been inserted, to be driven home on the morrow. Of his purpose at the moment

Arrival of Marshal Ney.

there is further evidence. During the afternoon had arrived at the French headquarters one who was destined to play a leading part in the events of the next few days. Marshal Ney had been received back into the Imperial service; the Emperor affected to have forgotten the ugly incident of the iron cage; but he left him without a command in the army of invasion. Napoleon, however, had a kindly feeling for *la bête noire*, as he now called the Marshal; on 11th June he wrote to Davout, bidding him say to Ney that if he wished to be present in the first battles, he must report himself at Avesnes on the 14th. Ney required no second summons; following the Emperor from Beaumont, he overtook him at Charleroi. "Good morning, Ney," was Napoleon's abrupt

The Emperor gives him command of the left wing.

greeting. "I am glad to see you. You will take command of the 1st and 2nd Corps d'armée. I give you also the light cavalry of my Guard, but do not employ them. To-morrow you will be joined by Kellermann's cuirassiers. Go and drive the enemy along the road to Brussels and take up a position at Quatre-Bras." Read in connection with this the *Bulletin de l'Armée*, issued at Charleroi on the evening of 15th June—"The Emperor has given command of the left wing to the Prince of Moskowa (Ney), who has fixed his headquarters at Quatre-Bras on the road to Brussels"—and most people will agree with M. Houssaye that further evidence as to the Emperor's immediate intention is unnecessary. He meant to force his way to Brussels between the two armies opposed to him, and in dictating this order on the evening of the 15th, assumed—or pretended to assume—

that Ney had done his part by establishing himself at Quatre- ANN. 1815.
Bras. After giving the left wing to Ney, the Emperor
removed Grouchy from command of the cavalry, and verbally And com-
gave him the right wing, with instructions to take possession mand of
the right
of Fleurus; but, after Gilly had been taken, Vandamme, wing to
commanding the 3rd Corps, declared his men were tired, Grouchy.
and refused to advance further under orders of the General
of cavalry.

Ney, also, failed to possess himself of Quatre-Bras.
General de Perponcher, commanding the Dutch-Belgian
division on Wellington's extreme left, being convinced that
the enemy's attack was no feint, as had been at first supposed,
took on himself the responsibility, the Prince of Orange being
absent in Brussels, of placing the brigade of Prince Bernhard
of Saxe-Weimar at Quatre-Bras, instead of moving it, as he
had received orders to do, to Nivelles. Consequently, when
Ney's advanced guard arrived late in the evening at Frasnes,
they found Quatre-Bras occupied by a Nassau battalion and
a battery of horse artillery. The French had been under
arms since two in the morning; the very names, still more
the characters, of Ney's officers were unknown to him, and,
in a happy hour for the Allies, he decided to do no more that
night. Had he persevered, it is difficult to believe that the
weak detachment before him could have held their position,
and the whole character of the campaign must have been
altered. That it was not so altered, that the wedge was not
driven home that night, was not due to Wellington's dispositions, but to the prompt and unauthorised action of
General de Perponcher.

A sinister event marked the opening of the campaign for Desertion
the 4th French Corps. On the morning of the 15th, General of General
Bourmont.
Bourmont, commanding its leading division, deserted to the
enemy with his whole staff. Gérard had declared to the
Emperor that he would answer for his friend's fidelity with
his head. " Cette tête, donc, c'est à moi, n'est pas ? " said
Napoleon, playfully tapping Gérard on the cheek after

receiving his report of Bourmont's treachery, adding more gravely, " mais j'en ai trop besoin." On reaching the Prussian headquarters, Bourmont received a cold reception from Prince Blücher, who would not deign to speak to the renegade, although he had important intelligence to give.

The situation in Brussels.

The position of matters at the allied headquarters in Brussels now claims attention. By some misadventure or carelessness, which can never be explained now, the Duke of Wellington received no information of the French advance till three in the afternoon. The Prussians had been engaged since four in the morning; General Müffling, who was attached to the Duke's staff, has explained that General von Zieten, as soon as he was attacked, sent an officer off to Brussels, who arrived at 3 p.m., and that he, Müffling, at once apprised the Duke.* But from Charleroi to Brussels is only thirty miles; how did that officer spend eleven hours on the road? Above all, how did the Prince of Orange, commander of the left wing of the army, who ought to have been at the front, happen to be in Brussels, dining with the Duke of Wellington, when the news did at last arrive? Undoubtedly here is ground for the allegation, so indignantly repudiated by those who permit no reflection on their hero's infallibility, that Wellington was taken by surprise.

The Duke's orders to the army.

Müffling asked Wellington where he would assemble his army, observing that Blücher would certainly concentrate on Ligny. The Duke replied that he must wait for advice from Mons before fixing the rendezvous, but that he would order

---

* It well illustrates the value of evidence, and, at the same time, the kind of despair which almost overwhelms one who wishes to sift out of it the truth, that Sir William Napier, the historian of the Peninsular War, stated that it was Müffling himself who bore the message from Blücher to Wellington on 15th June. " I feel," he begins, " that I do not throw away what I am going to tell you, and it is from the Duke's mouth." He then quotes the Duke as having said, " I cannot tell the world that Blücher picked out the fattest man in his army to ride with an express to me, and that he took thirty hours to go thirty miles " (*Waterloo Letters*, No. 1). Müffling, of course, was in Brussels all day, being the Prussian Commissioner at the British headquarters, and received Von Zieten's express when it arrived, at last, from the front.

all to be ready to march at a moment's notice. Two hours later the Duke sent orders to his army to concentrate on its left; not on Quatre-Bras, however, where the main road from Charleroi to Brussels passed through his lines, but at Nivelles, seven miles to the west of that road.* Next, Müffling received a second despatch from the front, from Marshal Blücher this time, announcing that he was concentrating on Sombreffe, close to Ligny. The Duke approved, but still refused to fix his place of assembly before he heard from Mons.

"I went to my quarters," stated Müffling, "towards 10, drew up my report, leaving a place for the name of the rendezvous, and kept a courier's carriage ready at my door. Towards midnight the Duke called and told me, 'I have a report from General Dörnberg at Mons that Napoleon has moved on Charleroi with all his force, and that he, General Dörnberg, has nothing in his front. I have therefore sent orders for the concentration of my people on Nivelles and Quatre-Bras.'" †

There is, however, no mention of Quatre-Bras in these after-orders : ‡ the movement on Nivelles is confirmed. Yet at that moment Ney's advanced guard lay within two miles of Quatre-Bras, which place, had Wellington's orders been obeyed to the letter, the French might have occupied unopposed.

Readers of *Vanity Fair* (and what English man or woman English visitors in Brussels. has foregone the delights stored in Thackeray's masterpiece ?) must have acquired a pretty accurate idea of the state of society in Brussels when Napoleon crossed the Belgian frontier. The town was crowded with fashionable non-combatants. Numbers of English families—some drawn thither

---

* It is significant of the Duke's disbelief in the genuineness of the attack from the south that some of the movements indicated in the afternoon order are not to take place " until it is quite certain that the enemy's attack is upon the right of the Prussian army and the left of the British army " (*Despatches*, xii. 473).

† *Suppl. Despatches*, x. 510.

‡ *Despatches*, xii. 474.

out of solicitude for relatives in the army, others out of simple curiosity and love of excitement—thronged the hotels and lodging-houses.

The Duke of Wellington was most intimate with the Duke of Richmond's family, and the unpublished letters of the Rev. Spencer Madan, private tutor to the young Lennoxes, contain some interesting particulars of these days.

"Brussels, 13th June, 1815.

". . . Though I have given some pretty good reasons for supposing that hostilities will soon commence, yet no one would suppose it, judging by the Duke of Wellington. He appears to be thinking of anything else in the world, gives a ball every week, attends every party, partakes of every amusement that offers. (Yesterday) he took Lady Jane Lennox * to Enghien for the cricket match, and brought her back at night, apparently having gone for no other object but to amuse her. At the time Buonaparte was said to be at Maubeuge, thirty or forty miles off.

"14th June, 1815.

"The Duke of Wellington seems to unite those two extremes of character which Shakespeare gives to Henry V.—the hero and the trifler. You may conceive him at one moment commanding the allied armies in Spain or presiding at the conference at Vienna, and at another time sprawling on his back or on all fours upon the carpet playing with the children.

"His judgment is so intuitive that instant decision follows perception; consequently, as nothing dwells long upon his mind, he is enabled to get through an infinity of business without being embarrassed by it or otherwise than perfectly at his ease.

"In the drawing-room before dinner he was playing with the children, who seemed to look up to him as to one on whom they might depend for amusement. When dinner was announced they quitted him with great regret, saying, 'Be sure you remember to send for us the moment dinner is over,' which he promised to do, and was as good as his word."

Feasting and dancing went on every night; the Duke of

* Married Lawrence Peel, younger brother of the Minister, Sir Robert Peel.

Wellington had fixed 21st June as the date for a grand ball
he intended to give, but the Duchess of Richmond anticipated
him by selecting the 15th for her ball. The Duke of Richmond,* though a general officer, was in Brussels like many
other gentlemen, merely as a civilian spectator—an interested
one, indeed, for he had three sons in the army; one, Lord
March, on the Prince of Orange's staff, another, Lord George,
on the Duke's, and a third in the Blues. The Duchess's
brother, the last Duke of Gordon, was Colonel-in-Chief of
the 3rd (Scots) Regiment of Guards, while the 92nd Gordon
Highlanders,† with the 42nd and 79th Highlanders, formed
part of the 5th Division stationed as the reserve in Brussels.
Desiring to show her foreign guests a Highland reel, the
Duchess of Richmond engaged some of the sergeants and
privates of the 42nd and 92nd to perform one for their
entertainment. Before the summer sun had quenched the
ball-room lights, these poor fellows were trudging southwards,
some of them never to return.

Now it has been asserted that the Duke of Wellington,
although perfectly aware of Napoleon's movements, determined
to attend this ball in order to reassure people about the safety
of Brussels. General Müffling quotes him as having said at
midnight, after communicating to him the intelligence from
Mons, "The numerous friends of Napoleon (in Brussels)
will be on tiptoe; the well intentioned must be pacified;
let us therefore go to the Duchess of Richmond's ball, and
start for Quatre-Bras at 5 a.m."

---

* As soon as Wellington's promotion to Field Marshal gave him seniority over
the Duke of Richmond, that nobleman chivalrously offered to serve under his
former junior and secretary at the Irish Office—an offer which somewhat
embarrassed the Horse Guards, inasmuch as the Duke of Richmond had no
experience of active service.

† This fine regiment was raised by the fourth Duke of Gordon towards the
close of the eighteenth century. Recruits came in slowly at first; it is said that
only about a dozen men had been enrolled, when the Duchess, a celebrated
beauty and madcap, undertook to fill the ranks if the recruiting were left to her.
She gave out that every man who would take the King's shilling should receive
it in his lips from between hers. The story goes that in a very short time the
complement was complete.

Granted, then, that this was the Duke's object in attending a ball at such a moment, and permitting his officers to attend it, is there not proof in this that he was not aware of Napoleon's movements? All he knew was what he wrote to the Duc de Feltre at 10 p.m., that the Prussian posts at Thuin had been attacked, but that no news had reached him from Charleroi later than 9 o'clock in the morning, *two hours before it was captured by the enemy.* Picton still lay in Brussels with the reserve of the army, under orders to march, indeed, at short notice; but, had Wellington known the condition of affairs at the front, it would have been halfway to Quatre-Bras before the ball began. Had he realised that Napoleon's advanced guard was bivouacked within two miles of the left of his army, is it possible that he would have loitered or have permitted the Prince of Orange, to whom that left was entrusted, to loiter among the fiddles and champagne? Is it likely that Lord Hill, commandant of the right wing of the army, that Lord Uxbridge, commandant of the cavalry, that the Generals Picton, Ponsonby, Clinton, Byng, Cooke, Kempt, Pack, Maitland, and others would have been content to be absent from their divisions and brigades had the truth been suspected? It is perfectly clear from his own despatch that Wellington was completely deceived as to the nature of Napoleon's movements.

" I did not hear of these events (the attack on Thuin) till in the evening of the 15th, and I immediately ordered the troops to prepare to march, and afterwards to march to their left, as soon as I had intelligence from other quarters to prove that the enemy's movement on Charleroi was the real attack." *

It is not so certain when the real state of the case was revealed to him. Probably it is true, as reported, that news of the capture of Charleroi reached the Duke in the ball-room, and that he instructed his general officers to leave the place quietly, so as to cause no alarm, and it was then, towards

* *Despatches,* xii. 478.

two in the morning of the 16th, that the reserve was called
to arms and marched off; but it is not known certainly
whether this took place before, during, or after supper, at
which the Duke returned thanks for the toast of the allied
army proposed by General Alava.* Here, at all events, is
testimony from the journal of Lady Hamilton Dalrymple—
one out of hundreds of persons who scrutinised the Duke's
movements and expression on that memorable night.

"Although the Duke affected great gaiety and cheerfulness, it
struck me that I had never seen him have such an expression of
care and anxiety on his countenance. I sat next him on a sopha
a long time, but his mind seemed quite pre-occupied; and although
he spoke to me in the kindest manner possible, yet frequently in
the middle of a sentence he stopped abruptly and called to some
officer, giving him directions, in particular to the Duke of Brunswick and Prince of Orange, who both left the ball before supper.
Despatches were constantly coming in to the Duke . . . however, we remained till half-past two, and when I left the Duke
was still there. . . . At four o'clock in the morning . . . I went
to the window (it was the finest morning possible). I saw the
Highland Brigade marching out to the tune of 'Hieland
Laddie' . . . a number of British regiments followed, then
foreign troops, and at eight o'clock the Duke of Wellington and
his staff passed. . . ."

Even when the Duke left Brussels on the morning of the
16th he had not made up his mind that Quatre-Bras, and not
Nivelles, was to be the point of concentration, which is clear

* The late Sir William Fraser was strongly of opinion that he had identified
this historic ball-room as still in existence; but the late Dowager Lady de
Ros and Lady Louisa Tighe, both of whom were at their mother's ball, were
positive that the building had disappeared, and that the site of it is now
traversed by the Rue des Cendres. The story, so often repeated, that Lady
Louisa Tighe buckled on the Duke's sword before he set out for the front, has
been emphatically contradicted by her ladyship herself, who, happily, is still
alive. It is a pity that M. Houssaye has marred his fine narrative by giving
currency to a tale so misleading as to the Duke's simple character and dislike
of display.

from the fact that Picton had orders to halt the reserve division at Waterloo, where the roads to Nivelles and Quatre-Bras separate. Captain (afterwards General Sir George) Bowles, indeed, in his interesting memorandum of what took place, says that the Duke, before leaving Brussels, had fixed on Quatre-Bras; but the battle which took place a few hours later impressed the minds of men so powerfully with the name of Quatre-Bras, that it found its way into subsequent narratives more easily than any other.

"The Prince of Orange came back suddenly, just as the Duke of Wellington had taken his place at the supper table, and whispered some minutes to his Grace, who only said he had no fresh orders to give, and recommended the Prince to go back to his quarters and go to bed. The Duke of Wellington remained nearly twenty minutes after this, and then said to the Duke of Richmond, 'I think it is time for me to go to bed likewise;' and then, whilst wishing him good night, whispered to ask him if he had a good map in his house. The Duke of Richmond said he had, and took him into his dressing-room,* which opened into the supper-room. The Duke of Wellington shut the door and said, 'Napoleon has *humbugged* me, by G——! he has gained twenty-four hours' march on me.' The Duke of Richmond said, 'What do you intend doing?' The Duke of Wellington replied, 'I have ordered the army to concentrate at Quatre-Bras; but we shall not stop him there, and if so, I must fight him *here*' (at the same time passing his thumb-nail over the position of Waterloo). He then said adieu, and left the house by another way out. He went to his quarters, slept six hours, and breakfasted, and rode at speed to Quatre-Bras. . . . The conversation in the Duke of Richmond's dressing-room was repeated to me, two minutes after it occurred, by the Duke of Richmond, who was to have commanded the reserve, if formed, and to whom I was to have been aide-de-camp. He marked the Duke of Wellington's thumb-nail with his pencil on the map, and we often looked at it together some months afterwards." †

* It was the study.
† *Letters of the first Earl of Malmesbury,* ii. 445. The map was lost when the Duke of Richmond went to Canada.

No orders for the movement of troops on the 16th, or for their concentration upon any point towards the allied left, are extant, subsequent to the after-orders issued at 10 p.m. on the 15th, except those instructions dated 16th June, published in *Despatches*, xii. 474, to which the editor, Colonel Gurwood, appended the following note :—

Ann. 1815.<br>Welling-ton's orders to the army.

" The original instructions issued to Colonel de Lancey (Deputy-Quartermaster-General) were lost with that officer's papers. These memorandums of movements have been collected from the different officers to whom they were addressed."

Now these memoranda are five in number,* four being addressed to Lord Hill and one to Major-General Sir J. Lambert, and it is singular that those writers who have founded upon them the theory that Wellington, before leaving

* (1.)      *To General Lord Hill, G.C.B.*

                              " 16th June, 1815.

" The Duke of Wellington requests that you will move the 2nd Division of infantry upon Braine-le-Comte immediately. The cavalry has been ordered likewise on Braine-le-Comte. His Grace is going to Waterloo."

(2.)               *To the same.*

                              " 16th June, 1815.

" Your Lordship is requested to order Prince Frederick of Orange to move, immediately upon receipt of this order, the 1st Division of the army of the Low Countries, and the Indian Brigade, from Sotteghem to Enghien, leaving 500 men, as before directed, at Audenarde."

(3.)               *To the same.*

                           " Genappe, 16th June, 1815.

" The 2nd Division of infantry to move to-morrow morning at daybreak from Nivelles to Quatre-Bras. The 4th Division of infantry to move at daybreak to-morrow morning to Nivelles."

(4.)               *To the same.*

                              " 16th June, 1815.

" The reserve artillery to move at daybreak to-morrow morning, the 17th, to Quatre-Bras, where it will receive further orders."

(5.)      *To Major-General Sir J. Lambert, K.C.B.*

                              " 16th June, 1815.

" The brigade of infantry under the command of Major-General Sir J. Lambert to march from Assche at daybreak to-morrow morning, the 17th, to Genappe, on the Namur road, and to remain there until further orders."

Brussels, had ordered a concentration upon Quatre-Bras, seem to have overlooked the fact that three of them contain directions for movements to be carried out *not on the 16th but on the 17th;* further, that the only one which bears the place of origin is dated from Genappe, showing that the Duke was far on the road to the front before he issued it. This order, addressed to Lord Hill, directs the movement on the 17th of the 2nd Division from Nivelles to Quatre-Bras, and the 4th Division to Nivelles. This in itself disposes of the allegation that the Duke had issued orders for a concentration on Quatre-Bras before he left the ball-room in the early morning of the 16th. There is more. In one of these five memoranda Lord Hill is informed that the cavalry has been ordered to Braine-le-Comte, seventeen English miles to the west of Quatre-Bras. How is such a disposition to be reconciled with a concentration upon Quatre-Bras? Finally, it is inconsistent with such a concentration having been ordered early on the 16th that Picton remained at Waterloo with his division till after midday,[*] and that the Duke passed and left him there on his way to the front. The Duke, therefore, cannot have issued his final orders for a concentration on Quatre-Bras (which it has been surmised were lost with Sir W. de Lancey's papers) before he himself joined the Prince of Orange at that place.

"I found there the Prince of Orange with a small body of Belgian troops, two or three battalions of infantry, a squadron of Belgian dragoons, and two or three pieces of cannon, which had been at the Quatre-Bras since the preceding evening. It appeared that the picket of this detachment had been touched by a French patrol, and there was some firing, but very little; and of so little importance that, after seeing what was doing, I went on to the Prussian army, which I saw from the ground was assembling upon the field of Saint Amand and Ligny, about eight miles distant."[†]

[*] *Waterloo Letters,* p. 23.　　　　　　[†] *Croker,* iii. 173.

"In the meantime," wrote the Duke in his Waterloo de- Ann. 1815.
spatch, "I had directed the whole army to march upon Les
Quatre-Bras;" and goes on to say that Picton's division
arrived about half-past two. Now, there is a slight inaccuracy
here. We know that Picton's division, though it may have
been sighted at half-past two, did not arrive till half-past
three.* The position of Waterloo—Mont-Saint-Jean—is
just nine English miles from Quatre-Bras, the village of
Waterloo is a couple of miles further. Either distance could
be covered by a mounted officer in less than an hour; but
Picton's division, with guns, could not be reckoned on performing the march in less than three hours. It seems
probable, therefore, that it was not till the Duke had himself
inspected the position at Quatre-Bras, and satisfied himself
that the attack on Ligny was to be a genuine one, that he
issued final orders for the concentration of all his forces on
the Prussian right.

It is clear that the Duke had no right to reckon on Inactivity
Perponcher's weak detachment being left so long in undis- of the French on
turbed possession of Quatre-Bras; being permitted, indeed, the morn-
to regain on the morning of the 16th some of the ground ing of the 16th.
yielded on the 15th. The whole responsibility for this lache
must be borne by Ney. Making every excuse for that
Marshal on the ground that he was but newly arrived, had
been so suddenly placed in command of two corps d'armée,
had been compelled to improvise a staff from among officers
with whom he was imperfectly acquainted, and knew very
little about what Germans would term the "dislocation" of
his forces, the fact remains that he took no measures to
prepare for that advance which Soult, at half-past six in
the morning, informed him was about to be made. His
advanced guard, as we know, had touched Frasnes overnight, but the rest of his divisions were echeloned as far
to the rear as Marchienne-au-Pont, nine miles, and Thuin,
sixteen miles distant. Had Ney's columns been closed

---

* *Waterloo Letters*, p. 24.

to the front at an early hour on the 16th, he would have found nothing before him but Prince Bernhard's Dutch brigade, but at 10 o'clock Ney's troops were not even under arms.[*]

In like manner, if Napoleon had brought up his right into line with his advanced posts—if, in short, his army had bivouacked overnight in line of battle instead of in line of march—only one of the four Prussian corps, General Zieten's, was in position at Ligny to oppose him. Pirch I.'s, on the march from Namur, had only got as far as Onoz and Mazy, six miles from Ligny; Thielemann's was at Namur, fifteen miles off; whereas the fourth Prussian corps, Bülow's, was still at Liége, sixty miles distant. Napoleon had only to form his line of battle to the front early on that morning, and he would have brought 120,000 men to crush one Prussian corps d'armée and one Belgian Dutch brigade. Then he might have turned to demolish the British and Prussian forces as they arrived in succession. Instead of this, no effort was made to bring up the rear divisions from Charleroi and Châtelet till nearly midday on the 16th, when three-fourths of the Prussian army had assembled at Sombreffe and Ligny, and the attack was put off till the afternoon. Ney, on the left, timing his movements by the Emperor's, could but keep up an ineffective skirmish with his advanced guard, wasting the precious hours while the British were assembling before him. *Aliquando dormitant*—Wellington's unpreparedness, or, if that be too harsh a term, his miscalculation, on the 15th, was neutralised by Napoleon's inertness on the 16th; and thus the two greatest commanders of their age each inaugurated by a false move their first encounter with the other.

When Wellington perceived that all was quiet in front of Perponcher's division, he wrote the following letter to Prince Blücher :—

---

[*] *Houssaye*, 187, note.

"On the heights behind Frasne.
"June 16, 1815. 10.30 a.m.

"MY DEAR FÜRST,—My army is situated as follows: The Corps d'Armée of the Prince of Orange has a division here and at Quatre-Bras, and the rest at Nivelles. The Reserve is in march from Waterloo to Genappe, where it will arrive at noon. The English cavalry will be at the same hour at Nivelles. The corps of Lord Hill is at Braine-le-Comte. I do not see any large force of the enemy in front of us, and I await news from your Highness and the arrival of troops in order to determine my operations for the day. Nothing has been seen on the side of Binche, nor on our right.

"Your very obedient servant,
"WELLINGTON." *

After inspecting the Prince of Orange's position, the Duke, accompanied by his aide-de-camp, Sir Alexander Gordon, and two or three orderlies, rode over to inspect that of Blücher at Ligny, where he met Lieut.-Colonel Sir Henry Hardinge,† British Commissioner at the Prussian headquarters. *(Welling-ton visits Blücher.)*

"On the morning of the 16th I left Brussels and rode forward about five miles beyond Quatre-Bras to see the Prince of Orange's outposts.‡ After that, I went over to the Prussians about seven miles to our left from Quatre-Bras, and found them drawn up on the slope of the ground with their advanced columns close down to the rivulet of Ligny, the banks of which were so marshy that the French could only cross it at the bridges of three or four villages that lie along its course. I told the Prussian officers, in presence of Hardinge, that, according to my judgment, the exposure of the advanced columns and, indeed, of the whole army to cannonade, standing as they did displayed to the aim of

---

* This letter, quoted by Ropes (p. 106) from Von Ollech's history, was not published till 1876. It will be noticed that the position of the cavalry has been altered since the order sent to Lord Hill (see p. 15).

† Afterwards Field-Marshal Viscount Hardinge, G.C.B.

‡ He cannot have ridden due south, or he would have been landed within the enemy's outposts at Frasnes.

the enemy's fire, was not prudent.* The marshy banks of the stream made it out of their power to cross and attack the French, while the latter, on the other hand, though they could not attack them, had it in their power to cannonade them, and shatter them to pieces, after which they might fall upon them by the bridges at the villages. I said that if I were in Blücher's place with English troops, I should withdraw all the columns I saw scattered about in front, and get more of the troops under shelter of the rising ground. However they seemed to think they knew best, so I came away very shortly. It all fell out exactly as I had feared—the French overwhelmed them, as they stood, by a prodigious fire of artillery, and I myself could distinguish with my glass from Quatre-Bras a general charge of the French cavalry on their confused columns, in which charge it was that Blücher was ridden over and near killed." †

**And returns to Quatre-Bras.**

It has often been asserted that Wellington gave Blücher an unconditional promise of support, and that this decided Blücher to receive battle. Wellington, as has been shown, did not anticipate much trouble on that day at Quatre-Bras, and no doubt expected to be able to support Blücher when his own troops had collected. But his engagement was by no means unconditional. Müffling reports his last words as being—"Well, I will come, provided I am not attacked myself." As soon as he returned to Quatre-Bras, which he reached at half-past two or three o'clock, the Prince of Orange informed him that the French were in force in the wood before him, but that he did not expect they would advance that afternoon. At that moment loud cries of *Vive l'Empereur!* were heard, taken up in succession by brigades, and a loud voice could be heard distinctly crying— "L'Empereur recompensera celui qui s'avancera!"

"That," observed the Duke, "must be Ney going down the

---

* "If they fight here," said the Duke to Hardinge, "they will be damnably mauled" (*Stanhope*, 109).

† *De Ros MS.*

FIELD-MARSHAL VON BLÜCHER, AGED 72.
(*From a Pencil Drawing in 1814, by Major-General Birch.*)

[*Vol. ii, p. 20.*

line. I know what that means; we shall be attacked in five
minutes." *

And so it was. Immediately afterwards the French columns debouched from the wood in fine order, with drums beating, the Prince of Orange withdrawing his advanced light troops and guns before them.† As Wellington sat watching the enemy, he was surprised to see that instead of both corps, 40,000 or 50,000 strong, advancing against him, one of them, that opposite his own left, was moving off sharply to its right in the direction of Ligny. This, though it gratified him at the time, also puzzled him exceedingly; and the explanation was not apparent till many days later. It was this. In fixing 2.30 p.m. as the hour for Grouchy's attack on the Prussians at Ligny, the Emperor ordered Ney to fall on the Prince of Orange at the same time, to sever the British communication with Mons and Ostend, and to meet the Emperor at Brussels at seven o'clock the following morning. The Emperor, with the Imperial Guard in reserve, undertook to keep his eye on the movements of both Grouchy and Ney's columns, and support either according to the turn of affairs— "je me porterai sur l'une ou l'autre aile selon les circonstances." ‡ But at 3.15 p.m., after three orders had been despatched to Ney directing him to carry Quatre-Bras, the Emperor, through Soult, sent him a fourth, more urgent than the rest, commanding him to support Grouchy by directing his attack on the right flank of the Prussians at Ligny. "The fate of France is in your hands; therefore hesitate not a moment to move according to the Emperor's commands, and direct your march upon the heights of Saint-Amand and Brye."

---

* Houssaye describes Wellington as considering the situation at this moment as critical, and almost hopeless; but he misinterprets the meaning of a phrase used in the Duke's letter to Lady F. Webster : " We fought a desperate battle " (*Suppl. Despatches*, x. 501). English readers will perceive the difference between a desperate battle and a desperate situation (compare vol. i. p. 56, *note*).

† *De Ros MS.; Croker*, iii. 173.

‡ The Emperor's letter to Ney, 16th June. Napoleon sent nine despatches to Ney in the course of this day (*Houssaye*, 185).

Colonel Laurent, charged to carry this pencilled command to Ney, rode round by Gosselies. Fifteen minutes after he started Napoleon despatched another officer, Colonel de Forbin-Janson,* with orders direct to d'Erlon, commanding him to move upon the eminence of Saint-Amand and fall upon Ligny. " Monsieur le Comte d'Erlon," the note ended, " you are about to save France and cover yourself with glory ! " D'Erlon would gladly have exchanged this fine peroration for greater clearness in his instructions. *Portez vous . . . à la hauteur de Saint-Amand*—was not the intention *sur la hauteur ?* Forbin-Janson, an officer of but a year's experience, could throw no light on the meaning. He had ridden a shorter route than the messenger to Ney, and d'Erlon received his orders *three-quarters of an hour sooner* than Ney. He carried them out to the letter. Instead of marching upon the height of Saint-Amand—*sur la hauteur*—he advanced on a line with that hamlet—*à la hauteur*—sending Delcambre, the chief of his staff, to inform Ney of the change in his destination. Up to five o'clock Ney was under the delusion that d'Erlon was supporting him on the right, but at that hour Delcambre reached him with d'Erlon's message, announcing his change of direction. Five minutes later Colonel Laurent rode up with the Emperor's order of 3.15 to Ney, whose fury was without bounds. The balls from a British battery were ploughing up the ground round him. " Ah ! these English balls," he cried, " I wish they were all in my belly." He sent Delcambre back with positive orders to support Reille in his attack on Quatre-Bras, then in full progress.

It was too late. When Delcambre rejoined d'Erlon at six o'clock, the 1st Corps was almost within cannon-shot of Saint-Amand and in full view of the Prussians. D'Erlon had to choose between continuing the movement in compliance with the Emperor's direct command and obeying the

---

* *Houssaye*, 201, where a minute analysis is undertaken of the cause of the confusion. Mr. Ropes (p. 182) disbelieves in the Emperor's direct order to d'Erlon, but M. Houssaye produces convincing evidence in support of it.

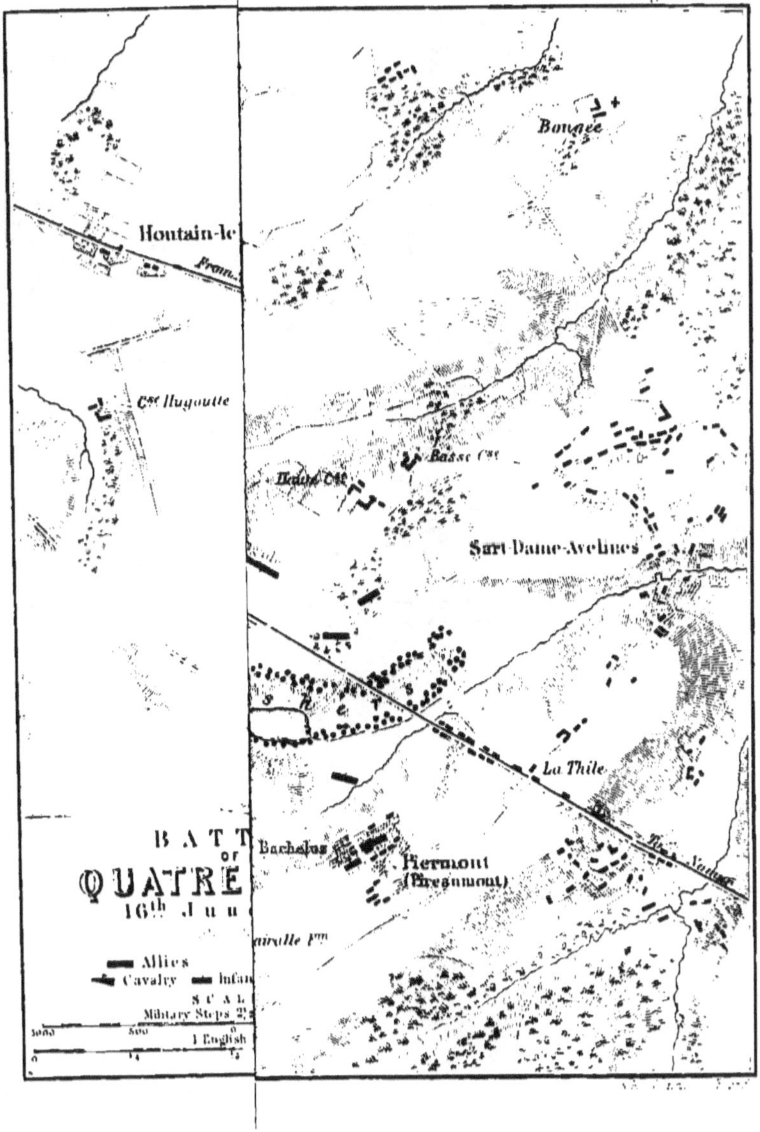

Bougée

Houtain-le

Front.

Cse Hugouite

Haute Cse   Basse Cse

Sart-Dame-Avelines

La Thile

S. R. C.

B A T T
or
QUATRE
16th Juu

Bachelus   Piermont
(Pireanmont)

airelle F^{m}

Allies
Cavalry   Infan
SCAL
Military Steps 2;
1000   500   0
0   1/4   1/2   1 English

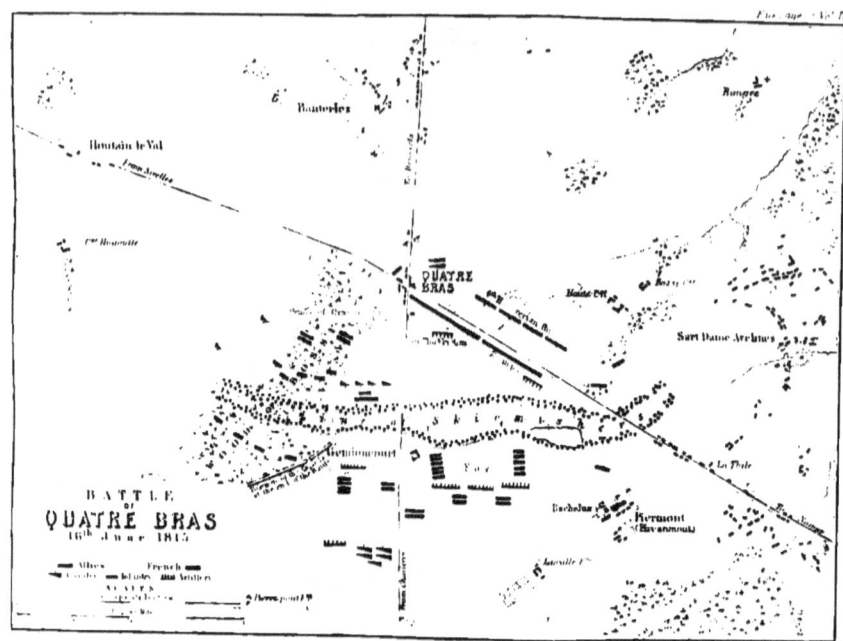

BATTLE
of
QUATRE BRAS
16th June 1815

imperative recall of his immediate superior.  The soldier's <small>ANN. 1815.</small>
duty seemed clear: he countermarched his columns, and,
leaving Fleurus which he had approached within two miles,
began the return to Quatre-Bras which was three times as
far off.  By no fault of its commander the whole energies of
the 1st Corps d'Armée, which, rightly directed, had been
irresistible at Quatre-Bras, was dissipated in fruitless oscil-
lation between the two battle-fields.*

Ney had begun his attack about three o'clock with a furious
onset upon the farm of Gémioncourt, situated on the Charleroi-
Brussels highway.  The fields were so deep with rye that it
was difficult to make out the exact positions of friend or foe,
a condition all in favour of the Allies, as concealing their
real weakness; for in truth the Duke began this action with
no more than 7,000 infantry and 16 guns, against 15,000 or
16,000 French.  Gémioncourt, weakly defended by a detachment of Nassau troops, was speedily taken, and Prince
Jérôme's division on the French left drove the Dutchmen out
of the wood of Bossu.  These two important points gained,
Ney ordered a general advance.  The conflict grew warm on
the allied left at Piermont, and the superior numbers of the
enemy soon began to prevail, until the 5th Division,† under

---

* Wellington's criticism on Napoleon's generalship on this occasion was severe
and just.  "I wonder what they would have said of me if I had done such a thing
as that.  I have always avoided a false move.  I preferred being too late in my
movement to having to alter it" (*Salisbury MSS.*, 1838).

† The divisions of the British army had been re-numbered since the close of
the Peninsular war.  On 15th June, the day before the battle of Quatre-Bras,
Wellington had consulted his Generals as to their desire to have them restored
to the old order.  Had there been time to effect this, Sir Thomas Picton's
division, the 5th, would have become again the 3rd, so long and gloriously
associated with his name.

| Peninsular Numbers. | Waterloo Numbers. | Generals. |
|---|---|---|
| 1 (the Guards) . . . | 1 . . . . | General Cooke |
| 2 . . . . . . . . | 4 . . . . | Sir C. Colville |
| 3 . . . . . . . . | 5 . . . . | Sir T. Picton |
| 4 . . . . . . . . | 6 . . . . | Sir L. Cole |
| 5 . . . . . . . . | 3 . . . . | Sir C. Alten |
| 6 . . . . . . . | 4 . . . . | Sir H. Clinton |

(*Despatches*, xii. 470).

old Picton, opportunely arrived from Brussels, 7,200 strong. Soon the Brunswick corps, nearly 7,000, marched in from Nivelles, and the Nassau contingent 6,900, making, with 1,200 of Van Merlen's horse, a total of some 22,000 Allies. By five o'clock Ney, who had begun the fight with overpowering superiority of numbers, was in turn outnumbered by 6,000 or 7,000. Nevertheless the Allies were at a great disadvantage in regard to cavalry. Lord Uxbridge's division had been directed to advance from Ninhove till the rear of the column had crossed the high-road from Mons to Brussels; but, owing to a misapprehension of the order, they were halted as soon as the head of the column touched it.[*]

The rest of the afternoon was spent in a series of encounters of exceeding severity, the course of which it is very difficult to follow. Personal impressions of every battle are confined to each man's sphere of observation; at Quatre-Bras the spheres of all men were unusually limited. Besides the deep corn, which concealed the infantry, there was the wood of Bossu, masking the attack of the enemy's left; and the successive arrivals of Wellington's forces render the sequence of events more than usually confusing. It must be confessed that there were departures as well as arrivals. Many of the Belgians and Dutch were Buonapartist at heart; others were indifferent or disaffected; nearly all believed Napoleon to be invincible. Thus it came to pass that the 2nd Dutch-Belgian Division, upwards of 7,000 strong, who had held such a brave front under the Prince of Orange in the fore part of the day, tired of the sport before evening, and quitted the field almost to a man. The chief feature of the fight was the steady endurance by British infantry of the repeated charges by French cavalry. Picton, to relieve the pressure on the squares of the 42nd, 44th, 79th, and 92nd, actually charged the French cuirassiers and lancers with the Royals, the 28th and 32nd Regiments. Ney had forfeited all the advantage he enjoyed in the morning: he had proved in anticipation the truth of Napoleon's verdict uttered at A.N. 1815. St. Helena, "Ney n'était plus le même homme." Still he was proud and brave: he held in his hand the Emperor's billet—"le sort de la France est entre vos mains." He knew that he was outnumbered before the heads of the 1st (Guards) Division, and the 3rd (Alten's) Division appeared about six o'clock coming up from Nivelles: mad with rage at the Emperor and chagrin at his lost opportunity, he must wrench victory even at the last hour. He sent for Kellermann.

"My dear General," said he, "the safety of France is at stake. We must make a supreme effort. Take your cavalry and fling yourself upon the English centre. Crush them!— ride them down!"

War-worn Kellermann was not the man to blench at such an order; nevertheless he pointed out that the enemy was now 25,000 strong, and that he had with him only a single brigade of cuirassiers, the other three brigades being far to the rear, in accordance with Ney's own commands.

"What does that matter?" roared Ney, above the thunder of the guns. "Charge with what you have; ride them down! I'll support you with all the cavalry I have. Go; go, I tell you!" *

Ten minutes later Kellermann's trumpets sounded the Charge of charge. In column of squadrons, eight hundred steel-clad Keller-mann's horsemen thundered down upon Sir Colin Halkett's brigade. cuirassiers. The first battalion, the 69th Regiment, was forming square in compliance with instructions from their Brigadier, when an officer of high rank rode up and asked what they were about.

"Preparing for cavalry, sir," was the reply, "by the Brigadier-General's orders."

"Oh, cavalry be d——d! There's none within miles of you. Reform column, sir, and deploy at once."

This fresh order was in the act of being carried out when

* *Houssaye*, 207, quoting Kellermann's narrative in the French *Archives de la Guerre.*

ÆT. 46. the cuirassiers swept upon the column, rode through it, and carried off the regimental colour.* The 30th and 33rd stood firmly in their squares, shoulder deep in rye; the cuirassiers rode past them, scattered the Belgian and Brunswick cavalry, and penetrated as far as Quatre-Bras, completely turning the allied position. On the left of Quatre-Bras the banks were lined by the 92nd Highlanders and some Hanoverians. The Duke of Wellington, dismounted, stood on the left of the Highlanders; then, moving round to the rear of the line, called out, "Don't fire, ninety-second, till I give you the word!" When the cuirassiers were within thirty yards he gave the order for a volley, which told with terrific violence, completely stopping and repulsing the attack,† and Keller-mann, being unsupported, drew off in great disorder, with the loss of one-third of his brigade. Reinforcements were arriv-ing in quick succession to the Allies, when Ney received positive orders from the Emperor by the hand of Colonel Baudus, that, happen what might to the left wing, d'Erlon was without fail to march to his right.‡ Ney was on foot, having had two horses shot under him, and, more like a madman than a cool-headed soldier, began rallying his broken infantry and leading them against Pack's Highlanders, con-tinuing the hopeless combat till nearly nine o'clock. Then he drew off, having been sacrificed by his master's interference with d'Erlon, but, in Napoleon's opinion, not sacrificed in vain. The 1st Corps had been neutralised, the 2nd beaten, yet in the Emperor's larger view the day had not been lost. On the contrary, his object had been attained; he had severed the armies of Blücher and Wellington and kept them apart, while he inflicted a severe defeat on the Prussians at Ligny—

* The 69th only brought one colour on the field, having lost the other at the disastrous affair of Bergen-op-Zoom in the previous year.

† *Waterloo Letters*, p. 386.

‡ "Il faut absolument que l'ordre donné au comte d'Erlon soit exécuté, quelle que soit la situation ou se trouve le maréchal Ney. Je n'attache pas grande importance à ce qui passera aujourd'hui de son côté. L'affaire est toute où je suis, car je veux en finir avec l'armée prussienne" (*Houssaye*, 212, quoting *Baudus MS.*).

the last and not the least characteristic in the long roll of Napoleonic victories. Had the positions of the two commanders been reversed, it may be safely said that Wellington, even at the price of attaining an important advantage, would never have compromised one of his Generals by withdrawing from him half his force at the moment of attack—would never have declared that "he attached little importance" to what befell that General.

On the other hand, it must be freely admitted that if Ney had shown ordinary alacrity in the morning and collected his forces in time to carry out the Emperor's earlier orders, he could have spared d'Erlon perfectly well, have cut to pieces or driven away the weak detachment of Perponcher, and probably no serious attempt would have been made to hold the position of Quatre-Bras against him. It was owing to Ney's culpable laxity that there was any battle of Quatre-Bras to be recorded.

The following is a return of the loss to the Allies, so far as known, in killed, wounded, and missing :—

| | |
|---|---:|
| British . . . . . . . . . | 2,275 |
| Hanoverians . . . . . . . | 369 |
| Brunswickers . . . . . . . | 819 |

3,463 officers and men.*

Of the casualties among the Dutch and Belgian troops no separate return could be made, most of them having deserted the field in the afternoon, spreading news of the total defeat of the Allies. The loss of the French was officially stated at 4,300.†

* *Siborne*, i. 160. Of the British regiments, the Highlanders suffered most severely; but, to judge from the following passage in a letter written from Brussels on 17th June by Lady Georgina Lennox (afterwards Lady de Ros) to Lady Georgina Bathurst, they were not of sufficient importance to cause much concern to the fashionable ladies in that town. "Thank God, my dearest G., all our friends are safe. There was a general action yesterday evening, the Guards were not engaged. . . . Poor Sir D. Pack is severely wounded, and the poor Duke of Brunswick died of his wounds. . . . The Scotch were chiefly engaged, so there are no officers wounded that one knows."

† *Houssaye*, 213.

The Duke of Brunswick fell at the head of his good Black Brunswickers, whose sable uniform and silver death's-head and crossbones bore witness how the duke's father had fallen in like manner commanding his hussars at the Battle of Jena. At the time Brunswick was killed, Wellington himself was in great peril. The Brunswick infantry, which had replaced the troops of Nassau in the first line, gave way under a

charge of French cavalry. Wellington rode up with the Brunswick hussars to cover them, but these also fell into disorder under a heavy fire of musketry, and fled before a charge of Piré's "red lancers." Wellington galloped off, closely pursued, and, arriving at a ditch lined by the Gordon Highlanders, called out to them to lie still. He set his horse at the fence and cleared it, bayonets and all.

Another incident in this hard day's work, harder than most men younger than the Duke would care to undertake on the morrow of a ball,* may be told in Wellington's own words.

"It was that same evening that I saw one of the strangest chances I ever recollect. A French regiment of cuirassiers, I suppose 600 or 700, came dashing up the Charleroi road to Quatre-Bras for the purpose of a reconnaissance—just where the Namur road forms the 'quatre bras;' there are some farm houses there, and also a large farm yard with a gate into the road. I had posted some infantry in the ditches at the cross-way, and these cuirassiers, being checked by their fire, turned off the head of their column into the gateway of the yard. I was looking attentively at their proceedings with my glass, in fact I was not more than a quarter of a mile distant, and, seeing they all followed into the gateway, I naturally concluded they had some way out at the back of the farm yard, by which they had

* The Duke had ridden from Brussels five miles beyond Quatre Bras, 29 miles, then 7 miles to Ligny and back, 43 miles in all, before the battle began. and remained in the saddle till nightfall. Colonel the Hon. Frederick Ponsonby, arriving late at night with his brigade of cavalry, found the wearied troops fast asleep in their bivouac, but Wellington was sitting in his tent, chuckling over the contents of some English newspapers which had just arrived. Truly an Iron Duke !

retired upon their army along the skirt of the wood.   But to <small>Ann. 1815.</small>
my great surprize on looking again, about ten minutes afterwards,
in the same direction, I saw them all rushing out full gallop at
the gateway, and returning by the very road they had come.
They lost several men by our infantry firing from their ditches,
but the main body escaped well enough.   It seems that when
they found there was no outlet from the farm yard into which
they had so heedlessly turned, without knowing the place in the
least, they quietly got into order, and seeing we took no notice
of them, waited a quarter of an hour and then effected their
escape in the manner I tell you.   Had we but thought it possible
they were there, we might have captured every man without
fail." *

About ten o'clock that night, Wellington sent his aide-de-
camp, Sir Alexander Gordon, who had been in the saddle
since early morning, with an escort of two squadrons of
the 10th Hussars, to find his way to the Prussian headquarters.   Riding as far as Sombreffe without hindrance, he
found General von Zieten's headquarters still in that village,
and the ground on which the Prussians had been beaten in
the morning was occupied only by a few French videttes
which he drove off.†   Blücher, the 4th Prussian Corps not
having arrived, had been so much weakened by his defeat
that he had been obliged to retire in the night upon Wavre.

Napoleon, whose constant practice it was to calculate the
future or the unknown by a percentage of chances,‡ was
almost sure that Blücher would retire upon his base on the
Rhine; but, while overrating the extent to which the
Prussians had suffered in the battle, he underrated their
staunch old Marshal's fidelity to Wellington.

* *De Ros MS.*
† *Ibid.*
‡ A good example of this mental habit may be seen at the beginning of the
Peninsular war, when Napoleon reckoned the odds in favour of Bessières at Rio
Scco as 75 to 25, and those of Dupont at Baylen as 80 to 20.

# CHAPTER II.

## THE SEVENTEENTH OF JUNE.

### 1815.

Confusion in Brussels.

MANY vivid descriptions have been given of the panic and confusion caused in Brussels by the fugitive Belgian and Dutch soldiers. The sound of artillery had been borne distinctly to the town on the sultry air.

"At first I was utterly incredulous; I could not—would not believe it; but, hurrying to the Parc, we were too soon, too incontestably convinced of the dreadful truth, by ourselves hearing the awful and almost incessant thunder of the guns apparently very near us. . . . Late as it was we went to see Mrs. H., whom we knew to be in great alarm. We found her sitting surrounded by plate, which she was vainly trying to acquire sufficient composure to pack up, with a face pale with consternation, and quite overcome with agitation and distress. . . . My brother had engaged horses, upon the condition of their being in readiness to convey us to Antwerp at a moment's warning by day or night, if required. . . . Thinking it prudent to be prepared, we had AN. 1815. sent our *valet-de-place* to *la blanchisseuse* to desire her to send home everything belonging to us early in the morning. *La blanchisseuse* sent back a message—'Madame,' said the valet, 'the *blanchisseuse* says that if the English should beat the French, she will iron and plait your clothes, and finish them for you; but if, *au contraire*, these vile French should get the better, then she will assuredly send them back *tout mouillés* early to-morrow morning.' . . . Great alarm continued to prevail all through the night, and the baggage wagons stood ready harnessed to set off at a moment's notice. . . . At six o'clock we were roused by a violent knocking at the room-door, accompanied by cries of 'les François sont ici! les François sont ici!' Starting out of bed, the first sight we beheld from the window was a troop of Belgic cavalry galloping from the army at the most furious rate, through the Place Royale, as if the French were at their heels; and instantly the whole train of baggage wagons and empty carts, which had stood before our eyes so long, set off full speed by the Montagne de la Cour, and through every street by which it was possible to effect their escape. . . . No language can do justice to the scene of confusion which the court below exhibited; masters and servants, ladies and stable-boys, valets and soldiers, lords and beggars; Dutchmen, Belgians and Britons; bewildered *garçons* and scared *filles-de-chambre;* enraged gentlemen and clamorous coachmen; all crowded together, jostling, crying, scolding, squabbling, lamenting, exclaiming, imploring, swearing and vociferating, in French, English and Flemish, all at the same time. Nor was it only a war of words; the disputants had speedy recourse to blows, and those who could not get horses by fair means endeavoured to obtain them by foul. The unresisting animals were dragged away half-harnessed. The carriages were seized by force, and jammed against each other. Amidst the crash of wheels, the volleys of oaths, and the confusion of tongues, the mistress of the hotel, with a countenance dressed in woe, was carrying off her most valuable plate in order to secure it, ejaculating, as she went, the name of Jesus incessantly; while the master, with a red night-cap on his head, and the eternal pipe sticking mechanically out of one corner of his mouth,

was standing with his hands in his pockets, a silent statue of
despair." *

Next morning Lady Hamilton Dalrymple notes in her
journal—

"17*th June.*—I again got up a little after four o'clock. What
a different sight from the morning before! An uninterrupted
chain of carts going helter-skelter—cars with wounded soldiers—
Belgian regiments seeming to be without any discipline or control
—all pouring into the town; wounded soldiers lying upon the
pavement, having got as far as the town, but unable to crawl
further—the dismay was universal. The morning was fine, but
about one o'clock the most dreadful storm of thunder and
lightning I ever recollect came on. We were obliged to shut the
shutters. . . . Lord Apsley came to me with a message from
the Duke of Wellington to say he had been obliged to retreat to
the last position before he gave up Brussels; that he hoped to
be able to retain it, but as it was very uncertain, he advised us
to have horses quite ready and all our things packed up. . . .
During the whole evening and night the rain fell in torrents. I
do not remember for a continuance of so many hours having ever
seen it so heavy; it was exactly as if pitchers of water were
pouring down. . . .

"18*th June.*—At six in the morning we procured horses and
set off to Antwerp. The road was nearly blocked."

D'Erlon's corps rejoined Ney after the cessation of fighting
on Friday evening, but the weary British were not disturbed
in their bivouac that night.

Was Wellington
surprised
by Napoleon?
Any attempt to review the incidents and results of the
fighting on the 16th is impossible without referring to the
heated controversy which has raged round them. Setting
aside the extreme advocates of the Duke's infallibility (for it
is clear that but for Ney's inactivity in the morning, and the
dislocation of his attack in the afternoon, the allied position

* *The Days of Battle, or Quatre-Bras and Waterloo, by an Englishwoman
resident in Brussels* (London, 1853), pp. 26–40.

must have been easily forced), there remain only three <small>ANN. 1815.</small> conclusions deserving consideration.

First: that the Duke of Wellington was actually surprised by Napoleon's advance across the Sambre.

Second: assuming that he was not surprised, that his tactics were faulty in neglecting to concentrate earlier on his left at Quatre-Bras, and that by selecting Nivelles as the rendezvous, seven miles west of the Charleroi to Brussels road, compromised both armies by admitting between them the head of Ney's corps d'armée.

Third: still assuming that his dispositions were so complete that he cannot be held to have been taken by surprise, that his adversary outmanœuvred him by a rapid and masterly concentration opposite the weakest point in the line of defence.

Wellington himself was always, as might be expected, exceedingly reticent on the subject. Although he never admitted that he had been surprised, except in the conversation in the Duke of Richmond's dressing-room,* he never denied it in any of his writings. He was on the watch, for we have his own assurance that from the moment he knew that the French were on the march, until he quitted Brussels on the morning of the 16th, he never went twenty yards from his own quarters, so as to be sure to receive the first intelligence coming from the front.† He was watchful enough, but not in what proved to be the direction of danger. The following extract from his strictures on Clausewitz's criticism of himself contains the key to the idea which dominated the whole of his dispositions, even after he knew of Napoleon's arrival on the frontier, and the concentration upon Maubeuge and Valenciennes,‡ up to, and even after, the very morning of Waterloo.

"The Duke of Wellington's letters, published by Colonel Gurwood, afford proofs that he was convinced that the enemy ought to have attacked by other lines than by the valleys of the

---

* See p. 14, *supra.*     † *Salisbury MSS., de Ros MS.*
‡ *Suppl. Despatches,* x. 436–481, passim.

Æт. 46. Sambre and the Meuse; and that even up to the last moment previous to the attack of his position at Waterloo, he conceived that they would endeavour to turn it by a march upon Hal. . . . It might be a nice question for military discussion, whether Buonaparte was right in endeavouring to force the position at Waterloo, or the Duke of Wellington right in thinking that, from the evening of the 16th, Buonaparte would have taken a wiser course if he had moved to his left, have reached the high-road leading from Mons to Bruxelles, and have turned the right of the position of the Allies by Hal. It is obvious that the Duke was prepared to resist such a movement." *

The hypothesis may be dismissed at once that Wellington deliberately left the position of Quatre-Bras open in order that Napoleon, in advancing upon Brussels, should expose both flanks to the armies on either side. The whole work of the 16th consisted in repairing the error of the 15th by assembling the Anglo-Dutch forces to prevent such an advance.

Reverting, then, to the three alternative conclusions to which one is shut up in examining the events of these days, one is forced to admit that the Duke of Wellington was both outmanœuvred and surprised. This plain fact remains, although the blame for the surprise be laid, not on Wellington, but on von Zieten's laggard messenger on the morning of the 15th, or on von Zieten for sending only one messenger, who must have lost his way. Remains the superiority of manœuvring. Wellington's adversary, who, with admirable skill, masked his movements along the whole western frontier

* *Suppl. Despatches,* x. 530. Mr. Ropes (p. 90) says that "some of the statements in this paper fairly take one's breath away;" but he refrains from mentioning more than one, namely, the Duke's statement that "having received intelligence of the French attack only at three o'clock in the afternoon of the 15th, he was at Quatre-Bras before the same hour on the morning of the 16th with a sufficient force to engage the left of the French army." It seems easy to take away the breath of some people. Surely it is obvious that "morning" was written here by a slip of the pen for "afternoon," especially as in another part of the same memorandum, which was written in 1842, the Duke mentions that he did not leave Brussels till the morning of the 16th.

of Belgium, timed the arrival of nine corps, distributed Ann. 1815.
between Lille and Metz, to coincide exactly with that of the
Imperial Guard from Paris, and selected for that concentration the weakest part in the allied lines, must surely be
credited with having outmanœuvred his opponent.  Up to
that point, Napoleon's conduct of the campaign was as
masterly and brilliant as anything in his military career.
Five years later Wellington frankly described it to Charles
Greville as "the finest thing that ever was done—so rapid
and so well combined." *

Imagine a parallel case arising in modern autumn manœuvres.  A red force is to guard the approach to Derby
of a blue force coming from the west of England.  Railroads
are barred ; the only means of locomotion are the soldier's
legs.  There are four routes by which the invasion may be
made—the high-roads through Northwich, Newcastle-under-
Lyne, Stafford, and Lichfield.  The red general has made up
his mind that his blue adversary will choose the route by
Stafford, at the same time keeping his army distributed along
the frontier, ready to concentrate at any point threatened.
His army consists of two corps, the 1st under General A——,
with headquarters at Stafford ; the 2nd under General B——,
with headquarters at Lichfield.  The blue general withdraws
his best troops from their cantonments opposite Northwich,
Newcastle-under-Lyne, and Stafford, and concentrates them
rapidly to the south of Lichfield, replacing them with some
militia battalions, without the red general being aware of
what is going on.  One afternoon, General B—— rides into
Derby and informs the red general that, early in the morning,
the enemy had approached his outposts in great force, but so
little serious did he think the movement that, instead of
sending word thirty miles back to Derby, he had brought
it himself, which would, and does, enable him to attend the
county ball in Derby that night.  General A——, commanding the 1st Army Corps, has also left his headquarters

* *Greville*, i. 39.

at Stafford, *the point where the red general expects the attack to be made*, in order to attend the ball. What does the red general do? He does not send Generals A—— and B—— back to their headquarters, but permits them to attend the ball with the chief officers of their staff and the generals of divisions and brigadiers. He sends orders to all his forces to be ready to concentrate at short notice, not on Lichfield, where the danger had appeared, but at Rugeley, because he believes the movement on Lichfield to be a feint, and because his judgment, whether founded or not on private information, still leads him to believe that Stafford is the route whence danger is most imminent. He then goes to the ball himself, and permits the officers of his staff and of the reserve in Derby to do the same, and it is past midnight before he hears that Walsall has been captured by the blue general thirteen hours previously. Would not the umpires pronounce that the blue general had outmanœuvred the red, and that the red general had been surprised?

Apply these conditions to the defence of Brussels. Does not the condition of the town itself, so graphically described in letters written home by the English girl quoted above, exclude every conclusion except that of complete surprise? Every incident of the 15th–16th June, after the arrival of the news in the ball-room, goes to show what had happened was as little expected by the military as by the civilian residents.

"The cavalry officers, whose regiments for the most part were quartered in villages about the frontier, ten, fifteen and even twenty miles off, flew from the ball-room in dismay, in search of their horses, and galloped off in the dark, without baggage or attendants, in the utmost perplexity which way to go, or where to join their regiments, which might have marched before they arrived." *

Wellington, therefore, was both outmanœuvred and surprised by Napoleon on 15th June; to deny it is to suppose

* *Days of Battle*, p. 20.

ANN. 1815.

him capable of voluntarily transgressing his own cardinal rule : " No army should ever be brought to its ground later than ten o'clock at night, nor should the columns of march be formed earlier than three in the morning, even when a forced march is necessary. With less than five hours' rest no soldier can endure the fatigue of marching, much less of fighting." [*]

Yet it must be remembered that, had the officer said to have been despatched by General von Zieten at 4 a.m. reached Brussels, as he ought to have done, at 7 a.m. instead of at 3 p.m., the reserve would have been at Quatre-Bras by 2 p.m. on 15th instead of 3.30 p.m. on 16th, and the concentration on the point threatened would have been timely, and well within the powers of the rest of the troops.

The morning of 17th June was one of intense and sultry heat. Wellington, having spent the night at Genappe, returned very early in the morning to Quatre-Bras, whence he sent Gordon once more with half a squadron along the Namur road to gain intelligence. Returning between seven and eight o'clock, Gordon found his chief striding restlessly up and down the high-road, and reported that he had pushed as far as Tilly, where he had seen General von Zieten, that the Prussian army was in retreat upon Wavre, and that the enemy were in force on the right of the road about two miles distant. This was the first intimation the Duke received of the direction of Blücher's retreat ; an officer sent overnight from the Prussian headquarters, having been wounded, failed to carry the news.

Wellington retreats from Quatre-Bras.

Now Ney, having been rejoined by d'Erlon with the 1st Corps, had more than 40,000 men in his command, whereas Wellington, after the Dutch troops had bolted, could not bring more than 25,000 into action. Clearly, then, having lost the support of the Prussians on his left, he could no longer maintain his position at Quatre-Bras.

" Old Blücher," said he, " has had a damned good hiding,

[*] *De Ros MS.*

and has gone eighteen miles to his rear. We must do the same. I suppose they'll say in England that we have been licked; well, I can't help that."

About ten o'clock orders were issued for the army to retire by successive brigades through the defile of Genappe into the position of Mont-Saint-Jean in front of Waterloo. The Duke, retaining with himself the cavalry and two battalions of the 95th Rifles, having sent out his orders, read some letters and papers which had arrived from England, and then lay down on the roadside, having covered his face with a newspaper, and fell asleep.[*] Awaking after a short nap, he rode down in front of Quatre-Bras, looking about through his glass, and expressing his surprise at the perfect quietness of the enemy. "It is not at all impossible," he said, "that they may be retreating."

Why was Wellington allowed so much time to begin his hazardous retreat? For two reasons. In the first place, Ney, deeply incensed with the Emperor for having interfered with d'Erlon's column at the most critical moment of his attack, had made no report of the failure of his own operations on the 16th. It was not till the Emperor's aide-de-camp, Count Flahault, returned to Fleurus about 8 o'clock a.m. on the 17th that Napoleon learnt the truth, and was told also that Ney knew nothing about the result of the battle of Ligny. Even then, late as it was, it was not too late to have attacked Wellington with immensely superior forces—Wellington, whom Napoleon had imagined was long since in full retreat upon Brussels—but there was another circumstance which

Cause of Napoleon's inactivity.

interfered. A great deal has been written, said, and surmised about the state of Napoleon's health at this time. In mental vigour it has been alleged that he was not equal to the victor of Austerlitz and Marengo—a suspicion which his conduct during the days from 12th to 16th June ought surely to dispel. Nevertheless these days had been a time of incessant mental and physical strain. Since daylight on the 12th,

* *Waterloo Letters*, p. 154.

when he started from Paris, the Emperor had taken little Ann. 1815. repose. He was suffering from a painful, but not a dangerous, malady, which made riding disagreeable exercise; he had grown stout, and was not capable of such long-continued bodily exercise as the Duke of Wellington underwent with impunity; but there is the testimony of General Foy that "he retained all the vigour of his mind, and his passions had lost little of their strength." On the morning of the 17th, when there was every reason for prompt and vigorous action, the Emperor's movements were leisurely and undecided—the loitering of a weary man.

"To-day," he directed Soult to write to Ney about 8 a.m., " will be needed to terminate this operation (viz. the occupation of Quatre-Bras), to supply ammunition, bring in stragglers, and call in detachments. Give your orders accordingly ; and see to it that all the wounded are cared for and taken to the rear. We hear complaints that the ambulances have not done their duty."

The Emperor had ordered overnight that the cavalry of Pajol and Exelmans should follow the Prussians and ascertain whether, as was probable, they were retreating on their own base at Liége and Namur, or whether, possibly, they would fall back so as to unite with Wellington for the defence of Brussels. About nine o'clock he left his quarters at Fleurus and rode upon the battlefield of Ligny, visiting the wounded and passing along the ranks of his troops paraded *without arms* in front of their bivouacs. Then he dismounted and discussed at length with Grouchy and other officers, not the prospects of the campaign, but, strangely enough, the course of politics in Paris. It was nearly eleven o'clock before it Napoleon's was reported to him that the troops at Quatre-Bras were not, Grouchy. as he had supposed, and as was the fact, merely Wellington's rear-guard, but his whole force on the ground. Not before that hour did he decide to support Ney in a fresh attack on Quatre-Bras with Loban's 6th Corps and the whole Imperial

Æt. 46. Guard.  At the same time he committed a corps of 34,000
men and 96 guns to Marshal Grouchy, giving him verbal
orders to pursue the Prussians in the direction of Namur.*

The
Duke's
retreat.

About two o'clock in the afternoon, the Duke, riding about
with Sir Hussey Vivian in front of Quatre-Bras, saw the
glitter of steel in the sun, and, turning his glass on the field
of Ligny, perceived heavy masses of the enemy moving upon
his own position.† Simultaneously the French under Ney
began to show themselves in front for the first time, just as a
heavy rain-storm was spreading over the sky.  The sun of
Austerlitz was about to be obscured, but the French position
was still brilliantly illuminated; only on Quatre-Bras and
the land to the north the storm-twilight had descended.  The
Duke at once ordered the 95th and the cavalry to fall back
steadily along the road to Brussels, and trotted on himself to
get some dinner which had been prepared for him in Genappe.
The storm had broken by this time; Lord Uxbridge had
opened fire with his guns upon Napoleon himself and his
staff; a battery of horse artillery of the Guard replied; the
reverberation shook the heavens; a deluge of rain began
which all witnesses agree in describing as without parallel in
their experience.

Cavalry
action at
Genappe.

The Duke was hardly seated at table when word came
from Lord Uxbridge that he was hard pressed, and required
the presence of the Commander-in-chief.  The Duke, mounting at once, galloped back to the high ground before Genappe,
where he found the 7th Hussars in much disorder, having
been repulsed with loss, and refusing to follow their officers
to a fresh attack.  Wellington brought up the Life Guards,

---

* No incident in this campaign has given rise to greater controversy than the
exact nature and sequence of the successive orders to Grouchy, and the degree of
Grouchy's responsibility for what followed.  In the present narrative I am not
concerned to balance nicely the evidence affecting the character of a French
marshal, and shall endeavour to state merely the bare facts as they appear to
have borne on the fortunes of the Prussian and Anglo-Dutch armies.  Those
who wish thoroughly to understand the question should have recourse to the
admirable narratives of Mr. Ropes and M. Houssaye.

† *De Ros MS.*

1. — MARÉCHAL GROUCHY.

who charged the enemy with success, and delivered the 7th Ann. 1815.
from an awkward predicament, for they had lost all formation, were jammed in the streets and defile of Genappe, and
could not retire because of the dense column behind them.

Having checked the forward movement of the enemy,
Wellington carried off Lord Uxbridge to share his dinner.
He afterwards expressed the opinion that the retreat of the
cavalry "would have been as uninterrupted and easy as that
of the infantry had been in the morning, had not Lord
Uxbridge taken it into his head to make that attack on the
French lancers as they were coming out of Genappe, which
ended so disastrously for the 7th Hussars." *

Napoleon, who rode at the head of the advanced guard Napoleon's
throughout the pursuit, was present in this affair, and certainly activity
betrayed no traces of the inactivity he had shown in the pursuit.
morning.

"One ought to have been witness," says the author of *Napoléon
à Waterloo,*† "of the rapid march of this army on the 17th—a
march more like a steeplechase than the pursuit of a retreating
enemy—to realise the energy to which Napoleon knew how to
inspire troops under his immediate command. Six pieces of the
horse artillery of the Guard, supported by the *escadrons de service,*
marched in the first line, and poured grape on the masses of the
enemy's cavalry as often as, taking advantage of some accident
of ground, he endeavoured to halt, take position, and check our
pursuit. The Emperor, mounted on a small and very active
Arab horse, galloped at the head of the column; he was constantly
close to the guns, stimulating the gunners by his presence and
his words, and more than once he was in the thick of the shells
and balls which the enemy's artillery poured on us."

The extraordinary rain soon rendered the going very
difficult over the cultivated land, which became one continuous swamp. This told in favour of the British, who were

* *De Ros MS.*
† An officer of the Imperial Guard, who remained near the Emperor all
this day.

far the lighter column, the rest of the allied army being already in position before Waterloo.

> "It rained in such a way as I never saw either before or since ; it seemed as if the water were tumbled out of tubs. . . . The ground was so soft that at every step our horses sank halfway to the knees, and in several places where we passed over fallow land, it had the appearance of a lake, the rain falling upon it faster than it could be absorbed or run off." *

Strength of the allied army.

It was nearly seven o'clock before Napoleon's advanced guard brought up on the elevated plateau in front of the position chosen by Wellington at Mont-Saint-Jean. General Picton opened fire with twelve guns on the head of the French column, which, being unable to retreat owing to the pressure behind, suffered for about half an hour. Two French horse batteries made reply, till the British fire ceased by order of the Duke. By this time the Anglo-Dutch army had assembled to the number of 67,661 of all arms, with 156 guns.† In addition to these, the Duke, always haunted by apprehension of a turning manœuvre on the part of the French, thought it expedient to keep a corps of observation at Hal, wholly detached, and thirteen miles to the west of his position at Mont - Saint - Jean. This corps consisted of 17,500 men, being some brigades of the 4th Division under General Colville and the corps of Netherlanders under Prince Frederick of Orange, who was directed on the 17th to defend the position between Hal and Enghien "as long as possible." ‡ This force, which might have been employed with advantage on the 18th, remained inactive on the whole of that day. The army in position before Waterloo was of very uneven material, largely composed of militiamen and young soldiers. It was made up as follows :—

* *Hamilton MS.*

† *Siborne,* i. 460. Brialmont gives a slightly larger total, having apparently made no allowance for the losses on 16th and 17th June.

‡ *Despatches,* xii. 476.

| | |
|---|---|
| British . . . . . . . . . . . | 24,991 |
| King's German Legion . . . . . | 5,824 |
| Hanoverians . . . . . . . . | 11,220 |
| Brunswickers . . . . . . . . | 4,962 |
| Nassau Contingent . . . . . . | 2,880 |
| Dutch-Belgians . . . . . . . | 17,784 |

67,661 men.

Against these Napoleon brought into the field, after detaching the two corps under Grouchy, 71,947 men. The discrepancy between the actual numbers on either side was scarcely enough to affect the prospects of the impending conflict; being, indeed, to a great extent only apparent, owing to the British returns including only effective rank and file, and non-commissioned officers, whereas the French always included in their returns officers, musicians, etc. But the French had a great superiority in cavalry, of which they had 15,000 of the best, and in artillery, having 246 guns. The general quality of the infantry, also, was far superior to that of the Allies, for Napoleon's old campaigners had flocked to the eagles, forming a homogeneous, seasoned body of troops— the finest army in Europe. Of this disparity in quality the Duke was well aware; he never concealed his dissatisfaction with the quality even of his British troops, and always said that " he started with the very worst army that had ever been got together." *  He acknowledged, however, that four or five of his old Peninsular battalions acted as a very rapid leaven on their young countrymen. The whole of the Hanoverian troops were militiamen, except some veteran battalions of the King's German Legion; and the Nassau men, though seasoned troops, actually fired on the Duke when, in the course of the battle of Waterloo, he attempted to rally them.†

Despite the consciousness of these disadvantages, the Duke

---

* *Palmerston's Journal.* p. 13.

† *Ibid.*, p. 14.  These three Nassau battalions were the same which had come over to the British from Soult's army during the operations round Bayonne in 1813.

of Wellington had chosen his own battlefield,[*] and was resolved to fight; but to the last moment, even when Napoleon's divisions were taking up their positions in his front, he was doubtful where the battle would take place. On the morning of the 17th, as soon as he discovered that Napoleon had neglected to occupy the field of Ligny, he had sent word to Blücher saying that he was about to fall back on Mont-Saint-Jean, and would give the French battle there, provided he had the support of one Prussian corps. Blücher, however, had been badly hurt in the battle of Ligny. Charging at the head of his cavalry, his horse was shot under him, he was twice ridden over by the French cavalry, and was believed to be killed or taken. He was carried, however, to the village of Mellery, where he spent the night in great pain and discomfort, in a little house crowded with wounded men. He was seventy-two years of age, and, being badly bruised, had to resign the command temporarily to his Chief of the Staff, Gneisenau. Now Gneisenau's confidence in Wellington had been grievously shaken on the previous day. When the Duke rode over to the Prussian headquarters on the morning of the 16th, not anticipating any serious work that day at Quatre-Bras, he undoubtedly did give a conditional assurance that he would support Blücher in the battle then imminent "provided I am not attacked myself." From this, taken in conjunction with a letter written to Blücher by Wellington three hours previously on his first arrival at Quatre-Bras, in which he said, "I do not see any large force of the enemy in front of us, and I await news from your Highness and the arrival of troops in order to determine my operations for the day,"[†] Gneisenau certainly

*Marginal note:* Gneisenau's distrust of Wellington.

---

[*] " The position occupied by us at Waterloo will attract many a John Bull, who will wonder why the devil that should be called a *position*, and return about as wise as he came. The Beau (a nickname borne by the Duke in this campaign) has a better eye, for he fixed upon it last summer (see p. 382, *supra*) in case of necessity to fight an action in the neighbourhood of Brussels, supposing the enemy to advance by the road he did; and one close to Hal, in case he advanced by Mons" (*Dumaresq MSS.*).

[†] This letter was first published by Von Ollech in 1876.

had drawn the inference that Wellington was not a man to he relied on. On the morning of the 17th he was very imperfectly acquainted with the course affairs had taken at Quatre-Bras, and he held the English General responsible for the defeat of the Prussians at Ligny.* Nevertheless he was unwilling at first to renounce all communication with the Anglo-Dutch army. While Blücher was disabled, Gneisenau took the important responsibility of ordering the 1st and 2nd Prussian corps (Zieten and Pirch I.) to fall back on Wavre instead of preserving the line of Namur; but on the 17th, when Blücher gallantly resumed the command in spite of his bruises, Gneisenau advised him to look after his own safety by falling back on Liége, and securing his communication with Luxembourg.† Blücher, however, was too staunch Blücher to desert his ally; supported by his Quartermaster-General keeps Grolmann, and acting in a spirit which can never be too highly tryst. admired, he ordered the concentration of the whole of his four corps d'armée upon Wavre. But at noon on the 17th, when Wellington's message arrived at Blücher's headquarters at Wavre, it was not known where the 3rd and 4th Prussian corps (Thielemann and Bülow) had got to; moreover, the reserve of ammunition had not come up. It was not, therefore, till shortly before midnight on the 17th, when Bülow's arrival at Dion-le-Mont had been notified, that Grolmann wrote Blücher's reply to Wellington, to the effect that Bülow would move at daybreak by Saint Lambert to attack the French right, supported by Thielemann; and that Zieten and Pirch I. would conform with their corps. It must have been about daybreak on the 18th before the Duke got this valuable assurance,‡ and it implies no little hardihood on his part

* It is admitted now on all hands that Blücher's decision to accept battle at Ligny was wholly independent of any assurance of support from Wellington, though no doubt he wished and hoped for it (see *Ropes*, p. 145).

† *Stanhope*, 110.

‡ The story that the Duke, after seeing his troops into their bivouacs at Mont-Saint-Jean on the evening of the 17th, rode over to Wavre and received personal assurance from Blücher of his support on the morrow, seems to belong to the

Æт. 46. that, before receiving it, he had resolved to stand his ground, because, for all he knew, "it was a perfectly possible thing that he might the next morning be assailed by a hundred thousand men,"[*] his information being that not more than 12,000 or 15,000 men had been detached under Grouchy to follow the Prussians.

Still the Duke would not bring in Prince Frederick's corps from Hal, and two letters written by him at 3 a.m. on the morning of the 18th, from his quarters in the village of Waterloo, betray considerable uncertainty and anxiety as to the course which events should take. The first of these is to the Duc de Berri, who was with the King of France at Ghent.

*Wellington anxious about his right.*

"It is possible that the enemy may turn us at Hal, although I have Prince Frederick's corps in position between Hal and Enghien. If that happens I beg your Royal Highness to march on Antwerp and canton yourself in the neighbourhood, and to inform his Majesty that I pray him go from Ghent to Antwerp by the left bank of the Scheldt . . . not on false rumours, but on receiving certain intelligence that the enemy has entered Brussels, in spite of me, by turning me at Hal."[†]

The second is to Lady Frances Webster in Brussels, for the Duke was not unmindful, even on the eve of battle, of the safety, and even the comfort, of his English friends there.

category of myth. Mr. Ropes, in his third edition (pp. 238–242), has carefully examined the evidence in support of it, and dismissed the story as a fable, although in previous editions he had expressed his belief in its truth. It is to be noted that the Duke, who had no possible reason for concealing the truth in this matter, never alluded to his alleged ride on that night of terrible rain, although he used to delight in discussing such incidents in his warfare. "It is impossible," says Greville (2nd series, ii. 41), "to convey an idea of the zest, eagerness, frankness and *abundance* with which he talked and told of his campaigns."

[*] *Ropes*, 235.
[†] *Despatches*, xii. 477.

"My dear Lady Frances,—As I am sending a messenger to Ann. 1815. Bruxelles, I write to you one line to tell you that I think you ought to make your preparations, as should Lord Mountnorris, to remove from Bruxelles to Antwerp in case such a measure should be necessary. . . . The course of the operations may oblige me to uncover Bruxelles for a moment, and may expose that town to the enemy; for which reason I recommend that you and your family should be prepared to move on Antwerp at a moment's notice. . . .

"Believe me, etc.,<br>"WELLINGTON.

"Present my best compliments to Lord and Lady Mountnorris." *

Many critics, from Napoleon downwards, have blamed the Duke for giving battle in such a position as Mont-Saint-Jean, whence, if beaten, it has been considered that he could not have retreated through the dense forest of Soignes upon Brussels. M. Thiers, also, in his *Histoire du Consulat et de* Brussels *l'Empire*, started the false idea, afterwards taken up by other was not the British writers, that the Duke's base of operations was Brussels. It base. was nothing of the kind; he had his headquarters there, but his base was Ostend and the coast. No doubt his chief object was to protect the capital of the Netherlands; but it will be observed that, in the letter last quoted, he speaks of the possibility of having to "uncover" it—not to retire upon it. That such was his intention was clearly explained at the dinner-table of Mr. Littleton (afterwards Lord Hatherton) at Teddesley, where the Duke was staying on 8th December, 1825.

"After dinner the conversation turned on the battle of Waterloo, and on those French writers who maintained that it ought never to have been fought on that ground at all, as, if beaten, the Allies could not have retreated through the forest of

* Suppl. Despatches, x. 501.

Soignes.   The Duke, speaking with much earnestness, said that was a mistake.

"'I knew every yard of the plain beyond the forest, and the road through it.  The forest on each side of the chaussée was open enough for infantry, cavalry, and even for artillery, and very defensible.  Had I retreated in that direction, could they have followed me?  The Prussians were on their flank, and would have been on their rear.  The co-operation of the Prussians in the operation I undertook was part of my plan, and I was not deceived.  But I *never contemplated a retreat on Brussels.*  Had I been forced from my position, I should have retreated to my right, towards the coast, the shipping and my resources.  I had placed Hill where he could have lent me important assistance in many contingencies, of which this was one.  Again I ask—if I had retreated on my right, could Napoleon have ventured to follow me?  The Prussians, already on his flank, would have been on his rear.  My plan was to keep my ground till the Prussians appeared, and then to attack the French position, and I executed my plan.'

" As the party left the room, Croker remarked, ' I never heard the Duke say so much on this subject before.' " *

* Note by Lord Hatherton, *Apsley House MSS.*

# CHAPTER III.

## WATERLOO.

## 18th June, 1815.

8 a.m. . . . . . Position of the allied army.
The advanced posts of La Haye, Papelotte, La Haye Sainte, and Hougoumont.

8—9 . . . . . . Napoleon prepares to attack.

10 . . . . . . . The Emperor's first order to Grouchy.
The French order of battle.

11 . . . . . . . Having marshalled his line of battle, the Emperor returns to Rossomme.

11.30 . . . . . . Attack on Hougoumont.

1 p.m. . . . . . Bülow's corps appears on the French right.
The Emperor's second order to Grouchy.

1.30 . . . . . . Ney receives the order to attack.

2 . . . . . . . . Advance of d'Erlon's corps d'armée.

2.15 . . . . . . Bylandt's Dutch brigade is broken.
Donzelot is repulsed by Kempt's brigade.

2.30 . . . . . . Death of Sir Thomas Picton.
Marcognet is repulsed by Pack's brigade.

2.40 . . . . . . Charge of the Union Brigade.

2.45 . . . . . . Death of Sir William Ponsonby.

2.40 . . . . . . Charge of Lord E. Somerset's brigade.

Repulse of Durutte's column at Papelotte.

11 a.m.—7 p.m. Well sustained defence of Hougoumont.

3.30 p.m. . . . . Second attack on La Haye Sainte.

4—6 . . . . . . Ney attacks with the cavalry.

4.30 . . . . . . Bülow's Prussian corps enters the field.

5 . . . . . . . . Engages Lobau's 6th corps, and carries Plancenoit.
Lord Hill moves up on the right.
Critical position of both armies.

5.30—7.30 . . . Plancenoit taken and retaken.

7.30 . . . . . . Zieten's Prussian corps begins to operate on the French right.
Final attack on the Allies.

8 . . . . . . . . Defeat of the Middle Guard.
General advance of the Allies.
Rout of the French.

9 . . . . . . . . Meeting of Wellington and Blücher.

*Appendix D.* . The Duke's Conversation about Waterloo.

*Appendix E.* . The Defeat of the Imperial Guard.

ÆT. 46. "THE people of England may be entitled to a detailed and accurate account of the battle of Waterloo, and I have no objection to their having it, but I do object to their being mis-informed and misled. . . . I am really disgusted with and ashamed of all that I have seen (written) of the battle of Waterloo. The number of writings upon it would lead the world to suppose that the British army had never fought a battle before; and there is not one which contains a true representation, or even an idea of the transaction; and this is because the writers have referred as above quoted (to stories picked up from peasants, private soldiers, indi-vidual officers, etc.) instead of to the official sources and reports." *

Twenty years later, after examining Major Siborne's model of Waterloo, now in the United Service Institution, the Duke made this confession: "It is very difficult for me to judge of the particular position of each body of troops under my command . . . at any particular hour." † Again: "Surely the details of the battle might be left to the original official reports. Historians and commentators were not necessary." ‡ "There is one event," he said to Lord Mahon, "noted in the world—the battle of Waterloo—and you will not find any two people agree as to the exact hour when it com-menced." § He used to say that he was accustomed to read so many conflicting descriptions of the battle that he would soon begin to believe he was not there himself.

*F. M. The Duke of Wellington to Walter Scott, Esq.* ‖

"Paris, 8th August, 1815.

"MY DEAR SIR,—I have received your letter of the 2nd regard-ing the battle of Waterloo. The object which you propose to yourself is very difficult of attainment, and, if really attained,

---

* Letter from the Duke to Sir J. Sinclair, 28th April, 1816 (*Suppl. Despatches*, x. 507).

† *Suppl. Despatches*, x. 513.        ‡ *Ibid.*, 530.

§ *Stanhope*, 88. The Duke himself seems scarcely to have known. In his official despatch (*Despatches*, xii. 481) he says "about ten o'clock;" in his letter to Walter Scott (*ibid.*, 508) he says "at eleven."

‖ In the published despatches this name is left blank.

is not a little invidious. The history of a battle is not unlike the history of a ball. Some individuals may recollect all the little events of which the great result is the battle won or lost : but no individual can recollect the order in which, or the exact moment at which, they occurred, which makes all the difference as to their value or importance. Then the faults or the misbehaviour of some gave occasion for the distinction of others, and perhaps were the cause of material losses ; and you cannot write a true history of a battle without including the faults and misbehaviour of part at least of those engaged. Believe me that every man you see in a military uniform is not a hero ; and that, although in the account given of a general action like Waterloo, many instances of individual heroism must be passed over unrelated, it is better for the general interests to leave those parts of the story untold, than to tell the whole truth. If, however, you should still think it right to turn your attention to this subject, I am most ready to give you every assistance and information in my power.

" Believe me, etc.,<br>" WELLINGTON."

" Paris, 17th August, 1815.

"MY DEAR SIR,—I have received your letter of the 11th, and I regret much that I have not been able to prevail upon you to relinquish your plan. You may depend upon it you will never make it a satisfactory work. I will get you the list of the French army, generals, etc. Just to show you how little reliance can be placed, even on what are supposed the best accounts of a battle, I mention that there are some circumstances mentioned in General ——'s account which did not occur as he relates them. He was not on the field during the whole battle, particularly not during the latter part of it. The battle began, I believe, at eleven. It is impossible to say when each important occurrence took place, nor in what order. . . . These are answers to all your queries : but remember, I recommend you to leave the battle of Waterloo as it is."

With these warnings, and many similar ones from the same source, ringing in his ears, how shall a writer, at this time of day, take up the well-worn theme, or hope to succeed where so many are held to have failed before him? Nothing more ambitious can be attempted than a synthetic sketch of the great scene, relying on those official reports which the Duke would have one regard as the only authentic materials for history, supplemented by his own subsequent memoranda and conversations, by incidents drawn from the numerous personal narratives, some already in print, others still in faded, tattered manuscript, and by the labours of those who have so industriously collated the official papers on both sides.

The rain continued to descend in torrents during the night of the 17th–18th, with violent thunder and lightning, drenching the troops of both armies in their comfortless bivouac on the miry fields.

"We arose with the daybreak," wrote an officer of the Scots 'Greys; "a miserably looking set of creatures we all were, covered with mud from head to foot, our white belts dyed with the red from our jackets, as if we had already completed the sanguinary work which we were about to begin." [*]

The rain stopped soon after sunrise on Sunday, 18th June, though the sky remained overcast. In the allied lines all was busy preparation from daybreak; the soldiers kindled fires with difficulty to cook breakfast, cleaned their rusted arms, and, a practice which Wellington disliked exceedingly but never succeeded in checking, instead of drawing the charges of their muskets, fired them in the air. At six o'clock the "fall in" sounded, and soon after the batteries, squadrons, and battalions took their appointed places in line of battle.

Lord Uxbridge, as next in seniority to the Commander-in-chief, came to the Duke and said that he should like to know his plans, because, if anything should happen to the Duke, the command would devolve on himself.

"Plans!" was the answer. "I have no plans. I shall be guided by circumstances."

* Hamilton MS.

Waterloo, where Wellington's headquarters were on the
night of 17th–18th June, is a small village, at that time
within the great forest of Soignes,* on the Charleroi-to-
Brussels paved road, about nine miles south of Brussels.
Two English miles further south is the hamlet of Mont-
Saint-Jean, where the *chaussée* to Nivelles branches off to the
south-west. From this point the Charleroi road, still running
south, ascends a gentle incline, till, nearly three-quarters of
a mile south of Mont-Saint-Jean, it is traversed at right
angles by the unpaved cross-road from Wavre and Ohain to
Braine-la-Leud, marking the crest of a low ridge running
due east and west. From this point the road dips into a
shallow valley, passing between a sandpit on the left,† and
the farmhouse and orchard of La Haye Sainte on the right,
crossing the hollow, and ascending through a slight cutting
a second ridge, parallel to that of Mont-Saint-Jean, and
distant from it at no point more than twelve hundred yards.
The cross-road from Ohain to Braine-la-Leud marked the
front of Wellington's position, and, although an insignificant
feature in unprofessional eyes, possessed at that time certain
qualities which proved of inestimable importance to the
defending force. To the east of the Charleroi *chaussée* this
cross-road was fenced with high and thick hedges now
removed; to the west it sank into a cutting between banks
five or six feet high.‡

To appreciate the merit of the Duke's position it must be
borne in mind that the cross-road from Ohain to Braine-la-
Leud runs along the edge of the plateau; that the ground
behind, that is, to the north, declines gently for a thousand
yards as far as the hamlet of Mont-Saint-Jean, and that the
ground in front, to the south, falls with a sharper descent into

* In 1815 the forest extended further to the south than it does now, and
encircled the village, which, at the present day, lies on its outskirts.

† Now partially filled up.

‡ Most unhappily these banks have been obliterated by the removal of soil to
form the huge mound marking the right centre of the allied position.

the little valley. It was the Duke's invariable custom, when possible, to keep his first line in shelter from fire, until immediately before it was engaged,* and the ground at Mont-Saint-Jean enabled him to carry out this principle. The first line of the Allies was placed on the reverse slope of the ridge behind the hedges and banks of the Ohain cross-road, the infantry being in quarter columns at deploying interval. The undulating ground behind them was occupied by the second line and reserves, including nearly all the cavalry, concealed from view of the enemy, and protected from his fire, by the land contour. The front was not protected by entrenchments, but the banks and hedges were pierced for the passage of cavalry and artillery.

The allied order of battle. Commencing from the centre of the allied position, to the east of the Charleroi road, Sir Thomas Picton held command with his 5th Division; Kempt's Light Infantry standing nearest the road; next them Pack's Highland Brigade, with Best's Hanoverian Brigade on their left; Wincke's Hanoverian Brigade further to the left, with Prince Edward of Saxe-Weimar's Nassau Brigade on their left opposite the farm of Papelotte; and Vandeleur's and Vivian's cavalry brigades covering the outer or left flank of the whole line. To the west of the Charleroi road, its left flank resting upon it, was formed Alten's 3rd Division, the brigades in succession from the left being Ompteda's King's German Legion, Kielmansegge's Hanoverians and Colin Halket's 5th Brigade. On Alten's right was drawn up the 1st or Guards Division under General Cooke, comprising the brigades of Maitland and Byng, with Byng's right resting on the Nivelles high-road. Beyond this road, and in reserve about Merbe-Braine, was Clinton's 2nd Division, composed of the brigades of Adam, Mitchell, Du Plat, and W. Halket. On the extreme right, and thrown back from the general alignment, Chassé's Dutch

---

* His chief criticism of Blücher's disposition before the battle of Ligny had been that the troops would suffer from the enemy's fire before they could be engaged.

division occupied the village and vicinity of Braine-la-Leud. ANN. 1815.
Lord Edward Somerset's brigade of heavy cavalry was behind
the centre of the line to the west of the Charleroi road, to the
east of which was Sir William Ponsonby's "Union Brigade"—
the Royal Dragoons, Scots Greys, and Inniskillens. Kruse's
Dutch cavalry was posted on Somerset's right.

It will be observed that, although the army had been
formally organised in two corps, the left being under command of the Prince of Orange, the right under Lord Hill, this
novel arrangement was not strictly adhered to in the line of
battle, the brigades being disposed so as to distribute as much
as possible the older and more trustworthy troops among those
of less experience. The Duke was careful to give his first
line the advantage of the shelter afforded by the ground, and
this was skilfully done. But to this there was one exception,
utterly unaccounted for to this day. Bylandt's Dutch brigade
was placed immediately on the east of the Charleroi road, on
the outer slope of the ridge, a hundred and fifty yards in front
of Kempt and Pack, and wholly exposed to the enemy's fire.
What these poor fellows suffered there must be remembered
when their subsequent behaviour has to be described.

Such being the general disposition of the first line of the
Allies, there remain to be described certain advanced posts
of great importance which the Duke caused to be occupied.
Abutting on the west side of the Charleroi road, three
hundred yards in front of the general line, is the farmhouse,
outbuildings, garden, and orchard of La Haye Sainte, enclosed in walls and hedges.* This was occupied as an
advanced post by four hundred men of the King's German
Legion, and an *abattis* was thrown across the high-road from
the southern angle of the enclosure. Four hundred yards in
front of the extreme allied left, Perponcher's Dutchmen

*The advanced posts.*

---

* The house and barn have been rebuilt since 1815, but much of the original
garden wall remains, in which, on the west side, may be traced the loopholes
made by its garrison. Even the two slight buttresses shown in the contemporary drawing remain to this day.

occupied the farms of La Haye and Papelotte, with a picket of the 10th Hussars thrown still further forward in the village of Smohain.

Coming now to the right of the allied position, there stand in the valley, five hundred yards in front of the Ohain cross-road, the château, walled garden, and farmyard of Hougoumont,* protected at that time on the south by a thick wood and copse, which has now disappeared. This quiet country house, with its rustic environment, was destined to lasting fame by reason of the long-drawn fury with which its possession was contested. It was occupied at first by the light companies of the 2nd Battalion Coldstream Guards and of the 2nd Battalion 3rd Guards,† a Nassau regiment, and some Hanoverian rifles. About noon, four more companies of the Coldstream, and, later still, the remainder of the 3rd Guards, were moved in to reinforce. During the night the loopholes in the garden wall were cleared out,‡ new ones were cut in the buildings; platforms and embankments were raised inside the garden walls to enable the men to fire over the top.

The Allies, then, showed a front of nearly three English miles towards the south, defined and strengthened by the hedges and banks of the Ohain cross-road, and with four advanced posts, La Haye, Papelotte, La Haye Sainte with its sandpit, and Hougoumont with its garden, orchard, and wood. On the right the line extended a mile further, but was thrown back nearly *en potence*, so as to face west-south-west.

Mounted on his famous charger, Copenhagen, the Duke rode with his staff along the lines as the brigades took up their positions. Crossing over to Hougoumont, he brought

---

* This is what philologers term a "ghost name." The real name was Château du Goumont, but it found its way into despatches, and thence, indelibly, into history, as the Château d'Hougoumont.

† Now the Scots Guards.

‡ Not made for the first time, as usually stated. They were part of the old defences of the place, having, as may be seen to this day, stone facings in the brickwork.

the Coldstream Guards back from the copse, posting them in ANN. 1815.
the orchard, garden, and buildings, and replaced them by
sending the Hanoverian and Nassau men into the wood. He
wore his usual exceedingly plain dress—blue frock, blue
cloak,* white pantaloons, black sword-belt, cocked hat without plume,† but with King George's black cockade and three
smaller ones in the colours of Portugal, Spain, and the
Netherlands, indicating the four services in which he held
marshal's rank. The one piece of dandyism he affected was
wearing a white cravat, fastened behind the neck with a
buckle, instead of the regulation black stock.

The Emperor Napoleon, before retiring to rest at the farm Position of
of Caillou shortly before midnight on the 17th, dictated to the French
Soult the order of battle for the morrow. After resting an army.
hour he rose again, and, accompanied by General Bertrand,
rode through the pouring rain right round his advanced posts.
He was uneasy lest the enemy should beat a retreat during
the night, but from the little tavern of La Belle Alliance,‡
distant only 1,400 yards from the centre of the allied line
along the Charleroi road, he saw the bivouac fires of
Wellington's army, and felt satisfied it was going to hold its
ground. Returning to the Caillou at dawn, he found a
despatch, sent off by Grouchy from Gembloux at ten o'clock,
announcing that the Prussians were moving in two columns,
one upon Liége, the other upon Wavre, and that he intended
to follow the Wavre column, to prevent it co-operating
with Wellington. All this was satisfactory enough. Half

---

* When Garrard was making an equestrian statuette of the Duke, Lord
Bathurst asked the Duke whether he wore a cloak at Waterloo. "It was a
showery day," replied he, "though it got finer in the afternoon. I had my
cloak on and off fifty times. I remember very well putting it on, because I
never got wet when I can help it. When it grew fine, I took it off and fastened
it on my saddle" (*Salisbury MSS.*, 1837).

† The Duke's cocked hat was made exceedingly low in the crown, and was
commonly covered with oilskin in bad weather.

‡ This name, which derived so much significance from the events of the day,
had its derisive origin in the marriage of a former proprietor, who was old and
ugly, with a pretty young woman in the neighbourhood.

Blücher's forces were falling back upon their communications
with Luxembourg; with the other half Grouchy assuredly
could deal, and prevent any interference with the defeat
Napoleon was about to inflict on the Anglo-Dutch army.
He little knew that Wellington and Blücher had been in
communication throughout the night.   The state of the
ground, however, in consequence of the rain, had seriously
retarded the march of the Emperor's divisions.   It had been
his intention to attack at daybreak, but now, at 5 a.m., he
issued orders for the men to make their soup, and for the
brigades to take up their positions in line of battle at nine
o'clock, " as indicated in his order of the previous evening." *
It was long after that hour before his array was complete.
The whole of the Imperial Guard, Lobau's corps d'armée,
Durutte's division, and Kellermann's cuirassiers had not
arrived from Genappe; the state of the roads and country
greatly retarded their march; but the mischief had its source
in the Emperor's fatal waste of the morning of the 17th.   Had
he advanced early on that morning on the 17th, he would
not only have interfered very gravely with the retreat of the
Allies, but, supposing them to have succeeded in retiring
safely upon the position of Mont-Saint-Jean, his various corps
would have been forward in time to begin the attack early on
the 18th.

The
Emperor's
breakfast
party.

The Emperor broke his fast at the farm of le Caillou with
Soult, Bassano, Drouot, and other Generals, the meal being
served on silver plate with the Imperial arms; after which,
at eight o'clock, maps were brought out, and the situation was
eagerly but leisurely discussed.

"The enemy," observed Napoleon, reverting to his favourite
calculation of the odds, "is one-fourth stronger in numbers
than we; † nevertheless the chances are ninety to ten in our
favour."   At that moment entered Ney, who had observed
some movements in the allied lines which looked like

---

* *Houssaye*, 279.

† This, of course, was not the case; probably Napoleon reckoned on Wellington
having brought in Prince Ferdinand's corps from Hal.

retreat, and urged the Emperor to hasten the attack, or the enemy would escape.

"You have seen wrong," replied Napoleon; "the time is past for that. Wellington would suffer destruction if he attempted retreat. He has thrown the dice, and they are in our favour."

Soult deplored the absence of Grouchy. He counselled the Emperor once more, as he had done the day before, to recall at least part of the 34,000 good men detached with that Marshal.

"You think," retorted the Emperor, roughly, "because Wellington defeated you, that he must be a great General. I tell you that he is a bad General, that the English are poor troops, and that this will be the affair of a *déjeuner.*"

"I hope so," replied Soult.

After this the party were joined by Napoleon's brother Jérôme and General Reille. The Emperor asked Reille his opinion of the English army. Reille certainly was not without experience of its quality: he said he thought that, well posted as they were, the British infantry were impregnable to a front attack, because of the excellence of their fire; but he believed they might be outmanœuvred. Napoleon liked this opinion no better than Soult's; with an impatient exclamation he broke up the gathering. The General of Engineers, Haxo, returned from reconnoitring, reported that the enemy had no entrenchments. He did not mention the natural features and buildings of which Wellington had taken full advantage to strengthen his position.

At this time only Reille's corps was in position; the other columns were still moving up from Genappe, labouring through the deep soil. Jérôme Buonaparte told the Emperor that on the previous evening the hotel waiter, who served him with supper at Genappe, repeated what he had heard an aide-de-camp say while Wellington was dining at the same house in the afternoon, namely, that the British and Prussian commanders had given each other the rendezvous before the

Æt. 46.

forest of Soignes, and that the Prussians would come up by way of Wavre.

"Bah!" said Napoleon; "after a battle such as that of Fleurus (Ligny) the junction of the English with the Prussians is out of the question for two days from now. Besides, the Prussians have Grouchy at their heels." Then, wearing his well-known grey paletôt over his usual uniform as a colonel of *chasseurs-à-cheval*, Napoleon got on his white charger Marengo,* and rode off to the front at La Belle Alliance, which he had fixed as the *point d'appui* of the right and left wings of his army. He took with him as guide Jean Decoster, who kept a small roadside tavern,† bound in the saddle of a troop-horse, and attached by a picket-rope to that of a mounted chasseur. Having scanned the allied position, and while his troops were still assembling, the Emperor rode back to the farm of Rossomme, where, seated

The Emperor's order to Grouchy.

at a small table in the open air, he wrote to Grouchy in reply to that Marshal's despatch of 10 p.m. on the 17th. Upon this letter of the Emperor's, and the interpretation put upon it by Grouchy, hinged, as it turned out, the issue of the day. To take any part here in the controversy between the apologists of Napoleon and the defenders of Grouchy would lie far outside the limits of the present work; that Napoleon's instructions to Grouchy were obscure, or at least ambiguous, is sufficiently proved by the widely divergent interpretation put upon their text by the historians who have most recently analysed it. This much, however, may be said. Napoleon himself, as is well known, laid the whole blame of the subsequent miscarriage upon Grouchy, but the initial error lay in the vagueness of the Emperor's orders to him when he was

---

* Marengo was a beautiful little Arab, measuring only 14 hands 2 inches. His skeleton may be seen in the museum of the United Service Institution, but one of his hoofs, mounted in silver gilt as a snuff-box, belongs to the mess of St. James's Palace guard. Marengo in the course of the day was wounded in the near haunch, on which Napoleon mounted his white Arab mare Marie.

† In some maps Decoster's tavern, situated a few hundred yards south of La Belle Alliance, is marked Maison d'Ecosse, a corruption of Maison Decoster.

ANN. 1815.

first detached on the 17th at Ligny to pursue the Prussians
"in the direction of Namur and Maestricht." But when,
early on the 18th, Napoleon became aware that Blücher had
baffled the French Marshal by a rapid concentration upon
Wavre, so far from summoning Grouchy to the support of the
main army, he directed him to follow the Prussians to Wavre.
Now Grouchy, with 34,000 men, had before him 75,000
Prussians, by no means in the dispirited and disorganised
condition imagined by the Emperor. This consideration
is not always present with those who reproach Grouchy
for not pressing the enemy more vigorously. But then
it is said that when he heard from Walhain (not Sart-à-
Walhain *) the cannonade opening at Mont-Saint-Jean, he
should at once have made all speed to support the Emperor,
as Gérard urgently desired him to do. Supposing he had
done so, which would have been directly to disregard his
instructions, must he not still have been too late to save the
battle, being sixteen miles distant from the field? When, at
4 p.m., he received the Emperor's morning order, it did but
confirm him in what he had undertaken: "You will direct
your movements upon Wavre, so as to approach us, act in
concert with us and keep communication with us, driving
before you the Prussian army which has taken that route,
and which may have halted at Wavre, *where you must arrive
as soon as possible.*" This command Grouchy carried out to
the letter by attacking and defeating Thielmann's corps at
Wavre, while the other three Prussian corps slowly but
steadily made their way towards Mont-Saint-Jean. "One
is compelled," says M. Houssaye, "to read into this letter
(Napoleon's morning order) that which is not in it, namely, an
order to Grouchy to manœuvre by his left in order to bring
him near the main body of the French army. . . . From the
tenour of this order it is manifest that, at 10 o'clock in the
morning, the Emperor neither summoned Grouchy to his
field of battle, nor reckoned on seeing him arrive." †

* *Ropes*, 256.     † *Houssaye*, 316, note.

However, whether Grouchy is to be blamed for disobeying the order dictated to Bertrand by the Emperor and sent to Grouchy on 17th June (an order which he afterwards repeatedly and falsely denied having received); whether, further, the construction which he placed on the Emperor's order of 10 a.m. on the 18th can be justified, is outside the scope of the present narrative; all that concerns it is that although Grouchy was within hearing of the guns at Waterloo, and was strongly urged by Gérard, commanding the 4th Corps, to move to the Emperor's support, he refused to do so, and spent the day fighting the 3rd Prussian corps under Thielmann at Wavre. A later and more imperative order sent by Napoleon at 1 p.m., when Bülow's attack on the French right flank was imminent, did not reach Grouchy till seven in the evening, when it was too late to do anything.

The French order of battle.

With drums beating, colours flying, and bands playing *Veillons au salut de l'Empire*, Napoleon's last army defiled past him into its position on the plateau of La Belle Alliance, affording to their adversaries beyond the valley an imposing display of force as the heavy columns wheeled and dressed with the deliberate precision of a holiday review. Each brigade as it passed by lowered its colours to the great chieftain, loud and long rang the shouts of *Vive l'Empereur!* louder and longer, said a veteran officer of the 1st Corps d'armée, than he had ever known before, for the men were determined that they should be heard among the brick-red lines which fringed the crest of Mont-Saint-Jean.

The position taken up by Napoleon was on the ridge, or plateau, of La Belle Alliance, corresponding in height, general direction, and character to that of Mont-Saint-Jean. The French centre, like that of the Allies, was marked by the Charleroi high-road; like that of the Allies, also, but not so accurately, the general alignment was marked by a cross-road. The force on the field consisted of the 1st (d'Erlon's four divisions), 2nd (Reille's three divisions), and 6th (Loban's three divisions) Corps, the Imperial Guard (three divisions), ANN. 1815. the heavy cavalry of Kellermann and Milhaud, and the light cavalry of Domon and Subervie—in all 71,947 men, of which 15,765 were cavalry and 7,232 artillery with 246 guns.

The army was disposed in three lines, the right wing of the first line being formed by d'Erlon's corps in dense columns under Allix, Donzelot, Marcognet, and Durutte, with its inner flank resting on the Charleroi road near La Belle Alliance, and with Jacquinot's light cavalry covering the outer flank opposite La Haye and Papelotte. Reille's corps of three divisions—Bachelu, Foy, and Jérôme—furnished the left wing of the first line, extending from La Belle Alliance to the Nivelles road, on which were Piré's light cavalry, opposite Hougoumont. After these troops had taken up their position, vigilant eyes in the allied army could perceive countless black specks appearing in the intervals along the front—those terrible *bouches-à-feu* which herald and enforce the operations of the sister arms.* In the centre of the second line, Count Lobau's infantry were massed in column on the west of the Charleroi road, balanced by the cavalry of Domon and Subervie on the east thereof. D'Erlon's infantry divisions had the support of Count Milhaud's cuirassiers in the second line; those of Reille that of Kellermann's. Further back, close to Rossomme, loomed the dark masses of the Imperial Guard in reserve, with cavalry on either flank.†

* It is needless to remind the reader that no display of this kind could ever be witnessed in modern warfare. It was sufficiently remarkable even in those days, for the English and French artillery were within easy range of each other the whole time.

† The infantry of the Guard wore their fighting dress this day—bear-skin cap without plume or hackle, blue trousers and long blue coats with red epaulettes. But each man carried in his haversack his parade dress, to be worn on entering Brussels, making his load, with musket and forty rounds of ammunition, nearly 70 lbs. avoirdupois. The Young Guard consisted of men of four years', the Middle Guard of men of eight years', and the Old Guard of men of twelve years' service and upwards.

Seldom, if ever, within historic times has such a mighty force been marshalled within so small a compass. Seventy-two thousand French, with 246 guns, were drawn up against sixty-eight thousand British and their allies, with 156 guns —one hundred and forty thousand men with four hundred cannon ; yet the whole space, from flank to flank, was less than three miles ; * at no point did the distance between the opposing armies amount to a mile ; three miles, measured along the straight Charleroi road, covered the distance between the rearmost reserves of both armies. The undulating ground between the two positions was deeply cultivated, without fences, as at this day, and covered with high and rich crops of rye and clover, soon to be trampled into a miry and bloody stubble. To one standing midway across the hollow between the two hosts, before they engaged, the preponderance of force would have seemed enormously in favour of the French, both because of their massive formation —quarter columns of double companies at short intervals— and because the first line of the Allies were screened by the hedges, and their second line, reserves, and most of the cavalry hidden by the reverse slope of the ridge.

It was close on eleven o'clock before the Emperor had completed his leisurely dispositions and returned to his post at Rossomme. There he issued the order which showed his disdain for Reille's caution. As soon as all the troops had come up from Genappe, which would be at one o'clock, the allied position was to be attacked in the centre ; the British infantry, whom Napoleon never yet had encountered in battle, were to be crushed and pierced by the very means which those who had so encountered them knew they were strongest in resisting ; and the superior manœuvring of the French, although repeatedly proved in former campaigns, was not to be employed in turning the enemy's left, where he was weakest, whereby also he should be separated from the possible approach of the Prussians from Wavre.

* Wellington held a front of nearly eight miles at Busaco with 36.000 men.

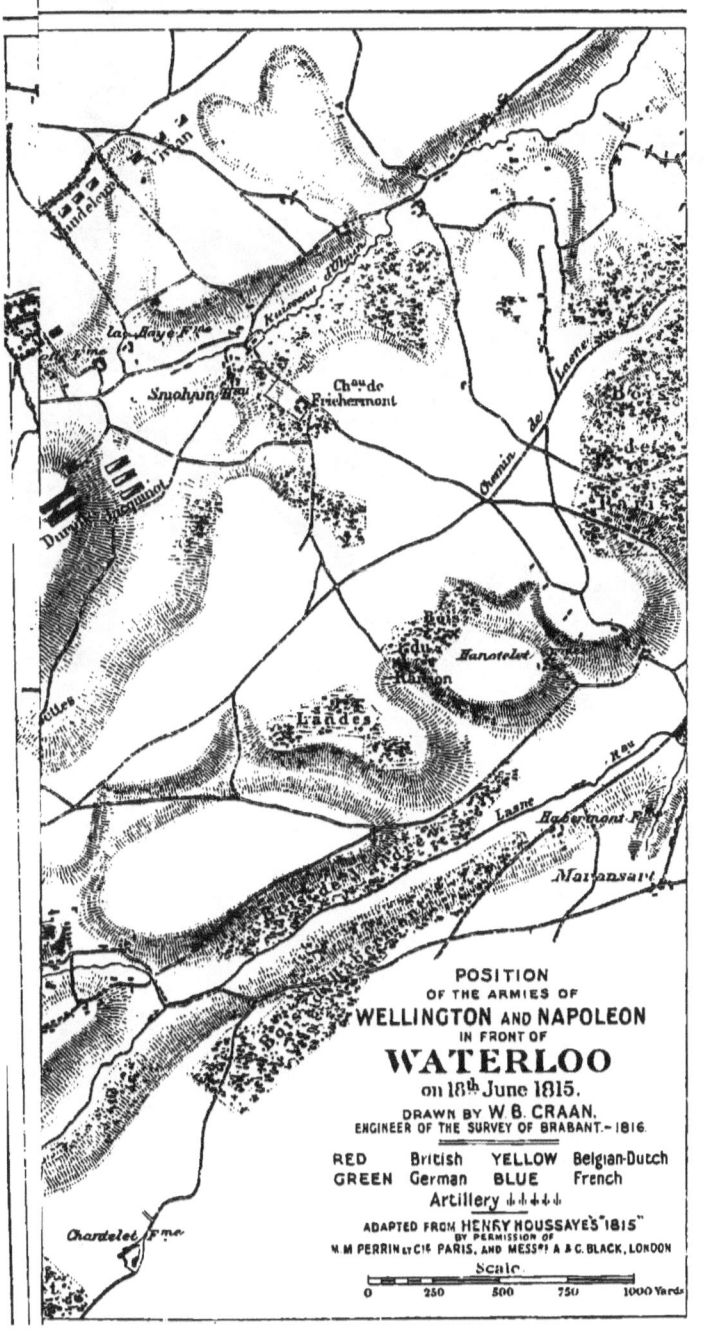

POSITION
OF THE ARMIES OF
WELLINGTON AND NAPOLEON
IN FRONT OF
WATERLOO
on 18ᵗʰ June 1815.
DRAWN BY W. B. CRAAN.
ENGINEER OF THE SURVEY OF BRABANT.—1816.

RED    British    YELLOW    Belgian-Dutch
GREEN    German    BLUE    French
Artillery ⚒⚒⚒⚒⚒

ADAPTED FROM HENRY HOUSSAYE'S "1815"
BY PERMISSION OF
M. M. PERRIN ᴇᴛ Cᴵᴱ PARIS, AND MESSᴿˢ A & C. BLACK, LONDON

Scale
0        250        500        750        1000 Yards

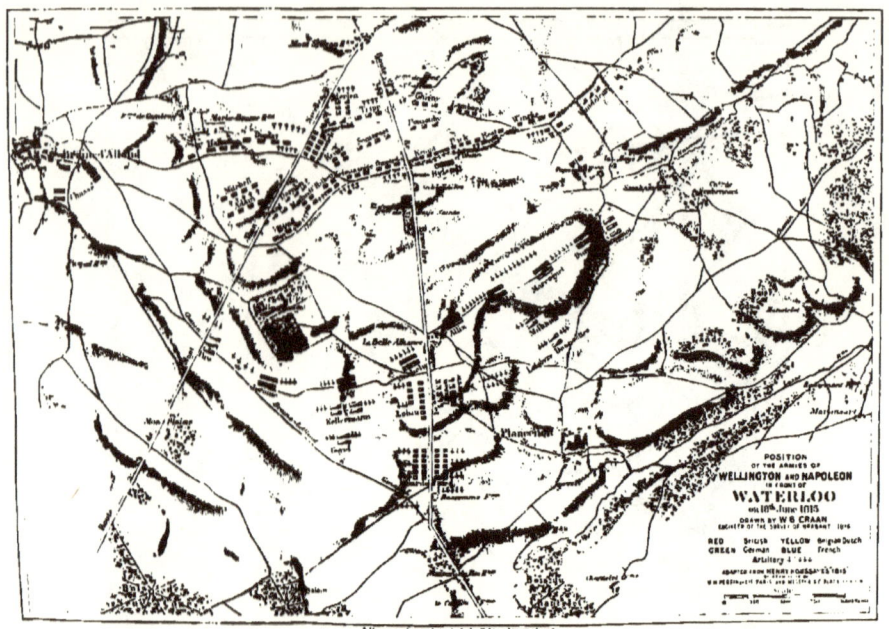

POSITION
OF THE ARMIES OF
WELLINGTON AND NAPOLEON
IN FRONT OF
WATERLOO
on 18th June 1815
DRAWN BY W.B.CRAAN
ENGINEER OF THE SURVEY OF BRABANT 1816

RED    British    YELLOW    Belgian Dutch
GREEN  German     BLUE      French
Artillery ᵒ ᵒ ᵒ ᵒ

ADAPTED FROM HENRY HOUSSAYE 1815

᛭ Position of mound on which the Belgian Lion is placed
● = Maison Brewster

In determining on this mode of attack, Napoleon had to
take into account the advanced posts of the Allies. To
induce Wellington, if possible, to weaken his centre, he
decided not to wait till his whole line was formed, but
directed Reille to possess himself of Hougoumont at once.

Shortly after eleven o'clock, coils of white smoke surged out
from the French left, and a mighty roar crashed along the dark
hedge of war. The British batteries on the allied right
made sonorous response : the ominous sound rolled as far
as Walhain, sixteen miles to the east, where Grouchy, having
finished a leisurely breakfast, was dallying with a dish of
strawberries.

Under cover of a terrific cannonade, Jérôme led a brigade
of four regiments in echelon of battalions, preceded by a
cloud of skirmishers, into the hollow before the copse of
Hougoumont, while Piré's lancers moved along the Nivelles
road. The Emperor had not intended Jérôme's attack to be
much more than a feint, but it developed into a furious
combat which lasted throughout the day. The tirailleurs of
the French 1ᵉʳ *léger* made good their footing in the skirts of
the wood, supported by the 3ᵉ of the line. Foot by foot they
fought their way through the thick copse ; after an hour's
murderous work the men of Nassau and a detachment of
Guards were driven back to the walls of Hougoumont, whence
a deadly fire poured upon the assailants. Reille sent orders
not to push further than the wood, but Jérôme persisted in
the endeavour to capture the château, sending up fresh battalions to the assault. Some of these outflanked the en-
closures, getting in rear of Hougoumont and firing out of the
deep rye at Colonel Smith's battery on the ridge above Byng's
brigade. More companies of the Coldstream Guards forced
their way in to reinforce the garrison, but no movement was
made from the allied centre, as Napoleon had hoped would
be the result of this attack.

While the combat raged round Hougoumont, preparations
went on for the grand attack in the centre. Eighty guns

were placed in battery in front of La Belle Alliance, and Ney's columns stood waiting the word to advance. The usual preliminary cannonade was about to open when, at one o'clock or thereby, Napoleon, ever anxiously looking for signs of Grouchy's approach, although he had no right to expect it, detected, about six miles to the north-east, a dark shadow on the heights—apparently a body of troops. The atmosphere was close and hazy; Soult was sure it was troops, probably Grouchy's; others of the staff thought it was only a wood. All doubts were set at rest by Marbot's hussars bringing in a Prussian sergeant whom they had captured, bearing a letter from Bülow to Wellington, announcing the arrival of the 4th Prussian Corps at Chapelle-Saint-Lambert. The junction, then, of the Prussians with Wellington's army, which Napoleon had derided in the morning as *paroles en l'air*, was on the point of accomplishment.[*] Instantly he detached the light cavalry of Domon and Subervie to reconnoitre, and Soult wrote at the same time to Grouchy, bidding him abandon his movement on Wavre, hasten to fall on Bülow's rear, and join the French right. "Ne perdez pas un instant pour vous rapprocher de nous et nous joindre, et pour écraser Bülow, que vous prendrez en flagrant délit."[†]

The apparition of the Prussian corps gave Napoleon more concern than surprise, because he had already received a despatch sent by Grouchy from Gembloux at six in the morning, announcing the general movement of the Prussian army either upon Brussels or to form a junction with Wellington at Mont-Saint-Jean. The Emperor, however, still cherished the hope that Blücher would not risk a movement upon Mont-Saint-Jean. "This morning," he said to Soult, "the chances were ninety to ten in our favour; they are

---

[*] Bülow's cavalry had been seen from the allied lines at an early hour in the morning, moving on the heights in front of Ohain. This was his advanced guard, the march of the main column being retarded by the wet ground and difficult defiles of Wavre.

[†] This despatch did not reach Grouchy till 5 p.m.

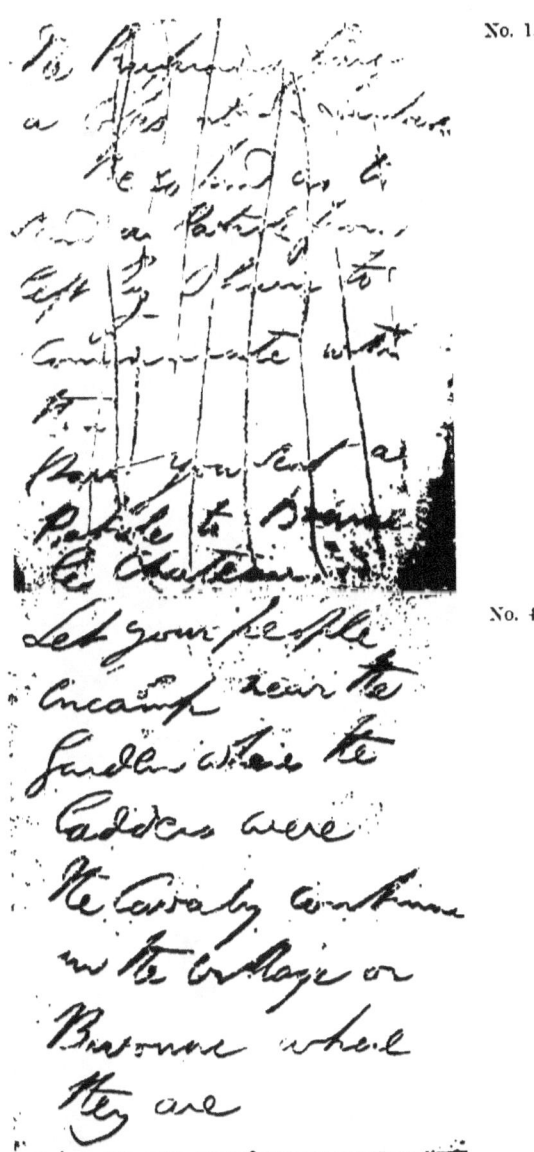

ORDERS PENCILLED BY THE DUKE OF WELLINGTON DURING THE BATTLE OF
WATERLOO.
No. 1 TO SIR H. VIVIAN, COMMANDING LIGHT CAVALRY BRIGADE ON THE LEFT.
No. 4 WAS WRITTEN AFTER THE BATTLE, BECAUSE ORDER No. 1 HAS BEEN
STRUCK OUT WITH THE PENCIL, SHOWING THAT No. 1 WAS ANTERIOR TO
No. 4.

still sixty to forty, and if Grouchy repairs the horrible fault he has committed by loitering at Gembloux, and marches fast, the victory will be all the more decisive, because Bülow's corps will be utterly destroyed."

Among the innumerable treasures of Apsley House none are more precious than three folded pieces of ass's skin, such as the Duke used to carry in his pocket during an action, and pencil his orders upon to his Generals. By great good luck these, which were used at Waterloo, were not sponged clean as was usually done, and at this day one may retrace the firm, clear characters as they were written in the very roar and tumult of the field. The first of them must have been sent out, probably to Sir Hussey Vivian, at this period of the battle.

"The Prussians have a corps at St. Lambert. Be so kind as to send a Patrole from our left by Ohain to communicate with them. Have you sent a Patrole to Braine-le-chateau?"

Napoleon could no longer neglect his right flank. Incessantly taking pinches of snuff, as was his custom in times of anxiety or excitement, and as he continued to do throughout this day, the Emperor wheeled up to the right the 6th Corps under Count Lobau to guard the approaches from Wavre and Saint-Lambert. Then he gave Ney the Ney order to begin his attack. The grand battery of eighty guns, receives posted on the edge of the plateau to the east of the Charleroi to attack. road, crashed continuously for half an hour in a cannonade to which the British and Brunswick batteries * made prompt response. At two o'clock the fire ceased, as d'Erlon's four Advance magnificent divisions of infantry, under the Generals Allix, of d'Erlon's corps. Donzelot, Marcognet, and Durutte, advanced 18,000 strong in echelon of divisions from the left at four hundred paces distance, Ney himself riding with d'Erlon at the head of the leading division (Allix). Napoleon rarely interfered with

* In 1815 batteries of field and garrison artillery were termed "brigades," and batteries of horse artillery "troops."

his Generals in their mode of executing movements which he
directed; on this occasion the usual formation for attack, in
columns of battalions at open or half distance, was exchanged
for a most objectionable one.   Each division was formed in a
single close column of battalions, with a front of 160 to 200
files, and a depth of twenty-four, a formation rigid and un-
wieldy, whence it was equally difficult to deploy or to
form square, and peculiarly ill-adapted for the deep and
broken ground to be traversed.*

   As each echelon in descending the slope cleared the line of
fire, the batteries behind reopened on Picton's 5th Division
and Bylandt's unfortunate Dutch brigade.   The French
covered their advance with a long line of skirmishers, and
soon the whole valley from Papelotte to the Charleroi road
was wrapped in flame and smoke, and filled with dreadful
noise—the musketry rattling below, the cannon bellowing
overhead.   Wellington watched the advance from under a
moderate-sized elm on the ridge, just in front of where the
Ohain road crosses the highway.†   In vain his staff urged
him to move away, seeing how dangerously the tree was
drawing the enemy's fire.   Of Allix's division, Quiot's brigade
Attack on<br>La Haye<br>Sainte. was engaged in a determined assault upon La Haye Sainte,
two hundred yards in front of the Duke.   Witnessing how
hard pressed were Baring's Germans in defending it, he sent
one of Ompteda's battalions to their relief, which, however,
was broken by a charge of Travers's cuirassiers, and he only
withdrew when the enemy's tirailleurs began firing from the
north end of the garden.‡   D'Erlon's massive columns

---

   * M. Houssaye (p. 338, note) suggests that d'Erlon's aide-de-camp, in carrying his order to the divisional generals, mistook the formation of *la colonne par
division*, i.e. column of double companies at half or wheeling distance, for *la
colonne de division*, i.e. eight battalions in a single close column.   But d'Erlon
must be held responsible, as the formation took place under his eye.

   † This elm is no longer to be seen, an enterprising Englishman having been
allowed to purchase it and enrich himself by the sale of its wood in snuff-boxes
and what not.

   ‡ *Waterloo Letters*, p. 33.

MAJOR-GENERAL SIR DENIS PACK, K.C.B.

*Vol. ii, p. 99.*

suffered terribly from artillery fire during their advance; Ann. 1815. nevertheless they pressed on, steadily ascending the slope. Allix's division drove two companies of the 95th Rifles out of the sandpit near La Haye Sainte. Next them Donzelot's men, with loud cries of *Vive l'Empereur!* moved upon Bylandt's Dutchmen, who had been grievously torn by the fire of the grand battery immediately opposite them at a range of not more than a thousand yards. These broke and ran up the slope, nor can they be justly blamed for doing so, seeing how cruelly they had been exposed. The fugitives passed through the ranks of the Cameron Highlanders, who, lying in shelter of the cross-road behind the advanced position, jeered them derisively, and many a sly prod from a bayonet quickened the movement of the broken battalions to the rear.

The French tirailleurs were now close to the hedges of the Ohain road; not a musket-shot betrayed what lay before them. Brave old Picton was there, with as much as Quatre-Bras had left him of Kempt's and Pack's brigades—three thousand light infantry and Highlanders. "Rise up!" he cried; the word was echoed by the brigade commanders, and Kempt's brigade * moved forward to the crest, sweeping before them the busy tirailleurs.

The congestion of the French columns had become un-Donzelot repulsed by Kempt's brigade. bearable. Donzelot halted his division, the second from the left, under the crest in order to attempt a deployment; he was in the act of carrying out this movement, so difficult from his peculiar formation, when a loud hurrah from the ridge above caused all to look up. Within forty yards stood the thin red line, far overlapping the flanks of the French column. A sharp command, and every musket was levelled at the "present;" another, and a torrent of lead tore through the crowded ranks. Donzelot's men wavered, began to fall back; then, in the comparative silence, for the French cannon

---

\* The 28th and 32nd Regiments, the 79th Cameron Highlanders, and 1st Battalion 95th Rifles.

Æт. 46. had suspended their fire as their own men climbed the slopes, was heard Picton's last word of command—"Charge hurrah!" He lived not to see the result: a musket ball entered his right temple, and he fell dead on the spot between the cross-roads and the sandpit.* The command was obeyed, though; with loud cheers the British line poured down the slope, forcing Donzelot's disordered mass into greater confusion.

Lord Palmerston has recorded Wellington's own words describing an incident at this period of the combat: they are instructive as showing, not only how he was exposed to fire as constantly as any of his fighting line—more so, because at no period of the day could he seek shelter by lying down— but also how the commander of a great army, when regimental officers are falling fast, must at times assume the direction of a mere handful of men.

"A column of French was firing across the road at one of our regiments. Our people could not get at them to charge them, because they would have been disordered by crossing the road. It was a nervous moment. One of the two forces must go about in a few minutes—it was impossible to say which it might be. I saw about two hundred men of the 79th, who seemed to have had more than they liked of it. I formed them myself about twenty yards from the flash of the French column, and ordered them to fire; and, in a few minutes, the French column turned about." †

Marcognet repulsed by Pack's brigade. This disposed of the second echelon of Ney's attack. While Donzelot was attempting to deploy, the third echelon, under Marcognet, came up on his right and passed him, crossed the Ohain road on the crest, and suddenly encountered

* "A rough, foul-mouthed devil as ever lived," was the Duke's elegy on this gallant officer, "but he always behaved extremely well; no man could do better in different services I assigned to him" (*Stanhope,* 69). The officers of the 2nd Battalion Connaught Rangers, the old 88th, still wear a black line in their gold lace, in mourning for their beloved Peninsular chief.

† *Palmerston's Journal,* p. 53.

*Lieut Gen.l the Earl of ....... G.C.B.*
*Governor & General of ........*

Pack's Highland brigade deployed in line.* Here, again, the A-N-N. 1815.
superiority of fire from an extended front told with fatal
effect on the French columns; Marcognet's men were checked.
Now was the moment for the cavalry, and they were ready
at hand. Sir William Ponsonby had wheeled his "Union Charge
Brigade" into line on the reverse slope to the east of the "Union
high-road—the Royal Dragoons, Scots Greys, and Inniskillens. Brigade."
The enemy's cavalry was threatening, and as Ponsonby's line
advanced the Highlanders were forming squares; but with
loud cries of "Scotland yet!" many of them seized the
stirrups of the Greys as they passed through the intervals,
and were carried forward in the charge. The heavy cavalry
fell upon both flanks of Marcognet's division, completing
their rout, forced back some heavy masses of French cavalry,
and rode on through the deep ground, often up to their girths,
against the French in position on the south side. They got
out of hand, as Wellington often complained his cavalry did,
and suffered in consequence from the enemy's batteries and
cavalry, finally being forced to retire with the irreparable loss
of their commander, Sir William Ponsonby.†

While the Union Brigade were thus occupied on the east Charge of
of the Charleroi road, Lord Uxbridge himself was leading Lord Lord E.
Edward Somerset's heavy brigade‡ against Travers's cuirassiers brigade.
and Allix's infantry upon and to the west of that road. The
cuirassiers had ridden up as far as the cross-road, and were
actually in it, in the hollow way, when the Household
Cavalry appeared on the bank above their heads. In order
to extricate themselves, the cuirassiers had to defile to the
right, and get upon the high-road between the allied position

* Third Battalion 1st Royal Scots, 3rd Battalion 42nd Royal Highlanders, 2nd
Battalion 44th Regiment, and 92nd Gordon Highlanders.

† Ponsonby's groom or orderly had not brought his charger in time or to the
right place, and Sir William was mounted on a hack. In leading a charge
against the Polish Lancers, the animal, overweighted, stuck fast in the mire;
Sir William and his aide-de-camp were killed on the spot.

‡ The 1st and 2nd Life Guards, the Horse Guards, and the King's Dragoon
Guards. Lord Uxbridge afterwards admitted that he made a great mistake in
leading this charge himself.

and La Haye Sainte.* Somerset's regiments charged them before they could re-form, scattered them, and drove Allix's infantry column back in disorder across the valley; but they, in turn, like their comrades in the Union Brigade, paid the penalty of disregard of trumpet and voice sounding the recall. "When I was returning to our position," said Lord Uxbridge, "I met the Duke of Wellington, surrounded by all the *corps diplomatique militaire*, who from the high ground had witnessed the whole affair. The plain appeared to be swept clean, and I never saw so joyous a group as this *troupe dorée*. They thought the battle was over." †

**Repulse of Durutte's column at Papelotte.**

Still there remains to be told the fortune of Durutte's division on the right of the French attack. It suffered less than the others, but having sustained the charge of Vandeleur's light brigade,‡ was obliged to draw off, though in good order, and without much loss. The grand attack of the whole French right wing had failed. A period of comparative calm, brief, but well marked, ensued. Only at Hougoumont, far on the British right, the conflict still raged furiously. The attack on this post, originally intended as no more than a diversion, had developed into the most sustained, and not the least murderous, of the day, owing to gross mismanagement on the part of Reille. No attempt was made to batter down the defences on the west with artillery, which would have been perfectly practicable, and must have rendered the position untenable. Hand to hand the combatants contested every yard of the copse; repeatedly driven to the shelter of the walls, the defenders as often sallied forth, until the wood and orchard became a sheer charnel-house. The barn caught

**The conflict at Hougoumont.**

---

\* This part of the ground has been grievously altered: the banks have disappeared, and the road is now level with the fields on either side. The direction taken by Travers's cuirassiers exactly corresponds with that of the modern tramway.

† *Waterloo Letters*, p. 9.

‡ The 11th, 12th, and 16th Light Dragoons; not the 13th as stated by M. Houssaye (p. 347), which was in Grant's brigade. During this charge the 11th Light Dragoons remained in reserve on the plateau.

fire, probably from some shells thrown in by the divisional
artillery of Jérôme. Wellington perceived it, and sent the
following pencilled order to Captain and Lieut.-Colonel
James Macdonell (Glengarry's third son) commanding the
Guards in the château :—

"I see that the fire has communicated from the Haystack
to the Roof of the Chateau. You must however still keep your
Men in those parts to which the fire does not reach. Take care
that no Men are lost by the falling in of the Roof, or floors.
After they will have fallen in occupy the Ruined walls inside
the Garden; particularly if it should be possible for the Enemy
to pass through the Embers in the Inside of the house."

But although this increased the suffering of the garrison,
many wounded men perishing in the flames, it gave no
advantage to the assailants. Furious at Jérôme's failure,
Reille sent forward Foy's division to reinforce, and, towards
evening, Bachelu's division also. It was all in vain: for
eight hours twelve hundred men held as many thousands
at defiance, and most nobly justified the Duke's choice of
Hougoumont as an advanced post.

About three o'clock Napoleon received a despatch from
Grouchy, written at 11.30 a.m., which gave him cause for
anxiety. Grouchy, when he wrote this, was still at Walhain,
eight heavy miles from Wavre. Bülow was already in position
at Saint Lambert, less than five miles from La Belle Alliance;
unless it should occur to Grouchy to move to his left on
hearing the guns of Waterloo, Bülow would presently be on
the right flank of the French. Time, esteemed so cheaply in
the morning, was of supreme value now; the English must
be beaten before Bülow could come into action. Before that
could be done, La Haye Sainte must be taken. D'Erlon,
having rallied and re-formed his shattered columns, Napoleon
committed the enterprise to Ney. Once more the great
battery discharged its thunder, while to the left Reille's
artillery opened on the west of the high-road. Ney led one
of Quiot's brigades, covered by one of Donzelot's extended as

AET. 46. skirmishers to the attack.  The skirmishers pushed forward
to the very crest of the allied position, but recoiled once
more from the fatal hedgerows.  The storm of La Haye Sainte
failed also, so busily Baring's Germans spread death around
them.  Here again, as at Hougoumont, it is past compre-
hension why more use was not made of artillery, which, in
ten minutes, should have reduced the homestead to a heap of
road metal.  Ney flew about like a madman.  The cannonade
at this period was terrific: the oldest soldiers had not heard
the like.  To save them from the fire, Wellington withdrew
some of his battalions behind the dip of the plateau.  Ney
mistook it for a movement of retreat, and called for a brigade
of cavalry.  D'Erlon's infantry was already ascending the
slopes.  By some misadventure, instead of a single brigade,
two whole divisions, 4,000 strong, including the light cavalry
of the Guard and the Red Lancers, were set in motion to the
front.  Great was the surprise of Wellington's staff to see
this preparation to attack infantry still in perfect order
in their position.  So far from any intention to retreat,
Wellington had just been strengthening his first line by
bringing up brigades from the second line and reserve, every
regiment lying down to avoid exposure to fire.

The men were called to their feet; squares were formed;
the gunners were ordered to keep up their fire till the last
moment, and then to run for shelter in the squares, leaving
their guns at the edge of the plateau.*  The French cavalry

* The behaviour of the artillery at this period was not perfect; indeed this is
one of the episodes of the battle which lay at the root of the Duke's firm determination never to countenance any history of it.  Writing to Lord Mulgrave,
15th December, 1815, in respect to a request which had been made for a mark of
special favour to the field officers of artillery present at Waterloo, he said: " In
my opinion, you have done quite right to refuse to grant this favour. . . . To
tell you the truth, I was not very well pleased with the artillery in the battle of
Waterloo.  The army was formed in squares immediately on the slope of the
rising ground, on the summit of which the artillery was placed, with orders not
to engage with artillery, but to fire only when bodies of troops came under their
fire.  It was very difficult to get them to obey this order.  The French cavalry
charged, and were formed on the same ground with our artillery, in general

No. 2.

I see that the fire has
communicated itself from the
Hay Stack to the Roof
of the Chateau
You must however still
keep your Men in those
parts to which the fire
does not reach.
Take care that no Men
are lost by the falling
in of the Roof or floors.
After they will have fallen
in occupy the Ruined walls
inside of the Garden, particularly if it should be
possible for the Enemy
to pass through the
Embers in the inside
of the House —

[Vol. ii. p. 75.

ORDER PENCILLED AND SENT BY THE DUKE OF WELLINGTON, DURING THE BATTLE OF WATERLOO, TO THE EARL OF UXBRIDGE, COMMANDING THE CAVALRY.

*Vol. ii. p. 75.*

advanced on the west of the high-road in echelon of squadrons from the right, slowly, because of the deep ground and
the high corn. It was a madcap—a cruel enterprise. The
batteries on the heights drove lanes of death through the
glittering masses of cuirassiers, of gay lancers and gallant
hussars; with faultless, yet fruitless, courage and discipline
these fine horsemen rode up to the batteries and through
them out on the plateau behind, where, far as the eye could
reach, the squares stood motionless, impregnably hedged with
steel. It is an hour for ever memorable in the annals of the
British infantry; perhaps the best, because the simplest,
account of it is contained in Wellington's own words to
Walter Scott, who was importunate for materials of history.

"The French cavalry were on the plateau in the centre between
the two high-roads for nearly three-quarters of an hour, riding
about among our squares of infantry, all firing (of artillery)
having ceased on both sides. I moved our squares forward to
the guns; and our cavalry, which had been detached by Lord
Uxbridge to the flanks, was brought back to the centre.* The
French cavalry were then driven off. After that circumstance,
repeated attacks were made along the whole front of the centre

within a few yards of our guns. We could not expect the artillery men to remain
at their guns in such a case. But I had a right to expect that the officers and
men of the artillery would do as I did, and as all the Staff did, that is to take
shelter in the squares of the infantry till the French cavalry should be driven off
the ground, either by our cavalry or infantry. But they did no such thing; they
ran off the field entirely, taking with them limbers, ammunition, and everything,
and when, in a few minutes, we had driven off the French cavalry, and could
have made good use of our artillery, we had no artillerymen to fire them; and,
in point of fact, I should have had no artillery during the whole of the latter part
of the action, if I had not kept a reserve at the commencement. . . . It is on
account of these little stories, which must come out, that I object to all the pro-
positions to write what is called a history of the battle of Waterloo" *(Suppl.
Despatches,* xiv. 618).

* The actual order of recall is here given in facsimile. "We ought to have
more of the Cavalry between the two high Roads. That is to say, three
Brigades at least, besides the Brigade in observation on the right, & besides
the Belgian Cavalry & the D. of Cumberland's Hussars. One heavy & one
light Brigade might remain on the left."

of the position by cavalry and infantry till seven at night; how many I cannot tell." *

The French cavalry renew their attack.

The French cavalry, with indomitable courage and perseverance, renewed their assault on the plateau a second, a third, and even a fourth time, with exactly similar result. The Emperor realised the terrible blunder that had taken place; he saw from La Belle Alliance what was going on beyond the valley. "That premature movement," he said to Soult, "may have a fatal effect on the fortunes of to-day."

"He has compromised us," growled Soult, "as he did at Jena."

"It is too early by an hour," continued Napoleon; "but we must support him now he has done it."

He ordered Kellermann to support Milhaud with four brigades of cuirassiers and carabineers. They gained the crest; they crowned the allied position; yet they could do no good when there, because they were not supported by infantry. Had the Emperor withdrawn one of Reille's divisions from the fruitless operations at Hougoumont, it must have gone hardly with the Allies, for it only wanted the fire of artillery and infantry to break the squares—the cavalry would have done the rest.† But Napoleon had his whole attention engrossed elsewhere at the time: he was obliged to leave Ney to deal with the enemy in front, in order that he himself might prepare to encounter danger from

Capture of La Haye Sainte.

another quarter. Meanwhile, the garrison of La Haye Sainte had exhausted all their ammunition. The precaution of making a postern in the western or northern wall of the enclosure had been neglected; ‡ it was found impossible to pass in supplies, and Baring, having spent his last cartridge,

* *Despatches*, xii. 610.

† It is only some fifty miles from Waterloo to Courtrai, where, in 1302, the Flemish pikemen first showed how infantry alone were the masters of cavalry alone, and, in the Battle of the Spurs, defeated Robert, Count d'Artois, and all the chivalry of France.

‡ *Stanhope*, 245.

LA HAYE SAINTE, FROM THE SOUTH.

(From a drawing made in 1815.)

[Vid. a. p. 76.]

collected the remains of his little force, forty-two men all told, and made good his escape to the general line. A serious loss, this, to the Allies. French sharpshooters swarmed into every part of the buildings and enclosure, whence they directed an injurious fire upon the right of the 5th Division. Ney established a battery there, which enfiladed the allied squares at less than three hundred yards range; Donzelot's skirmishers, crossing to the west of the high-road, pressed yet closer; some battalions of D'Erlon's wearied divisions moved forward once more; one of Reille's fresh columns might have decided the contest, but Reille was still wasting his energy on Hougoumont. Nevertheless, the danger was tremendous. General Ompteda fell dead near the high-road; Sir William de Lancey, the Quartermaster-General, riding beside Wellington, received mortal injury from a cannon shot; not far off, Sir Alexander Gordon took his death-wound; further to the right the Prince of Orange and General Alten were struck down; Kielmansegge's Germans, sorely pressed, began to yield. *The centre is open: vive l'Empereur!* It is a moment to test the steadiest nerve. The Duke remained calm, but very grave; beset on all sides by officers asking for instructions, he has but one answer for all: "There are no orders, except to stand firm to the last man."

Ney only required reinforcements to establish himself in the enemy's centre. He sent Colonel Heymès to ask them from the Emperor. "More troops!" shouted Napoleon; "where am I to get them? Does he expect me to make them?"

In truth Napoleon's position was as critical as Wellington's. It was about half-past four when he became aware that his right flank was imminently threatened. Blücher had joined Bülow's 4th Corps at Chapelle-Saint-Lambert about one o'clock, whence he directed his march upon Plancenoit, a village well in rear of the French right. When he began his attack here about five o'clock, the 2nd Corps under Pirch I.

ÆT. 46.    was only two miles behind him; Zieten's 3rd Corps was drawing near in front of the French right along the ridge from Ohain, while Thielemann's 4th Corps was fighting Grouchy at Wavre.  The Emperor's anxiety deepened; while the impression in the allied army became very general that the day was lost.  Towards the right of the allied line, many of the troops not actually engaged began to turn restive under prolonged exposure to artillery fire.  The Duke's attention was concentrated on the conflict on the central plateau, where the slightest failure of staunchness on the part of the infantry, exposed to prolonged and repeated assaults of cavalry, must have involved irrevocable defeat.

"At this time the action was evidently all against us. . . . Lord Uxbridge was gone, and all his staff; the Duke of Wellington was shut up occasionally in squares,* all his staff disabled, being either killed, wounded or dismounted; there was therefore no one to report anything that occurred in the centre of the army." †

There was much misgiving and perplexity; happily, the great majority of British and Hanoverian officers behaved with the dignity of their rank, and a common spirit of gallantry and endurance seemed infused into the rank and file, down to the youngest recruit.  But there are black sheep in every flock, and there can be no doubt that not a few officers and men rode quietly off the ground to Brussels, and an undue anxiety was shown by others to accompany escorts of prisoners and wounded to the rear.‡  The Duke of Cumberland's Hussars deserted the field *en masse.*

---

* It has been denied that the Duke entered a square at any time during the day, but there is his own statement in writing to show that he did (*Suppl. Despatches*, xiv. 619).

† *Hamilton MS.*

‡ *Ibid.* It is unnecessary to repeat the instances of personal cowardice described by Mr. Hamilton, but so much unfavourable comment has been passed by English writers on the conduct of the Belgian-Dutch and Nassau troops, that it ought to be clearly explained once for all that misconduct was not confined to them alone, as may be seen from the following extract from the general order thanking the troops " for their conduct in the glorious action : " —

About four o'clock Wellington, no longer apprehending A̲ₙ̲ₙ̲. 1815. danger on his right, had desired Lord Hill to move up to the Lord Hill support of the troops in Hougoumont. They were in time to moves up on the repulse a new attack to which Ney, after the fourth failure right. of his cavalry to break the allied line on the plateau, had ordered up a fresh infantry division (Bachelu's) and a brigade of Foy's division. It was too late. These six thousand troops which, at an earlier hour, might have followed the cavalry with good effect, for the allied guns were temporarily silenced each time the cavalry passed them, were cut to pieces and dispersed by the converging fire of Hill's guns and of his infantry line.

To meet the Prussian menace on his right, Napoleon had Bülow brought forward the 6th Corps from its position in the second engages the French line on the west of the high-road, and caused Lobau to form right. it on a new front towards the east. Against this Blücher caused Bülow to direct his attack; who, manœuvring by his right, turned the outer flank of the 6th Corps, dislodged the brigade which held Plancenoit, and took possession of this important post, which gravely affected the Emperor's whole position and compromised his line of retreat. Napoleon sent Conflict Duhesme with eight battalions of the Young Guard to re- at Plance- capture Plancenoit, which was effected after a fierce encounter, noit. with house-to-house fighting. Shortly after, the Young Guard in turn were driven out of the village, upon which the Emperor detached two battalions of the Old Guard (the 1st

"The Field Marshal has observed that several soldiers, and even officers, have quitted their ranks without leave, and have gone to Bruxelles, and even some to Antwerp, where, and in the country through which they have passed, they have spread a false alarm in a manner highly unmilitary and derogatory to the character of soldiers. The Field Marshal requests the General officers command- ing divisions in the British army, and the General officers commanding the corps of each nation of which the army is composed, to report to him in writing what officers and men (the former by name) are now or have been absent without leave since the 16th instant" (*Suppl. Despatches*, x. 538).

Brialmont, Jomini, and other writers have described the road to Brussels in rear of Mont-Saint-Jean as being so crowded with fugitives that Wellington had no choice but to hold his ground, retreat through the forest being impossible.

of the 2nd Grenadiers and the 1st of the 2nd Chasseurs), who once more retook Plancenoit, the Young Guard rallying under their shelter.

Then, and not before, Napoleon was free to turn his mind to the attack on Mont-Saint-Jean. It was past seven; he had lost the support of Lobau's corps, which must remain on the defensive; yet, as he scanned the opposing ridge through his glass, fortune seemed to smile on the tricolor. On his right, Durutte's division held La Haye and Papelotte, with skirmishers extended to the very crest of the plateau; d'Erlon's other divisions were busy and well forward on Durutte's left; in the centre, the gunners and sharpshooters at La Haye Sainte were diligently raking the allied position on their right and left; to the west of the road Ney crowned the height; Wellington's front was broken and disordered—probably he had used up all his reserves; there was yet time to snatch victory by a supreme effort. The Emperor had still in hand twelve battalions of the Guard, two others being engaged in holding Plancenoit. Leaving three more as a reserve near La Belle Alliance, he caused Drouot to advance into the valley with the other nine formed in squares, riding himself at the head of the leading battalion.

Again too late! Half an hour earlier, when Ney implored reinforcements, this noble column might have turned the day; but the moment *à frapper juste* was past. Wellington had re-established his line, bringing Chassé's Dutch division in from Braine-la-Leud, Vandeleur's dragoons and Vivian's hussars from the extreme left, and calling up Wincke's infantry brigade and four Brunswick battalions from the reserve. Moreover, the 1st Prussian Corps had reached Ohain an hour previously. Wellington had sent Colonel Fremantle to bid them hasten to his support; but their commander hesitated, for some of his staff had brought him word that the English were beaten, and that the road to Brussels was one mass of fugitives. Happily, Müffling had ridden towards the left to look out for his countrymen. Perceiving that Zieten

WATERLOO, JUNE 18, 1815.

(From a Lithograph by Reiffe.)

was moving to support Bülow, he galloped over to him, and A.N.N. 1815.
succeeded in persuading him to come to Mont-Saint-Jean.
When the first six battalions of the Middle Guard descended
into the valley, Zieten's advanced guard was already at
Smohain.  This caused the Emperor to post one of these six Napoleon's last card.
battalions to the west of the Charleroi road, and committed
the other five to Ney for the final attack on the right centre
of the Allies.  He led them, still in squares,* in echelon of
battalions from the right, with a pair of eight pounders in
each interval of the echelon, not straight across to the nearest
and weakest part of the enemy's line, but diagonally athwart
the undulating ground between the Charleroi and Nivelles
roads, against the troops on the allied right which had
suffered least during the day.  Reille ought surely to have
supported their advance by sending forward some brigades
on their left, but by some mismanagement these superb
battalions went to their doom alone.  Of cavalry they had
but the support of a squadron or two.  A captain of
French carabineers left his regiment, galloped across the
valley among the skirmishers of H.M. 52nd Regiment,
calling out, "Vive le Roi! look out! that —— Napoleon
will be upon you in half an hour with his Guards."

Sorely torn by the converging fire from the allied line, the
first square of the Middle Guard ascended the slope, slippery
with blood and mire, and obtained a momentary advantage
over the Brunswickers and the British 30th and 73rd.  Wellington himself, always at hand where the stress was sorest,
rallied the Brunswickers, and General Chassé, once an officer
in Napoleon's service, charged with a Dutch brigade, and
drove the French in confusion over the declivity.†

---

* The statement that the Imperial Guard moved in squares, a formation most
unsuitable for crossing uneven ground under a heavy fire, has been called in
question; but M. Houssaye quotes from the MS. of General Petit of the
Imperial Guard, who assisted in carrying out the formation prescribed by Ney,
and is positive on the subject.

† It is scarcely to the credit of English historians that this fine performance of
Ditmer's brigade has been little noticed, considering how much has been said

The second echelon (4th Grenadiers) coming up on the left of the first during this contest, engaged in a hand-to-hand conflict with Sir Colin Halkett's brigade.

An important change had been made in the formation of the allied infantry on this part of the plateau. The attack of the French infantry columns had been met and repulsed in line two deep, the fighting formation peculiar to British troops. When the cavalry ascended the slopes, squares were formed; but the fire of squares is ineffective against infantry; when the line was attacked by cavalry and infantry combined recourse was had to a new formation, which, while preserving an extended front to deal with infantry, possessed some of the weight of a square to sustain the impact of cavalry. The battalions were formed in line four deep.

The 33rd began to yield; Halkett seized one of their colours and, loudly calling on them to bear themselves like men, restored their formation, and the French advance was stayed.

The third and fourth echelons had become fused together during the advance through the deep, uneven ground, and reached the crest as a single column, containing the 1st and 2nd Battalions of the 3rd Chasseurs.* There was nothing in their front, apparently, and they had neared the cross-road, when Wellington's voice was heard clear above the storm, "Stand up, Guards!"† Then, from the shelter of the way-

---

uncomplimentary to our Belgian-Dutch allies. It was the 1st Battalion of the 3rd Grenadiers which they defeated.

* So many and conflicting are the narratives of this period of the combat that the exact position of the troops and sequence of incidents can never be positively determined. The 1st British Guards received the title of Grenadiers in honour of having defeated the Grenadiers of the Imperial Guard; but the third echelon of the attack, which came in contact with H.M. 1st Guards, were undoubtedly Chasseurs. Where all bore themselves so well, the victors may be well content to divide the honours equally.

† This is the origin of the theatrical "Up, Guards, and at 'em!" The Guards were lying down, as it was the Duke's orders all troops should do under fire, when not actually engaged. Having bidden them rise, he then gave the commanding officers orders to attack (*Croker*, iii. 281).

side banks rose the line of Maitland's brigade of Guards, four deep and fifteen hundred strong, which poured a withering volley into the square, and charging, swept them out of the combat.

Near the foot of the slope pursued and pursuers encountered the last and left echelon (4th Chasseurs) still unbroken. The British Guards obeyed the command to retire, which they did in double time and in considerable disorder. Regaining the crest, they re-formed on the flank of Colin Halkett, and to the left of Adams's brigade (52nd, 71st, and 95th). Colonel Colborne * immediately changed his battalion front one-eighth of a circle to the left, so as to bring his whole fire to bear on the last echelon in its advance, a movement which set the seal on the failure of Napoleon's last attack.† Just as the splendours of sunset were flowing over the scene, the last body of Frenchmen that reached the plateau of Mont-Saint-Jean were broken and scattered.‡

At the moment when the leading echelon was pressing back the Brunswickers, the 30th and the 73rd, Ney's fifth horse was shot under him, and General Friant was severely wounded. Believing that the heights had been carried, he rode slowly back to where the Emperor sat between Belle Alliance and Haye Sainte, and reported to him that all was going well at the front. Napoleon was about to lead in person three more battalions of the Guard § to reinforce the fighting line. While they were being marshalled for attack— one battalion deployed with a battalion in close column on either flank—he kept his glass turned upon the conflict in which he was about to bear a part.

* Afterwards Lord Seaton.

† Here, again, professional opinion is irreconcilably divided as to the exact proportion borne by the 52nd and the rest of Adams's brigade, compared with that to be credited to Peregrine Maitland's Guards. Colborne claimed that the 52nd changed front and opened fire *before* the charge of the Guards (*Waterloo Letters*, 287).

‡ See Appendix E, p. 93.

§ 1st Chasseurs, 2nd Grenadiers, and 2nd Chasseurs.

Suddenly his hand fell.

"Mais ils sont melées!" he exclaimed in hollow accents to his aide-de-camp, Count Flahault, who was under no illusion as to what troops were meant. The sun had just set. There was no radiance to prevent all men seeing what was going on out there in the north-west.

**Defeat of the Imperial Guard.**
First the trampled corn was sprinkled, then it was covered with a confused mass of men moving south; behind and among them the sabres of Vivian's hussars and Vandeleur's dragoons rose and fell with direful diligence. "La garde recule!" sounded like a sob in the motionless ranks of the Old Guard, and sped with astonishing swiftness to every part of the field. "La garde recule!" cried the men of Allix, Donzelot, and Marcognet, and began to melt away from the vantage ground they had so nobly won. "La garde recule!" whispered Reille's columns, still unbroken on the left. Far on the right, Durutte's battalions, suddenly confronted by the heads of Zieten's columns, where they had been told to look for Grouchy's, caught up the word. Next, the uneasy murmur, "Nous sommes trahis!" was heard—for was there not treason? Had not General Bourmont and his staff and sundry other officers openly gone over to the enemy? "La garde recule!" Oh, fatal cry! soon swelling into one still more dreadful—last tocsin of the soldier's agony—"Sauve qui peut!" Papelotte and La Haye were abandoned, and from the east, as already from the west, the wreck of the Last Army rolled towards the Charleroi road.

Not ashamed some, in the delirium of success, others under the sheer pang of remembered defeat, to revile the great commander by declaring that before the battle was fairly lost he rode off the field and abandoned to destruction the army which had made him their god. No need to quote from tales of which the tellers had better have held their peace. Nothing jars more harshly on English ears than slander of a
**Last stand of the Old Guard.**
beaten foe. Napoleon did his duty to the last. He broke the brigade of the Old Guard into squares, and placed them

across the line of flight to the west of the Charleroi road,* ANN. 1815.
hoping to rally behind them at least their comrades of the
Middle Guard; and, holding in hand his four *escadrons de
service* of light cavalry till the pursuit drew near, he launched
them, but in vain, against Vivian's hussars.

Ney comes along with the crowd—Ney, who has been
seeking death and finding no friendly bullet to end this
frenzy of defeat—Ney, bareheaded and in rags, shrieking to
d'Erlon as they are borne together in the crush, "If you
and I come out of this alive, d'Erlon, we shall be hanged!"
then succeeds in rallying some of Durutte's division. "Come
and see how a marshal of France dies!" But these, too,
fall away from him. Covered with blood and mud and black
powder, with a broken sword in his hand, he enters one of
the squares of the Old Guard—the only steadfast objects in
the hideous torrent of panic and pursuit.

When Wellington recognised the supreme moment, he rode General
forward to the crest of the ground, and, above the smoke- advance of
wreaths, clearly defined as a bronze statue against the bright the allied line.
western sky, held his cocked hat aloft and forward. No mere
theatrical gesture this, we may be sure, but the signal—more
rapid than word of mouth—for a general advance, and straight-
way the whole allied army, except the Highland brigade, the
Germans of Ompteda and Kielmansegge, and some batteries
which were so built in with corpses that they could not move,
descended from the heights where it had patiently endured
the fiery storm for nine hours. The battalions closed their
thinned ranks as they marched; far in advance of the general
line was Colborne's 52nd; and on their left the cavalry swept
the ground, doubling up the flank of Durutte's scattered array.
Of the enemy, only Reille's corps on the left and three squares
of Napoleon's Old Guard at La Belle Alliance remained in
formation. Ney himself fought dismounted in the ranks of
the Middle Guard not far from the Charleroi road. Men fell
thick and fast around him, yet he remained unwounded:

* *Houssaye,* 402.

Æт. 46.  destiny had marked him for a darker fate. His false move
earlier in the day, by exhausting Napoleon's reserve of
cavalry, told with fatal effect after the failure of his attack
with the Guard.

All kinds of wild stories have found harbour in this final
act of the tragedy of Waterloo. Lamartine has told an
admiring public that the Duke drew his sword and charged
at the head of the cavalry. His sword was never out of
its scabbard all day.* Here are his own words describing
the last act in the drama.

"The Infantry was advanced in Line. I halted then for a
minute in the bottom that they might be in order to attack
some Battalions of the Enemy still on the Heights. The Cavalry
halted likewise. The whole moved forward again in very few
moments. The Army did not stand the attack. Some had fled
before we halted. The whole abandoned their Position. The
Cavalry were then ordered to charge and moved round the
flanks of the Battalions of Infantry. The Infantry was formed
into Columns and moved in pursuit in Columns of Battalions."†

Napoleon
leaves the
field.

The dusk began to deepen. The Middle Guard had
re-formed its squares, and easily kept the cavalry at bay.
But when the allied infantry came up, Napoleon, weary of
the useless slaughter, and seeing these squares riven with a
dreadful fire, gave them the order to retreat. He himself,
despairing of rallying his flying troops, rode into the square
of the 1st Battalion of the 1st Grenadiers, which, with the
other two squares of the Old Guard, slowly retreated along
the Charleroi road, followed by General Adams's brigade and
a battalion of Hanoverian militia. Colonel William Halkett,
commanding this militia, attacked the square commanded by
General Cambronne, calling on it to surrender. The summons not being complied with, he treated them to a dose of

---

* *Croker*, iii. 281.

† Memorandum by the Duke on Siborne's model of the field of Waterloo,
written in 1836 (*Suppl. Despatches*, x. 513).

RETREAT OF THE IMPERIAL GUARD

(From a Lithograph by Raffet.)

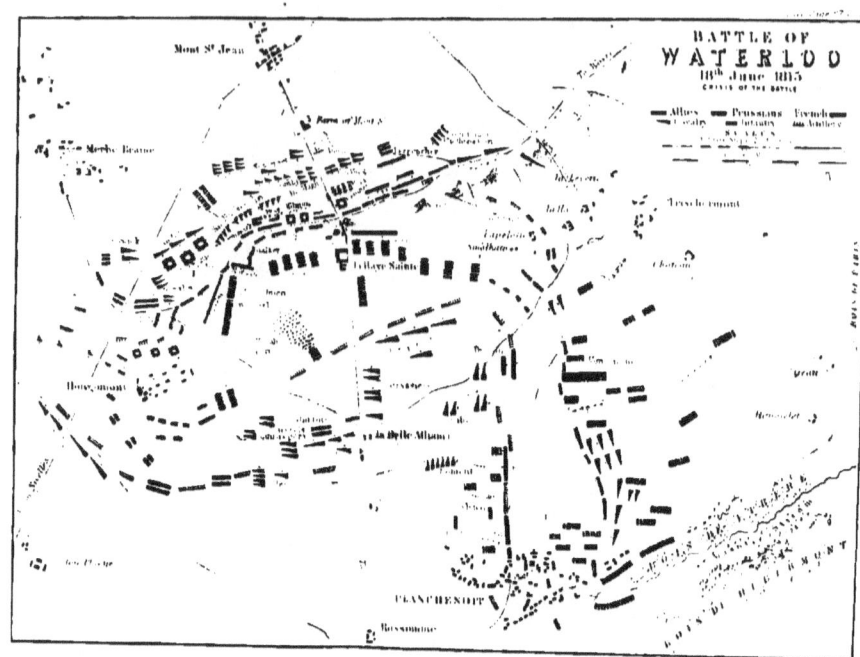

musketry, on which the square broke up, leaving the General A.N. 1815. and two other officers unprotected. Halkett galloped up to the General, and made as if to cut him down, on which he yielded himself prisoner.*

While this was the state of affairs between Rossomme and La Belle Alliance, the Prussians were driving the Young Guard out of Plancenoit. The fugitives fled along the Brussels road, crowding round the squares of the Old Guard, who, to preserve their own formation, had the cruel task of driving them off with bayonets and even with bullets. This cross current of fugitives took the pressure of the pursuit off the Old Guard, and the Emperor rode out of his square of Grenadiers, pacing in advance of their retreat with Soult, Drouot, Bertrand, and a few *chasseurs à cheval* as escort. At the farm of Le Caillou he joined a battalion of chasseurs of the Old Guard, and continued his course with it in the direction of Genappe.

The Prussians recapture Plancenoit.

Shortly after nine o'clock Wellington met Blücher in the dark in the neighbourhood of La Belle Alliance. The old Prince saluted the Duke warmly on both cheeks, and offered to relieve his troops in the pursuit. Wellington willingly accepted the offer, for his people had been fighting for ten hours. Blücher's men had endured a hard day also, having marched fifteen miles fasting over execrable ground, and fought their way from Frischermont to Plancenoit. It had been no easy matter for him to keep tryst. His men had eaten nothing since the day before; it was only his constant presence and encouragement that had given them the spirit to carry the artillery through the marshes of Lasne.

Meeting of Wellington and Blücher.

* It is an unpleasant task to dispel romantic illusions, but *le mot de Cambronne* was something less chivalrous than the traditional "La garde meurt, mais ne se rend pas!" The Duke of Wellington used to laugh at it, and told how Cambronne was brought to him just as he was sitting down to dinner in Waterloo village. The Duke told him he was sorry he could not receive him as a guest until he had made his peace with King Louis, who had made him a viscount. The Duke used to add that there was a set of ladies at Brussels, partisans of the Prince of Orange, called *la vieille garde*, of whom it was said, "Elles ne meurent pas et se rendent toujours!" (*Salisbury MSS.*, 1836).

"Come, lads," he cried to some gunners labouring at the wheels of a piece deeply bogged; "you would not have me break my word!"

**The Prussians take up the pursuit.** So Gneisenau went forward with his dragoons, reaping the harvest of death by the light of the summer moon, and Blücher followed with Bülow's infantry. At Genappe they captured the Emperor's carriage and a vast amount of baggage and artillery. Wellington, in his official despatch, made honourable acknowledgment of what he owed to his faithful ally.

"I should not do justice to my own feelings or to Marshal Blücher and the Prussian army, if I did not attribute the successful result of this arduous day to the cordial and timely assistance I received from them. The operation of General Bülow upon the enemy's flank was a most decisive one; and even if I had not found myself in a situation to make the attack which produced the final result, it would have forced the enemy to retire if his attacks should have failed, and would have prevented him from taking advantage of them if they should unfortunately have succeeded." *

After the battle the Duke went to the little inn in Waterloo, where some dinner was prepared for him and the survivors of his staff. Sir Alexander Gordon † had been brought thither mortally wounded; the Duke caused them to lay him on his own camp-bed, while he himself lay down in the outer room, wrapped in his cloak.

Before going to rest the Duke directed Dr. Hume to bring him the list of casualties in the morning, in order that he might include it in his despatch. Dr. Hume brought it about 5 a.m., and, finding the Duke asleep, left the paper beside him. Returning later in the morning, he found the Duke awake, having perused the list. His countenance was apparently unchanged, except that under his eyes were two whitish streaks. He had not washed his face since the

---

* *Despatches,* xii. 484.      † Brother of the Earl of Aberdeen.

battle; it was still covered with the mud and grime of
the field, and those streaks were the traces of tears he had
shed for his lost soldiers.*  After writing his despatch at
Waterloo early on the morning of the 19th, Wellington called
for his horse, and rode into Brussels.  Lady Georgina Lennox,†
calling early on 19th, was struck by the Duke's exceeding
sadness—no elation of victory, only sorrow for the lives of so
many brave soldiers.  It was the countenance, not of a conqueror, but of a fallen General.

Indeed, the loss was frightful enough to cast a shadow on
the most glorious triumph of arms.  The killed and wounded
were reckoned among the Allies thus:—

|  |  |
|---|---:|
| British and Hanoverians . . | 11,678 |
| Prussians . . . . . . . | 6,999 |
| Netherlanders . . . . . . | 3,178 |
| Brunswickers . . . . . . | 687 |
| Nassau Contingent . . . . | 643 |

Total   23,185 officers and men.

Out of twenty-four officers the Scots Greys lost seven
killed and nine wounded.  Captain Cheney, on whom the
command of the regiment devolved during the last three
hours, had five horses shot under him in half an hour.  The
Cameron Highlanders, out of forty-two officers, lost five killed
and twenty-six wounded; the Royal Scots, six killed and
twenty-five wounded out of thirty-nine, and so on.  The
accounts of the French losses vary between 18,000 and 30,000
killed and wounded.  It is certain they lost 227 cannon.

The Duke was as constantly exposed throughout the day
as any one; more so, indeed, for he was ever present where
the battle was at its closest; yet he remained unhurt.  When
a cannon-shot took off Lord Fitzroy Somerset's right arm, he ·
was riding with his left arm touching the Duke's right.
Again, when Lord Uxbridge lost his leg, the cannon-shot
which struck him passed first over the withers of Copenhagen.

* See Appendix D, p. 91.          † Afterwards Lady de Ros.

" By God! I've lost my leg," cried Uxbridge. " Have you,
by God?" was all the Duke's reply.* De Lancey also
received his mortal wound from a cannon-shot when riding
by the Duke's side; and his mind must have been more or
less than human had he shown no sense of gratitude for the
number and narrowness of his escapes. Nothing is rarer in
the vast mass of his correspondence than appeals, or even
references to the Almighty, though it cannot be denied that
he often swore by His name; but at 3 a.m. on the morning
after the battle, writing to Lady Frances Webster to tell her
she might remain in Brussels in perfect safety, after enumerat-
ing the chief losses he had sustained, he added, " The finger of
Providence was upon me, and I escaped unhurt." †

Among all the learned disquisitions and fanciful rhapsodies
about this great battle, the Duke's simple, homely description
of it to his old comrade-in-arms, Lord Beresford, condenses
the whole affair into a single paragraph.

" You will have heard of our battle of the 18th. Never did
I see such a pounding match. Both were what the boxers call
gluttons. Napoleon did not manœuvre at all. He just moved
forward in the old style, in columns, and was driven off in the
old style. The only difference was that he mixed cavalry with
his infantry, and supported both with an enormous quantity
of artillery. I had the infantry for some time in squares,
and we had the French cavalry walking about us as if they

---

* *Greville*, 2nd Series, i. 135.

† When Colonel Gurwood was editing his twelfth volume he paid £50 to an
impecunious barrister for the Duke's two letters to Lady F. Webster, and asked
the Duke whether he approved of their being printed. The Duke at first replied
that he did not care whether they were published or not, provided the names
were not given, adding, " *The finger of Providence* ought to be omitted." Afterwards he wrote (1st September, 1838) to say they had better be suppressed, as
" containing nothing of publick or military interest " (*Apsley House MSS.*).
The letters, however, were printed after the Duke's death in the *Supplementary
Despatches* (x. 531). Lady F. Webster was a very pretty woman, daughter of
the first Earl of Mountnorris, and wife of an officer in the 9th Light Dragoons.
Her husband was on the staff of the Prince of Orange at Waterloo.

had been our own. I never saw the British infantry behave Ann. 1815.
so well." *

Before his crowning victory, the Duke's countrymen had Further
exhausted the catalogue of honours which could be heaped recogni-
on a single individual. Parliament now purchased the the Duke's
mansion and estate of Strathfieldsaye and bestowed it on the services.
conqueror of Napoleon, to be held by him and his heirs for
ever, on condition of presenting a tricolor flag to the Sovereign
at Windsor annually, on 18th June. Of the innumerable
monuments erected in his honour, perhaps it is only necessary
to allude to one, the bronze statue of Achilles in Hyde Park,
which was subscribed for by the countrywomen of the Duke,
and made out of guns taken at Vitoria and elsewhere.
Mention may also be made of one of the Prince Regent's
gifts, the colossal marble statue of Napoleon by Canova,
which Louis XVIII. gave to the Prince Regent after the
peace of 1814, and now stands in the staircase at Apsley
House. When some critic observed to Canova on the dis-
proportionate smallness of the orb representing the globe,
which the figure holds in the left hand, the sculptor replied—
" Ah ! but you see Napoleon's world did not include Great
Britain."

## Appendix D.

### *The Duke's Conversation about Waterloo.*

The following notes of a conversation at Walmer have been
preserved in Lady Salisbury's journal for the year 1836 :—

*Lady S.* " I suppose you must have felt secure of the victory
when the Guards withstood the famous charge. What was your
feeling at the moment ? Did it not surpass all that one can
imagine ? "

---

* *Despatches*, xii. 529. The original of this letter was sold by auction in
August. 1809, for £21.

*The Duke.* "It is very singular, but I have no recollection of any feeling of satisfaction. At the time I was by no means secure of the victory, nor till long afterwards : I can recollect no sensation of delight on that day—if I experienced it. My thoughts were so entirely occupied with what was to be done to improve the victory, to replace the officers that were lost, to put everything in proper order, that I had not leisure for another idea. I remember our supper that night very well, and then I went to bed, and was called about three in the morning by Hume,* to go and see poor Gordon, but he was dead before I got there. Then I came back, and had a cup of tea and some toast, wrote my despatch, and then rode into Brussels."

*Lady S.* "But now, while you were riding there, did it never occur to you that you had placed yourself on a pinnacle of glory ?"

*The Duke.* "No. I was entirely occupied with what was necessary to be done. At the door of my own hotel † I met Creevey : they had no certain accounts at Brussels, and he called out to me, 'What news?' I said, 'Why, I think we've done for 'em this time.' . . . I staid all that day in Brussels, making different arrangements ; among other things there was a mutiny among 3,000 prisoners we had in the gaol, with only 600 troops to guard them. I sent orders to the commanding officer that, if they attempted to break a single bar, he was to fire in among them, and I sent them word that I had done so. We heard no more of them after that. Then the Mayor came in great alarm. His people had seen some troops they mistook for French, and fancied they were coming upon them. I told them there was no fear ; that Napoleon's army was scattered to the devil, and half way to Paris by that time. I left Brussels next morning at four o'clock ; the second night I slept at Malplaquet ; the third I took Perronne ; the fifth day I joined the Prussians before Paris. But it was not till ten or twelve days after the battle that I began to reflect on what I had done, and to feel it."

*Lady S.* "But the feeling of satisfaction must have come at last. I can't conceive how it did not take possession of your mind immediately—that you did not think how infinitely you had raised your name above every other."

---

* One of the medical staff.        † In the Rue Montagne du Parc.

*The Duke.* "That is a feeling of vanity ; one's *first* thought is
for the public service."

*Lady S.* "But there *must* be a lasting satisfaction in that feeling of superiority you always enjoy. It is not in human nature it should be otherwise."

*The Duke.* "True. Still, I come constantly into contact with other persons on equal or inferior terms. Perhaps there is no man now existing who would like to meet me on a field of battle ; in that line I am superior. But when the war is over and the troops disbanded, what is your great general more than anybody else? . . . I am necessarily inferior to every man in his own line, though I may excel him in others. I cannot saw and plane like a carpenter, or make shoes like a shoemaker, or understand cultivation like a farmer. Each of these, *on his own ground*, meets me on terms of superiority. I feel I am but a man." *

Appendix E.

*The Defeat of the Imperial Guard.*

General Petit's statement, quoted by M. Houssaye, that the Middle Guard attacked in five squares, will be keenly disputed by students of military history. Most British eyewitnesses testify to the formation being in two columns, but it is easy to imagine that the original formation of squares in direct échelon would be disordered in the advance under a heavy fire across undulating and muddy ground, covered with crops. The dense smoke must have interfered with such a formation being accurately judged from the British position.

"I cannot describe positively," wrote Lieut. Gawler of the 52nd Regiment, "from my own observation the formation of the enemy, for, when the right of the 52nd subsequently crossed the summit, the smoke was very dense ; but it has been

* *Salisbury MSS.,* 1836.

confidently stated in the regiment that, as seen from *this* side,
it was in two columns in direct échelon—the left considerably
to the rear. It has also been stated that at first the opening
between the two columns was distinctly visible." [*]

On the other hand, Lieut. S. Reed of the 71st Regiment,
which was on the right of the 52nd, and supported it in its
charge, wrote—

"The Imperial Guard, I think, were either in square or
column. I do not think they were in line. . . . We charged
three squares of the Guard, whom we broke and pursued. . . .
The French squares having separated, the 52nd pursued what
had been their right square; the other two fell to our
lot." [†]

The third battalion in Adams' brigade was the 2nd of the
95th Rifles. Corporal Aldridge, who served twenty-two
years in that regiment, said, "The French came up in three
columns abreast of each other; they looked like quarter-
distance columns." [‡] Now, a square in movement is not easily
to be distinguished from a column at quarter distance, but the
fire from the flank of a square when halted is very much more
powerful than anything that can be effected by the flank
files of a column. When the Guard did halt, its flank fire
was most intense, causing a loss to the 52nd of about one
hundred and fifty men in less than four minutes. Such a
fire could never have come from the flank of a column.

As to the timeworn controversy between the 52nd and
the Grenadier Guards for the chief honour in routing the
Imperial Guard, his would be an intrepid judgment that were
offered to decide it. The case for the 52nd has been set
forth at large and in detail in Mr. Leeke's two volumes
on *Lord Seaton's Regiment at Waterloo;* while the First
Regiment of the Guards—*beati possidentes*—derive their title

---

[*] *Waterloo Letters*, 289.          [†] *Ibid.*, 298.
                    [‡] *Ibid.*, 302.

of Grenadiers from the general order of 29th July, 1815, Ass. 1815. which declares that the Prince Regent has been pleased to confer that title upon them in commemoration of their having defeated the Grenadiers of the Imperial Guard at Waterloo. In such a noble rivalry, arising from sources so complex and so remote, let the countrymen of these brave troops pronounce the verdict—" Honours easy!"

# CHAPTER IV.

## THE ARMY OF OCCUPATION.

### 1815–1818.

FAR different was the manner in which the glorious tidings found its way from Waterloo to London from the way news of battle is flashed about the globe at the present time. We can imagine how field correspondents would feed the wires for us now; how the evening papers with rapid editions would keep us abreast of every movement and intensify the

Lady Elcho   Mrs. Tennant   Lady D. Somerset

agony of every ominous phase; how the offices would be Ann. 1815. besieged by eager crowds all night, and the best or worst be known before another sun. Fourscore years ago the utmost speed at man's command lay in the legs of a good horse.*

Almost the only individual of Wellington's staff remaining How the uninjured at the close of the day was the Hon. Henry Percy.† news came<br>to Eng- He had left the Duchess of Richmond's ball, and ridden to land. Quatre-Bras without having time to change even his shoes, and him the Duke charged to carry to England the despatch announcing the victory. His mission was anticipated. The financial house of Rothschild, with shrewd business eye to Stock Exchange movements, had a fast sloop lying off Antwerp, which reached England some hours before Percy.‡ Landing at Dover, Percy posted with all speed to London, with two eagles § of the Imperial Guard sticking out of the windows of his chaise, one on either side. Arriving at the Horse Guards late in the evening, he was told the Duke of York was dining out. He went on to Lord Castlereagh's; the Foreign Secretary was dining at the same house as the Commander-in-chief in St. James Square. Arriving there, he found the Prince Regent was of the dinner-party; he demanded an immediate audience, and was shown into the dining-room carrying his papers and the French eagles.

"Let the ladies leave the room," said the Prince Regent as soon as he perceived Percy; then, holding a hand out to the travel-stained soldier—"Welcome, *Colonel* Percy!"

"Go down on your knee," exclaimed the Commander-in-chief, "and kiss hands for the step you have obtained."

---

* Pigeon-flying, as a means of conveying intelligence, though well known at that time, does not seem to have been employed during the campaign. The semaphore telegraph was used sometimes between ships and fixed points on shore.

† Son of the Earl of Beverley. His eldest brother succeeded to the dukedom of Northumberland, on the death of the 4th Duke, in 1865.

‡ Consols stood at 58⅛ when Rothschild's messenger arrived. Enormous profits were realised on the rise.

§ Every French regiment possessed an eagle, but, as each regiment consisted of five battalions, every eagle represented the equivalent of five stands of colours.

Æt. 46.

Next, and before the despatch was opened, numberless inquiries were addressed to him about different officers. His answer was so often "dead" or "severely wounded" that the Prince Regent burst into tears.

Napoleon arrived at Charleroi about daybreak, on 19th June, with a small mounted escort. Halting at Laon on the 20th, he held a council of war. He desired to assemble there the remains of his army. Prince Jérôme had collected 20,000, and Grouchy, who had renewed the combat with Thielmann at Wavre on the 19th, till apprised of the defeat of the *grande armée*, had been ordered to march on Laon with all speed; but the opinion of his Generals being adverse to further resistance, Napoleon continued his flight to Paris, handing over to Soult the command of such troops as he could collect. There is no occasion to retrace here the dismal close of the Hundred Days; of the fallen Emperor's reception in his capital; of his abdication for the second time on 22nd June, in favour of his son; of the rejection of that son by the Chamber of Representatives, and the election instead of an Executive Commission of five. Still believing himself to be the Man of Destiny, and "regarding himself still as the first soldier of the nation," he offered his services as General to defend France with 70,000 men still under arms; but they were refused, and on the 3rd July Napoleon was at Rochefort, seeking a passage to America. Baffled by the vigilance of the British cruisers, he surrendered himself on the 15th a prisoner to Captain Maitland of the *Bellerophon*, and penned his famous letter to the Prince Regent, desiring to "seat himself at the hearth of the British people."

On 21st June the allied army crossed the French frontier; Valenciennes and Quesnoy being promptly blockaded by the British, Maubeuge and Landrecy by the Prussians. Cambray was taken by escalade on the 24th, on which day King Louis, in consequence of Wellington's invitation, joined the British headquarters at Le Cateau. On the 26th the Duke received overtures from the French Commissioners for a suspension of hostilities, which Blücher and he declined,* believing the Ann. 1815. abdication to be only a trick to gain time. The Commissioners were informed that no armistice could be granted as long as Napoleon Buonaparte was in Paris and at liberty, and the Allies continued to advance on Paris with 120,000 men. On 2nd July Wellington fixed his headquarters at Gonesse. M. Brialmont has attributed the rapidity of their advance to a concerted scheme between the British and Prussian Marshals for the political purpose of obtaining the submission of Paris before Russia and Austria could enter the field, thereby obtaining for Great Britain and Prussia a preponderating influence in the settlement of the affairs of France. The refutation of this innuendo, so far as Wellington is concerned, is contained in his letter to Prince Blücher of 2nd July, in which, after dissuading the Prince from his project of attacking Paris at once, he observes—

"It is true we shall not have the vain triumph of entering Paris at the head of our victorious troops; but, as I have already explained to your Highness, I doubt our having the means at present of succeeding in an attack upon Paris; and, if we are to wait till the arrival of Marshal Prince Wrede to make the attack, I think we shall find the Sovereigns disposed, as they were last year, to spare the capital of their ally (Louis XVIII.), and either not to enter the town at all, or enter it under an armistice, such as it is in your power and mine to sign this day." †

Napoleon being finally off the scene, the way was open for an armistice. Accordingly, on 3rd July, the Convention of Paris was signed, in which the chief conditions were—a suspension of arms, the evacuation of Paris by the 50,000 or 60,000 troops therein, the withdrawal of all the French forces to the south of the Loire, and the peaceable occupation of the capital by the Allies. Meanwhile, the Provisional Government, in order to conciliate the army, had proclaimed Napoleon II. as Emperor; but Wellington having intimated

The Convention of Paris.

* *Despatches*, xii. 512, 522, 533.     † *Ibid.*, xii. 527.

Æt. 46. to them that the Allies could not treat with Napoleon or any of his house, the Commissioners, secretly inspired by Fouché, asked whether, if, instead of King Louis XVIII., some other prince of the Royal House were called to the throne, the Allies would raise any objection. The fact is that among the French people there was no kind of enthusiasm for the House of Bourbon, least of all for Louis XVIII., who, while personally the object of no admiration on the part of the allied Sovereigns, was regarded with actual dislike and hostility by the Emperor of Russia.

Wellington told them bluntly that they had best bring back their legitimate King, instead of trying any more usurpers, and be quick about it, as the surest means of attaining the peace of Europe.\* Fouché tried to insist on the adoption of the tricolor as the flag of the Bourbons, to which the Duke replied that "the tricolor had become the flag of rebellion, and could not be adopted by the King." The interview lasted from eight in the evening till five in the morning, and the Commissioners separated without coming to any conclusion. Next morning the Duke had an interview with King Louis, and advised him, in order to facilitate his immediate restoration, to confer an appointment on Fouché. Talleyrand was accordingly directed to make out his appointment as Minister of Police. The Commissioners met the Duke again at Neuilly that evening, when Fouché began raising fresh difficulties. Said the Duke, " Mais avant d'aller plus loin, lisons un peu ce papier que tient Monsieur de Talleyrand." The change was instantaneous; all difficulties vanished.†

Occupation of Paris by the Allies and restoration of Louis XVIII.

On 6th and 7th July the armies of Wellington and Blücher took peaceable possession of Paris ; General Müffling was appointed Governor of the city, and Louis XVIII. returned to his capital as King on the 8th.

Well was it that Napoleon had quitted Paris and its environs before the Allies entered, for it is doubtful whether the British Marshal's influence over his fiercer colleague

\* *Despatches*, xii. 534.          † *Salisbury MSS.*

would have prevailed to avert a tragedy. *Mortui non mor-* A.N. 1815.
*dent** was an aphorism which occurred to many others besides
the bluff Blücher about the quondam prisoner of Elba. "To
conclude," wrote Liverpool to Castlereagh † on 21st July,
"we ‡ wish that the King of France would hang or shoot
Buonaparte as the best termination of the business." § As it
was, Wellington had a delicate task in restraining Blücher's
heavy hand. Ever since he had risen to high command,
Wellington had set the example of moderation and humanity
in conquest ; ‖ but besides this high principle there was the
circumstance that the British had no wrongs to avenge on
the French. It was otherwise with the Prussians : the
column of Austerlitz and the bridge of Jena recalled too
bitterly the injuries of a conquered fatherland and the exactions levied by the Emperor on the city of Berlin. Prince
Blücher, accordingly, felt that he was only performing an
act of equity in imposing a levy of one hundred million
francs on the city of Paris, and setting his engineers to mine
the arches of the Pont de Jena. Wellington vigorously

---

* " Dead men don't bite."

† Lord Castlereagh was still British Minister at the Tuileries.

‡ The Cabinet.

§ *Suppl. Despatches*, xi. 47.

‖ In spite of his uniform humanity towards an enemy and his insistence on
his army paying its way in a foreign country, the Duke was by no means
ignorant of the rights of conquerors under the law of nations. as the following
passage from a letter to Mr. Canning, written in 1820, will show : "I believe
it has always been understood that the defenders of a fortress stormed have no
claim to quarter; and the practice which prevailed during the last century of
surrendering a fortress when a breach was opened in the body of a place, and
the counterscarp had been blown in, was founded upon this understanding. Of
late years, however, the French have availed themselves of the humanity of
modern warfare, and have made a new regulation, requiring that a breach
should stand one assault at least. The consequence of this regulation was to
me the loss of the flower of the army in the assaults of Ciudad Rodrigo and
Badajos. I certainly should have thought myself justified in putting both
garrisons to the sword ; and if I had done so to the first, it is probable I should
have saved 5,000 men in the assault of the second. I mention this to show you
that the practice of refusing quarter to a garrison which stands an assault is
not a useless effusion of blood " (*Civil Despatches*. i. 94).

ÆT. 46.

remonstrated.  In regard to the first, he urged in a letter of admirable tact and tone that the levy, if made at all, should be made with the general consent of the Allies; and in regard to the second, he pointed out that one of the articles in the Convention reserved all public monuments and buildings to be dealt with according to the will of the allied Sovereigns.*  Luckily, Prince Blücher was neither thin-skinned nor jealous of the renown of his puissant colleague; he was essentially what is known as "a good fellow," and suspended his project in both respects, though grumbling mightily, until the arrival of the Sovereigns.  Not the less did Wellington, as the more distinguished of the two commanders, incur the odium of having been the author of both schemes, and was execrated by Frenchmen of all parties for the threatened injuries which, in fact, he was the sole agent in averting.

There were other circumstances which tended to bring the Duke into disfavour with the Court party.  It appeared to the allied Sovereigns that France, if not dismembered, must at least be reduced to such limits as would prevent her being in future a menace to the peace of Europe; indeed, Lord Liverpool advocated that she should be deprived of the territory annexed by Louis XIV.†  To this project Wellington offered strenuous resistance.  His letters on the subject must be studied in order to understand how far his views extended beyond the limits of his profession—how great he was in statesmanship as well as in strategy.  While agreeing that the Revolution and the Treaty of Paris had left France too strong for the rest of Europe, weakened and bankrupt as the other continental Powers had become from the long strain of Napoleonic war and exaction, and by the destruction of all the fortresses in the Low Countries and in Germany, he argued that the Allies neither had the right to make any material alteration in the Treaty of Paris, nor would they attain peace by demanding cessions which Louis XVIII. might summon his people to resist.

Moderation of the Duke's views.

* *Despatches*, xii. 552.　　　　　† *Suppl. Despatches*, xi. 32

"That which has been the object of the Allies has been to put an end to the French Revolution, to obtain peace for themselves and their people, to have the power of reducing their overgrown military establishments, and the leisure to attend to the internal concerns of their several nations, and to improve the situation of their people. The Allies took up arms against Buonaparte because it was certain that the world could not be at peace as long as he should possess, or should be in a situation to obtain, supreme power in France ; and care must be taken, in making the arrangements consequent upon our success, that we do not leave the world in the same unfortunate situation respecting France that it would have been in if Buonaparte had continued in possession of his power. . . . Revolutionary France is more likely to distress the world than France, however strong in her frontier, under a regular Government ; and that is the situation in which we ought to endeavour to place her. With this view, I prefer the temporary occupation of some of the strong places, and to maintain for a time a strong force in France, both at the expense of the French Government and under strict regulation, to the permanent cession of even all the places which in my opinion ought to be occupied for a time. These measures will not only give us, during the period of occupation, all the military security which could be expected from the permanent cession, but, if carried into execution in the spirit in which they are conceived, they are in themselves the bond of peace."

Ann. 1815.

This temperate counsel prevailed and was acted on, but Wellington received no credit for its leniency, either from the French people or the courtiers of King Louis. On the contrary, the royalist party deeply resented his action in obtaining the restoration to office of the regicide Fouché, who was, moreover, more than suspected of having been in the plot to bring back Napoleon. Fouché, a member of the Convention which ordered the execution of Louis XVI., had been created by Napoleon Duc d'Otrante, and served under him during the Hundred Days. A thorough time-server, he now was anxious to obtain high office under Louis XVIII. It has been asserted persistently that Wellington had long been in

Unpopularity of the Duke with the French.

secret communication with this individual, had received from him secret intelligence of the movements of the Emperor during the Hundred Days, and had disposed his troops accordingly in anticipation of the campaign of Waterloo.[*] The whole fable is dispelled, and the Duke of Wellington's part in the restoration of Fouché explained, by what he wrote to General Dumouriez on 25th September, 1815.

" Before my arrival near Paris in July, I had never seen Fouché, nor had any communication whatever with him, nor with those connected with him. . . . The fact is that all the Powers, England among others, had been trying during the spring and summer to persuade the King to take Fouché into his service, as a means of conciliating a great number of persons towards his Majesty, and, notwithstanding that I never could see that he carried the influence attributed to him, I carried out that which the others desired. . . . On my arrival near Paris I knew that the Allies were not agreed in favour of the King ; that the Russians especially were hostile to the restoration ; that neither the army nor the Assemblies were favourable to him ; that four provinces of the realm were in open rebellion ; and that others, including the city of Paris, were very cold. It was clear to me that if I could not gain Fouché's interest in the King's restoration, his Majesty must have remained at Saint Denis, at least till the arrival of the Sovereigns, which would have been greatly to the detriment of his authority and dignity, should he ever reascend the throne. Therefore I advised his Majesty to take Fouché into his service, in order that he might make his entry with dignity and without an effort on the part of the Allies, and I am perfectly certain that he owes his tranquil and dignified restoration to this advice." [†]

While the Duke's action in regard to Fouché thus incurred the ire of the Court party, circumstances connected with the fine art collection in the Louvre brought upon him the deep

---

[*] This is stated confidently in Alison's *History of Europe* and in Walter Scott's *Paul's Letters to his Kinsfolk*.

[†] *Despatches*, xii. 649.

animosity of Frenchmen in general and citizens of Paris in Ann. 1815. particular. It had transpired that, previous to the capitulation of Paris, King Louis had volunteered a pledge to the King of the Netherlands that, in the event of his own restoration, he would replace in the churches and galleries of The question of the galleries. Holland and the Low Countries those works of art of which Napoleon had despoiled them as a conqueror. The fulfilment of this pledge was claimed by the King of the Netherlands at a conference of the Powers, whereupon Prince Blücher declared that his master, the King of Prussia, had an equal claim in respect to the works of art carried off from his dominions, and claims were lodged also on behalf of Italy. This was tantamount to the dissolution of the collection in the Louvre; but Wellington, unable to conceive the King of France departing from his promise, was equally unable to perceive any equitable grounds for the retention in Paris of works of art belonging to other Powers who had not received a similar promise. The Prussians, therefore, were allowed to help themselves, and removed all the pictures belonging to their nation and other German principalities. Wellington undertook the negociations with the Prince de Talleyrand and the Duc de Richelieu for the removal of the property of the King of the Netherlands. The King shuffled, and declined to issue any orders on the subject; and finally, the Duke was told that if he must have the pictures, he must take them with an appearance of force in order to screen the King. Accordingly a working party of British soldiers was employed to take down and pack the Netherlands pictures, which, having the appearance of an act of spoliation on the part of the British, excited extraordinary resentment among the people of Paris, the odium of which was thrown on the Duke. He was far too loyal and far too indifferent to public opinion to explain, as he might have done, that it was the King of France, and not he, who was responsible, but he was careful to make known to his own Government the true history of the affair.*

* *Despatches*, xii. 641.

Æt. 46.
It is said that those of Napoleon's Generals who had become Royalists turned their backs upon the Duke at the Court of the Tuileries. Observing this, King Louis made some excuse for their rudeness, but the Duke replied lightly, " Sire, ils sont si accoutumés à me tourner le dos, qu'ils n'en ont pas encore perdu l'habitude ! " *

Trial and execution of Marshal Ney.
There remains to be noticed another event in relation to which the Duke of Wellington's conduct excited attention and some unfavourable comment far beyond the limits of France. When Louis XVIII. was restored in 1814, his return to the capital was signalised by none of those punitive, still less vindictive, measures which usually follow the re-assertion of legitimacy, as in the case of Ferdinand VII.'s restoration to the throne of Spain. The Revolution and the Empire had been overcome after a long struggle, but those who had taken active parts in them were not treated as rebels, save that Napoleon himself had been placed under restraint. But the events of the Hundred Days had been marked by acts of such flagrant treachery on the part of those in high military command that to condone them altogether would have been to admit that every private soldier executed for desertion or disobedience had been the victim of murder. The capitulation of Paris, indeed, had provided that the lives, liberty, and property of the inhabitants should be respected by the allied Generals and their troops, but this by no means could be held to preclude the established French Government from such disciplinary acts as might be determined on. Nevertheless, when in November a list of persons proscribed was published by Fouché, an attempt was made to prove that the clause in the capitulation referred to was of the nature of a general amnesty, and that the Duke of Wellington, as one of the parties to the capitulation, was guilty of a breach of faith in permitting the proscription.

Among the persons so proscribed were Marshal Ney and

---

* " Sir, they are so much accustomed to turn their backs upon me, that they have not yet lost that habit ! "

Colonel Labedoyère, who had both betrayed, in a singularly disgraceful way, the trust of a command accepted from Louis XVIII. Neither of these persons was found in Paris after the capitulation, and it was to persons so found that the capitulation exclusively referred. Ney and Labedoyère both left Paris under feigned names before the Allies entered it, but both were indiscreet enough to return. No doubt the King's Government would have been glad to let them leave the country quietly, but they did not choose to do so; their presence was denounced by zealous officials in the provinces; they were tried and condemned to death.

Ney and his wife made passionate appeals to the Duke of Wellington to interfere. He declined to do so. Why? Not, assuredly, because he bore resentment against the brave General whom he had encountered and defeated on so many fields. Not because there was any tinge of cruelty in his character; his whole career is one long testimony to his natural clemency, but is also a testimony to justice. Had Ney been unjustly condemned, Wellington undoubtedly would have exerted the influence he had so often used over the actions of King Louis, and obtained a pardon. He did intercede with the King on behalf of General le Comte de Lobau, because, he said, "although a faithful servant of Buonaparte, and perhaps the most active and useful, he was never employed by the King, and therefore did not betray him." But Ney's treachery had been of a peculiarly heinous kind. At the very moment that he set out from Paris, proclaiming loudly that he would bring back Napoleon in an iron cage, he was in secret league with the invader. Had Wellington interfered he would have felt that he was acting unworthily in obtaining for an officer of the highest rank that which he could not have asked had the culprit been a private soldier caught in the act of deserting to the enemy. It was the subject of his frequent complaint that, under the British military code as it then was, officers often escaped the punishment due to their breaches of duty, while the non-commissioned and private ranks enjoyed no such immunity. It cannot have been agreeable to the Duke to resist the appeals made to him on behalf of his ancient antagonist, especially considering the chivalrous relations which always prevailed between soldiers of all ranks in the British and French armies; to the public clamour he was indifferent; his private inclination he was accustomed to control, and he refrained from any interference in a case where there was not the slightest suspicion of injustice.*

The army of occupation. On 20th November, 1815, a convention was signed by the representatives of the Powers, and by the Duc de Richelieu as representing King Louis's Government, providing for the withdrawal of all the foreign troops from France, except an army of occupation of 150,000 men, to be fed and paid at the expense of France, and to be maintained for a period of five years within the frontiers of that country on a line extending from the Upper Rhine through the departments of Moselle, Meuse, Ardennes, Nord, and Pas de Calais, subject to a limit of three years, should the Powers agree to shorten the period. In addition to the charge of maintaining these troops, it was agreed that France should pay an indemnity of 700,000,000 francs (£28,000,000) to the late belligerents. That the negociations on which this treaty was based were ever carried to a unanimous issue must be attributed in equal measure to the admirable harmony with which Castlereagh and Wellington always worked together, and to the support given them by Count Nesselrode, representing the Emperor of Russia, in moderating the more rigorous demands of Prussia and Austria. That the occupation itself did not bring about fresh disturbance was chiefly owing to the choice by the

---

* Mr. Gleig says that, while the trial was going on, the Duke expressed himself, " both openly and in private circles, adverse to the execution of Ney " (*Brialmont*, iii. 17). Probably this amounted to no more than a friendly hope that Ney would escape the capital sentence; in later years, at all events, the Duke entertained no doubt that the Marshal suffered rightly. " It was absolutely necessary," he said to Lady Salisbury in 1838, " to make an example " (*Salisbury MSS.*).

Powers of a Commander-in-chief of the allied forces. It was ANN. 1815. arranged that Great Britain, Austria, Prussia, and Russia should each furnish a contingent of 30,000 men, and the Welling-ton is appointed to the chief command. smaller German States in the aggregate a like number, which, by common consent, were placed under command of the Duke of Wellington.

The eventful year of 1815 had drawn to a close, and Napoleon was playing inoffensive whist for sugar-plums with the ladies at Longwood * before the various corps composing the army of occupation had taken up their allotted positions, and France was relieved from the presence and expense of maintaining nearly a million foreign troops. The Duke, fixing his headquarters at Cambrai, at once set about, by a mixture of tact and firmness, establishing in his composite command those principles of moderation and strict respect for property which, however alien from the practice of continental armies, it was ever his first object to insist on his troops observing. The military part of his obligations, difficult and complicated as it was, formed but a small part of his labours. His correspondence at this period, extending to the affairs of most European nations, and to the relations of Spain and Portugal with their American colonies, is amazing in its volume and detail. Among other questions submitted to him was the reduction of the British army contemplated by the Cabinet in consequence of the brighter prospects of enduring peace. It is usually calculated that it takes twice as long to make an efficient cavalry soldier as it does to train a foot soldier, but the Duke seems to have held a different opinion, as expressed in writing to Lord Bathurst.

" My opinion is that the best troops we have, probably the best in the world, are the British infantry, particularly the old infantry that has served in Spain. This is what we ought to keep up, and what I wish above all others to retain. The cavalry, that which is the expensive branch of the cavalry—the

* As described in letter from Admiral Sir George Cockburn, 22nd October, 1815.

horses—may be put down in peace; and upon the renewal of
war it is more easy to recruit them, or even horses for the
artillery, than it is to get together a good body of infantry.   For
this reason I would recommend you not to lose your good infantry
if you can keep it ; and to reform (? reduce) rather the horses
of your cavalry and artillery to the utmost, and all the expensive
parts of your establishment." *

Appointed
Chief Com-
missioner
of Arbitra-
tion and
Finance.

It had become customary whenever a difficulty of unusual
magnitude arose in European politics to call in the aid of
the Duke of Wellington.   Under the Convention of Paris
a commission of diplomacy and finance was appointed,
consisting of Sir Charles Stuart, Count de Goltz, Baron de
Vincent, and General Pozzo di Borgo, representing respectively
Great Britain, Prussia, Austria, and Russia, and charged with
the settlement of claims sent in by nearly every Government
in Europe on behalf of every town and village, every province
and parish, where French troops had made their presence felt
during the revolutionary and Napoleonic wars.   Against these
had to be weighed counterclaims on behalf of the French
Government, and in the complicated calculations which arose,
the Commissioners freely availed themselves of the Duke's
advice.   Still they made but slow progress: at the end of
nearly two years of deliberation it became obvious that the
allied Sovereigns had under-estimated the extent of these
claims, which, by midsummer of 1817, already amounted to
fifty millions sterling, although the claims of Great Britain,
Spain, and Portugal had not yet been lodged.   Clearly, the
resources of France would prove unequal to meet these
demands, added to the cost of the indemnity and the expense
of the army of occupation.   Thus matters were drifting to a
deadlock, when, on 30th October, 1817, the Emperor of
Russia wrote under his own hand to the Duke of Wellington
as to one who, " placed at the head of the military forces of
the European alliance, had contributed more than once, by
the wisdom and moderation which distinguished him, to the

* *Despatches*, xii. 668.

reconciliation of weighty interests," * expressing his desire
that the Duke should defer to the wishes of the allied
Powers and of all interested parties by placing himself at the
head of the Commission, and arbitrating on the claims with a
view to arriving at a speedy and practicable means of liquidat-
ing them.† He accepted this post—*une position nouvelle en
Europe,*‡ as he justly termed it—and from this point his
despatches become simply bewildering in their number and
the intricacy of the calculations set forth and received from
his correspondents. No idea can be formed of the nature
of his labours, or of the amount of personal consideration
bestowed by him on details, except by an examination of the
letters in 1817 and 1818. Not only did he succeed in con-
solidating the claims against France into one manageable sum,
but he arranged that, although this was a large reduction
from the aggregate of claims, France should be held to have
liquidated them when she made payment of that amount to
the Allies, who should undertake settlement with the
creditors; and to enable the French Government to make
this payment, Wellington negociated a loan for them with
the leading financiers of Europe.

"Since Baring left me, as I generally spend the greatest part
of every morning now with money-changers, Rothschild has been
with me; and he says that he is certain that the French Government will experience no difficulty in realising within the year,
that is, twelve months, the whole sum which they want." §

The pages of history may be searched in vain for a parallel Unique
to the position of Wellington. Great conquerors, like position
attained
Alexander or Napoleon, have wielded more extensive powers, by the
Duke.
but the voluntary assignment of undisputed ascendency by
crowned heads and diplomatists to the subject of an alien
monarch is unique in the history of civilisation. At the age
of eight-and-forty Wellington was the most conspicuous

---

* *Suppl. Despatches,* xii. 119.  † *Ibid.,* 156.
‡ *Ibid.,* 212.  § *Ibid.,* 261; 9th Feb., 1818.

ÆT. 48. figure—the most exalted individual in the world. His good
sword had won him equal rank with the greatest captains;
his capacity for rule, his inflexible rectitude, his superiority
to all intrigue and suspicion of self-seeking, his far-seeing
sagacity—these drew upon him the choice of the Sovereigns
to place him in the most critical post of administration and
diplomacy.*

His
scrupulous
avoidance
of selfish
ends.

It is to be noted how scrupulous the Duke was not to turn
the trust reposed in him to his private advantage, and this in
small matters as well as in great. When the Governments
of allied States conferred on him high military rank, carrying
with it handsome emoluments, in accepting the rank he
invariably declined the pay. As Spanish Generalissimo he
had been entitled to draw £8,000 a year; instead of which he
allowed the money to accumulate, and, at the close of the
war, handed it over as a fund for the benefit of the Spanish
army. In the same spirit he expressed quick displeasure on
hearing that certain horses of the pontoon train had been
employed to draw the carriages of the Duchess of Wellington
and the Duchess of Richmond from Valenciennes to Cambrai,
on their way to a review.

"As one of these carriages is mine," he wrote to Sir George
Wood commanding the artillery, "and this example may be
drawn into a precedent of using for private convenience the
horses belonging to the public, than which nothing could be
more injurious to his Majesty's service, I am anxious to take
this opportunity of recalling your particular attention to his
Majesty's orders and regulations on the subject; and I beg that

* In Lady Salisbury's interesting notes of conversations with the Duke there
is one of an observation describing the illuminant process of a penetrating
intellect. "There is a curious thing that one feels sometimes; when you are
considering a subject, suddenly a whole train of reasoning comes before you like
a flash of light : you see it all (moving his hand as if something appeared before
him, his eye with its brightest expression), yet it takes you perhaps two hours
to put on paper all that has occurred to your mind in an instant. Every part
of the subject, the bearings of all its parts upon each other, and all the consequences, are there before you " (*Salisbury MSS.*).

on all future occasions . . . those sent in charge [of horses Ann. 1818.
belonging to the public] may have orders in writing not to allow
them to be employed for the convenience of any officers in his
Majesty's service, or of any of his Majesty's subjects, without an
order in writing signed by me." *

It was not in the nature of things that one in such a His un-
peculiarly influential position as the Duke of Wellington popularity
should avoid incurring the hostility of parties and persons. in France.
The Court party resented the counsels of clemency which he
urged in regard to the regicides ; royalists, as well as Buona-
partists and revolutionaries of every degree, chafed more and
more because of the hateful presence of the army of occupation, of which he was the head, and because of the stipulated payments in exacting which he had been appointed the
chief agent. Lastly, there was a mass of officers on half-pay
and disbanded soldiers on no pay, seething with discontent,
a fertile soil for a rank crop of conspiracy. Many of the
persons obnoxious to the restored monarchy of France had
been excluded from that country, and received passports
requiring them to reside in Brussels, more or less under police
supervision. These persons published a series of libels in
certain newspapers, for which, as they imputed base and mischievous acts and motives to the Duke in his public as well
as in his private character, it was necessary to prosecute and
punish them. It then became apparent that an extensive
revolutionary plot was in process of maturing at Brussels,
that many of those engaged in it were on intimate terms with
persons in the confidence of the Belgian Government, and
were receiving assistance and encouragement from at least
one British nobleman. One of the leaders of the conspiracy
was Comte Victor de Cruquenbourg, whose brother was aide-
de-camp to the Prince of Orange, and the Prince himself
was known to be indisposed to interfere with the utmost
freedom of political opinion and its expression. His liberal

* *Suppl. Despatches*, xii. 92.

Æт. 48. proclivities were destined to sustain a severe shock by an event which took place early in 1818.

Already, on 25th June, 1816, an attempt had been made to destroy the Duke's house in the Rue des Champs Elysées, on the occasion of his giving a ball to the French princes. Smoke was perceived issuing from the cellar shortly after midnight; on search being made a quantity of combustibles and explosives, including a barrel of oil and bottles filled with gunpowder, were found to have been laid there and a match applied. It was a narrow escape, because the explosion of the powder would have interfered with any attempt to extinguish the flames, had the discovery been delayed but a few minutes. The affair, however, was hushed up; the Duke had previously arranged to start for England next day, in order to take a course of Cheltenham waters, and no attempt was made to bring to justice the miscreants, who were generally supposed to be Buonapartist malcontents.

Attempted assassination of the Duke. The second attempt on his life was more nearly successful, and was distinguished by certain very disquieting circumstances. Lieut.-General Sir George Murray, serving once more under his old chief, received a letter written in Brussels on 30th January, 1818, by Lord Kinnaird, a gentleman who had made himself conspicuous by his avowed sympathy with the revolutionary conspirators and by liberal contributions to their money chest. He told Murray that a French refugee, under sentence of death, had desired him to obtain the interest of the Duke of Wellington to procure for him liberty to return to Paris, but that he (Kinnaird) had declined "both because I believed the Duke did not interfere, and because there seemed to be no pretence whatever for asking such interference." The fellow then asked if Kinnaird would intercede for him with M. de Cazes, if he revealed a plot which was about to be put in effect against the Duke's life. All the man wanted was a safe conduct to carry him to Paris, when he would undertake to point out to the police within twenty-four hours the hired assassin who had been

waiting his opportunity for more than four months.* The Ann. 1818.
Duke, when Murray laid the matter before him, made
very light of it; there never was a less likely subject for
intimidation than he. Murray was directed to reply that,
unless Lord Kinnaird knew to the contrary, his acquaintance
was probably "a mere humbug, and will obtain nothing by
the line he has taken." † He expressed, in addition, the wish,
not unnatural in the circumstances, that Lord Kinnaird
should communicate the name of his informant.

Lord Kinnaird's letter was received on the morning of 8th
February; Murray's reply was written in the afternoon. Two
days later, on the 10th, the Duke dined with Sir Charles
Stuart, at whose house, among others, he met Marshal Grouchy
and Madame De Staël. The Duchess of Wellington was not
residing in Paris at this time. His own hotel has long
since been improved off the plan of Paris: it stood in the
Rue des Champs Elysées, and was entered by a *porte cochère*
at an awkward angle to the street, and so narrow that the
two sentries were obliged to fall back each time a carriage
passed in, the sentry boxes being outside the gate. The
Duke returned from dinner soon after midnight, and just as
the carriage turned into the entry, a fellow stepped forward
and fired a pistol in at the window.

The coachman instantly whipped up his horses and dashed
into the courtyard. The Duke, who had been leaning back
in his carriage, heard the report, but did not see the flash.
Thinking his coachman had knocked down one of the sentries,
whose musket had gone off, on alighting he asked him what
on earth he meant by driving in at such a pace, and told him
he had knocked down a sentry. "I saw a man fire at your
Grace," replied the coachman.

Two of the Duke's servants coming along the street heard the
report, saw the flash, and the assassin running away; one of them
proposed to stop him. "No, no," said the other; "it's only a
row between some damned Frenchies; best keep out of it." ‡

* *Suppl. Despatches*, xii. 274.      † *Ibid.*, 260.      ‡ *De Ros MS.*

The French Government were, or affected to be, incredulous of the genuine character of the attempt, but warnings had arrived from other sources than Lord Kinnaird, which left no doubt whatever of the existence of an extensive conspiracy against the Duke's life. He had, besides, received numerous anonymous letters, to which he had paid not the slightest attention; * but, the attempt having been made, he insisted on due diligence being shown in order to discover the culprits. He sent Lord Kinnaird's letter to be laid before the King of the Netherlands, that nobleman having explained that his sense of honour would not permit him to reveal the name of his informant. The worst part of the affair was that the Prince of Orange—the Duke's brother-in-arms at Waterloo—was implicated in the conspiracy by the extent he was known to have encouraged and sheltered the French refugees. In reply to the Prince's letter of hot disclaimer (which, curiously enough, was not written till two months after the outrage), the Duke replied calmly—

"I assure your Royal Highness that the idea never did nor never could have entered my mind that you had any knowledge of the plot, which I believe nobody now doubts was formed by the French refugees in the Netherlands, to assassinate me. Those who know me best will do me the justice to say that, whenever the idea was suggested in my presence, I always answered that I would as soon suspect my own son as I could your Royal Highness; but I will not conceal from your Royal Highness that this occurrence has brought your name into discussion in a way very disagreeable to your friends."†

Lord Kinnaird's connection with the conspirators led him into a good deal of trouble. As he persisted in refusing to give up the name of his informant, orders were issued by the Belgian Government for his arrest. Leaving Brussels secretly, he took his informant with him to Paris, choosing to construe a passage in a letter from the Duke to Lord Clancarty,

* *Stanhope*, 76.        † *Suppl. Despatches*, xii. 480.

FREDERICK WILLIAM, PRINCE OF ORANGE,
AFTERWARDS FIRST KING OF THE NETHERLANDS.

*(Vol. ii. p. 116.*

British Minister in Brussels, as an efficient safe conduct for
his companion.* On arriving in Paris, both were arrested,
but Lord Kinnaird was released at the request of the Duke,
who took him into his own house, otherwise, as he wrote to
Lord Bathurst, " he would probably have been lodged in the
Conciergerie, which I certainly should not have liked." † His
lordship made but a shabby return for the Duke's protection.
He left Paris on 15th April, telling his host he was going to
Brussels. ‡ This was merely a blind to deceive the police,
because it was found that he had gone two stages along the
road to Amiens. He left a sting behind him. On the day Lord
of his departure he addressed a letter, and an exceedingly Kinnaird
accuses the
long memorandum, to the French Chamber of Peers, accusing Duke of
bad faith.
the Government and, by implication, the Duke of Wellington
of breach of faith in the arrest of the informer Marinet.
Wellington simply characterised this malicious document,
drawn up by one enjoying his hospitality and protection at
the moment, as " certainly a very impudent production, but
I think I ought not to give it any answer." §

The judicial inquiry was prolonged for many months both
in Paris and Brussels. It was ascertained beyond all moral
doubt that the man who fired the shot was one Cantillon, an
ex-sergeant of dragoons, and that he acted in the pay and
under the direction of a large number of persons, chiefly old
officers *en demi-solde* of Napoleon's armies; but although many
of them and Cantillon himself were kept in custody for a long
time, no one was punished. Cantillon was committed for
trial, but was acquitted by the French jury, which was not

* " It may be proper to mention to you that the French Government are
disposed to go any length in the way of negociation with the person mentioned
by Lord Kinnaird, or others, to discover the plot, and to co-operate with the
Government of the King of the Netherlands on the subject " (*Suppl. Despatches*, xii. 328).

† *Suppl. Despatches*, xii. 382.

‡ *Ibid.*, 479.

§ *Ibid.*, 535. Lord Kinnaird acted very indiscreetly, and incurred suspicion
of much from which the Duke freely acquitted him. But when he returned to
England Lady Holland dubbed him " Oliver " Kinnaird.

surprising, considering the amount of popular sympathy he
had secured.    Among the swarm of squibs—straws which
show the direction of the wind—the following doggerel affords
a fair sample of the quality and spirit :—

> " Mal ajuster est un defaut ;
>     Il le manqua—et voici comme,
> L'imbecile visa trop haut,
>     Il l'avait pris *pour un grand homme !* " *

In the mind of one man, at least, there can have been no
doubt of Cantillon's guilt, for Napoleon added a codicil to his
will at St. Helena, devising 10,000 francs to him in acknowledgment of the service he had attempted to render his
country by the murder of Wellington !

"Cantillon," ran this precious document, "had as much
right to assassinate that oligarchist, as Wellington had to
send me to perish on the rock of St. Helena," a parallel
which, as Sir Walter Scott pointed out, betrays a reasoning
either infirm or insincere.    "If both were wrong, why reward
the ruffian with a legacy ? but if both were right, why complain of the British Government for detaining him at St.
Helena ? "

The
British
Govern-
ment recall
the Duke
from Paris. Lord Bathurst communicated to the Duke the unanimous
instruction of the British Cabinet that he should avoid further
risks by withdrawing from Paris to his headquarters at
Cambrai,† and, in a separate letter, conveyed the Prince
Regent's commands to the same effect.

"His Royal Highness, deeply impressed with the conviction
that the preservation of a life of such inestimable importance is
paramount to all other considerations, has commanded me to
inform your Grace that it is his pleasure that you should,

---

\* " Aiming badly is a blunder ;
    The idiot missed, and cheated fate ;
He aimed too high—and little wonder !
    He thought his man was something *great.*"

† *Suppl. Despatches,* xii. 325.

without delay, quit Paris and proceed to the headquarters at Ann. 1818.
Cambrai." *

Hence arose the solitary instance on record of disobedience The Duke's one
to the orders of his superiors on the part of this great act of dis-
disciplinarian. obedience.

" I only regret," ran his reply to Bathurst, " that the Cabinet
did not, as they usually have done, consult my opinion before
they decided on a case in which I am principally and personally
concerned, and on a line of action depending on particular circumstances existing here at the moment, of which I must be
a better judge than anybody else. It is very hard to place me
in the situation of being obliged to disobey, or even to delay
to obey, the positive order of the Prince Regent; but I must
do the latter at all events, as I conceive the public interests
require it." †

No doubt the Duke was doing valuable public service in
Paris by bringing about the liquidation of international claims
and hastening to a close the foreign occupation of France, but
one can read between these lines the repugnance of a proud
spirit to the faintest suspicion of being intimidated, and this
is still more apparent in other passages of this letter.

" It must not be supposed that the allied Ministers here are
very cordially united, either in their objects or councils, because
they don't break out. The truth is that I keep them together;
but if I were to withdraw from Paris altogether, and particularly
if I were to do so in a manner which should shake the public
respect for me, you would no longer see that union of councils
and objects which has prevailed here since the peace. In short,
I have no hesitation in stating it as my opinion that, after
assassination, the greatest public and private calamity which
could happen would be to obey the order of the Prince Regent.
Indeed, I don't know that I should not prefer that the assassin
should have succeeded, as at least I should have died respected." ‡

---

* *Suppl. Despatches*, xii. 326.     † *Ibid.*, 333.     ‡ *Ibid.*, 335.

Ær. 48. Thus, calmly defiant, Wellington remained at his post in Paris till the end of April. By that time he had succeeded in persuading the Powers to accept a sum of 240,000,000 francs (£9,600,000) as settlement in full of all claims instead of the gross amount of 800,000,000, outside the expenses of the army of occupation. He had also carried towards completion the negociation of loans to the French Government by the English houses of Hope and Co. and Baring Brothers. In connection with the last matter, he went to London early in May, and by the middle of that month was back at Cambrai. In September following the representatives of the Powers met in conference at Aix-la-Chapelle to take into consideration the propriety of withdrawing the army of occupation. The Duke had previously resisted proposals which had been urged, not only by the French Government, but by the Emperor of Russia,* for the anticipation of the term of three years, which had been fixed under the Convention of Paris as the minimum, although he had consented to a reduction of the force in 1817 by 30,000 men. Negociations proceeded so smoothly that, on 5th October, the Duke was able to write to Lord Bathurst asking for ships to be sent at once to Calais, Antwerp, and Ostend for the embarkation of the

**Evacuation of France by the Allies.** British contingent. On the 30th he issued from Cambrai his *Ordre du jour*, bidding farewell to the troops of different nationalities, and thanking them for their excellent behaviour while under his command.† Of his own part in conducting the occupation, so hazardous in its nature, to a pacific close, ample recognition was expressed by the pen of Lord Bathurst, which lent itself on this occasion to terms more characteristic of French or Spanish documents than the frigid officialism of English despatches. "Amidst the signal achievements

* Repetition in history is proverbial. The recent action of the present Emperor of Russia by inviting the Powers of Europe to confer on a project of universal disarmament is singularly akin to that of Alexander I., whose project of a Holy Alliance included the settlement of all international disputes by periodical conferences of crowned heads.

† *Suppl. Despatches*, xii. 795.

which will carry your name and the glory of the British Empire down to the latest posterity, it will not form the least part of your Grace's renown that you have exercised and concluded a command unexampled in its character with the concurrent voice of approbation from all whom it could concern." *

### Appendix F.

### *Influence of Wellington on the Character of the British Army.*

The close of the Duke's long warfare seems a fitting opportunity to appraise the permanent effect of his command upon the British land forces.

First as to the officers, his early complaints of their inefficiency, their inattention to orders, and their neglect of regimental duties, contrast in a marked degree with what we are accustomed to read at the present day in despatches; but it was inevitable, having regard to the absence of all previous training and the system of appointment and promotion. They were gallant to a fault—*sans peur, mais sans avis;* examples of misconduct in action were as rare among officers as among their men: practically they formed a *quantité negligeable.* It was Wellington's part to instil into regimental officers that sense of duty which appears now inseparable from the profession; to awaken in them pride in knowledge of tactics and acquaintance with interior economy, which, in the early years of the century, were considered creditable only in sergeants. In short, he established, or at least revived, the tradition of proficiency as inseparable from the dignity of a commission.

There were exceptions, of course, to the general level of incompetency which he found prevailing in the service—young officers like the three Napiers of the Light Division,

*Duties of officers.*

---

\* *Suppl. Despatches,* xii. 852.

Fletcher, Jones, and Chapman of the Engineers, Ramsay and Ross of the Artillery; senior officers, too, like Hope, Graham, Beresford, Hill, and George Murray; gifted staff officers like Waters, Fitzroy Somerset, and Alexander Gordon, whose hearts were in their profession, who looked upon it as something more than a mere mill of brutal discipline for turning yokels into marching machines, who cordially welcomed the Duke of York's reforms, and ardently longed for more. Sir John Moore had already shown what the British infantry might become, fashioning the 43rd, 52nd, and 95th Regiments at Shorncliffe into an ideal brigade, hereafter to develop into the world-famed Light Division. But the average regiment was no better than could be expected from a system which tolerated ignorance and indolence in the officers, while it exacted slavish obedience from the men.

Promotion.

Wellington accepted, and even approved, the recognised effect of family influence upon promotion, which, in these plainer-spoken days, we should stigmatise as jobbery, but he claimed vehemently that military character and service should count for something also. For instance, there was a certain Captain Lloyd of the 43rd whose promotion he frequently urged on the Horse Guards, speaking "both as a general officer and on the part of the Lord Lieutenant of Ireland;" but his recommendation was persistently neglected.

"It would be desirable, certainly," he wrote to the Military Secretary, "that the only claim to promotion should be military merit; but this is a degree of perfection to which the disposal of military patronage has never been, and cannot be, I believe, brought in any military establishment. The Commander-in-chief must have friends, officers on the staff attached to him, etc., who will press him to promote their friends and relations, all doubtless very meritorious, and no man will at all times resist these applications; but if there is to be any influence in the disposal of military patronage, in aid of military merit, can there be any in our army so legitimate as that of family connexion, fortune, and influence in the country. I acknowledge, therefore, that I have been astonished at seeing Lloyd, with every claim that an officer can have to promotion, still a captain; and others, connected with the officers of the staff, promoted as soon as their time of service had expired. . . . I, who command the largest British army that has been employed against the enemy for many years, and who have upon my hands certainly the most extensive and difficult concern that was ever imposed on any British officer, have not the power of making even a corporal!!! . . . . Even admitted that the system of promotion by seniority, exploded in other armies, is the best for that of Great Britain, it would still be an advantage that those who become entitled to it should receive it immediately, and from the hand of the person who is obliged to expose them to danger, to enforce discipline, and to call for their exertions." *

The allusion to the disuse of promotion by seniority in other armies is not quite clear, seeing that in 1839 the Duke wrote to Lord Hill—

"Seniority regulates the service of all armies. This rule is the safeguard of authority against the influence and power of pretensions however founded. The enforcement of it is essential to the meritorious officer on service. . . . I must say that of all the difficulties with which I had to contend in the Peninsula, the greatest was the advanced rank in the Portuguese service given to our officers, and the relations of command in which they consequently stood towards the officers of the British army." †

It is very remarkable, considering how frequently and bitterly the Duke complained of the average ignorance of officers of the army, that he set no store by professional education. He held the opinion, since so clearly expounded by Guyau,‡ that the object of education is not to fill a head but to form it, conscious, no doubt, that his own professional

*Military education.*

---

* *Despatches,* vi. 305.
† *Apsley House MSS.*
‡ "Outside the sum total of the narrow and positive science indispensable in practical life, all restricted scientific instruction is sterile."

eminence had been attained, not by means of the instruction he received at school, but by knowledge acquired subsequently by the exercise of a strong will. Probably he would have given assent to Mr. Ruskin's doctrine that "the first use of education is to enable us to consult with the wisest and the greatest men on all points of difficulty;" but in effect he expressed himself more simply, that "the best education for the military and all other professions was the common education of the country." *

The Duke's personal influence. A volume might be filled with wise maxims gathered from the Duke's letters of advice, remonstrance, or censure addressed to officers under his command. Let a single instance suffice, remembering that, although the Duke never was what could be termed a popular commanding officer, men of all ranks had such perfect confidence in his experience and judgment that every word he wrote or spoke was laid to heart and quoted from lip to lip. When Marshal Beresford complained to him more bitterly than usual about an officer under his command who was in the habit of sending home false and injurious reports, Wellington replied, "There is only one line to be adopted in opposition to all trick; that is, the steady, straight line of duty, tempered by forbearance, lenity, and good nature." †

Sometimes, in his later years, the Duke's injunctions to his officers were too paternal not to provoke a smile. His counterblast in 1845, though not so prolix, but equally ineffective as that of James VI., became almost equally famous, and for a while tobacco-stoppers, carved in his likeness, became very popular.

"G.O. No. 577.—The Commander-in-Chief has been informed that the practice of smoking, by the use of pipes, cigars, and cheroots, has become prevalent among the Officers of the Army, which is not only in itself a species of intoxication occasioned by the fumes of tobacco, but, undoubtedly, occasions drinking and,

---

* *Salisbury MSS.*, 1838.         † *Despatches*, iv. 441.

tippling by those who acquire the habit; and he intreats the Officers commanding Regiments to prevent smoking in the Mess Rooms of their several Regiments, and in the adjoining apartments, and to discourage the practice among the Officers of Junior Rank in their Regiments."

The wits of *Punch* made merry over this, declaring that the officers were in dismay, " dreading the possibility of being thrown upon their conversational resources, which must have a most dreary effect."

In one respect the Duke's influence upon the habits of officers is open to criticism. When he rose to high command in the army the usual dress of an officer, even when not on duty, was his uniform, as it remains now in Continental armies. The Duke's example, arising out of his personal dislike of display, first set the fashion of "mufti," or plain clothes. For instance, in 1814, when Louis XVIII. attended the Odéon theatre with the Royal Princes and a brilliant suite, the Duke occupied the box opposite the royal one, and was the only officer in the building not in uniform.

The Duke attached almost higher importance to the non-commissioned officers than to any other rank in the service. Time, and the change which it has wrought in the professional zeal of regimental officers and in the habits of non-commissioned officers, have removed some of the grounds for the Duke's reliance on the inferior ranks; but his opinion is still worth quoting, were it only as a warning against relapse into the old indolent system.

*Non-commissioned officers.*

"The Guards are superior to the Line, not as being picked men like the French—for Napoleon gave peculiar privileges to his guardsmen and governed the army with them—but from the goodness of the non-commissioned officers. They do, in fact, all that the commissioned officers of the Line are expected to do— and don't do. This must be so as long as the present system lasts—and I am all for it—of having gentlemen for officers; you cannot require them to do many things that should be done.

They must not speak to the men, for instance—we should reprimand them if they did; our system in that respect is so very different from the French. Now all that work is done by the non-commissioned officers of the Guards. It is true that they regularly get drunk once a day—by eight in the evening—and go to bed soon after, but then they always take care to do first whatever they were bid. When I had given an officer in the Guards an order, I felt sure of its being executed; but with an officer in the Line, it was, I will venture to say, a hundred to one against its being done at all." *

One day the Duke had been quoting the saying of a certain sergeant, and added, " I have served with all nations, and I am convinced that there would be nothing so intelligent, so valuable, as English soldiers of that rank, if you could get them sober, *which is impossible.*" †

He was always very anxious to maintain the dignity of the non-commissioned ranks, and to preserve the due proportion in their pay to that of the rank and file. Thus in 1812 he wrote earnestly on the subject to Lord Liverpool.

" The foundation of every system of discipline which has for

* *Stanhope,* 17. The Duke would have altered his opinion had he lived to see the great change in the habits and attainments of line officers, brought about by the general elevation of the spirit of the service which we owe, in large measure, to the influence of the late Prince Consort. The following instance, described to me by an officer of the regiment who was present, took place some time in the 'forties, and illustrates the kind of thing which was not at all uncommon. The regiment, a fine one, which lost at Waterloo fourteen killed and wounded out of twenty-six officers, was paraded for inspection in the Phœnix Park. After riding down the ranks, the inspecting officer directed the Colonel to put the battalion through some manœuvres, beginning with a change of front. The Adjutant began giving the necessary words of command, upon which the General, unreasonably exacting, desired that the Colonel should direct the movement himself. Now Colonel —— knew only one movement, namely, how to form square from line or column. Instead. therefore, of changing front, he promptly brought the battalion into square, and gave the command for file firing, which, continuing till all the ammunition was expended, effectually silenced the remonstrances of the inspecting officer.

† *Salisbury MSS.,* 1837.

its object the prevention of crimes must be the non-commissioned officers of the army. But I am sorry to say, that notwithstanding the encouragement I have given to this class, they are still as little to be depended on as the private soldiers themselves; and they are just as ready to commit irregularities and outrage. I attribute this circumstance very much to the lowness of their pay in comparison with that of the soldiers. Within my recollection the pay of the soldiers of the army has been increased from sixpence to one shilling per diem; while that of the corporals, which was eightpence, has in the same period been raised only to one shilling and twopence; and that of the sergeants, which was one shilling, has been raised only to one shilling and sixpence. . . . Your Lordship will observe that the old proportions have not been preserved; and the non-commissioned officers of the army not only feel no inclination to preserve a distinction between them and the private soldiers, but they feel no desire to incur the responsibility, and take the trouble, and submit to the privations of their situation for so trifling a difference in their pay. . . . The remedy for this evil is to increase the pay of the corporals and sergeants, so as at least to restore the old proportions." *

These representations prevailed in the end, though not until after much resistance on the part of the Treasury had been overcome. It was feared that demands might follow for an increase in the pay of ensigns and lieutenants.

Turning now to the rank and file, Wellington's despatches and general orders bear testimony that the difficulty he found in enforcing discipline was second only to that which he encountered in getting officers to learn and attend to their duties. He succeeded in overcoming both difficulties, but the way was hard, and he did not endear himself to soldiers in the process. Vauvenargues, nearly a hundred years before, had cried in the wilderness, "If you would raise the character of men, you must raise them to consciousness of their own prudence and strength;" but the lesson had not been laid to heart. Military punishment ran upon a scale of mediæval,

*Rank and file.*

* *Despatches,* ix. 228.

of demoniac ferocity.   To realise its horrors one has to look
up such a case as was sanctioned by a commanding officer of
singular mildness and thoughtful nature.   Charles Napier,
commanding the 50th Regiment, writes to his mother in
June, 1808—

"You know my antipathy to flogging: you know that it is
unconquerable. . . . This antipathy gains strength from principle
and reason, as I am convinced it could be dispensed with.   Still,
as other severe punishments do not exist in our army, we must
use torture in some cases, until a substitute is given by our
government.   Mark this narrative.   A robbery was committed
in the regiment, and the thief was discovered in a few hours. . . . I
resolved to make a severe example. . . . He was sentenced to
nine hundred lashes.   Yet there was not one positive proof of
the robbery, all was presumptive evidence: but I charged him
with breaches of discipline which could be proved, and my resolve
was to punish or not, according to my own judgment, a commanding
officer being in truth despotic.

"Two days I took to consider every circumstance, thinking,
if he should be afterwards proved innocent, it would be disagreeable to have bestowed nine hundred lashes wrongfully. . . .
Yesterday he was flogged in the square. . . . When he had
received 200 lashes he was promised pardon, if he told where
the money was.   No! God in heaven was his witness he was
innocent. . . . In this manner he went on.   I was inexorable;
and it is hardly credible that he received 600 lashes, given in
the most severe manner . . . praying for death to relieve
him. . . . At six hundred lashes he was taken down, with the
seemingly brutal intention of flogging him again in a half-healed
back . . . the greatest torture possible. . . . Directions were
given that he should be kept solitary to lower his spirits. . . . Pain,
lowness and the people employed to frighten him succeeded:
he confessed all, and told where the money was hid." *

The same author testifies in another place that when he
was a subaltern he frequently saw 600, 700, 800, 900, and

* *Life and Opinions*, i. 87.

1,000 lashes sentenced by a *regimental* court-martial, and generally every lash inflicted. He had heard of 1,200 inflicted, but never saw it. Writing in 1837, he rejoiced that even a general court-martial could no longer inflict more than 200 lashes, and that it was no longer legal to bring a poor fellow out of hospital to receive the balance of his sentence. Of his experiences of the old system he writes as follows :—

"I have seen many hundreds of men flogged, and have always observed that when the skin is thoroughly cut up or flayed off, the great pain subsides. Men are frequently convulsed and screaming during the time they receive from one lash to three hundred lashes, and then they bear the remainder, even to eight hundred or a thousand lashes, without a groan. They will often lie as if without life, and the drummers appear to be flogging a lump of dead, raw flesh. Now I have frequently observed that, in these cases, the faces of the spectators assumed a look of disgust; there was always a low whispering sound, scarcely audible, issuing from the apparently stern and silent ranks; a sound arising from lips that spoke not."

Such was the system devised to encourage recruiting at the beginning of the present century; it is scarcely credible to us at the end of it. It was the system which Sir Arthur Wellesley had to administer in taking command of an European army. How did he apply it? Not exactly as an enlightened commander would do at the present day. He did not abolish the lash—far from it; to the end of his days he never believed that it could be safely dispensed with. Charles Napier himself dared not advocate its abolition *on active service.* Neither did the Duke entertain a high opinion of the possibility of raising the common soldier's morality or self-respect. "The scum of the earth; all English soldiers are fellows who have enlisted for drink—that is the plain fact—they have all enlisted for drink."* He used the only

*Wellington's opinion of the lash.*

* *Stanhope,* 14.

means which military law, as he found it, gave him to enforce discipline; but his sense of humanity and justice was as strong as his discipline was inflexible.  His general orders in the Peninsula abound in instances where a prisoner having been sentenced to death or flogging for desertion, insubordination, or plunder, the Commander-in-chief confirms the sentence, but pardons the culprit, either because his regiment has been behaving well in recent operations, or because offences of the kind have lately been rare, or because of some slight irregularity in the proceedings.  Plundering of peaceful inhabitants was the one crime he detested and was determined to put down.  The country round Copenhagen was devastated by Lord Cathcart's troops, without an effort made to stop it; but in the detachment under Sir Arthur Wellesley, when a man of good character in the 43rd stole some cherries off a tree in front of his billet, he was sentenced to receive 25 lashes *—not worth taking off a fellow's jacket for, officers of the old school would have said.

Still, the Duke remained to the last an uncompromising advocate of corporal punishment; he was unable to imagine discipline maintained in a volunteer army without that *ultima ratio.*  It seems never to have occurred to him that, while it was a more or less effective deterrent from crime, it was also a deterrent to voluntary enlistment, except by "the scum of the earth."  So strongly did he feel on this subject that, when in Opposition in 1833, hearing that Lord Grey's Government were about to propose an alteration in the Mutiny Act, whereby "corporal punishment should be restricted, if not entirely abolished," in the British services, he wrote a very strong memorandum to the King, stating his opinion that no punishment could be substituted for corporal punishment without causing the army, at least, to fall into a state of hopeless indiscipline.†  Three years later, appearing as a witness before the Royal Commission on Military Punishments in 1836, he gave his opinion emphatically that

* *Life and Opinions,* i. 80.          † *Apsley House MSS.,* 1833.

flogging was the only effective deterrent, because, unlike solitary confinement, imprisonment with hard labour, or other punishments which had been introduced during his experience of the army, it was inflicted in public, and every man knew what was before him if he incurred a sentence of corporal punishment.

"I have no idea of any great effect being produced by anything but the fear of immediate corporal punishment. I must say that in hundreds of instances the very threat of the lash has prevented very serious crimes. It is well known that I have hundreds of times prevented the most serious offences by ordering the men to appear in their side arms. When I found any great disorder going on, the first thing I did was to order that all the men must appear, if they appeared in the streets at all, in their side arms; that was the first thing. I then ordered that the rolls should be called every hour; and all these restraints were enforced by the fear of the lash. . . . Then, after that, if this did not do, I ordered them all under arms, and kept them standing near their arms. It is well known that I have done that very thing frequently. All these things were ordered to prevent the mischief in the first place; and in the next place, I was quite sure that no man would venture to disobey it, because he knew that if he ventured to disobey it, he would come to corporal punishment.

*Q.* "Supposing the power of corporal punishment had not been in your hands at that time, could you by any other means have established that discipline in the army?

*A.* "No; it is out of the question. . . . Having had this subject in contemplation for six or seven years, I have turned it over in my mind in every possible way, and I declare that I have not an idea of what can be substituted for it.

". . . When I marched up to Paris with the Prussian army upon my right, they were obliged to quit the country in which they were living. Both armies were living by requisition, and we went and lived in that same country, because my army was in a state of discipline, and order, and regularity, and obedience, and the Prussian was not.

" Towards the close of the Peninsular campaign, by discipline, and by care and attention, the army was brought into such a state of discipline that every description of punishment was almost discontinued altogether. I always thought that I could have gone anywhere and done anything with that army. It was impossible to have a machine more highly mounted and in better order. . . . When I quitted that army on the Garonne, I do not think it was possible to see anything in a higher state of discipline, and I believe there was a total discontinuance of all punishment."

The discipline and performances of the British army at the present day have gloriously falsified the predictions of those who pronounced it impossible ever to abolish corporal punishment; none the less it is certain that at the beginning of the century the very existence of a British army abroad depended upon its existence. Civilisation and education have told upon the classes from which the army is recruited, with an effect as marked as that which professional pride and sense of duty has had upon its officers. It is impossible to imagine in the British army, as we know it, the prevalence of a practice very common when Sir Arthur Wellesley first took command of European troops, namely, the chastisement of soldiers by their officers. From the first Wellesley sternly repressed this habit; had it continued, it is not difficult to believe that, without corporal punishment officially administered, neither discipline nor due respect for commissioned officers could have been maintained.

The Duke of Wellington, then, must be held to be justified in his opinion that corporal punishment was indispensable to restoring discipline to the army as he found it, with officers for the most part uninstructed in their duties and indifferent to the personal welfare and comfort of their men; although, as soon as he had succeeded in establishing discipline, and convincing the general body of regimental officers that it was disgraceful to neglect the details of their profession, he found it possible practically to suspend the use of the lash altogether.

Where time has proved the Duke to be in error, is in his disbelief in the possibility of raising the self-respect of the private soldier, so that he could ever be ruled except by the terrible dread of corporal punishment.

In spite of his somewhat harsh expressions about the irredeemable character of the average rank and file, the Duke was never indifferent—no good officer can be so—to the soldier's welfare and personal comfort. At Saint-Jean-de-Luz, in 1814, when it came to his knowledge that a private had been discharged from the headquarters of his battalion in a destitute condition, he directed a very sharp rebuke to be sent to the officer responsible, followed by the admonition, "The attention of a commanding officer, and the credit of the corps, should always be considered connected with the soldier's welfare till the last hour of his service, and omission on any points relating to that end cannot fail to prove prejudicial to the interests of the corps." * Welling-ton's solicitude for the soldier.

Although indifferent to details of uniform, no matter affecting the soldier's comfort or efficiency was so minute as to escape his attention. Thus in 1813, although tents had been provided for the men, they could not be carried for want of mules; the three animals allowed by regulation for each company being loaded with heavy iron camp kettles. Wellington caused light tin kettles to be made, one for each mess of six men, and provided each man also with a tin canteen, thus enabling three tents to be carried for each company.

The Duke was inflexible in his belief in the impossibility of shortening the soldier's service, without sacrificing efficiency. In 1847, Lord John Russell having submitted to him as Commander-in-chief a plan for the discharge of soldiers after ten years' service, the Duke replied—"It is very painful to me to be under the necessity of troubling your lordship at this moment, but it is absolutely impossible for me to be the Duration of service.

* *Suppl. Despatches*, xiv. 372.

instrument of carrying into execution a project which will destroy the efficiency of the small army which her Majesty's Government has at its disposition." *

Rewards and medals.

Closely cognate to the subject of punishment is that of rewards and decoration, and in order to understand the apparent austerity of the Duke in this matter one must bear in mind the altered view in which it has come to be regarded since the days of his service. All honours and orders, by the laws of chivalry, derived their whole value from the Sovereign —the fountain of honour—and that value was held to depend on their exclusive and select character. War medals, being of the nature of a chivalrous order, would have been considered to lose much of their value if they were made common, and in fact no regimental officer who had not commanded a battalion in action, or served within prescribed rank on the staff, was eligible to receive a war medal before the battle of Waterloo. Nay—it was not sufficient to have been in action, as Lord Fitzroy Somerset reminded Lord Beresford in 1833, when he applied for a decoration for some officer. He quoted the instances of Sir Rowland Hill, who commanded a corps d'armée at Busaco, of Sir Miles Nightingale's brigade and of the brigade of Guards, all of which troops, though they suffered severely from artillery fire, never actually were exposed to the fire of small arms. Consequently neither Hill nor Nightingale, nor any of their officers, nor those of the Guards, received the Busaco clasp.† After Waterloo, the Duke of Wellington recommended that a medal should be granted to all officers *and men* who had taken part in that great victory,‡ and the Prince Regent directed that such a

* *Apsley House MSS.*

† Unpublished letter from Lord F. Somerset to Lord Beresford.

‡ "I confess that I do not concur in the limitation of the order (of the Bath) to field officers. Many captains in the army conducted themselves in a very meritorious manner, and deserve it; and I never could see the reason for excluding them either from the order or the medal. I would likely beg leave to suggest to your Royal Highness the expediency of giving to the non-commissioned officers and soldiers engaged in the battle of Waterloo a medal. I

medal should be struck and distributed.* Every man present at Waterloo was also entitled to reckon two years' additional service towards discharge and pension. Strange to say, no such recognition of the long warfare of which Waterloo was but the epilogue was made till 1848, when the Queen presented a medal to those who still survived to claim it, covering the operations in the period from 1793 to 1814. Honours are more lavishly bestowed at the present day, and it would be wrong to interpret the Duke's policy in the regulation of rewards by the sentiment which governs it under a different state of things. The chief value of a decoration in A.'s eyes is the fact that it has been conferred on B., C., and D., who, he may feel, are not better entitled to it than himself.

As a matter of fact, the Duke never objected, as it has been asserted he did, to a Peninsular medal being granted to all ranks. He did object, and felt it necessary to interfere, when the officers of the army petitioned the House of Lords to move the Sovereign to grant them medals, for he considered that an infringement of the royal prerogative; but, as he explained to Lord John Russell, as soon as he was "informed that it was the wish of the Sovereign and her Ministers, I eagerly adopted the plan, and suggested means to facilitate its execution." †

The dress and equipment of the soldier was regulated by the Duke of York and the Horse Guards; Wellington had little time to bestow on matters of taste or even of comfort, and he expressed his views very seldom on the subject. Only once, when a change of uniform was contemplated for the cavalry, he wrote home begging that it might be made as different as possible from French uniforms, to avoid awkward

*Equipment and dress.*

am convinced it would have the best effect in the army; and, if that battle should settle our concerns, they will well deserve it" (*Despatches*, xii. 520: 28th June, 1815).

* *Suppl. Despatches*, xi. 343.

† 10th December, 1846 (*Apsley House MSS.*).

mistakes. It is true that he is credited with having cut off
the pigtails of his soldiers when he disembarked in the
Mondego in 1808; but he made no remonstrance, apparently,
against his men being obliged to serve under a southern sun
wearing cruel black leather stocks and preposterously high
and heavy head-dresses.

Arms.    With regard to improvements in arms the Duke was
exceedingly conservative. He regarded Colonel Congreve's
invention of rockets with great suspicion, though they had a
decided success at Bayonne,* and he retained an almost super-
stitious admiration for Brown Bess, which might have been
shaken had he lived to witness its inferiority before the
Russian Minié rifles in the Crimea.

*The Duke of Wellington to Lord Fitzroy Somerset.†*

"Walmer Castle, 9th November, 1835.

"I return the books and papers which you sent me; and as the
Master-General desires to have my opinion, I give it; but I do so
with great diffidence; and deference for the superior judgment of
others. I have always considered the Alteration of the Armament of the British Infantry, including the Indian Army, and
scattered as it is, in all parts of the World, as a most serious
undertaking. I considered our Arm as the most efficient that
had yet been produced. The fire from it undoubtedly is acknowledged to be the most Destructive known. It is durable, it bears
all sorts of Ill-usage, is easily repaired, and kept in Repair and
serviceable; and besides its Power as a Missile, its length is an
advantage in the use of the Bayonet. When I knew more of
these Details than I do now we had in Store some Hundreds
and Thousands of these admirable Arms; and I confess that
I always considered undesirable any alteration of them, much
more any change of them for others of different Calibre, Length,
etc. in reference to the Expence to be incurred, in Comparison
with the advantage to be acquired. . . .

* It is not generally known that a British rocket battery was engaged in the
battle of Leipsig.
† Afterwards Field-Marshal Lord Raglan.

" For instance in case of Wet—which Musquet will recover soonest—the one with the Flint and the Steel lock, or the one with the lock for the use of Detonating Powder ? I recollect having had a Trial with Manton's plugs on that point. The Musquet with the Flint and Steel lock commenced its fire the soonest. . . . Can the Soldier be entrusted to take care of the 60 or 75 Rounds of Priming composed of Fulminating Powder ? Will it bear all the vicissitudes of heat, cold, wet to which he must be exposed ? Where is it to be kept in order that he may get at it for use with certainty and celerity ? . . . I do not hesitate to declare my opinion that it would be absolutely impossible to venture to rely upon the Priming Ammunition whether in our Fleet or our Armies. . . . In respect to cutting balls into four or more parts,* I think that the Spanish Guerillas practised this method. I can recollect that the Impression upon our minds at the time was, that it was not fair. That Impression may have been erroneous. It is certain that the Wound received was a bad one." †

The Duke was justly proud of the fire of his infantry, which was steadier and more effective than that of any other European troops. When Lord Salisbury asked him how he accounted for the French having refrained from attacking him during the retreat from Burgos, he replied, " Because they had found out that our bullets were not made of butter ! " ‡

In all his campaigns, except that of Waterloo, the Duke Cavalry. was weak in cavalry, and was supposed to be indifferent to that arm. Even in India, where he sometimes had the assistance of large bodies of native horse, they gave him nearly as much trouble as they did service, owing to their want of discipline. British cavalry were trained to execute all their movements at high speed, which might be considered a point in superiority to those of other nations, but in fact it

* The cuts did not divide the balls, but gave them the effect of an expanding bullet.

† *Apsley House MSS.*

‡ *Salisbury MSS.*, 1837.

was the reverse. It unsteadied the men, especially the sup-
ports; the horses, often fed on green forage, got blown, and
Wellington frequently complained that officers had such an
unconquerable belief in the necessity for charging at full
speed that he lost all control over his cavalry after they were
employed in a battle. He probably shared Jomini's opinion,
that far more is lost by the disarray caused by high speed in
a charge than is gained by the additional impetus. "All our
movements," he wrote to Lord Combermere in 1816, "are too
quick for those of large bodies of cavalry . . . I wish you
would turn your mind . . . to keep the charge, as well as all
other movements, at the pace at which 'at least the middling
goers, if not the slowest, can keep up." *

The Duke favoured Lord William Russell's idea of
employing cavalry in single, rather than in double rank.
He advocated, as the original and ordinary formation, three
squadrons in single lines one behind the other, at a distance
of 400 yards, and in discussing the question with Lord
William left an interesting memorandum of his own practice
in the use of the mounted arm.

"My practice in regard to cavalry was this: first, to use them
upon advanced guards, flanks, etc., as the quickest movers, and
to enable me to know and see as much as possible in the shortest
space of time; secondly, to use them in the momentary pursuit
of beaten troops; thirdly, to use them in small bodies to attack
small bodies of the enemy's cavalry. But I never attacked with
them alone, always with infantry, and I considered our cavalry
so inferior to the French from want of order, although I consider one squadron a match for two French squadrons, that I
should not have liked to see four British squadrons opposed to
four French; and, as the numbers increased, and order of course
became more necessary, I was more unwilling to risk our cavalry
without having a great superiority of numbers. For this reason
I used my cavalry even less than Buonaparte did his, for he gained
some of his battles by the use of his cuirassiers as a kind of

* *Suppl. Despatches*, xi. 454.

accelerated infantry, with which, supported by masses of cannon, he was in the habit of seizing important parts in the centre or flanks of his enemy's position, and of occupying such points till his infantry could arrive to relieve them. He tried this manœuvre at the battle of Waterloo, but failed, because we were, not to be frightened away; and in fact (we) attacked the cuirassiers, who were in possession of the line of our cannon, with the squares of infantry; and when once we moved them, I poured in our Life Guards, etc. This shows the difference of his principles and mine; but it was to be attributed to his having his cavalry in order. Mine would gallop, but could not preserve their order, and therefore I could not use them till our admirable infantry had moved the French cavalry from their ground." *

With regard to the Duke's general practice as a tactician, this has been so closely analysed by many competent authorities as to render superfluous any review of it in this place, so profoundly have the altered conditions of armament, transport, and communication modified all considerations of that nature. Nevertheless, two main objects must always remain of chief importance, and were never absent from the Duke's mind: First, in a campaign, the maintenance of lines of communication; second, in battle, what he expressed in his own words—"The great secret of battle is to have a reserve. I always had, with the infantry sometimes eight or ten deep, and with the cavalry—no end to the reserve." †

* *Civil Despatches*, iii. 353.

† *Salisbury MSS.*, 1837. Sir Walter Scott has a note to similar effect in his journal—27th April, 1828. " I heard the Duke say to-day that the best troops would run now and then. He thought nothing of men running, he said, provided they came back again. In war he had always his reserves."

# CHAPTER V.

## WELLINGTON AS CABINET MINISTER.

### 1818–1822.

THERE are not wanting those who hold the opinion that, had the assassin's bullet cut short the great Duke's career at its zenith, his renown would have suffered no whit in the esteem of later generations, but, on the contrary, would have retained some lustre which became overcast in the murky atmosphere of political life. It may be so. It may be that if, like his great counterpart Nelson, he had been struck down when scarcely past his prime, and with the first gloss still fresh on his laurels, the story had gained something in dramatic symmetry; there had remained more direct suggestion of the heaven-born in the life-work both of England's greatest sailor and her greatest soldier: Wellington's task would have been pronounced *teres atque rotundus.*

But in that case his countrymen would have missed the reve-
lation of a type of character—the noblest form of aristocrat.
Hitherto all Wellington's doings had been far from our shores.
All men had heard of him, comparatively few had seen him;
he was not a familiar figure in festivals, in Parliament, or any
public place. When he sheathed his sword at the close of
the military occupation of France, he returned home as a
soldier, single of purpose, ready to take the field again should
the summons come, but with a strong disinclination towards
political life.

"The Duke told me," wrote Lady Salisbury in her journal of
1836, "that when office was first proposed to him by Lord
Castlereagh after the Congress of Aix-la-Chapelle, he had the
greatest dislike to accepting it, and the only thing that determined
him was the assurance that, if he refused to join, he should
weaken the Ministry and become a rallying-point for the
disaffected." *

The world had been so long at war that no man could
reckon on the endurance of the measures devised to secure
peace; nevertheless, little as he expected or desired it, the
Duke of Wellington, in returning to England, was crossing
the threshold of a new sphere of energy and influence, and
a whole generation was to be born and grown up for whom he
should become the embodiment of English political life, to
whom he should set the pattern of an English gentleman.
"The Duke" *sans phrase*—"the Duke" without territorial
designation—came to denote the individual as precisely as did
the titles "the King" or "the Speaker."

In all his campaigns, from the time immediately preceding The Duke
the dethronement of Tipú Sultan in 1798 down to the Congress joins the
of Aix-la-Chapelle in 1818, Wellington had displayed con- Cabinet.
spicuous sagacity and adroitness as an administrator, and
Lord Liverpool was not slow to perceive how much strength
his Cabinet would derive by the addition of a soldier-statesman

* *Salisbury MSS.*

of such wide experience. Accordingly, on 23rd October, when the Congress was on the eve of completing its labours, he wrote to the Duke offering him the post of Master-General of the Ordnance, which Lord Mulgrave cheerfully and handsomely consented to vacate for his acceptance, coupled with a seat in the Cabinet. The Duke replied that, although he wished, for many reasons, that the arrangement could have been postponed, he would "make no objection to the appointment taking place," inasmuch as the Government attached importance to a prompt settlement. Such a frigid acceptance of Cabinet rank conferred on an individual for the first time must surely be almost unique in the experience of Prime Ministers; but the remarkable sentences which follow have scarcely received the attention they deserve, containing, as they do, the key to a good deal which earned for the Duke in after years the displeasure of the Tory party.

"I don't doubt that the party of which the present government are the head will give me credit for being sincerely attached to them and their interests; but I hope that, in case any circumstance should occur to remove them from power, they will allow me to consider myself at liberty to take any line I may at the time think proper. The experience which I have acquired during my long service abroad has convinced me that a factious opposition to the government is highly injurious to the interests of the country; and, thinking as I do now, I could not become a party to such opposition, and I wish that this may be clearly understood by those persons with whom I am now about to engage as a colleague in government. I can easily conceive that this feeling of mine may, in the opinion of some, render me less eligible as a colleague, and I beg that, if this should be the case, the offer you have so kindly made to me may be considered as not made, and I can only assure you that you will ever find me equally disposed as you have always found me to render you every service and assistance in my power." *

* *Suppl. Despatches*, xii. 813.

Returning to England shortly before Christmas, the Duke Æt.1818. took up his residence in Apsley House, which he had bought from Lord Wellesley some years previously, and which meantime had undergone, at the hands of the architect Wyatt, a drastic transformation from the original structure of the brothers Adam to the building as it stands at this day. About the bill for the alterations, amounting to £130,000, the Duke observed, " It would have broken any back but mine ; " and he seems never to have taken any pride in his palace, nor to have had any of the affection for it which he bore to Strathfieldsaye and Walmer.

British home politics, when the Duke returned to take State of Great Britain in 1818. active part in them, were passing through an ominous phase. As long as the war lasted, employment was plentiful and prices ruled high ; the national spirit rose nobly to the occasion, and Ministers received almost uniformly admirable support from the country. Not the less surely, however, though silently, the revolutionary leaven had been spreading through the lower ranks, and assuredly there was plenty of material to feed it. The brutality of the military scale of punishment has been commented on elsewhere in these pages ; a more certain source of danger was the severity of the criminal code. Horse and sheep-stealing, the theft of the value of five shillings from a shop or of forty shillings from a dwelling house, were capital offences ; prisoners charged with these, or with any one of other two hundred offences, were not permitted to be heard in defence through counsel, and the horrors inseparable from detention in prison or hard labour in the hulks rendered transportation a doom greatly coveted by evil doers.

At the beginning of the war in 1792 the public debt of Great Britain and Ireland stood at £239,650,000, imposing an annual charge of £9,301,000 on Great Britain and £131,000 on Ireland ; at its close in 1815 it had swollen to the unparalleled sum of £861,000,000, without reckoning terminable annuities, and the yearly burden to £32,645,618, or, if the

The fall
in prices.

sinking fund be taken in account, to more than £46,000,000. Nevertheless, the full weight of this burden was not perceptible till the close of the war which had caused it. The first effect of peace was a heavy fall in the price of agricultural products and of manufactures. British imports were reduced by nearly 20 per cent. in 1816, and exports by 16 per cent. The price of copper fell from £180 to £80 per ton, of iron from £20 to £8, of hemp from £118 to £34. Wheat, which had often stood as high as £6 per quarter during the war, was worth but 52s. 6d. at the beginning of 1816, though a wet season raised the price to 80s. at the end of April, thereby destroying the solitary alleviation to the hardships of the masses—that of cheap bread.

European markets were closed to British goods by sheer reason of the impoverishment of buyers; the home markets fell flat because of the diminished resources of the land-owning class, whose rents, having rolled up handsomely under the stimulus of war prices,* now came down with a run, necessitating curtailment of expenditure of every kind. Mills and factories were closed, and multitudes of artisans wandered over the country destitute and discontented, creating serious riots in many places; reduction in the land and sea forces added nearly a quarter of a million to the ranks of the unem-ployed,† and upon farmers and rural labourers the pinch came with terrible severity. In a single parish in Dorsetshire, as stated in the House of Commons, out of 575 inhabitants 419 were in receipt of relief from the rates.

In the highest level of society there was little to counteract the peculiar stress which lay so heavily on the country, or to attach the subjects to the monarchy. The old King, indeed, still lived, but blind—deaf—hopelessly mad—he was but the

---

* In Scotland alone, where the gross rental amounted to £2,000.000 in 1795, it stood at £5,278,000 in 1815.

† By a single stroke of the pen the navy was reduced from 100,000 men in 1815 to 33,000 in 1816, the army was put on a peace footing, and the militia was disembodied.

husk of the kindly, shrewd country-gentleman who had once ANN. 1818.
so admirably fulfilled what Englishmen desire in their
Sovereign. His virtues, if not forgotten, had been almost
effaced by the odious profligacy and shameless extravagance
of his eldest son, the Prince Regent. Even these might have
been atoned for and forgiven, for the English people are
liberal in making allowance for young blood; but they are
impatient of open scandal in married lives. The relations
between the Prince and Princess of Wales had long been
cynically disgraceful. A separation took place before the
birth of their only child, Princess Charlotte; the Prince
resumed his former ill-regulated life; the Princess took up
her abode in a villa at Charlton, where an unfortunate levity
of manner and undue freedom with persons of inferior rank
gave occasion for the most unfavourable surmise. The Prince,
desirous of occasion for a divorce, sought diligently for evidence
against her; when his Whig friends came into office in 1806,
they appointed a secret commission to examine upon the
Princess's conduct, but the charges completely broke down.
Another inquiry was instituted under the Privy Council in
1813, and in 1814 the Princess went to live on the shore of
the Lake of Como. Whatever truth may have lain under
the charges against the Princess of Wales, there can be no
doubt that her conduct was culpably careless and unbecoming
to any lady, let alone the future Queen of Great Britain.
Nevertheless, her husband's habits were so notorious, and his
attempts to make out a case against the Princess so unlovely,
that the popular sympathy was all on her side. She and her
daughter were greeted everywhere with cheers by the populace; whereas a moody silence prevailed whenever the Prince
appeared in public.

In their attempts to keep order by the strong hand Ministers Habeas
incurred extreme unpopularity. The Habeas Corpus Act Corpus
was suspended in England and Scotland from February, 1817, pended.
to March, 1818, an extreme measure which has never since
been resorted to in Great Britain; penal acts to repress sedition

# THE LIFE OF WELLINGTON.

**Æt. 49.** and prohibit assemblies were carried through Parliament against vehement opposition; even the Cambridge Union— the undergraduates' debating society—was suppressed by the edict of the Vice-Chancellor. For the first, and perhaps for the last, time in history the Government armed themselves with powers to rule Great Britain more forcible than those they wielded in Ireland under the Insurrection and Peace Preservation Acts. Upon no Minister did the odium of these proceedings fall with so much weight as on Lord Castlereagh, the leader of the House of Commons; his long and meritorious public service was unjustly requited by an opprobrium which darkened his later years, and finally helped to drive him out of existence. By the commencement of 1818 matters had begun to mend. True, the Government had failed in nearly all the prosecutions under the new Acts; the amelioration was due, not to the suspension of the constitution, but, in spite of it, to a fall in the price of food stuffs and to a marked revival in trade. To these, also, must be attributed, as well as to the restricted nature of the electorate, the comparative immunity with which Lord Liverpool's Government passed the ordeal of a general election at midsummer. They came back to power with a loss of only fourteen seats, representing twenty-eight votes on a division.

In the following year, however, the distressing conditions returned. Tens of thousands of willing hands were idle, and the proverbial mischief was not far to seek. Reform was scarcely considered by members of Parliament as within range of practical politics. Sir Francis Burdett's motion was rejected in a languid House by 153 votes to 58. Yet the Radical party turned to their own purposes the abounding discontent out-of-doors; mass meetings were held in the Midlands and northern counties demanding Reform and the repeal of the Corn Laws. They were the first mutterings of a storm which was to acquire a violence threatening every revered institution in the country. On 16th August 50,000 or 60,000 persons assembled in St. Peter's Field near

The "Peterloo" affair.

Manchester; the Cheshire Yeomanry, two troops of the 15th <sub>AN.1819.</sub>
Hussars, and two guns were placed at the disposal of the
magistrates. When it was judged necessary to disperse the
meeting, the yeomanry were ordered to march into the crowd
in single file; immediately they were rendered helpless by
the pressure, many of them were unhorsed; the senior magistrate called on Colonel l'Estrange with his hussars to save
the yeomanry. The order was promptly obeyed: the same
trumpets which had rung out at Waterloo sounded the charge
in this ignoble strife; the crowd were piled and crushed
together, many were injured, six persons were killed outright,
and the affair, ironically named the battle of Peterloo, took
a permanent place in the annals of England.

The Duke seems to have taken little part during his first
year of office in directing the policy of the Cabinet. His
attention was concentrated on the affairs of his department,
in advising Lord Bathurst as to the defences of Canada and
other Colonies, in carrying out the reduction of the forces, and
in the settlement of numerous claims on the part of his old
officers for distinction, promotion, or compensation for loss.
Castlereagh, also, continued to take confidential counsel with
him respecting the affairs of the Continent, especially what
he termed the "most hazardous notion" of the Emperor of
Russia of establishing a Conference of the Powers for the settlement of all disputes. Although the odium incurred by the
repressive measures framed and carried by the Government
in 1819 fell chiefly on Castlereagh, nevertheless that Minister's
"Six Acts" had the approval and support, not only of all
Ministerialists, but of a large proportion of the Whig
opposition, so dire was the apprehension excited by the
doings of the Radicals. The Duke urged Lord Sidmouth,
the Home Secretary, to carry into execution without delay
the new law against unauthorised military training. "Don't
let us be reproached again with having omitted to carry into
execution the laws." * He believed that the country was "not

* *Civil Despatches,* i. 89.

far removed from a general and simultaneous rising in different parts," and was concerned that, although the lieutenants of counties had been warned to be on the alert, and officers commanding troops had instructions to support the civil power, no specific plan of operations had been laid down. The country was practically at the mercy of the insurrection which seemed to be brewing in the northern counties. Sidmouth perceived the peril, but was helpless to avert it. Wellington offered to write instructions to Sir John Byng, commanding the Northern Districts. Sidmouth gratefully agreed, upon which the Duke drew up a scheme for the disposition of troops, having first in view the security of the King's garrisons, castles, and magazines, and providing next that no detachments should be stationed anywhere except within easy reach of support. "It is much better that a town should be plundered, and even some lives lost, than that the whole country should be exposed to the danger which would result from the success of the mob against even a small detachment of troops." *

Political moralists have exhausted the vocabulary of invective in denouncing the coercive policy of Lord Liverpool's Cabinet at this time, but it is not easy to point out an alternative course, which, under the circumstances of the day, would have averted a violent revolution. No measure of electoral reform would have alleviated the suffering arising out of events beyond the control of Ministries; and the accusation that the Cabinet interfered with the right of public meeting because they were "afraid of demonstration," is merely an uncomplimentary description of the precautions taken in face of such vaunts as that of Watson when haranguing a meeting at Smithfield, that 800,000 armed Radicals were resolved on liberty or death. The country was passing through one of those phases which demand extraordinary courage and nerve on the part of its rulers; it came through it with hardly any bloodshed, a result which must be attributed

* *Civil Despatches,* i. 81.

in great part to the organisation imparted by the Duke to the ANN. 1820.
forces at the disposal of the Government.

By the beginning of 1820 affairs had greatly settled
down. Writing to the Baron Vincent on 5th January, the
Duke observed—

"Thanks to God and to our miraculous institutions (*nos miraculeuses institutions*) we are at an end of our troubles, and you may
believe that the danger which threatened us, and was imminent,
has passed away. They have tried to copy our institutions in
other countries; but I am tempted to believe that what people
describe here as ancient abuses, which modern reformers wish to
get rid of, and which our neighbours and liberal imitators decline
to copy, are the very things which give us a remarkable support
in all our difficulties." *

Sedition, however, though repressed in the provinces, The Cato
assumed a more nefarious character in the metropolis. What Street<br>plot.
is known as the Cato Street conspiracy was concocted under
the direction of a Radical leader named Arthur Thistlewood.
This fellow had once held a commission in a line regiment,
resigning which, he went to Paris in 1790, and was concerned
in some of the worst passages in the French Revolution.
Returning to England in 1814, he engaged in the Radical
agitation, and was arrested in 1818 for complicity in the Spa
Field riot. As soon as he was released, he sent a challenge
to Lord Sidmouth to fight him with sword or pistol. Sidmouth wished to take no proceedings, but his colleagues,
regarding the offence as one against the constitution, directed
his prosecution, and Thistlewood received sentence of a year's
imprisonment. On his release, finding that the "Six Acts"
interfered with his former course of action, he collected a
number of desperadoes, and laid plans for the assassination
of the whole Cabinet, the seizure of London by an armed
mob, and the formation of a provisional government. Warning was conveyed by informers that a Cabinet dinner, to be

* *Apsley House MSS.*

held at Lord Harrowby's house in Grosvenor Square on 23rd February, had been fixed as the occasion for the massacre. Fourteen men, armed with hand-grenades and other weapons, were told off for the job; one of them was to ring the door-bell, and, while he parleyed with the servant, the others were to rush in and slay every one in the dining-room. The Duke urged that the dinner should be allowed to proceed. He advised that during the night of 22nd a body of constables should be concealed in the house, without the knowledge of any servant, that every minister should have a brace of loaded pistols in his despatch-box, and shoot down the conspirators as they entered the dining-room, while the constables took them in rear. Such heroic counsel found little favour with his colleagues, and was overruled; indeed, it is obvious that its adoption would have involved bloodshed, probably not only of the assailants. The preparations for the dinner were allowed to go on, but another dinner was cooked in Downing Street, where the Ministers assembled. In the mean time measures had been taken to capture the gang in their den in Cato Street.* Mr. Birnie, the Bow Street magistrate, went there after dusk with fourteen constables. He was to have been supported by a party of the Grenadier Guards, but, owing to a misunderstanding, these were not ready at the moment, and he proceeded without them. The constables, obtaining access by a ladder to the loft in Cato Street, found between twenty and thirty armed men, and, in the *melée* which ensued, one constable was killed and three wounded. The detachment of Guards came up in time to secure most of the gang, of whom six afterwards paid the penalty of death.† Previous to this affair the Duke of Wellington had very narrowly escaped assassination. One of the gang had been told off to slay him, and, waiting one

---

* Cato Street exists no longer. It was a narrow lane running into John Street parallel with the Edgware Road.

† It is said that Thistlewood uttered the following laconic prayer on the gallows: "O God—if there be a God—save my soul—if I have a soul!"

evening till the Duke came out of the Ordnance Office, followed ANN. 1820.
him along Pall Mall, intending to stab him in the back as he
walked across the Green Park, as was his custom, to Apsley
House. Fortunately, Lord Fitzroy Somerset happening to
come along, the Duke made him turn, and the two gentlemen
proceeded into the park arm-in-arm. The assassin's courage
failing him, he gave up the attempt for that time.

The horror inspired by this scheme of massacre, so nearly
carried into effect, served to silence criticism on the coercive
Acts and to restore Ministers to some degree of popular
favour—to what degree was about to be tested, so far as a
general election under the franchise of 1688 could be accepted
as a test of national sentiment.

The old King died on 29th January, just before the Cato Death of George III.
Street conspiracy was disclosed. Under the constitution as
it then was, the demise of the monarch involved the dissolution of Parliament, which took place in March.

The first matter of moment submitted to the new Parliament
was of a nature to bring shame and confusion on the whole
nation. Among the earliest duties of the Privy Council on
the beginning of a new reign is the re-editing of the prayers
for the Sovereign and the Royal Family in the Book of
Common Prayer. George IV. strictly prohibited any reference
to his consort in the prayers, and desired his Ministers
to institute immediate proceedings for his divorce. With
the first command the Cabinet complied, on the proviso
that the second should not be insisted on. This did not
suit the King's views at all; he dictated a vigorous remonstrance to the arguments of his Ministers, and gave them
to understand privately that unless they went on with the
divorce, he would either dismiss them or retire to his
dominions of Hanover.* The Cabinet met on Sunday, 13th
February, when, after sitting for thirteen hours, Ministers

---

* The kingdom of Hanover was an appanage of the crown of Great Britain
until 1837, when, the succession being limited to heirs male, it passed to the
eldest surviving brother of William IV., the Duke of Cumberland.

Æt. 51.

Proceed-
ings
against
Queen
Caroline.

declined to comply with his Majesty's desire. The general conclusion was that the Government was out, but the King gave way with a wry face. Howbeit, the unsavoury question was not laid to rest.

The Queen announced her intention of returning to England, and sent warrants appointing Henry Brougham and Thomas Denman her Attorney and Solicitor - General. Brougham, convinced of the dangers inseparable from her return, persuaded Lord Liverpool to undertake to settle £50,000 a year on her for life provided she should not enter British dominions nor assume the title of Queen. Probably this offer might have been accepted, but unhappily the disgust with which George IV. had inspired his subjects revived the reflex sentiment of the masses in favour of the consort whom he was held to be persecuting. She might be all that her accusers tried to make out, but no industry could whitewash the private morals of the King; the rough mob chivalry was enlisted on the weaker side, with cheers for Queen Caroline, and jeers for Mrs. Fitzherbert and other ladies of reputation lower than hers.* On Monday, June 5th, Queen Caroline landed at Dover, where the officer commanding the garrison, having no direct orders to the contrary, fired a royal salute, and an immense crowd which assembled drew her carriage to the inn. Her progress through Kent was triumphal; at Canterbury the mayor and corporation, in official robes, presented an address; the officers of cavalry stationed there escorted her out of the town; the clergy in gown and bands waited on her at Sittingbourne, and all along the route church bells rang out a welcome. She entered London in a shabby carriage, with Alderman Wood, a fishmonger, seated beside her, the streets thronged with crowds frantically enthusiastic. Over Westminster Bridge, through Whitehall to Pall Mall, the strange procession passed, constantly increased by the

---

* It was generally understood that George IV. had actually married Mrs. Fitzherbert, but that the Protestant ceremony of marriage through which they had gone was not valid in her case, as she was a Roman Catholic.

addition of more vehicles. The very sentries on Carlton ANN. 1820.
House, the King's residence, presented arms, and the crowds
did not disperse till the Queen, alighting at Alderman Wood's
house in South Audley Street, appeared on the balcony, and
bowed her repeated acknowledgments. Lord Sidmouth,
driving home from a Cabinet with the Duke of Wellington,
could not get into his own house, and the mob broke the
carriage windows.*

The popular ferment increased as days went by. There Mutiny in the Guards.
was no police force in London at that time; the Government
relied on the Guards for maintaining order, and at this very
time one of the battalions of this *corps d'élite* mutinied. This
drew from the Duke a memorandum which led to the first
steps in forming a regular police for the metropolis, afterwards
carried into effect by Sir Robert Peel.

"We know not, and cannot know under existing circumstances,
whether seeds of discontent are laid or not in other corps, and
the Government depend for their protection against insurrection
and revolution, and individuals for their personal safety and
property, upon the fidelity of 3,000 Guards, all of the class of
the people, and even of the lowest of that class. In my opinion
the Government ought, without loss of a moment's time, to form
either a police in London or a military corps, which should be of
a different description from the regular military force, or both." †

The Guards were a privileged corps, but the privileges were
confined to the officers. Really, to consider the existing
conditions of military service, the heartless system of punishment and low rate of pay, is to be amazed, not that isolated
cases of mutiny should have occurred, but that disaffection
was not chronic and universal.

"I would recommend," continues the Duke, "some new arrangement of the duties. . . . Besides the King, who sends his own
commands through Bloomfield, there are the following officers

* *Croker*, i. 174.     † *Civil Despatches*, i. 128.

who send orders to these unfortunate troops :—the Secretary of
State; Commander-in-Chief; Field-Officer in Waiting; Gold
Stick, Silver Stick—to the two regiments of Horse Guards only.
The consequence is that when there is a disturbance in the
town . . . nobody knows who is on or who off duty, all the troops
are harassed, and the duty is ill done after all. Only last night,
after I had received Lord Sidmouth's directions for the duties of
the night, at eight o'clock in the night I found that somebody
had altered what was ordered, and that the guard at the Horse
Guards was doubled, whether for any or what necessity I cannot
judge. . . . The sergeants and corporals of the Guards are
certainly excellent soldiers, and their conduct is exemplary on all
occasions. But it must be observed that they are taken from the
ranks, and of the class of the people, and liable to be influenced
by the views and sentiments of the people. If the officers of the
Guards could perform duties required from the officers of the Line
there is no doubt that the sergeants and corporals of the Guards
would perform their duty even better than they do now. . . . I
think therefore that it might be desirable that the duty of the
officers of the Guards should, as far as possible, be assimilated to
that of officers of the Line."

Negocia-
tions with
the Queen.
On the Queen's return to London negociations were
resumed in order to induce her to leave the country quietly.
Her Majesty consented on condition that her rank and privileges as queen should form the basis of any agreement. Lord
Liverpool replied that "whatever appertains to her Majesty
as queen must continue to appertain to her so long as it is
not abrogated by law." Thereupon the Queen, having proposed that the matters in dispute should be referred to arbi-
tration, the Lords Fitzwilliam and Sefton were appointed to
act for her Majesty, and the Duke of Wellington and Lord
Castlereagh to represent the King's Government. The party
character imparted to the quarrel by the fact of two Whig
lords acting for the Queen was not diminished when, at the
Duke's suggestion, these were replaced by her official representatives, Brougham and Denman.

The negociations broke down after five days' conference. Ann. 1820. The King yielded to his Ministers so far as to make large concessions from his original demands. The name and rights of a queen were to be conceded to Caroline and formally notified to the Court of the country in which she should reside in future, and she was to receive the thanks of Parliament for acceding to its wishes. But on what seemed the minor point of restoring to the Liturgy the name of "our most gracious Queen Caroline," King George was inflexible. "You might as easily move Carlton House," said Lord Castlereagh when Brougham raised that point.

Pending the negociations, there had been a suspension of arms on the question in Parliament and the country. On 19th June Ministers made the announcement that the proceedings had ended in failure. In the Commons Wilberforce moved an address to the Queen, in the hope of averting what was rapidly assuming the character and menace of social strife. In the course of the debate it was suggested that, even if the Queen was not mentioned by name in the Liturgy, she might be considered as comprised in the general prayer for the royal family. "If her Majesty," replied Denman in words which echoed the general feeling out-of-doors, "is included in any general prayer, it is in the prayer for all who are desolate and oppressed."

Wilberforce's mediation was ineffective, and the affair continued its squalid course. On 5th July Lord Liverpool introduced a bill "to deprive her Majesty Queen Caroline Amelia Elizabeth of the title, prerogative rights, privileges and exemptions of Queen Consort of this realm, and to dissolve the marriage between his Majesty and the said Caroline Amelia Elizabeth," the second reading being fixed for 17th August. The London populace were not the only section of the people infuriated by what they looked on as the King's tyranny. Meetings were held in all parts of the country. The Duke of Wellington, on being taken to task for refusing, as Lord-Lieutenant of Hampshire, to convene a county meeting

Bill of divorce introduced.

replied with injudicious bluntness that, having already presented a petition in the Queen's favour signed by 9,000
persons in that county, he did not see that any good
purpose could be served "by going through the farce of a
county meeting." This phrase was never forgotten. In after-
years it was brought against him at every turn; for although
he did not intend any slight on the people of Hampshire, it
expressed the small respect he really entertained for popular
demonstrations, which he was at all times too much disposed to repress by force, if indifference should not quell
them.

The
Queen's
trial.

The scene at Westminster on 17th August, the day fixed
for the Bill of Pains and Penalties, was one to test the
courage of Ministers; but Lord Liverpool and his colleagues,
whatever their shortcomings, have never been suspected of
pusillanimity. A vast crowd filled all the approaches to
Parliament; two regiments of Life Guards occupied Palace
Yard, the Coldstream Guards were stationed in Westminster
Hall, and a battery of field artillery was kept at hand.
Luckily, the utmost good humour prevailed in the crowd;
they cheered the Queen and hooted the Duke of Wellington,
but no violence of any sort was threatened. The proceedings
on the bill were a curious mixture of the judicial and the
parliamentary. Evidence was taken both for the prosecution
and defence; the verdict was contained in the division on the
second reading. This took place early in November, when
the bill was carried by 123 votes to 95, but even this in-
sufficient majority dwindled in the committee stage to one of
fifteen only, and Ministers discreetly refrained from forcing
this most unpopular measure further.

Of the Queen's guilt or innocence of the charges made
against her no opinion need be expressed in this place; this
only need be said, that if they were unfounded, no woman
had ever done more to wreck her reputation in contempt of
all the observances which ensure and justify respect to rank.
Parliament, in allowing her, as Princess of Wales, £35,000

a year, had made ample provision for maintaining her dignity; A.D. 1820.
it had been her choice to lead the life of a common tramp.

On 23rd November Parliament adjourned for a month ;
when it reassembled the Ministry had been weakened by the
resignation of Canning, who disapproved of the proceedings
against the Queen.   The popular agitation, however, had
greatly subsided, the Queen's conduct having damped the
ardour of her warmest supporters.   At the conclusion of her
trial, she had boldly declared, by Brougham's advice, that she
would never consent to receive a subsidy from a Parliament
which excluded her name from the Liturgy.   Reflection
brought a change of mind: she wrote and asked Liverpool
for an allowance; an annuity of £50,000 was voted and a
residence provided at the public expense ; nobody could say
that, short of being restored to her full rights as royal consort,
she was illiberally treated, and people turned their thoughts
to other matters.

It is difficult to gather any evidence as to the feelings of The Duke's part in the proceedings.
the Duke of Wellington throughout these proceedings, be-
cause, being in daily intercourse with his colleagues, very
few written communications seem to have passed between
them.   It is true that he told the King he had nothing to
do with the appointment of the Milan Commission, sent out
to collect evidence against the Queen, and that he did not
know of its existence till long after he had taken office.   But
he undoubtedly supported the Cabinet throughout their proceedings in relation to the Queen, and imparted confidence
to his colleagues in facing the popular tumult, which he
despised, and supported them in the loss sustained by the
defection of Canning.   No man ever carried out more fully
than Wellington the precept of "honouring the Crown, though
it hangs on a bush," and never, perhaps, was that precept
more hardly strained than in regard to George IV.   Wellington had received many favours and the highest possible
honours from the hands of the King, but there never was
trust or affection between them.   The King, indeed, relied

greatly on the Duke, but he feared him, and at times was unable to conceal his dislike. A strong sense of duty attached the Duke to the King's service, but his confidential letters are full of expressions showing how little reliance he placed on him.

It is immediately after the breakdown of the proceedings against Queen Caroline that we come on the first evidence of the Duke advising the King independently of his colleagues in the Cabinet. The King, furious at the abandonment of the Bill of Pains and Penalties, was inclined to dismiss his Ministers.

"I am very far from wishing," ran this singular letter from the Master of the Ordnance, "to persuade your Majesty not to change your government if your Majesty thinks that others can conduct your Majesty's affairs with more advantage. But I entreat your Majesty, for the sake of your own honour, and, I will add, your own independence in relation to their successors, not to deprive your servants of their power till they have concluded the business in which they are engaged." *

Parliament had adjourned until 23rd December, when the King insisted that it should at once enter upon the question of the Queen's provision and other issues collateral on the abandonment of the Bill of Pains and Penalties. The Duke was urgent for prorogation on 23rd December in order that the bill might expire in the ordinary course, and the remaining matters be discussed without its shadow remaining on the notice paper. In a letter of great length he argued against the prudence of discussing the Queen's affairs while the public mind was still agitated by the provisions of the discredited bill. Then he returned to the King's intention of changing his Ministers.

"No persons could serve your Majesty, excepting those now in your service, without dissolving the Parliament; and I need not point out the consequence of coming to a discussion of all the

* *Civil Despatches,* i. 150.

difficult questions relating to a provision for the Queen, and to A.xx. 1821. the Milan Commission, and others collateral to the recent inquiry in the House of Lords, in a Parliament elected during the existence of the present ferment in the public mind.  But those to whom your Majesty would naturally look as the successors to your present servants are, and have long been, their political rivals and opposers, particularly in their recent measures regarding the Queen; and it cannot be expected that they will not take advantage of every circumstance, however trivial, and of every action of every inferior agent, however low and corrupt, of the Milan Commission, to destroy the reputation of their predecessors in office, and, through them, that of your Majesty yourself. . . . It appears to me to be not only the height of impolicy, but the greatest degree of unfairness, to hand these servants over to their rivals and opponents for the trial of their conduct in these transactions." *

It is not apparent whether Liverpool knew of the Duke's intention to write this letter; probably he did, because it would scarcely have been consistent with Wellington's loyalty to his chief, which was without flaw, that he should address the King behind backs, as it were: but it is a sign of the extraordinary ascendency to which he had attained in home politics *per saltum*, that the King should have yielded to the remonstrance of a subordinate member of the Cabinet, and retained the services of Liverpool, whom, however, he never received into favour again.

The Coronation, which George's anxiety to be rid of his Coronation of George IV. Queen had made it inexpedient to hold in the previous year, was celebrated with prodigious splendour on 17th July, 1821,† and here we catch sight for the last time of the unhappy Caroline, presenting herself at the portals of Westminster and turned away amid the jeers of the populace. Yes, the jeers, for the people had wearied of her griefs, and were intent on getting the most out of the pageant; so that the organ

* *Civil Despatches*, i. 153.

† The sum voted for George IV.'s coronation was £243,000; a reformed Parliament showed its sense of economy by allowing only £70,000 for Queen Victoria's.

Æт. 51. pealed within, the King made his oblation at the altar and received the Sacrament, while his Queen was driving sadly home to die. She expired on 7th August, while the King was on his way to Ireland. He did not suffer the news of her death to interrupt the uproarious festivities with which he was received in Dublin, and in which he took a part more remarkable for energy than dignity.

The Duke revisits Waterloo.

During this summer the Duke went on a tour of inspection round the fortresses of the Netherlands, and afterwards visited Paris, where he had an interview with Louis XVIII. on the subject of the troubles which King Ferdinand's capricious absolutism had brought upon Spain. Louis considered himself bound to support the Bourbon dynasty in that country, and was eager to invade it, but he entertained a vast respect for Wellington, and yielded to his persuasion to unite with Great Britain in an attempt at friendly mediation.

Thereafter the Duke met George IV. at Brussels, and conducted him over the field of Waterloo. A singular contrast it must have been between these two figures on that historic ground—the florid, still handsome, but bloated and diseased voluptuary, and the lean, keen-eyed soldier-statesman; one self-styled, the English people know with how much justice, "the first gentleman in Europe;" the other, *vainqueur des vainqueurs*—the first soldier in the world.

Movement for the recall of Canning.

The Queen having been removed from the scene, the Prime Minister was pressed by members of his Cabinet and others to procure the restoration of Canning to office. Liverpool, though he dreaded his late colleague, yet relied greatly on his ability, and put the necessity of strengthening his Cabinet by the re-admission of the only debater who could meet Brougham on equal terms. The King flatly refused to listen to the proposal. He had not forgiven Liverpool for his failure in the matter of the divorce; far more active was his resentment against the Minister who had left his service rather than be party to the proceedings against the Queen. Thereupon Liverpool told the Duke that he intended to resign.

Wellington held Canning in high esteem at this time, and A.N.N. 1821. was fully convinced of the advantage of bringing him back to office, but he did not approve of staking the existence of the Government upon it.   He wrote a long letter to his chief, which gives a curious insight into the methods of Georgian government.

"There is no doubt that Mr. Canning is not very popular with the party, and although they in general would wish for his assist- ance, they would be much disappointed and displeased to find the power of the country transferred to the hands of the Whigs and Radicals, because we could not prevail upon the King to re-admit Mr. Canning into his Councils. . . . Then the question arises, ought you to make it (a threat of resignation) without being determined to carry it through?   Your continued opinion, mine, that of several others of your colleagues, and of many of your friends, that it is highly desirable that Mr. Canning should be in the Government, and the claim preferred in the last letter of the 29th of June to bring his name again under the King's view, show that you ought to propose him to the King; not only under present circumstances, but whenever an opportunity may offer; his own conduct and opinions in relation to the Government being the same as they are at present.   I would recommend you to propose him to the King, then, not in the spirit of hostility, not as an alternative to be taken between Mr. Canning and us, or anything else the King can find as a Government, but as you did at first, as an arrangement calculated for the strength of the Government, the benefit of the country, and the honour of the King himself." *

The Duke then alluded to the King's desire to appoint Lord Conyngham to high office, the husband of a lady whose relations with the King were a public scandal.

"In respect to Lord Conyngham, your line is quite clear; you have nothing to propose, but you desire to remonstrate if the King should propose to appoint him Lord Chamberlain.  This,

* *Civil Despatches*, i. 193.

you may rely upon it, he will not be allowed to do. If he does, I think the appointment of Lord Conyngham, unaccompanied by a satisfactory arrangement of the question of Mr. Canning or of the Government, would give you a good ground for quarrel. But why should *we* look for a quarrel? Is it not rather our duty to endeavour to settle this petty question, which, after all, is a mere trifle, and can [not] affect us, and never was considered as affecting us, except as a point of honour? I don't mean to depreciate the importance of a point of honour to the Government; but, I would observe, that the prevention of this particular appointment became a point of honour and importance to the Government, after the rejection of Canning in June, the questions of the Irish peerages and of the green ribbons, and all the follies of the coronation. . . . As I told you at Walmer, the King has never forgiven your opposition to his wishes in the case of Mr. Sumner.* This feeling has influenced every action of his life in relation to his Government from that moment; and I believe to more than one of us he avowed that his objection to Mr. Canning was, that his accession to the Government was peculiarly desirable to you. Nothing can be more unjust or more unfair than this feeling, and as there is not one of your colleagues who did not highly approve of what you did respecting Mr. Sumner,† so there is not one of them who would not suffer with you all the consequences of that act. . . . It must not be forgotten, however, that we have a duty imposed upon us which was never thrown on any of our predecessors. The question for us is not—whether we shall bear with many inconveniences and evils resulting from the King's habits and character, and which none of our predecessors ever bore, or make way for others equally capable with ourselves of carrying on the public service? but—whether we shall bear all that we have to endure, or give up the government to the Whigs and Radicals, or, in other words, the country in all its relations to irretrievable ruin? " ‡

---

* Afterwards Bishop of Winchester.

† Lord Liverpool had declined to give advancement in the Church to Mr. Sumner, who was tutor in Lord Conyngham's family, when Lady Conyngham had asked for it.

‡ *Civil Despatches*, i. 195.

There, in a single sentence, is the key to the whole of the Ann. 1822. Duke of Wellington's political career, with the exception of a . remarkable transaction, presently to be noticed. This was his guiding principle on many subsequent occasions, wherein a lesser man might have been judged as having taken a certain line out of desire for office and power. The fact is that the Duke could never, till his latest breath, view a Whig or Radical Government as consistent with the safety of the throne or the welfare of the country. One may smile at the apprehensions he expressed as to the results of the slightest tampering with the constitution or the increase of popular political power; but light is the task of upholding the throne as we know it compared with that of its defenders under George IV. Had there been no stout hearts and steady heads to stem the tide of change when it seemed about to overwhelm all landmarks, we might now be speculating on the former grandeur of the ruins of that edifice which it is our privilege to beautify and enlarge. Wellington was by no means singular in his dread of democratic change, but he was far more frank about it than others at a time when to be frank required a high degree of courage. The sentiments of Lord Bacon and Thomas Carlyle were equally outspoken on this question, but the first did not risk much when he owned to having a strong dislike for the word "people," nor the second when he made disparaging reference to " the collective wisdom of individual ignorances."

Lord Liverpool yielded to Wellington's advice and continued Illness and death of Castlereagh. to conduct the King's Government, till, at the close of the session of 1822, an event occurred which revived the urgency for the return of Canning. The closing days of the session were saddened for the Duke by the alarming condition of his closest friend and most trusted colleague. Throughout the most eventful years of his life, through the shadows of disfavour cast by the Convention of Cintra, through those periods of anxiety when the continued support to the army in the Peninsula was most precarious, Castlereagh's confidence in

ÆT. 53. Wellington had never wavered; never, under any circumstances, had these two men ceased to rely on each other. It
would be difficult to say which of them had served the other
best—Castlereagh, in supporting Wellington in the field and
in the conduct of the war, through good report and ill—
Wellington, in crowning with success by his splendid generalship the foreign policy of Castlereagh. Without the services
of the soldier, the statesman must have bowed his neck to
Buonaparte—without the friendship of the statesman, the
soldier's talents must have been buried with those of Burrard
and Dalrymple. This noble fellowship was about to be
severed. The strain of anxiety caused by the state of the
country after the peace, and by the humiliation brought on
the Government by the trial of the Queen, proved more than
a mind, sapped by private misery of a peculiarly distressing
kind,* could sustain; and, shortly before the prorogation of
Parliament, the leader of the House of Commons alarmed his
friends by symptoms of approaching insanity. On 9th August
the Duke of Wellington, then on the point of starting for
the Netherlands, saw Lord Castlereagh,† who was also on the
eve of his departure to take part in the Congress of Vienna.
Castlereagh began an extraordinary complaint, that all his
friends had conspired against him, that somebody had sent
his horses up to town that he might fly, and that it was
necessary for him to fly.

" Depend upon it," said the Duke, " this is all an illusion.
Your stomach is out of order. Ring your bell and ask if
your horses are in London; convince yourself."

Castlereagh rang the bell furiously, and shouted at the
servant who answered it—

" Who dared to order my horses up to town ? "

" They are not in town, my lord," replied the man ; " they
have not been ordered."

---

* It is known that Lord Castlereagh fell into a nefarious stratagem, which
exposed him to a peculiarly cruel system of blackmail.

† I retain the title by which he is best known in history, though he had
shortly before succeeded his father as Marquis of Londonderry.

"There," said the Duke, when the man had gone, "you see Ann. 1822. it's as I said;" upon which Lord Castlereagh flung a handkerchief over his face, threw himself back on the sofa, and burst into tears.*

"Well," he sobbed, "since *you* say so, it must be so."

The Duke then offered to put off his journey to the Netherlands in order to stay with him, but Castlereagh would not hear of it; so on leaving the Duke wrote an urgent note to Dr. Bankhead, requesting him to see Lord Castlereagh at once. The doctor called that night, and let blood according to the approved practice of the day. The patient's razors and every dangerous instrument were carefully removed; but there was a knife in one of his despatch-boxes, with which, on 12th August, he put an end to his life.

Thus ended one of Wellington's few intimate friendships, one which was never overcast by coldness save once. This was caused by the evil influence of Lord Castlereagh's brother, Lord Stewart,† whose intrigues against his chief in the Peninsula have been briefly referred to in the account of General Craufurd's death.‡ It was on one of the numerous occasions on which Lord Liverpool threatened to resign; Castlereagh naturally expected to succeed him as Prime Minister, but his brother insinuated to him that the Duke of Wellington intended to become head of the Government. Thereupon, and for some time after, Castlereagh treated the Duke with marked coolness, till one evening, when they were driving down together to dine with Sir William Curtis at his villa, the Duke spoke with so much frankness and cordiality of the affairs of the approaching Congress of Vienna, that Castlereagh told him of the attempt that had been made to

---

* *Salisbury MSS.*

† Succeeded as third marquess on his brother's death, having been previously raised to the peerage as Baron Stewart in 1814.

‡ Vol. i. p. 253. The Duke discovered Lord Stewart's insincerity on more than one occasion, but he continued to address him in correspondence as "My dear Charles" until the final political rupture of 1846. after which he became "My dear Lord Londonderry."

set them at variance, and that nothing should ever shake
his confidence in his friend again.* For Castlereagh's public
and private character Wellington retained to the last the
highest esteem. "He possessed a clear mind, the highest
talents, and the most steady principle—more so than anybody I ever knew. He could do everything but speak in
Parliament ; *that* he could not do." †

On Castlereagh's death the Duke of Wellington received
the King's commands to attend the Congress of Vienna in his
place, but his departure was delayed by a sharp attack of
illness. In the mean time the vacancy in the Cabinet and at
the Foreign Office had to be filled, and there were but two
men between whom the choice of Lord Liverpool must lie—
Peel and Canning. The state of Peel's health made it doubtful if he were equal to the labours of such an important
department, conjoined with those of leading the House of
Commons. Besides, he could not talk French, and was wholly
unaccustomed to foreign affairs. The King's displeasure with
Liverpool rendered that Minister the worst advocate of
Canning's claims ; upon Wellington, therefore, was laid the

The Duke task of overcoming his Majesty's resistance. Canning, mean-
prevails on while, had accepted the appointment of Governor-General of
the King
to give India, and the King wrote from Scotland declaring that his
office to decision was "final and unalterable," that to India he should
Canning.
go. Undaunted by this, the Duke, though confined to bed
by illness, addressed his Majesty immediately upon his return
to London.

* *Salisbury MSS.*, where illustrations abound of the manner in which the
third marquis acted so as to forfeit the Duke's confidence. At the first Congress
of Vienna, Lord Londonderry (then Lord Stewart), who was serving under the
Duke, wrote home despatches constantly criticising and reflecting on the proceedings, without showing them to his chief, who only discovered it when, on
arriving to command the army in Flanders, he received duplicates of these very
papers among the despatches which came from Vienna, which Lord Castlereagh
had desired him to open. He did the same thing at the Congress of Verona ;
and Canning, who received the despatches, gave information of it to the Duke.
Metternich put the Duke on his guard against Stewart, saying. "C'est la plus
mauvaise pièce que vous avez."
† *Salisbury MSS.*

*The King to Field-Marshal the Duke of Wellington.*　　　Ann. 1822.

"Carlton House, 5th September, 1822.

"MY DEAR FRIEND,—I was very glad to learn by the *friend* whom I sent to your bedside yesterday that you were rather better, and I hope that I shall have your further amendment confirmed by him to-day.

"He gave me a most faithful and detailed account of your opinion and kind feelings under the painful embarrassment in which we are at present placed; and I must confess that it has produced a stronger conviction on my mind than anything that had previously been urged by others. If I could get over that which is so *intimately connected with my private honour*, all might be well, but how, my friend, is that to be effected? I have a perfect reliance in your dutiful affection towards me as your Sovereign; I have the most unbounded confidence in your sentiments of regard towards me as your friend; my reliance therefore on you is complete.

　　　　　"I am, with great truth,
　　　　　　　　"Your affectionate
　　　　　　　　　　　"G. R."

"Carlton House, 7th September, 1822.

"MY DEAR FRIEND,—If you are quite well enough to come out to-day, of course I shall be most anxious to see you; but let me desire of you in the strongest manner not to leave your room at any hazard.

"I have written to Lord Liverpool to say that I shall defer my interview with him until I shall have had the pleasure of seeing you. My friend, whom I again send with this, will receive from you, in the interim, any new sentiments or opinions that further reflection may have induced you to form on the painful subject under consideration. I am most sensibly impressed with your dutiful and affectionate attention to my interests and happiness.

　　　　　"Believe me, with great truth,
　　　　　　　　"Your affectionate
　　　　　　　　　　　"G. R."

Wellington, being still confined to his room, wrote a long and clear letter, acknowledging that it had been "with pain

Æt. 53. and difficulty" that he had brought himself to recommend
the recall of Canning to office, knowing as he did the King's
reasons for objecting to it, but expressing his conviction that
there was no other arrangement which would enable the
Cabinet to face another session.

"The honour of your Majesty consists in acts of mercy and
grace, and I am convinced that your Majesty's honour is most
safe in extending your grace and favour to Mr. Canning. . . . I
really believe, as I have before told your Majesty, that Mr.
Canning never intended to do anything displeasing to your
Majesty, and I feel assured that he would be too happy to explain
any part of his conduct which might have had that effect. But
I confess that I doubt that any explanation would be satisfactory
to your Majesty, and I am quite certain that the call for it, or
even the admission of it, would not be so consistent with your
Majesty's dignity, and would not give such ease to your Majesty's
mind, as the act of royal grace which I have taken the liberty
of suggesting." *

Canning
and Peel
join the
Cabinet.

Lord Eldon was bitterly opposed to the restoration of Mr.
Canning, but the Duke had the last word with the King, and
it prevailed. Canning took the seals of the Foreign Office and
the post of leader of the House of Commons, while Lord
Sidmouth made way for Peel at the Home Office, retaining
his seat in the Cabinet without a department.

*The King to Field-Marshal the Duke of Wellington.*

"Carlton House, 4 p.m., 13th September, 1822.

"MY DEAR FRIEND,—I am glad to find by my friend that you
are better to-day; and I hope and trust that the indisposition is
nearly over.

"Lord Liverpool has just been with me, and the affair respecting Canning may be considered as concluded. . . . Thus ends
the last calamity; my reliance is on you, my friend; be watchful,
therefore. God bless you.

"Your sincere friend,

"G. R."

* *Civil Despatches.* i. 274.

# CHAPTER VI.

## THE FEUD WITH CANNING.

### 1822–1827.

THE Duke of Wellington went to the Congress of Vienna (afterwards of Verona) under instructions which Lord Castlereagh had drafted when about to proceed thither himself.* The Congress of Vienna.

* *Civil Despatches,* i. 284.

Mr. Canning, after assuming the seals of the Foreign Office, made it appear as if the policy of his predecessor had been uniform support of absolutism wherever a people was in conflict with its Government, and assumed credit for imparting a more liberal spirit into the relations of Great Britain with other nationalities; nevertheless there is not to be found in these instructions any of that blind support of absolutism of which Canning assumed the credit of purging the foreign policy of the Government.  Canning, it is true, was avowedly anxious to recognise the independence of Greece; Wellington's instructions were, not to hinder it, but "first, to prevent a rupture between Russia and the Porte; secondly, to soften, as far as possible, the rigour of the war between the Turks and the Greeks; thirdly, to observe a strict neutrality." In regard to Spain, where a democratic constitution had been forced upon King Ferdinand, "there seems nothing to add to or vary in the course of policy hitherto pursued.  Solicitude for the safety of the royal family, observance of our engagements with Portugal, and a rigid abstinence from any interference in the internal affairs of that country," were the principles to be observed by the British plenipotentiary.  The Duke himself had succeeded, when in Paris in the autumn of 1821, in dissuading Louis XVIII. from his projected invasion of Spain to prop the failing power of the Bourbon king.  As to the recognition of the revolted Spanish colonies as belligerents, that, ran the instructions, "may be regarded rather as a matter of time than of principle;" and in regard to the revolutions in Italy, "we may regard the duty of the British plenipotentiary upon Italian affairs as limited to informing himself of what is going on, and taking care that nothing is done inconsistent with the general system of Europe and the observance of treaties."

The Duke's instructions as plenipotentiary.

In short, it would scarcely be possible to frame directions more consistent than these with a policy of non-interference, subject to respect for treaty obligations.  But the Emperor of Russia, formerly in the van of liberal sentiment, had

greatly modified his views in the seven years since the A.N. 1822.
Convention of Paris. He had ranged himself with the rest
of the rulers of Europe in a desire to repress by force the
revolutionary current which was surging among all the
nations. He told Wellington that he regarded Spain as
"the headquarters of revolution and Jacobinism; that the
King and royal family were in the utmost danger, and
that so long as the revolution in that country should be
allowed to continue, every country in Europe, and France in
particular, was unsafe," * and he protested against Great
Britain's policy of non-interference as inconsistent with the
safety of society. We have, therefore, the evidence of the
Duke's despatches, describing at great length his resistance
to the views of the Emperor of Russia, upon principles formu-
lated and laid down by Lord Castlereagh, and showing that
the doctrines which Mr. Canning's partisans have claimed
that he imparted into the foreign policy of Great Britain, were
recognised and acted on in large measure before Canning had
any hand in it, and that it was Castlereagh and not Canning
who inaugurated a system of honourable adherence to treaties,
of resolute non-interference with the internal affairs of other
countries, and of discouragement of any attempt to stamp out
Liberalism in any nation.

In October the scene of the Congress was transferred to
Verona. Of this period Mr. Gleig tells an amusing incident, no
doubt narrated by the Duke himself. When the Congress was
on the eve of leaving Vienna, the suppression of the slave trade
being one of the chief subjects under deliberation, an eminent The Duke
Quaker, Mr. William Allan, waited on the Duke one morning. and the
Quaker.

"Friend," said he, "I must go to Verona."

"Impossible, I'm afraid," replied the Duke. "Have not
you seen the order that nobody is to be allowed to enter the
town unless he is a member of one of the embassies?"

"Friend, I must go to Verona, and thou must enable me to
do so."

* *Civil Despatches,* i. 343.

"How can I do that? You don't hold any office and I have none to give you."

"Friend," persisted the Quaker, "I must go to Verona, and thou must carry me thither."

"Well," returned the amused Duke, entering into the spirit of the thing, "if I must I must. If you like to ride as one of my couriers you may do so."

And Mr. Allan actually rode into Verona as the Duke's *avant coureur*, taking advantage of his official position to obtain audience of the Emperors of Russia and Austria and the other dignitaries assembled.

The negociations which went on until the end of November, though of much moment to the peace of Europe at that time, entailing a copious correspondence and constant vigilance upon the British plenipotentiary, retain little interest for general readers at the present day. Returning by way of Paris, Wellington received Canning's instructions to renew the offer of mediation by Great Britain with the view of averting the invasion of Spain, for which the French Government had been massing troops on the frontier for some time back. Wellington pointed out that the offer had already been rejected at Verona, and advised that it should not be renewed; but Canning was urgent, and the result was that mediation was again declined, and the war went on.

Good under-standing between the Duke and Canning.

The most important feature in this correspondence is the perfect cordiality and frankness which is apparent on the part of both Ministers. The time had not come, though it was near at hand, when the Duke should imbibe that distrust of his colleague's sincerity and motives which ultimately wrecked the Ministry. The years of external peace following on Waterloo had begun to tell favourably on the internal resources of Great Britain, notwithstanding the civil disturbances which prevailed at first. The partial repayment of the Austrian loan in 1823 and the redemption of £75,000,000 of 4 per cent. stock, landed Mr. Robinson, the Chancellor of the Exchequer, with handsome surpluses in his budgets of

that year and the following. But towards the close of that
year the Cabinet, already divided on the Roman Catholic
claims for emancipation, showed signs of further cleavage.
Not only on that, but on other questions, Ministers were
ranged practically in opposing camps, and a bitter feeling set
in when Mr. Canning adopted the practice of seeking support
from Brougham and the Opposition against his old Tory
colleagues. From this period may be traced Wellington's
distrust of the Minister and dislike of the man. Lord Liverpool, whose failing health had begun to tell on his powers,
listened alternately to each set of counsellors, who were thus
brought into direct antagonism.

The first triumph of the Canningite party came at the close
of 1824, when Canning wished to persuade his colleagues
to announce in the King's speech the recognition of the
independence of the Spanish-American colonies. Canning
gained over Lord Liverpool to his view, and a paper was sent
round the Cabinet on the subject, which produced an earnest
remonstrance addressed by the Duke of Wellington to the
Prime Minister. He reviewed the principles which had
hitherto restrained the Government from recognising the
revolted colonies of their ally; he entreated him to ascertain
the real opinion of his colleagues on the question, believing
as he did that all, except one (Canning), were indisposed to
the step proposed or indifferent to it, and, lastly, urging that
the project was highly distasteful to the King, "you will find
it most difficult to obtain his consent to pledge his Government to any measures for finally separating these States from
the mother country."

He concluded by expressing his distress at differing in
opinion from his leader, and offered to resign.

"As for my part, I came into the Government to support
yourself and the principles on which you had been acting, and
for which we had struggled in the field for such a length of time.
I should wish to go on as I have done, and nothing makes me

Æᴛ. 51. so unhappy as to differ in opinion from you. But as you know, I am not inclined to carry these differences further than necessary. I have advised, and shall invariably advise, his Majesty to follow the advice of his Cabinet. But I can easily conceive that it must be equally irksome to you to have a colleague whose opinion on many subjects is so decidedly different from yours; and I am ready, whenever you wish it, to ask the King's leave to retire from his service." *

Lord Liverpool begged the Duke not to think of resigning.† When he submitted to the King the proposal about the Spanish Colonies, the King asked if the Cabinet were unanimous, and, on the state of matters being explained to him, expressed a desire to see the Duke of Wellington. The Duke, accordingly, had an audience at Windsor, of which the result may be traced in a communication dated the same day, 17th December, expressing his Majesty's regret that he must differ with *the majority* of the Cabinet on this subject, but, inasmuch as he always desired to concur with the opinion of his Ministers, he would not oppose the projected measures, provided previous notice were conveyed to his Allies and the King of Spain "in such language and manner as may make the communication as little obnoxious to their feelings as possible." ‡ And so the matter passed, but not without significant evidence of the internal relations of the Cabinet, especially as between Wellington and Canning. "To do Mr. Canning justice," wrote the Duke to the King, "I must say that in the original draft of the Minute laid before your Majesty there was a proposition that the measure should be communicated to your Majesty's Allies, and it was struck out at the desire of Lord Westmorland principally, who was anxious to keep the measure secret as long as possible." §

The rift widened, but the cleavage between the old Tories, represented by Eldon, Peel, and Wellington, and the Liberal

* *Civil Despatches*, ii. 361. † *Ibid.*, 366. ‡ *Ibid.*, 368.
§ *Ibid.*, 374.

Tories, headed by Canning, became complicated on the revival Ann. 1825. of the Catholic claims for emancipation. On that question, at least, the Duke's views were more conciliatory than those of the colleagues most in unison with him on projects of Free Trade and Reform. His long experience abroad had divested his allegiance to Protestant ascendency of insular intensity; theological arguments at no time exercised the slightest influence on his opinions; he looked upon Roman Catholic disabilities merely as political safeguards; and, although he had never offered, as Peel did during the first fourteen years of his public life, an active hostility to the Catholic claims, he took part in the resistance to them as long as he considered resistance practicable and consistent with harmony between the two branches of the legislature. He cannot have been ignorant of Pitt's intention to emancipate the Catholics when he effected the Union, an intention frustrated only because of George III.'s unconquerable resistance; it has been shown that in Wellington's early days in the Irish Parliament he spoke in favour of a limited measure of relief introduced by the Government;[*] and it may be assumed that, so far as he had hitherto allowed the question to occupy his thoughts, he shared the views of his brother, Lord Wellesley, whom Lord Liverpool had sent as Lord Lieutenant to Ireland on purpose to propitiate the Catholic party.

It might have been expected that the Duke of Wellington, by birth an Irishman and having held office as Irish Secretary, would have taken a forward part in the consideration of Irish politics; but he never did so willingly until they forced themselves on his attention. It must be confessed that he was destitute of any special love for Ireland as his native country; he never returned there after resigning office as Chief Secretary in 1809; he always spoke of himself as an Englishman, and took a gloomy view of the possibility of reconciling the Irish people to English rule.

But in 1823 the state of Ireland compelled every one

[*] See vol. i. p. 7.

charged with ministerial duties to take up a definite attitude on the future position of Roman Catholics in relation to the constitution. Lord Wellesley's appointment as Lord Lieutenant had given deep offence to the Orangemen, stirring them to feverish activity, and causing formidable riots at Armagh, in Dublin, and elsewhere. The truculence of the Orangemen roused the Catholics to action; under the leadership of Daniel O'Connell the Catholic Association was organised; matters became so threatening that the Irish Insurrection Act was renewed, and the Government consented, on Lord Althorpe's motion, to a Commission of Inquiry into the causes which rendered repressive legislation necessary.

The King wrote to Mr. Peel, who, as Home Secretary, was specially charged with the Government of Ireland, pointing out that the action of the Catholic Association was "what may be fairly termed intended rebellion," and complaining that an idea had been permitted to circulate that his Majesty was not unfavourable to Roman Catholic claims.

"It is high time for the King to protect himself against such an impression, and he has no hesitation in declaring that if the present proceedings continue, he will no longer consent to Catholic Emancipation being left as an open question in his Cabinet. This indulgence was originally granted on the ground of political expediency, but that expediency dissolves when threatened rebellion calls upon the King for that which the King will never grant. The sentiments of the King upon Catholic Emancipation are those of his revered and excellent father; from these sentiments the King never can and never will deviate." *

Wellington, to whom Peel, by the King's command, first showed this letter, made light of the difficulty.

"The King told me that he had given or sent such a letter after it had reached you, but before I had seen it. I told him

* *Peel Letters.* i. 349.

that it appeared to me that there never was a moment in which ANN. 1825. the Catholic question as a parliamentary question was so little to be apprehended as at present, and that it would be most unfortunate if he were at this moment to involve himself and his authority in it, that his intention not to allow this question any longer to be considered open went to destroy the principle on which the Government was founded, and that I really believed that many of those most opposed to the Catholics considered a Government thus formed better able to defeat the Catholics than if formed exclusively of persons opposed to what was called the Catholic question. I do not think the King intends what his letter states. At all events his intention is founded on a hypothesis, and I am certain that we shall find him very little disposed to carry such an intention into execution." *

Events, however, soon caused the Duke to alter his mind The question becomes urgent. as to the urgency of the question. Year by year the majorities in favour of Roman Catholic relief had been growing in the House of Commons. The King had allowed his Cabinet to leave it an open question; but his Majesty's uncompromising hostility to concession barred the way to a settlement, and the strange spectacle was renewed each session of Ministers passionately advocating a policy and a measure which their colleagues rose from the same bench to denounce. Even in the Lords the majorities against the motion were dwindling. In 1824, Lord Lansdowne introduced a bill conferring the franchise on English Roman Catholics, a privilege which Irish Catholics already enjoyed, and another to enable Catholics to hold Revenue offices, both of which received the support of five Cabinet Ministers, but were thrown out by the Lords. In Ireland, where the question, of course, was really a burning one, although crime and disturbance had diminished in a remarkable manner, not the less was the situation exceedingly alarming. The whole of the people, except in Protestant Ulster, were banded together in and under the absolute control of the Catholic

* *Peel Letters*, i. 350.

Association—an organisation which, as the Duke of Wellington perceived, had all the attributes of a party protected by a foreign Power. Something having to be done to prevent the two parties flying at each other's throats, in March, 1825, an Act was passed, declaring illegal all associations in Ireland constituted for the redress of grievances in Church or State, "renewing their meetings for more than fourteen days, or collecting or receiving money." This was ingeniously phrased to deprive the Act of the appearance of being aimed at Roman Catholics alone, inasmuch as it brought the Orange Society within its scope: the sting lay in its application.

*Suppression of the Catholic Association.*

In no part of the world are the cycles of political recurrence so clearly marked as in Ireland. As the Land League, suppressed by Mr. Gladstone's Government in 1881, rose from its ashes and fulfilled all the purpose of its founders as the National League, so the Catholic Association underwent some changes of structure to enable it to pass through the meshes of the Act of 1825.

King George had recently sanctioned certain concessions to his Roman Catholic subjects in Hanover, which probably caused the Duke of Wellington to believe that his Majesty's repugnance to emancipation was evaporating. This, conjoined with the obvious peril of the situation in Ireland, and the growing difficulty of resisting the measures laid before Parliament, induced him to draw up a scheme of legislation, showing how far he was ready and even anxious to go in 1825. Apparently this document was prepared for the consideration of the Cabinet, though perhaps it never came before it. It is of great length and of remarkable ability, containing first a review of the whole situation, including the growth in number both of the advocates of complete emancipation and of former opponents who had become indifferent; the inexpediency of endeavouring to maintain resistance in the House of Lords against repeated declarations of opinion by the House of Commons; and the wisdom of making concessions, not, as hitherto, in time of war and

*The Duke's scheme of Catholic relief.*

difficulty, but during a period of external peace and internal ANN. 1825.
tranquillity. It goes on to show that the recent suppression
of the Roman Catholic Association made it a peculiarly
favourable moment to deal with the question, and there
follows a complete scheme of relief and religious equality
founded on the principle of concurrent endowment. As for
the charge of inconsistency which would be incurred by a
Tory Cabinet undertaking such legislation, the Duke brushed
that lightly aside.

"I go further, and say that the King's present servants are
the men who ought to consider of it, and to decide it as far as
circumstances will enable them. . . . If this be true, it is surely
more manly and consistent with our duty to our Sovereign and
the public so to conduct ourselves as to be able to render most
service in the particular crisis of time, than to be looking about
to see what imputations can be brought against us of supposed
attachment to office, founded upon our continuing to hold our
offices after a question has been carried . . . contrary to our
opinions, by our own friends in Parliament, and by the influence
of those acting in the Cabinet with us. I really cannot think
we ought to quit the King in such a crisis, or that it can be any
satisfaction to our friends the Protestants that the loss of the
Roman Catholic question should be attended by the additional
misfortune of our retirement from office." *

Wellington knew the influence he possessed over the King
well enough to feel assured that his resistance might be overcome; but there was another member of the royal house,
next in succession to the Crown, not to be conciliated so
easily. The Roman Catholic Relief Bill of 1825 passed
the third reading in the Commons on 10th May; it was
believed so generally that the Lords would accept it that
Peel actually had sent in his resignation, and the Cabinet
seemed on the verge of breaking up, when the Duke of York,
in presenting a petition against the bill from the Dean and

* *Civil Despatches,* ii. 595.

Æt. 57.

The Duke of York's declaration.

Chapter of Windsor, made a declaration of invincible hostility to all concession to Roman Catholics, winding up with the forcible words—"These are the principles to which I will adhere, and which I will maintain, and that up to the latest moment of my existence, whatever may be my situation in life ; so help me God ! "

The effect of this speech from the heir presumptive awakened all the languishing Protestant spirit in the country. It might have proved a hazardous thing for a royal prince to interfere in such a concern, but the English people easily condoned the constitutional impropriety in their gratitude for a bold, outspoken sentiment : the press rang with applause : the Peers for once championed the popular cause against the House of Commons, and the bill was thrown out.

In his memorandum above quoted, the Duke of Wellington had expressed the opinion that it would not be easy to revive public feeling in the country against the Roman Catholic claims, and that the majority in their favour would increase in each successive Parliament. The effect of the Duke of York's manifesto caused him to change his opinion on this point ; he strongly and repeatedly urged Lord Liverpool to dissolve Parliament at once, and take advantage of the excitement in the country in favour of a policy of no concession, with which, though not one which the Cabinet would make a test question, the Tory party in general was identified.

General Election of 1826.

The Duke's advice was not taken : the Parliament was allowed to run to its natural conclusion in 1826, when enough effect remained from the Duke of York's speech to return a House of Commons which in the following year rejected, by a majority of four, the same bill of relief which their predecessors had passed.

In this year the Duke of Wellington was called on once more to serve on a foreign mission. His health, since he had exchanged service on the field for political life, had been very uncertain : he had passed through one attack which, if not cholera, was nearly akin to that complaint : his frame, at no

time other than spare, had wasted to a degree which caused ANN. 1826.
anxiety among all his acquaintance. He took pride in never
allowing illness to master him, and no doubt, by dint of his
strong will, he worked through many attacks which would
have disabled less resolute men. But the strongest of us are
at the mercy of the frailty of our organs, and the Duke had
to sustain a trial this year which endured to the end of his
life. One effect of his disturbed health was a troublesome deaf- The Duke's
ness in one ear. Probably in no branch of scientific surgery deafness.
has so little advance been made, even during the present
century of rapid enlightenment, as in the treatment of hearing.
The Duke had recourse to the best advice, but in vain. At
last a specialist persuaded him to submit to the injection into
the ear of a strong solution of caustic. The effect was instantaneous; the sense of hearing was restored with extraordinary
acuteness, but violent inflammation set in, and, in the end,
the patient became, and remained for ever after, stone deaf
of that ear.

Now the reason which induced the Duke to submit to such
a hazardous remedy for partial deafness was his haste to
render himself fit for a duty which certain events in Europe
induced Canning and the King to select him to perform.
The Emperor Alexander of Russia died in December,
1825. The relations between the courts of St. Petersburg
and London had been cooling ever since Mr. Canning, with
his enthusiasm for Greek nationality, had been at the head of
the British Foreign Office. At the conference of the Powers
held at St. Petersburg in 1824, Great Britain had not been
represented, and the subsequent reserve of the Russian
ambassador at St. James on the subject of his master's intentions in regard to Greece gave rise to the belief that the
Emperor was preparing to go to war with Turkey. On
Alexander's death, it was desirable, in the interests of European
peace, to ascertain, and, if necessary, to modify, the projects of The Duke's
the new Emperor Nicolas. Accordingly, the King chose the mission to
Duke of Wellington, as "an individual peculiarly acceptable burg.

to his Imperial Majesty," * to convey his condolences and congratulations to the new Emperor. He was charged also with long and detailed instructions from Mr. Canning,† the chief object of which was to obtain the Emperor's assent to the pacific intervention of Great Britain between Turkey and insurgent Greece, and to dissuade him from persevering in his father's plan of European conferences, which had proved anything but conducive to international harmony. The correspondence preceding the Duke's appointment throws some light on the relations prevailing between the King, Canning, and himself, and on the apprehension felt by the King of a rupture between his two Ministers. In a long letter marked, somewhat pleonastically, "Most secret and confidential *and for yourself alone*," the King explains how the proposal came to be made to himself by Mr. Canning before the Duke was consulted.

"I must in justice to Mr. Canning add, that every expression he made use of was in a very friendly and proper tone. *My fear was* that you might think that the proposal originated with *me*, and therefore that you might consider it as something in the shape of an *official order* without any previous private consultation on *my part, with you my friend, as to that* which might be *agreeable* to *your feelings*, and of which, I do entreat of you to believe, that I am wholly and entirely incapable.

"Mr. Canning's *fear*, on the other hand . . . seems to have arisen from *this*—the apprehension that if this proposal was not, in the *very first instance*, made to *you*, *you* might possibly suppose that, from some unjustifiable reason, he had overlooked your superior consequence, pretensions, and ability; and therefore that he might be deemed as guilty of not showing to you *all* that high consideration and respect which *are no more than your due*, and with which, as well as with private regard for you, he not only expresses himself, but appears to be, strongly impressed." ‡

* *Civil Despatches.* iii. 84.     † *Ibid.*, 85.     ‡ *Ibid.*, 53.

Canning wrote to Lord Granville, the British ambassador A.D. 1826. at Paris, describing how the Duke received the invitation.

"I have determined to send the Duke of Wellington to Petersburg. I proposed it to the. King almost as soon as the event was known ; but his Majesty doubted—solely, however, on the ground of the Duke's health. I persuaded his Majesty to let me try the question upon the Duke. . . . The Duke not only accepted, but *jumped*, as I foresaw that he would, at the proposal. 'Never better in his life,' 'ready to set out in a week,' and the like expressions of alertness, leave no doubt upon my mind that the selection of *another* person would have done his health more prejudice than all the frosts and thaws of the hyperborean regions can do to it. . . . I am perfectly satisfied, and so, I believe, is he : he with my intentions, and I with his disposition to execute them, not only fairly but strenuously." *

The Duke wrote briefly to say he was at all times ready to serve the King in any station where he could be useful. To Lord Bathurst he wrote more fully.

" Excepting in the way of conciliation, which is certainly very desirable at the commencement of a new reign, I don't expect to do much good in my mission. But I don't see how I, who have always been preaching the doctrine of going wherever we are desired to go, who had consented to go and command in Canada, could decline to accept the offer of this mission." †

The negociations were entrusted exclusively to the Duke, Lord Strangford, the British ambassador at St. Petersburg, being instructed to that effect.‡ In spite of warnings the Duke received at Berlin, where he spent a few days on his journey out, that it was impossible for Russia to avoid going to war, in order to allay the seditious movement in her own army, he found the Emperor Nicolas much disposed to accept the friendly mediation of Great Britain, and willing to avoid

* *Stapleton.* 470.     † *Civil Despatches.* iii. 113.     ‡ *Ibid.*, 93.

a Turkish war if the Porte could be persuaded to comply with the treaty of Bucharest. After a month spent in constant interviews and negociations, the Duke left St. Petersburg with the conviction that, whatever may have been the intentions of the late Emperor, Nicolas had no intention of going to war on behalf of the Greeks, and that if war did break out between Russia and Turkey, it would be solely to enforce the just rights of his empire under treaty. Before leaving he obtained the agreement of the Emperor to a joint protocol, under which Russia and Great Britain were to offer their mediation between Turkey and Greece, on the basis of Greece becoming a Turkish dependency, paying a fixed tribute to the Sultan, but enjoying freedom of religion and of trade.

Death of the Duke of York.   On 5th December, 1826, the Duke of York died. Of all the sons of George III., he was the only one who had secured in any degree the affection of the public and the esteem of his friends. As a General in the field he had proved an admitted failure, but during his long tenure of office as Commander-in-chief he had earned the confidence of the army and the character of a good administrator. His interference upon the Roman Catholic question, although not to be defended on constitutional grounds, had undoubtedly won for him a degree of popular favour which he would not have earned by attending more exclusively to the duties of his office.

Some months before the Duke of York's death the King had told the Duke of Wellington that it was his wish that he (Wellington) should become Commander-in-chief in the event of the Duke of York's death; and as neither the Duke of Cambridge nor the Duke of Cumberland could be considered in relation to such an appointment, public opinion universally assigned that post to the Duke of Wellington. The Duke, however, begged the question might not be discussed till it arose for settlement, and he was not at all surprised, upon the Duke of York's death, to find that the King coveted the appointment for himself. Peel wrote in dismay at such a

project :* Liverpool denounced it as "preposterous," † but ANN. 1827.
Wellington merely observed in reply to Peel—

"However extraordinary the arrangement is which you tell
me his Majesty has in contemplation, I suspected that something
of the kind was in agitation, and I determined to go out of
town. . . . I have always considered that the conversation
which passed between his Majesty and me, like many others,
as so many empty and unmeaning words and phrases ; and I
consider his Majesty perfectly at liberty to make any arrangement
for the command of his army that may be thought proper by his
government." ‡

Lord Liverpool found little difficulty in convincing the Wellington
King that the objections to his assuming the office were becomes
insuperable, and his Majesty at once conferred it on the Duke Com-
of Wellington. In order that the Duke's services might not mander-in-
be lost to the Cabinet, it was arranged that he should retain chief.
the civil office of Master of the Ordnance, although drawing
the salary of one only of these appointments. Simultaneously
with his appointment as Commander-in-chief, the Duke
received from the King the colonelcy of the Grenadier
Guards.

A very characteristic incident marked the Duke's advent
to this new command. Sir Henry Torrens, who, it might be
supposed, should have better understood the man with whom,
as Military Secretary, he had been in correspondence for so
many years, wrote to the Duke enclosing the draft of a
general order which he suggested it would be proper to issue
on the occasion. It was exceedingly long, containing an
elaborate panegyric on the late Duke of York, and bore as
little resemblance as possible to any general order that ever
appeared above the signature "Wellington." In reply to
Sir Henry, the Duke civilly declined to adopt his suggestion—
"I dislike to come before the army and the world with this

---

* *Civil Despatches*, iii. 531.      † *Ibid.*, 535.      ‡ *Ibid.*, 532.

Æt. 57. parade"—and enclosed the following pithy document, with the request that it might be published at once :—

"G. O.—In obedience to his Majesty's most gracious command, Field-Marshal the Duke of Wellington assumes the command of the army, and earnestly requests the assistance and support of the general and other officers of the army to maintain its discipline, good order and high character."

Almost the first official act of the new Commander-in-chief deserves mention as showing his solicitude for his old brothers-in-arms, whom he has sometimes been accused of neglecting. The Duke of York had left debts to the amount of £200,000, and no means of defraying them. Lord Londonderry proposed to open a subscription among officers of the army to pay the creditors. The Duke emphatically condemned the project, and reasoning mercilessly, showed that although the honour of the royal family might be considered as involved in the contraction of these debts, it could not be redeemed by laying the burden on other shoulders.

"The creditors, indeed, will be satisfied, and their complaints will be silenced. So far, we shall hear no more of the fact of the Duke of York having died leaving his debts unpaid. But still the fact remains. Let us now see whether this subscription ought to be set on foot. . . . Let us only look at the situation of the General officers and officers of the army in general. There may be from a dozen to twenty of us capable of subscribing a sum of money for any purpose. But the great majority of General officers have from £300 to £400 a year. Those best provided for, among those not having private fortunes, have from £700 to £1,000 a year! The distress of the creditors relieved  . . would fall upon this meritorious body of men, who neither could nor would resist the call if made upon them, whatever might be the distress it would occasion to them and their families. . . . I earnestly deprecate it, and I may do it with the more freedom as there are two persons now alive who know that I was willing to come forward, if others would, to arrange the Duke's debts some years ago, if he would allow of their being A.D. 1827. arranged." *

Fresh differences in the Cabinet.

The unnatural internal condition of the Liverpool Cabinet was brought to a crisis by certain events which occurred early in 1827. The old Parliament had grown more or less tolerant of the anomalous arrangement under which the Roman Catholic question, one of the most pressing topics of the day, was treated as an open one, pressed forward and resisted by Ministers sitting together on the Treasury bench. It was inevitable that a new House of Commons should exhibit restiveness under such ambiguous leading, and the Old Tories, owning Eldon, Wellington, and Peel as their chiefs, received a fresh shock in the attitude assumed by the Canningites on the question of the corn duties. The Ministry were pledged to a revision of these duties, but during the summer of 1826 Mr. Huskisson, President of the Board of Trade, had anticipated the proposals of the Cabinet by announcing to a meeting of shipowners in Liverpool that the duties were to be largely reduced, and committed himself and his colleagues to a policy of free trade or something very near it. This produced at the time a vigorous protest from the Duke addressed to Lord Liverpool, whose position between the two parties in his Cabinet was becoming intolerable. " I beg leave to recall to your recollection that you and your Government are pledged to this and no more, viz., that the Corn-laws shall be reconsidered in the next sessions of Parliament. There has been no decision of the Cabinet on the object and result of the intended revision of the Corn-laws . . . but you will see from this document that the head of the Board of Trade . . . tells his constituents and the world, in so many words, that the whole question is settled, that the trade in corn is to be free." † Lord Liverpool approached the King with a view to his resignation, but his Majesty's resentment against him had so far been overcome by his usefulness

---

* *Civil Despatches,* iii. 552.  † *Ibid.,* 342.

Æт. 57.

as a buffer on the Roman Catholic question, that he persuaded the Prime Minister to retain office at least during another session.* The immediate difficulty was got over by taking the Government bill for amending the Corn Laws out of the hands of Huskisson, who, in the ordinary course, would have become responsible for its conduct through the House of Commons, and placing it in those of Canning. But Lord Liverpool's troubles had worn him out. On 17th February he had a fit of apoplexy, and although he lived for some time longer, he never recovered his faculties, and his long service in office was at an end.

Liverpool's last illness.

The question, of course, arose at once, and was eagerly canvassed, Who was to succeed him? Canning's debating powers set him head and shoulders above every ministerialist in either House of Parliament; but Canning had incurred the hostility, not only of the country party, wherein lay the Tory strength, on account of his henchman Huskisson's declaration on the corn duties, but, by his own intrigues with the Opposition, of those very colleagues who, in 1822, had wrung from the King unwilling consent to his re-entering the Cabinet.†

Canning's position, however, with the King was very different now to what it had once been. His Majesty's repugnance to the first acts of Canning's foreign policy had given way to a conviction that that policy "had placed this country in a position with respect to Europe in which it had never stood before." ‡ And, in proportion as the King had adopted Canning's views on foreign policy, his former sentiments of personal resentment and distrust towards the Minister, arising out of the old affair of Queen Caroline's trial, had been exchanged for confidence and affection. In

Canning regains the King's favour.

* Lord Londonderry's memorandum of his audience with the King (*Civil Despatches*, iii. 632).

† "I took great pains," the Duke told Lady Salisbury, "to persuade the King; but I did not know Canning then" (*Salisbury MSS.*, 1835).

‡ Memorandum by Canning of an interview with the King, 27th March, 1827 (*Stapleton*, 582).

proportion, also, to this change in relations with Canning, the Ann. 1827. King's intimacy with the Duke of Wellington had lessened : there was a cessation of the frequent conferences which he used to hold with the Duke on foreign affairs as long as " the continental system was in vogue ; " * and there is no doubt that the King found intercourse with his Foreign Minister far more easy and agreeable than with his formidable Master of the Ordnance, of whom he always stood in great awe.

Under these circumstances Canning would have been looked on as the natural successor to Lord Liverpool, but for a single consideration. The King could not entertain the idea of appointing at the head of his Government one who did not share his own views on the Roman Catholic claims. After a long interview with his Majesty on 27th March, Mr. Canning drew up the following minute :—

" For the Cabinet—
    "That his Majesty is desirous of retaining all his present servants in the stations which they at present fill ; placing at their head, in the station vacated by Lord Liverpool, some peer professing opinions upon whom his Majesty's confidential servants may agree, of the same principles as Lord Liverpool." †

This, then, was the understanding on which matters proceeded, and it was natural that the Duke of Wellington should be regarded, and regard himself, as most completely filling the part of a peer " of the same principles as Lord Liverpool." The Duke's subsequent conduct has been attributed, not, it must be confessed, without appearances to justify the inference, to chagrin at being passed over. The real cause, however, lay further below the surface ; it was the Duke's indignation at what he considered insincere treatment. His distrust of Canning had deepened, as his correspondence with Liverpool

---

* Memorandum by Canning of an interview with Sir W. Knighton, 27th April, 1825 (*Stapleton*, 443).

† *Stapleton*, 586.

Æт. 57. and Peel bears witness, in proportion as Canning had been gaining the King's favour. Canning owed his seat in the Cabinet chiefly, as the King himself testified, to Wellington's advocacy; and it has been held by some that he was galled by the sense of this obligation into undermining the Duke's influence with his Majesty. It is an unworthy imputation, not justified by anything that has come to light. On several important questions, on the Roman Catholic claims, on the corn duties, on certain points in foreign policy, the views of Canning were diametrically opposed to the policy pursued by the Duke. He could scarcely be blamed if, since his admission to the Cabinet, he had been industrious in advancing men of his own opinions, and to that extent thwarting the policy of his Eldonite colleagues. From the moment of his entry the Ministry had been practically a coalition. Canning was neither of the temper nor the intellectual stature to suffer his influence to be a passive one; in endeavouring to extend it over the King, which he succeeded in doing, he was acting very much as any other Minister—as Wellington himself —would have felt to be his duty, had the positions been reversed. Indeed, we have seen that the Duke's private judgment on the Roman Catholic question was much the same as Canning's, and it was not destined to be very long before he acted on the conviction that neither religious disabilities nor corn duties could be retained with safety to the country. Canning only anticipated his doughty colleague by a few years in trying to carry his convictions into effect.

But it is unjust to the Duke to impute to him the slightest attempt to intrigue for his own advancement to the head of the Government. So far from that, he discouraged those gentlemen who tried to induce him to put himself forward. The Duke of Buckingham wrote on his own behalf and Lord Londonderry's, as representing the anti-Catholic peers, expressing their wish to assist in forming "a balanced Government without Mr. Canning's assistance." Their advances were coldly received.

*The Duke of Wellington to the Duke of Buckingham.*    

" London, 21st March, 1827.

" MY DEAR DUKE,—I did not return from the House of Lords last night till after eight o'clock, when I did not perceive your letter ; and I have therefore opened it only this morning.

" I hope you will allow me to return it to you, and to consider it *non avenue !*

" I am going to Windsor to dine and pass to-morrow with his Majesty. It is most probable that his Majesty will not talk to me upon any business ; and that he will continue in that state of reserve in which he has kept himself towards all his Ministers, I believe without exception, upon the subject of his successor to his Prime Minister since the misfortune occurred which has deprived his Majesty of the services of Lord Liverpool.

" Believe me, etc.,

" WELLINGTON."

The King, however, who is certainly entitled to some sympathy in his difficulties, did discuss the situation with the Duke, telling him that he was prepared to name any head of the Government who might be agreed upon among Ministers, and bidding him take counsel with Canning and Peel. Unhappily the relations between Canning and the Duke had become very bitter by this time—witness, for example, a letter written by Canning to Lord Liverpool as early as 16th October, 1826, referring to a complaint by the Duke that " he knew nothing about the state of Portugal except what was to be learnt from the newspapers, which was not the state of information in which he ought to be to render his opinion of any use to Mr. Canning or anybody else," and requesting that papers might be communicated direct from the Foreign Office to Apsley House.*   Quarrel of the Duke and Canning.

* *Civil Despatches*, iii. 420. " I understand," wrote the Duke in this letter, " that it is true that my servants at Apsley House will not tell where I am to be found, though they always know. I conclude that they will not give the information because I have long and repeatedly given directions that they should not communicate my movements to the newspapers, and this from the desire of

ÆT. 57.   "The D. of W.," wrote Canning to Lord Liverpool, "will of course complain that despatches are anticipated by the newspapers; but I humbly answer, I cannot help it, until he can contrive to give me the command of wind and waves, or to put down the French telegraph.* . . . I really do not understand what he would have. Is he contented that the despatches should go to him next in order after the King and yourself? They are ordered so to do; but then you let the F. O. know where you are—they can therefore judge when they are likely to have the despatches again. There is no such calculation to be made of the D. of W.'s movements; and so far from the despatch being always returned to a day—— But there is no use in discussing these by questions; there is something else, though I protest I know not what, at the bottom of the D. of W.'s temper. His extraordinary fretfulness upon this matter, his repeated reference, and those of his *alentours*, to the approach of critical times, and other language which I know both he and the Chancellor have held very lately about the state of the Government, satisfy me that there is a looking forward to some convulsion in the Government, not wholly unmixed, perhaps, with some intention of bringing it on. Be it so. I confess I have no idea how the Government will be carried on in the House of Commons, in the sense in which it has been carried on for the last three years, with the whole patronage of the law, the greater part of the Church, and all the Army in the Chancellor's and the D. of W.'s hands.

"I am aware, too, that the D. of W. is very angry at my coming here (Paris). Two years ago he interfered with the King to prevent my doing so. But I suppose he felt that after he had himself been here in the interval, and after Westmorland had been preaching here for two months his ultra and philo-Turkish principles, I was not likely to be again so easily turned from my purpose. I am right glad that I came, not only for the immediate and unforeseen advantage of my presence here

avoiding to be made the show in every part of England which I might visit: and I believe it has happened more than once that the runners of the newspapers have made enquiries about me at my house, professing to be the Queen's messengers."

\* Not the electric telegraph, but the semaphore.

during the discussion with Spain, but because I have been able <sub>Ann. 1827.</sub>
to assure myself, to absolute conviction, that had the Govern-
ment been rightly understood here in 1822–3, the invasion of
Spain would never have taken place. In this faith I shall
die." *

Here were brewing many elements of the storm soon to
break. Canning carried his principle of non-intervention
between rulers and rebellious subjects to a greater extreme
than the Tories could sanction. The Duke, while he would
not raise a finger in support of despotism, could never feel
indifferent to the overthrow of authority. After all, he had
borne a large part in establishing the system of "continental
balance" and maintenance of dynasties; and although he
had consented at last to the recognition of the revolted
colonies of Spain, not the less did he distrust and resist the
extension of this precedent to European countries. The
spectacle of the widening breach between these two strong
spirits—Canning and Wellington—is a sorrowful one, all the
more because it engendered personal distrust and dislike.

It becomes evident from this point how greatly the Duke's The
habit of command had unfitted him for acting as one of a Duke's<br>habits of<br>command. Cabinet. He possessed mental grasp and penetration, almost
unerring in matters of his own profession, but far from infal-
lible in his civil capacity. As a soldier, he had not been accustomed to have his will disputed; when he came to encounter
opposition in the Cabinet to his view of the national policy,
he held that view so strongly and clearly that he was unable
to subordinate it to that of any other man, except the
King or the Prime Minister. He owed no submission to any
other; the very intensity of his own opinion was inseparable
from a certain narrowness, and the opposition he encountered
seemed to him to savour, if not of insubordination, at least
of hostility. Upon colleagues unaccustomed to military
obedience the Duke's brusque and peremptory intimation of

* *Stapleton.* 527.

his will acted with centrifugal effect. As he himself remarked to Lady Salisbury on a later occasion, "One man wants one thing and one another; they agree to what I say in the morning, and then in the evening up they start with some crotchet which deranges the whole plan. I have not been used to that in all the early part of my life. I have been accustomed to carry on things in quite a different manner; I assembled my officers and laid down my plan, and it was carried into effect without any more words." *

It has been shown how quick Sir Walter Scott was to recognise the military genius of young General Wellesley; † with equal penetration he discerned how far that very genius unfitted him for political life. "Lord Liverpool holds much by . . . the Duke of Wellington, but the Duke is a soldier —a bad education for a statesman in a free country." ‡

As an illustration of the different methods and mental habits of the soldier and the statesman, an incident may be quoted from Mr. Stapleton's narrative. Canning, waxing impatient under the difficulty of conducting the House of Commons with the whole legal and military patronage in the hands of his ultra-Tory colleagues the Chancellor and the Duke of Wellington, wrote rather a fiery letter to Lord Eldon, and told Mr. Stapleton, his private secretary, to copy it and send it "immediately."

"It seemed, however, in the ticklish state in which one party of the Cabinet was towards the other, that, however just and reasonable the complaint, yet, unless it were intended (which I knew that it was not) to produce a crisis, it would be unwise to send a letter written under the influence of angry feelings; so I ventured to keep it back. A few hours afterwards I said to him, 'I have not sent your letter to old Eldon.' 'Not sent it!' he angrily inquired, 'and pray why not!' I replied, 'Because I am quite sure that you ought to read it over again before you send it.' 'What do you mean?' he sharply replied, 'go and get

* *Salisbury MSS.*, 1835.　　　　† Vol. i. p. 127, *supra.*
‡ Scott's *Journal*, 8th October, 1826.

it.' I did as I was bid; he read it over, and then I saw the Ann. 1827. smile of good humour come over his countenance. 'Well,' he said, 'you are a good boy. You are quite right. Don't send it; I'll write another.' " *

All the Duke's subordinates knew him too well to have ventured on such a proceeding. Compare Canning's behaviour in this instance, one of deliberate disobedience, to the Duke's treatment of Norman Ramsay after Vitoria, where the disobedience was unintentional and unconscious.

At his interview with the King on 27th March, Canning, finding his Majesty as resolutely hostile to the Catholic claims as ever, advised him to choose a Ministry "conformable" to his own determination. Canning next, on 2nd April, made a suggestion to the Duke of Wellington that Mr. Robinson, Chancellor of the Exchequer, should be removed to the House of Lords and become First Lord of the Treasury and Prime Minister; a proposal which, though the Duke does not appear to have expressed any opinion upon it at the time, found very little favour with him. A week of silence followed, during which Mr. Canning increased his influence over the King, and the following correspondence was the outcome.†

*The Right Hon. George Canning to the Duke of Wellington.*

" Foreign Office, 10th April, 1827, 6 p.m.

"My dear Duke of Wellington,—The King has, at an audience from which I am just returned, been graciously pleased to signify to me his Majesty's commands to lay before his Majesty, with as little loss of time as possible, a plan of arrangements for the reconstruction of the administration.

"In executing these commands it will be as much my own wish, as it is my duty to his Majesty, to adhere to the principles on which Lord Liverpool's Government has so long acted together.

* *Stapleton*, 530.

† The notes in brackets are paragraphs from the memorandum drawn up by the Duke on 13th April, on which was founded his speech to the Lords on 2nd May.

" I need not add how essentially the accomplishment must depend upon your Grace's continuance as a member of the Cabinet.

" Ever, my dear Duke of Wellington,

" Your Grace's sincere and faithful servant,

" GEORGE CANNING."

[" It will be observed that this note did not state of whom it was intended that the proposed administration should be formed, although I have since learned that this information was conveyed to my colleagues ; nor who was to be at the head of the Government ; nor was I invited as others were, to receive further explanations, nor referred to anybody who could give them ; nor, indeed, did I consider the invitation that I should belong to the Cabinet to be conveyed in those terms to which I had been accustomed in my constant intercourse with Mr. Canning up to that moment, nor to have been calculated to induce me to continue in the administration about to be formed."]

*The Duke of Wellington to the Right Hon. George Canning.*

" London, 10th April, 1827.

" MY DEAR MR. CANNING,—I have received your letter of this evening informing me that the King had desired you to lay before his Majesty a plan of arrangements for the reconstruction of the administration, and that in executing these commands it was your wish to adhere to the principles on which Lord Liverpool's Government had so long acted together.

" I anxiously desire to be able to serve his Majesty as I have done hitherto in the Cabinet, with the same colleagues. But before I can give an answer to your obliging proposition, I should wish to know who the person is whom you intend to propose to his Majesty as the head of the Government.

" Ever, my dear Mr. Canning,

" Yours very sincerely,

" WELLINGTON."

[" It will be observed that I stated my anxious desire to form part of a Cabinet with *the same colleagues;* but that I postponed to give any answer to Mr. Canning's *obliging proposition* till I

should know the name of the person intended to be recom- ANN. 1827.
mended by Mr. Canning to his Majesty as the head of the
administration."]

*The Right Hon. George Canning to the Duke of Wellington.*

" Foreign Office, 11th April, 1827.

"MY DEAR DUKE OF WELLINGTON,—I believed it to be so
generally understood that the King usually entrusts the formation
of an administration to the individual whom it is his Majesty's
gracious intention to place at the head of it, that it did not
occur to me, when I communicated to your Grace yesterday the
commands which I had received from his Majesty, to add that,
in the present instance, his Majesty does not intend to depart
from the usual course of proceeding on such occasions.

"I am sorry to have delayed some hours this answer to your
Grace's letter: but from the nature of the subject I did not like
to forward it without having previously submitted it (together
with your Grace's letter) to his Majesty.

"Ever, my dear Duke of Wellington,

"Your Grace's sincere and faithful servant,

"GEORGE CANNING."

["I will only observe here that this answer did not tend to
remove the impression which Mr. Canning's first note had made
upon my mind, viz. that he did not wish that I should belong to
his Cabinet."]

*The Duke of Wellington to the Right Hon. George Canning.*

" London, 11th April, 1827.

"MY DEAR MR. CANNING,—I have received your letter of this
day; and I did not understand the one of yesterday evening as
you have now explained it to me. I understood from yourself
that you had in contemplation another arrangement,* and I do
not believe that the practice to which you refer has been so
invariable as to enable me to affix a meaning to your letter which

---

* The advance of Mr. Robinson with a peerage to the head of the Government.

Æt. 57. its words did not, in my opinion, convey. I trust that you will have experienced no inconvenience from the delay of this answer, which, I assure you, has been occasioned by my desire to discover a mode by which I could continue united with my recent colleagues.

"I sincerely wish that I could bring my mind to the conviction that, with the best intentions on your part, your Government could be conducted practically on the principles of that of Lord Liverpool; that it would be generally so considered; or that it could be adequate to meet our difficulties in a manner satisfactory to the King and conducive to the interests of the country.

"As, however, I am convinced that these principles must be abandoned eventually, that all our measures would be viewed with suspicion by the usual supporters of the Government, that I could do no good in the Cabinet, and that I should at last be obliged to separate myself from it at a moment at which such separation would be more inconvenient to the King's service than it can be at present, I must beg you to request his Majesty to excuse me from belonging to his councils.

"Ever yours, my dear Mr. Canning, most sincerely,

"WELLINGTON." *

*The Duke leaves the Cabinet.* Now, there is nothing surprising in this correspondence, nor in the first result thereof—the resignation of the Duke of Wellington, followed by that of Eldon, Bathurst, Melville, Westmorland, Bexley,† and Peel. It was only natural that the section of the Cabinet opposed to the Roman Catholic claims should refuse to serve under a Prime Minister who was their most eloquent and industrious advocate; but one is puzzled to detect in Canning's letters above quoted cause for the deep personal offence which the Duke received from *And resigns command of the army.* them. Far more bewildering was his next act. On the day following the resignation of his seat in the Cabinet, the Duke wrote to the King resigning the offices of Master-General of the Ordnance and Commander-in-chief, in consequence, as he

* *Civil Despatches*, iii. 636.
† Lord Bexley afterwards withdrew his resignation.

said, of ceasing to be in the Cabinet, and "adverting to the tenor of the letters which I have received from your Majesty's Minister by your Majesty's command." He persisted in reading "terms of taunt and rebuke" * into Canning's second letter, and in considering that the rebuke came direct from the King, in which opinion he continued to the end of his days, though it is difficult for the ordinary reader to perceive in the letter anything more than a frigid and business-like civility.

"I remained still in the office of Commander-in-chief, which I might have continued to hold, whatever might be the difference of my political opinions with his Majesty's Minister. But in addition to political differences, the tone and temper of Mr. Canning's letters, and of that of the 11th particularly (which had been previously submitted to his Majesty, and which, therefore, was a communication from the King), were of a nature to render it impossible for me to retain the command of the army. I could not exercise that command with advantage to his Majesty, the Government and the public, or with honour to myself, unless I was respected and treated with that fair confidence by his Majesty and his Minister which I think I deserve ; and nobody will consider that I was treated with confidence, respect, or even common civility, by Mr. Canning in his last letter." †

It is painful for all who have followed the Duke from height to height, in the course of his long service to his country, to be forced to admit that his action at this juncture was unworthy of himself and inconsistent with the principles he always avowed. He was right in refusing to join Mr. Canning's administration; he had carried compliance and forbearance with a policy he could not approve as far as he could do with honour. He expressed this to the King with perfect propriety in his letter of resignation.

---

* *Civil Despatches*, iv. 51.
† The Duke's memorandum on leaving office (*Civil Despatches*, iii. 639).

"To recommend to your Majesty to appoint Mr. Canning Secretary of State for Foreign Affairs, and to entrust to him all the conduct of your Majesty's Government in the House of Commons, is one thing; and to act under him as your Majesty's Minister is another." *

But to throw up a command entirely disconnected with party politics was to import into the army that very spirit of party which he had earnestly denounced as its bane, not only at the beginning of the Peninsular war, but on many subsequent occasions; † and to land the King suddenly in the acknowledged dilemma of finding a successor to him in the command was to prove unfaithful to his own leading doctrine, that the maintenance of the King's government, military as well as civil, was paramount to all other considerations. It was the act of an angry man, a conclusion which is rather confirmed than dissipated by a passage from a subsequent letter to Mr. Canning.

"I considered your letters to me, and most particularly the one of the 11th of April, in which, be it observed, you state that you had previously submitted it to his Majesty, to have placed me in such a relation to his Majesty, and towards yourself as his First Minister, as to render it impossible for me to continue in my office of Commander-in-chief. . . . I am not in the habit of deciding upon such matters hastily or in anger, and the proof of this is that I never had a quarrel with any man in my life." ‡

When did an angry man ever admit that he was angry?

The public and the press were unanimous in surprise and disapproval of the Duke's action. Of his friends, Arbuthnot

---

* *Civil Despatches*, iii. 631.

† "*Easter Day*, 1838.—At breakfast the Duke was speaking of the shameful use made by the Whigs of patronage in the Army and Navy for political purposes, and the contrast it presented to former practice. George IV., after the war, objected to giving a regiment to Sir Ronald Fergusson, a violent Whig; but I told him he *must*, and he *did*" (*Salisbury MSS.*).

‡ *Civil Despatches*, iv. 26.

and others, who desired nothing better than that Canning Ann. 1827. should be landed in a difficulty, applauded; but others, whose views were unclouded by party strife, deplored the construction which the newspapers put on the affair.

### *Viscount Palmerston to the Countess of Jersey.*

"The only thing that I do *grieve* over is the D. of Wellington's abandonment of the army. That is a Loss which cannot be supplied, and which seems to me to have been quite unnecessary. I wish to God Hamilton Place had not been quite so near Apsley House.* I am quite sure, too, that the Duke himself will repent it always. He must know that he is the only man fit for the situation, and when he sees, as he may do some Day, other Things doing which he may disapprove of, he will blame himself for having quitted his Post." †

The press was always on the side of Canning, who, by inclination as well as policy, had always cultivated its support. The London papers were unsparing in their imputations on the Duke's motives, insomuch that he, usually loftily indifferent to what was printed about himself, made an elaborate personal explanation in the House of Lords on 2nd May. He was especially anxious to remove the impression, which it cannot be doubted was a false one, that he had coveted the first place in the Government for himself. At the outset of his speech he committed the indiscretion and, as must be added, the injustice of alleging as his excuse for troubling their lordships, "the manner in which I have been treated by the corrupt press in the pay of the Government." Now, this was indiscreet, because no public man in this country could affect, even seventy years ago, to be above criticism in the public journals; and it was unjust because, having ceased only within three weeks to be himself a member of the Cabinet, if the newspapers were

---

* Apparently alluding to Lord Londonderry's influence.
† Original at Middleton Park.

corrupt he must be held responsible for the existence of such corruption.

The Duke's defence in the House of Lords.

"Do your Lordships suppose that, having raised myself to the highest rank in the profession which I had previously followed from my youth . . . I could be desirous of leaving it in order to seek to be appointed the head of the Government, a situation for which I am sensible that I am not qualified, and to which, moreover, neither his Majesty, nor the right honourable gentleman, nor any one else wished to see me called? . . . It must be obvious to your Lordships that, not being in the habit of addressing your Lordships, I should have been found, besides other disqualifications, incapable of displaying as they ought to be displayed, or of defending the measures of the Government as they ought to be defended in this House. . . . My Lords, I should have been worse than mad if I had thought of such a thing."

This speech, which the Duke had printed and circulated as a pamphlet, was followed by a wordy correspondence with Mr. Canning. Sir Herbert Taylor used his good offices, and Renewed offer of the command of the army. elicited from the Duke the admission that the only bar to his resuming command of the army was the implied rebuke in Canning's letter of 11th April, and that he was willing to take it again if that rebuke were cancelled or withdrawn. Taylor showed this letter to Canning, who immediately got the King to write the following, without, however, laying the Duke's letter before the King :—

"St. James Palace, 21st May, 1827.

"My dear Friend,—I learn from my government, as well as from other quarters, that you have obligingly expressed your readiness to afford your advice, if required, upon any matters of military importance or detail that might occur. These circumstances renew in me those feelings towards you, which God knows (as you must know) I have so long and sincerely felt, and I hope on all occasions proved; at least it was always my intention so to do. I cannot refrain therefore from acquainting you that the

command of *the army* is still open, and if you choose to recall <small>ANN. 1827.</small>
that resignation which it grieved me so much to receive, you have
my *sincere* permission to do so.

" Ever your sincere friend,

"G. R."

Unhappily, from not having read the Duke's letter to Sir
Herbert Taylor, the King missed the point on which the
Duke laid so much stress—the withdrawal of the implied
rebuke. It scarcely admits of doubt that Canning designedly
suffered the King to remain in ignorance of the true root of
the Duke's resentment. He and the Duke were now open
enemies; and although Canning certainly desired the Duke's
return to the Horse Guards as a strength to the executive, his
temper was up, and he was as little disposed to admit himself
in the wrong in having caused, as the Duke was to acknowledge his fault having made, the resignation. He was careful,
however, to resist the King's revived desire to become
Commander-in-chief of his own army.

Permission to resume the command was not what the
Duke sought: he desired a complete removal of all shadow of
reproach.

"I earnestly hope," he wrote in reply to the King's letter,
"that your Majesty will have the goodness to refer to the reasons
which I stated to your Majesty on the 12th of April, and more
fully to your Majesty's minister on the 6th of May, as having
imposed on me the painful necessity of offering to your Majesty
my resignation of the command of your Majesty's forces. I
humbly entreat your Majesty to bear in mind that those reasons
still continue in force, and that were I under such circumstances
to recall my resignation, I should by that act admit that I had
not been justified in retiring." *

Canning, having disarmed the Whig opposition, albeit he
failed at first in his overtures towards a regular coalition,

* *Civil Despatches,* iv. 37.

Æt. 58.

Recon-
struction
of the
Cabinet.

succeeded during the Easter holidays in getting together a Ministry. His tenure of the post he had coveted so ardently and so honourably was stormy and brief; its close sudden and tragic. The hardest blow dealt to his administration came, though in a measure inadvertently, by the hand of the Duke. When the Corn Bill, prepared by Lord Liverpool's Cabinet, was in Committee of the House of Commons, the Duke wrote to Mr. Huskisson, the Minister in charge of the measure, suggesting an amendment to prevent corn being taken out of bond until the price had risen to 70s. a quarter. Huskisson objected on the ground that such a provision would enable any owner of foreign corn in a port "to lay a veto upon the sale of all corn warehoused subsequent to his in that port until the price reached 70s." He went on to say that personally he should not object to a proposal that no corn should be allowed to be entered for home consumption till the average price had touched 66s.; but he added that such an amendment would probably prove fatal to the bill in the Commons. When the bill came for consideration in the Lords, Wellington moved an amendment in the terms which he believed Huskisson to have approved. Lord Goderich *
declared at once that its acceptance would be fatal to the bill,

Defeat of
the Go-
vernment
on the
Corn Bill.

upon which the Duke produced Huskisson's letter. The effect of this was that four subordinate members of the Government voted for the amendment, the exact majority by which it was carried on a division, and the bill was lost. Canning took his revenge on the Duke and the Peers by declaring in the House of Commons that "he could conceive no species of faction more inexcusable, more blamable, or more wicked than that which would make a subject touching the vital interests, and involving the prosperity of the whole community, a ground for exciting party feelings, or exasperating party animosities."

Peel, while giving Canning his support in re-affirming in the Commons the principles of the lost bill, warmly defended

* Mr. Robinson had been raised to the peerage under this title.

the Duke of Wellington against the charge of factious Ann. 1827.
opposition. Canning's speech was almost his last public
utterance. The brilliant, stormy course was nearly run.
Parliament was prorogued on 2nd July; on 8th August Death of
George Canning expired in the Duke of Devonshire's house Canning.
at Chiswick, in the very room where Fox had breathed his
last twenty years before.

This event came with startling suddenness on the Ministry
and the nation. All eyes turned upon the Duke of
Wellington and Mr. Peel, one of whom it was thought
certain would be called upon to lead the Government. The
general opinion inclined to the Duke being the more probable,
owing to an incident which took place while Canning was
lying in his last illness at Chiswick. It had been intimated
to the Duke, then at Strathfieldsaye, that the King felt some
surprise that he had never waited on his Majesty since
resigning his offices. The Duke, accordingly, interpreting
this as a command, rode over to Windsor to pay his respects
on Coronation Day. The King received him graciously,
although the impression made on the Duke was that his
Majesty's "displeasure against those who would not submit
to be tricked by his Majesty and Mr. Canning last April was
as strong as ever, although expressed in moderate terms." *
This visit, in the words of Sir Herbert Taylor, "excited very
general hopes and expectations" of the Duke's return to the
Horse Guards. This, and a knowledge that Canning's supporters were circulating reports that the Duke had visited
the King without invitation, induced the Duke to draw up
a fresh memorandum, which he placed in the hands of his
brother, Lord Maryborough.

"26th July. 1827.

"It is my opinion that Mr. Canning is now endeavouring to
prevail upon the King to adopt the new arrangement for the
command of the army.† . . . The adoption of this arrangement

---

\* *Peel Letters.* ii. 5.
† That the King should become Commander-in-chief.

will be forced on him, unless I consent to take command of the army unconditionally ; that is to say, without an apology from Mr. Canning. This I neither can nor will do as long as Mr. Canning is the Minister. It matters not to me in what channel the apology comes, provided it is clear and distinct, and so conveyed that it can be communicated to all mankind. It is absolutely necessary that it should be as public as the offence has been, and as my return to office would be." *

This deplorable wrangle was hushed in the silence of the death-chamber at Chiswick ; but the Duke's recent visit to Windsor was not forgotten, and was taken by the Whigs as indicating his Majesty's reconciliation with his old servants. The Tories feared a patch-up of the existing Cabinet, and a renewal of the offer of the army to Wellington. Arbuthnot wrote to Peel on 12th August—

"The King pretended great misery at not being reconciled to the Duke. The Lady † did the same, and Knighton ‡ went further, and said it was absolutely necessary to have the Duke to fly to in case of need. This case of need suddenly arrives. They think not of sending to him. They prove that all they wanted was to inveigle and cajole him back to the army, for the exclusive purpose of giving strength to Canning. . . . I shall die of despair if he allows himself to be so misused. . . . The truth is the King in his heart hates the Duke and he hates you, and like most kings he will try and surround himself with men of no name or power, because with such men he may do whatever he pleases." §

Lord Goderich becomes Prime Minister.

What Arbuthnot and the Old Tories dreaded was exactly what came to pass. The King laid his commands on Lord Goderich, who placed a list of the new Ministry before his Majesty on 13th August. Two days later the King wrote to

* *Civil Despatches,* iv. 65.
† Lady Conyngham.
‡ Sir William Knighton, the King's private physician, confidential secretary, and keeper of the Privy Purse.
§ *Peel Letters,* ii. 4.

the Duke, offering his "dear friend" the command of the Ann. 1827.
army; Lord Goderich wrote that "from the bottom of his
heart" he hoped the Duke would accept the offer. These
letters were brought together to the Duke at half-past seven on
the morning of the 17th, and, without consulting any one or
leaving his bedroom, he wrote his answers at once, accepting
the appointment, which, indeed, he had no excuse nor motive
for declining, Mr. Canning being no longer on the stage.
Mr. Arbuthnot did not die of despair, but he expressed to
Mr. Peel bitter chagrin at the result.

"I should have been rejoiced if the Duke had felt himself at The Duke
Liberty to refuse. He had placed himself at the head of the resumes
command
great Tory party in the House of Lords, and in a way that had of the
no connection with his military character. I trust the result army.
for him will not be that he will be taken from his friends and
given to his enemies. Should this unfortunately happen, his
private happiness will be interfered with, and all those in the
House of Lords who revered his great name . . . will be disappointed and displeased." *

How imperfectly may a man's warmest friends take fore-
thought for his welfare and renown! The Duke of Wellington
was the man in all England for command of the army;
had he been reserved for that alone, how peerless had
remained the record, its lustre undimmed by those clouds
which are never absent from the troubled firmament of party!

* *Peel Letters*, ii. 10.

# CHAPTER VII.

## THE DUKE AS PRIME MINISTER.

### 1828–1829.

Jan. 8, 1828. Resignation of Lord Goderich.

„ 9 . . . . The King sends for the Duke of Wellington. Repeal of the Tests and Corporations Acts.

March . . . . The Corn Duties.

May 20 . . . Mr. Huskisson resigns. And is followed by four other Ministers. New appointments in the Cabinet. The Clare Election.

August 11 . Peel alters his opinion on the Roman Catholic question, but desires to resign office.

Jan. 12, 1829. Peel agrees to retain office.

February 1 . The King consents to repeal of the disabilities.

February 23. The Attorney - General refuses to draw the Bill.

March 4 . . . Interview of Ministers with the King and their resignation.

5 . . The King consents to the Bill proceeding: Ministers resume office.

„ 21 . . The Duke's duel with Lord Winchilsea.

„ 22 . . Dismissal of the Attorney-General.

„ 31 . . The Relief Bill introduced in the Lords.

April 2 . . . The Emancipation Bill in the Lords.

B EFORE the close of his last session Mr. Canning had effected a formal coalition with the Whigs by inducing Lord Lansdowne and Lord Althorpe to join the Administration; but, with a new hand on the reins, the team soon became unruly. Early in December, Goderich, distracted by the disunion of his Cabinet and embarrassed by the consequences of the battle of Navarino, laid his resignation before the King, who accepted it, and sent for Lord Harrowby. That nobleman having declined the task he was invited to undertake, Goderich consented to remain at the head of affairs,

Lord Goderich resigns and resumes office.

but with Wellington as an unfriendly critic on his flank.
Among the Duke's papers is a memorandum, comparing
Goderich's position with that of Canning.  Mistrust he had
none of Goderich's sincerity, nor any of the personal dislike
which he had borne latterly to Canning on the score of
temper, spirit of intrigue, inclination to radical measures and
alliances, and "avowed hostility to the landed aristocracy
of the country."  Not the less did the Duke consider
Goderich's Government founded on "false pretences" as
surely as that of his greater predecessor.

"There is in the Cabinet avowedly a majority of members of
the Roman Catholic opinion; and they tell the King that the
Roman Catholic question shall not be carried.  How must they
avoid it? by an agreement among themselves that it shall not
be proposed.  Will they proclaim this agreement to Parliament
and the public?  If they keep it concealed, as they must, they
will be acting under a false pretence.  Such a Government cannot
conciliate the support of the public or of the gentlemen of the
country.  It must be weak.  No man can avow his connection
with those who are practising a deceit upon the public or acting
upon a false pretence.  There will not be against Lord Goderich
the same personal objections as against Mr. Canning.  It is true
that he will be supported, for a time at least, by the Radicals
here, and applauded by the discontented all over the world; but
this will be as the friendly successor, and because he lends himself
to keep out of office those who resigned rather than serve with
Mr. Canning, and whose position and strength in Parliament kept
him in check." *

Goderich did not so lend himself for long.  Probably the
false position in which he felt himself had as much to do with
his final retirement as his inability to reconcile the differences
of his motley Ministry.  On 8th January, 1828, he renewed
his resignation, and the King, on Lord Lyndhurst's advice,
sent for the Duke of Wellington, although the formation of

* *Civil Despatches*, iv. 179.

Æт. 58.
a purely Whig administration under Lord Lansdowne was thought imminent.* The Duke found the King at Windsor ill and in bed, wearing a dirty silk jacket and a turban night-cap, but in high good humour. "Arthur, the Cabinet is defunct!" he cried, and proceeded to give a ludicrous account of the behaviour of his late servants in taking leave of him, mimicking the peculiarities of each with much animation.†

The King lays commands on Wellington.

On receiving his Majesty's commands, the Duke craved leave to consult his friends, and at once sent for Mr. Peel, who personally was as much disinclined for the task as was the Duke, in view of the difficulties of the situation. The Duke, as he afterwards wrote to the Prince of Orange, felt that he had been summoned to a "most arduous situation and in most critical times; a situation for the performance of the duties of which I am not qualified, and they are very disagreeable to me." ‡ Peel described himself as obeying, "though not without great reluctance, the summons thus received. I had no desire whatever to resume office, and I foresaw great difficulty in the conduct of public affairs, on account of the state of parties, and the position of public men in reference to the state of Ireland and the Catholic question." §

Again, in writing to Lord Eldon, Peel said—

"My return to public life has been no source of gratification to me. In common with the Duke of Wellington, hitherto at least, I have had nothing to contemplate but painful sacrifices, so far as my private feelings are concerned." ‖

Men called to mind the Duke's exaggerated declaration in the House of Lords, pronounced only nine months previously, that he felt his unfitness for the first post in the Government, and would " be worse than mad if he had thought of such a thing;" but the removal of Mr. Canning seems to have dissipated the Duke's own scruples upon that score.

The attempt to form a purely Tory administration having

---

* *Croker,* i. 399.     † *Raikes's Journal.*     ‡ *Civil Despatches,* iv. 335.
§ *Peel Letters,* ii. 28.     ‖ *Ibid.,* 33.

Alvorsley

January 12 - 1887

My dear January.

I have to thank you for your message sent
since consideration. the following arrangement
for an information be in conformity with

been dismissed as impracticable, Peel co-operated with the
Duke in obtaining the assistance of the Canningites, and
having secured the good-will of Mr. Huskisson, succeeded so
well that, on 12th January, Wellington wrote to the King as
follows :—

> " London, January 12, 1828.

" I now submit for Your Majesty's most gracious consideration
the following arrangement for an Administration in conformity
with Your Majesty's Commands communicated to me on Wednesday last.

" Lord Chancellor Lord Lyndhurst.

" President of the Council The Earl Bathurst, K.G.

" First Lord of the Treasury

" Secretaries of State Home     Mr. Peel.

                Colonial Mr. Huskisson.

                Foreign The Earl Dudley.

" I would humbly submit to Your Majesty that before Your
Majesty finally determines upon this last appointment you
should wait till we shall have seen the Instructions on the late
Affairs in Greece. This delay will be creditable to the Gov' as
well as to Lord Dudley.

" President of the Board of Control Viscount Melville.

" Master General of the Ordnance The Earl of Rosslyn.

" The Lord Chancellor has according to Your Majesty's desire
seen the Earl of Carlisle to offer him to retain his Seat in Your
Majesty's Councils. Lord Carlisle was much flattered by Your
Majesty's most gracious recollection of him, as well as by the
mode in which I had executed Your Majesty's instructions ; but
he desired to delay to give his Answer till to-morrow. From
the Lord Chancellor's report of the Conversation I am apprehensive that he will decline to accept the offer. If he should accept
I humbly submit to Your Majesty that he should fill the Office
of Privy Seal. If not I would humbly submit to Your Majesty
that your old Servant the Earl of Westmorland should be
appointed to fill this Office.

" I would humbly submit to Your Majesty that Your Majesty
would be most graciously pleased to grant a Pension of the

first Class to Lord Bexley; and that His Lordship should be called upon to resign the office of Chancellor of the Duchy of Lancaster; and that Mr. Herries should be appointed to that office; and that Mr. Goldborne should be appointed Chancellor of the Exchequer. This arrangement will greatly facilitate Your Majesty's Service.

"Lord Palmerstone to be Secretary at War with a Seat in the Cabinet.

"I humbly sollicit Your Majesty's Permission to make communications to the persons interested in case these arrangements should obtain Your Majesty's most gracious approbation; and I will submit those which remain for consideration upon another occasion, the various claims upon Your Majesty's favour having rendered it difficult to make them immediately.

"All of which is Humbly submitted for Your Majesty's pleasure by Your Majesty's most dutiful and devoted Subject and Servant

"WELLINGTON." *

After some changes, the list finally stood as follows:—

| | |
|---|---|
| Lord Chancellor. . . . . . . | Lord Lyndhurst † |
| Lord President . . . . . . . | Earl Bathurst |
| Chancellor of the Exchequer . . | Mr. Goulburn |
| Chancellor of the Duchy . . . . | Earl of Aberdeen |
| Secretaries of State { Home . . | Mr. Peel |
| Foreign . . | Earl of Dudley † |
| Colonial . . | Mr. Huskisson † |
| President Board of Trade . . . | Mr. Grant † |
| Lord Privy Seal . . . . . . . | Lord Ellenborough |
| Secretary of War . . . . . . | Viscount Palmerston † |
| Master-General of the Ordnance . | Lord Beresford |
| India Board . . . . . . . . | Viscount Melville |
| Lord Lieutenant of Ireland . . . | Marquis of Anglesey † |

The common object of the Duke and Mr. Peel was thus fairly attained of effecting a continuity of the Liverpool policy of

---

* *Apsley House MSS.* The Duke's original letter to the King (of which the first page is here given in facsimile) was returned to him on the death of George IV.

† Members of the Goderich Administration.

moderation and conciliation. But it was not effected without offence to the Old Tories. The admission of Huskisson, Ellenborough, and Palmerston was almost as distasteful to them as the exclusion of Eldon, Londonderry, Westmorland, and Buckingham.

*Ann. 1828. Dissatisfaction of the Tories.*

"It grieves me to think," wrote Lord Sidmouth, "that an opportunity of forming an Administration which would have given entire satisfaction to the country has been lost. The admissions and omissions are deeply to be deplored."

"I sincerely hope," wrote Wellington to the Duke of Newcastle, "that this Ministry, although not exactly in all its parts such as your Grace suggested, will conciliate your confidence, than which nothing will tend more to its stability and efficiency. I assure you that this reunion with the old servants of the Crown in Lord Liverpool's Administration has been made without any sacrifice of principle on either side, on any subject whatever." *

But the Duke's imperious nature was not well calculated to conciliate critics. At an earlier stage Newcastle had communicated his views on the composition of the new Cabinet, and the Duke had treated them with scant consideration. "I was wrong," he said afterwards to Lord Salisbury on one of the few occasions when he admitted himself to have been in error; "Newcastle addressed me a letter on the subject of forming an administration, and I treated him with contempt. No man likes to be treated with contempt." † Newcastle made response—"Any Ministry which excludes Lord Eldon and includes Mr. Huskisson cannot gain my confidence."

To the following letter, Lord Londonderry, then British Ambassador at the Tuileries, replied, expressing his "bitter mortification" that his claim to high office had been overlooked, calling to mind the Peninsular days, and reproaching the Duke with forgetfulness of an old comrade.

---

\* *Apsley House MSS.*         † *Salisbury MSS.*

*The Duke of Wellington to the Marquis of Londonderry.*

"London, 21st January, 1828.

"MY DEAR CHARLES,—You will have heard that on the dissolution of the late Ministry the King had sent for me to desire me to assist him in forming a new one, and I inclose the arrangement approved by H.M., which was finally concluded only last night.

"I hope that this arrangement will conciliate your confidence. It is not exactly the arrangement that you would have wished for perhaps : but we must observe that we cannot form a Ministry as we do a Dinner or a party in the Country : we must look to its Stability, and its capacity to carry on the King's Business in Parlᵗ, and to carry with it the respect of the Country and of Ireland and of foreign Nations. . . .

"Yours most sincerely and affecᵧ,

"Wⁿ" *

**Lord Hill appointed Commander-in-chief.** Curiously enough it seems never to have occurred to the Duke that his position as Prime Minister was inconsistent with the retention of that of Commander-in-chief. When Peel and others made this clear to him, he recommended the King to appoint "Daddy" Hill, in writing to whom the Duke said—

"I certainly did not contemplate this necessity as being paramount when I undertook for his Majesty the service of forming his Government, . . . and it is useless to regret that I did not make the retention of my office a condition without which I would not serve his Majesty as he desired I should." †

It is certainly remarkable that the Duke, with his experience of civil and military business, should have thought it possible for one human being to discharge effectively the duties of both offices. Before he had been Prime Minister many months he was writing to Lord Camden—"If I could do in twenty-four hours the business that could be done by

---

* Original at Wynyard Park.        † *Civil Despatches*, iv. 253.

another man in seventy-two hours, I should not have time to Ann. 1828. do all that is required of me." *

Huskisson's re-election at Liverpool gave rise to an incident ominous for the harmony of the Cabinet. He was reported as having explained his adhesion to the new Government by stating that the Duke of Wellington had given him "positive and special pledges that a particular line of policy should be followed, and that his Grace should tread in all respects in the footsteps of Mr. Canning." † Taken to task for this by Lord Eldon in the House of Lords, the Duke repudiated the statement attributed to his colleague.

"If my right honourable friend had entered into any such corrupt bargain as he was represented to describe, he would have tarnished his own fame as much as I should have disgraced mine. No guarantee was required, and none was given on my part."

Huskisson afterwards explained to the House of Commons that he had been misunderstood; that the only guarantee he had sought and found was in the composition of the Cabinet itself. Not the less surely had the root of fresh bitterness been planted, nor was it long in bearing fruit.

However, before any outward severance took place, the Government had to deal with two important questions. Under the law as it stood, all persons, before taking any office, civil or military, under the Crown, were required to receive the sacrament of the Lord's Supper according to the rites of the Church of England; whereby not only Dissenters, but members of the Established Church of Scotland were technically excluded from the public services. Although, this notwithstanding, many Dissenters and Presbyterians actually did hold such offices, they did so in virtue of the annual passage of an Indemnity Act, not inaptly described by Lord John Russell as one "passed yearly to forgive good men for doing good service to their country." Nevertheless, *Disabilities of Dissenters.*

---

* *Civil Despatches*, v. 487.          † *Annual Register*, 1828.

the system worked smoothly enough, and Dissenters submitted to the Test and Corporation Acts the more willingly
because they foresaw in their repeal a precedent for concession
to the Roman Catholics. The question, however, having been
raised in Parliament in 1827, Lord John Russell took it up in
1828, and his motion was carried against Ministers, although
most of them abstained from voting, by a majority of 44.
The Government had to choose between resigning office and
bringing in a bill to give effect to the resolution of the House
of Commons. They adopted the simpler alternative. When
Lord Eldon sought to amend the bill in the Lords by inserting
a provision requiring every person accepting office to declare
himself a Protestant, the Duke of Wellington withstood the
amendment, using the memorable words—

"There is no person in this House whose feelings and sentiments are more decided than mine are with respect to the Roman
Catholic claims, and I must say that until I see a great change
in that question, I must oppose it. But no man, on the other
hand, is more determined than I am to give his vote against any
proposition, which, like the present, appears to have for its object
a fresh enactment against the Roman Catholics."

The significance of the last part of this quotation is clear
enough: the Duke would not hear of anything to preclude
Roman Catholics holding commissions in the army: his
experience was there to prove that they were as loyal and
true as officers of any other persuasion. But the expressions
in the first part were affected by that exaggeration to which
persons not eminent in public speaking are prone. The
Duke's memorandum on the Roman Catholic claims, drawn
up in 1825, was in existence to prove how far he was in
advance of some of his colleagues in readiness for concession.
His speech conveyed far more than it must be believed he
intended; it allayed the suspicions of the anti-Catholics at the
time; twelve months later it embittered their resentment at
having been hoodwinked, as they considered, by the Duke.

For good or for ill—for ill as the Tory party long believed, A̅x̅.1828.
for good as the strictest Conservative is now constrained to
admit—the first step had been taken in the long march of
reform. The monopoly of the Church of England had been in-
fringed upon, the advanced guard of more formidable invasion.
In 1827 the House of Commons had thrown out by a majority
of four the bill for the relief of Roman Catholics, in the teeth
of Canning's eloquent advocacy; on 12th May, 1828, the
same House affirmed a resolution in their favour by a majority
of six. Three Cabinet Ministers voted Aye and three voted
No, and Peel, feeling it impossible to continue leader of the
House in which he was in the minority on "the most important of domestic questions," resolved on resignation at an
early date.* Circumstances, however, immediately followed
which induced him to stand fast by the Duke's Ministry.
The evil of divided counsels had gone far during the few
months the Cabinet had been in existence. The Corn Duties The Corn
had to be dealt with, and the following letter illustrates, Duties.
perhaps more clearly than anything which has yet been
published, how little considerations of revenue actuated the
Tory party—how exclusively they were taken up with maintaining wheat at a remunerative price to the home producer.

### The Duke of Wellington to Lord Westmorland.

"March 23rd, 1828.

"I have had some very disagreeable work with corn; but
I hope that we shall bring forth a measure that will answer;
though it will not give universal satisfaction, it will be much
better than that of last year. The truth is that no measure that
can be adopted will insure a high price of corn. If the measure
adopted were a positive prohibition, whether by duty or otherwise,
up to a certain high price, such as 70s. or 80s., the Gov$^t$ would
be under the necessity of interfering at every moment in order
to provide for the supposed wants of the country. . . . I think
the proposed measure will give that security for nearly the

* *Peel Letters,* ii. 46.

Æt. 58. monopoly of the home market at a reasonable price, as will revive a trade in British-grown corn." *

Already, before arriving at a common ground of agreement on the duties, the difference had become so acute that Huskisson took his resignation to the King, and only withdrew it on hearing, at the very time his interview was in progress, that Grant had agreed to compromise the dispute. In consequence, an Act was passed modifying the corn duties to 20s. a quarter when the average price of the quarter went as low as 60s., which landowners then considered the lowest price compatible with the existence of British agriculture.

Corrupt boroughs. The storm was only dispelled in order to reappear in another and wholly unexpected quarter. Liberal as Mr. Canning had been in his views on many subjects, he was immovable on any proposal for change in the constitution of Parliament; and in 1827, when the flagrant corruption prevalent during the elections for Penryn and East Retford † occupied the attention of the House, he firmly opposed the motion for their disfranchisement. An amendment, however, was carried against him, whereby Penryn should lose its two members. The measure did not reach the House of Lords and was dropped; but in 1828 it was introduced again. The Cabinet failed to agree as to the disposal of the seats taken from the peccant boroughs, Peel wishing to swamp their corruption by throwing them into the adjacent hundreds, Huskisson having pledged himself to assign additional members to Manchester and Birmingham. The question was left an open one, with the result that Huskisson, Palmerston, and Lamb voted against their leader in the House of Commons. Immediately after the division, Huskisson wrote to the Duke

---

* *Apsley House MSS.*

† It required a pretty strong scandal to disturb the conscience of an unreformed Parliament, and Penryn certainly had managed to supply one. It was proved that the recognised custom was that the two members returned for this village should disburse twenty guineas for every vote given them, so that the elector who voted for both the successful candidates received forty guineas.

to say that he would "lose no time in affording him an opportunity of placing his office in other hands." [*] The Duke took Huskisson sharply at his word, and laid the letter before the King, upon which Huskisson wrote to explain that he had not intended to express his own intention of resignation, but merely to put it in the Duke's power to fill his place by making a fresh appointment. Lord Dudley and Lord Palmerston, loyally anxious to avoid a split, tried to convince the Duke that Huskisson had meant only to give him the option of his resignation; but the Duke, weary of perpetual bickerings with his Canningite colleagues, refused to make the slightest overture to retain Huskisson, to whom he wrote in exceedingly cold terms. The only expression in his two letters which could be construed as regretful was one to the effect that the resignation had "surprised him very much, and had given him great concern." [†] Huskisson's resignation was followed by that of Palmerston, Grant, Dudley, and Lamb. The affair was a blunder from beginning to end, little credit-able to the Duke's statecraft. He would have been glad enough to get his colleagues back, but his punctilio, and perhaps a ruffled temper, restrained him from making the first move. "I told Dudley and Palmerston," he said to Croker, at that time Secretary to the Admiralty, "that I had no objection, nay, that I wished, that they and Huskisson could get out of the scrape, but that I begged on my own part to decline taking a roll in the mud with them."

The first thing to do was to replace the retiring Ministers. Sir Henry Hardinge took Palmerston's place at the War Office; another old war-comrade of the Duke's, Sir George Murray, followed Huskisson at the Colonial Office; Lord Aberdeen became Foreign Secretary instead of Lord Dudley; Lord Francis Leveson-Gower Chief Secretary for Ireland in place of Lamb, a berth greatly desired by J. W. Croker; and Vesey Fitzgerald went to the Board of Trade. Of these men the last-named was least known, yet was he destined by

[*] *Civil Despatches,* iv. 449.          [†] *Ibid.,* 449.

ÆT. 59. a strange chance to become the most conspicuous figure in the crisis. A wealthy Irish landlord, he had always supported the Roman Catholic claims, and, in vacating his seat for County Clare on taking office, nobody dreamt of any obstacle to his return.

"We are going on very well here," wrote the Duke to his brother Henry, who had been raised to the peerage as Lord Cowley and was Minister at Vienna; "the Government is very popular, and indeed there is but little opposition." *

The Clare election. There ensued a prodigy and a portent. The Duke had no suspicion of the mine that was about to be sprung on his Ministry. Daniel O'Connell, with the whole Catholic Association perfectly organised at his back, with dramatic suddenness stepped into the ring as candidate for County Clare. Fitzgerald, after maintaining for some days † a contest which was hopeless from the moment his opponent appeared, threw up the sponge, and left the seat in possession of the Roman Catholic champion. O'Connell being debarred on account of his religion from taking the oaths, and thereby from taking his seat in the Imperial Parliament, the Roman Catholic question at once acquired an urgency which it had never possessed before. The franchise of Ireland was much wider than that of Great Britain. The forty-shilling freeholders, admitted by the Act of 1793, practically included the mass of the small tenantry of Ireland; hitherto they had voted with their landlords, but now it was clear that they were at the beck of the priests. What had happened in Clare would be repeated in every county in Ireland except in Ulster. Peel, as Home Secretary, was specially concerned, as the Cabinet was constituted in those days, with the affairs of Ireland.

"However men might differ," he wrote, "as to the consequences which ought to follow the event, no one denied its vast

---

* *Civil Despatches*, iv. 499.

† At that period the polling-booths were kept open for fourteen days.

importance.   It was foreseen by the most intelligent men that the Ann. 1828.
Clare election would be the turning-point in the Catholic question,
the point *ubi se via findit in ambas."* \*

Henceforth the Irish constituencies, hitherto returning three
Tories for every Whig member, would send to Parliament
nominees of the Catholic Association in the same proportion.
Disfranchise the forty-shilling freeholder, cried irresponsible
Tories, forgetting the impossibility of persuading the House
of Commons to such a reactionary course.   The Lord
Lieutenant of Ireland, Lord Anglesey, was no coward; maimed
of a leg at Waterloo, he was not the man to quail in the
presence of danger, real or imaginary; yet he wrote to warn
the Government that they were on the eve of civil war.

"There may be rebellion.   You may put to death thousands.
You may suppress it; but it will only be to put off the day of
compromise. . . . The present order of things must not, cannot
last.   There are three modes of proceeding.   1st: That of trying
to go on as we have done.   2ndly: To adjust the question by
concession and such guards as may be deemed indispensable.
3rdly: To put down the Association and to crush the power of
the priests.
    " The 1st I hold to be impossible.
    " The 2nd is practicable and advisable.
    " The 3rd is only possible by supposing that you can reconstruct
the House of Commons; and to suppose that is to suppose that
you can totally alter the feelings of those who send them
there. . . . I abhor the idea of truckling to the overbearing
Catholic demagogues . . . but I do most conscientiously and
after the most earnest consideration of the subject, give it as my
conviction that the first moment of composure and tranquillity
should be seized to signify the intention of adjusting the
question." †

This letter was laid before the Cabinet by Peel, and it was
determined that the King should see it.   Peel, a consistent

---

\* *Peel Letters*, ii. 47.          † *Civil Despatches*, iv. 521.

opponent of Roman Catholic claims, announced his opinion to the Duke that the time was come when the question must be taken up and settled by concession, but he added that, in view of his past record, his was not the hand to conduct such a measure through the House of Commons. He volunteered his retirement from office, promising his hearty support to "a measure of ample concession and relief," and enclosing the draft of what he considered such a measure should be. Simultaneously with this declaration, which was dated 11th August, Mr. Dawson, member for Derry, brother-in-law of Mr. Peel, one of the staunchest Tories, and hitherto most resolute in opposing concession, made a speech to his constituents in which he told them his conviction that resistance could be carried no further and that the disabilities must be removed. Wellington, retiring to Cheltenham to drink the waters, told Peel that he would be prepared to discuss the situation with him and Lord Lyndhurst in the month of September. That his mind was already made up is clear from the existence not only of a memorandum on the state of Ireland, submitted to the King on 1st August,[*] showing the necessity of measures for the pacification of that country, but also of another long memorandum describing the nature of these measures, which, although prepared before 7th August for presentation to the King, was withheld on account of his Majesty's ill health till 16th November.

**The Duke undertakes Roman Catholic emancipation.** It has been commonly supposed and frequently stated that the Duke of Wellington was converted on the Roman Catholic question by the apprehension of a rebellion in Ireland. It is doing him a grievous injustice to associate his action with any such motive. He entertained, it is true, a passionate horror of civil war, but no man was less likely to alter his course under terrorism. His true motive was briefly expressed in a letter to Lord Camden written on 31st March, 1829, the day the Emancipation Bill came before the House of Lords, one of many written in answer to objections raised to the

[*] *Civil Despatches,* v. 565.

change of policy.   Lord Camden had written to tell the Duke Ann. 1828. that Lord Chatham considered the time unfavourable for dealing with the question.

"I don't know whether this letter will answer Lord Chatham's objection as to the time.   The truth is there was no time to be lost.   Matters were getting worse every day.   I don't think they were tending directly to rebellion.   The leading agitators were too well aware of the relative strength of the parties, and of their own peril, to venture upon that extremity.   But the state of society was becoming worse daily, and we should very soon have had the resident Protestants crying out for a settlement." *

Another misconception of the true course of events is that under which warm admirers of the Duke attribute his changed attitude on emancipation to the timid counsels of Peel. Certainly Peel was not so bold as the Duke on this question, not in that he was more disposed than he to yield to the Roman Catholics, but because he hesitated to go so far.   He had much rather have resigned his office than undertaken concession; it was fidelity to and confidence in his chief that induced him to face the task; having faced it, his influence on the Duke's scheme was to diminish its scope and to shear from it some of its most valuable safeguards.   The Duke was prepared to subsidise the Irish priesthood to the extent of £300,000 a year; Peel could not approve of setting up a dual Church establishment in Ireland.   In other respects the draft was modified to reconcile it to Peel's assent, and the measure submitted to Parliament was far less thorough and effective than the Duke, if single-handed, would have made it.

Reflection during his retirement at Cheltenham confirmed the Duke in his judgment that the position of a Cabinet, divided on what had become the chief question in domestic politics, was no longer tenable.   None knew better than he

* *Civil Despatches*, v. 501.

the hazards of retreat in the presence of an enemy; almost more hazardous was a change of front. Yet the front must be changed before the next general election, else the Roman Catholic forces would be strengthened so as to carry all his defences. Steadily, silently, the Duke came to the conclusion that the King must be brought to brook concession. Did this imply any sacrifice of principle on the Duke's part? The answer must be—None. It has been shown that his private opinion had long been far from hostile to concession; practically it was identical with that of William Pitt, although he did not feel so strongly about it as to allow, as Mr. Pitt did, the King's opposition to concession to drive him out of office. Better, as we judge him now, had he done so; better for his reputation for consistency; better for his standing with anti-Catholic Tories who reposed their entire trust in him, and were filled with rage and dismay at his desertion of the post.

Having made up his mind that the position must be abandoned, the Duke set to work with Lyndhurst and Peel to arrange the order of retreat. But he allowed no suspicion of what was coming to leak out: just as when compelled to fall back from Quatre-Bras he concealed his movement to the last moment, so up to the close of 1828 all the indications pointed to defending what Peel and he had come to the conclusion was indefensible. Curtis, the Roman Catholic bishop of Armagh, for whom the Duke had conceived an esteem, fully reciprocated, in the far-off days of Salamanca, wrote earnestly and reasonably, urging that the question might be taken up and dealt with; * the Duke replied that he was indeed sincerely anxious to witness a settlement, but that party had become mixed up with the matter to such an extent that he saw no prospect of one.† The troops in Ireland were reinforced and more guns sent over there; Lord Anglesey, who had shown some indiscreet encouragement towards members of the Catholic Association, was

* *Civil Despatches,* v. 308.        † *Ibid.,* 326.

deprived of office, and the Lord Lieutenancy was conferred Ann. 1829. on the Duke of Northumberland, who, having always voted against the Roman Catholic claims, was not suspected of entertaining the really enlightened views he expressed to the Duke of Wellington on accepting the office.* All the symptoms on the surface indicated an inflexible policy of repression; yet all the time, as often as the King's health allowed of his attending to business, the Duke pressed on him, by letter and interview, the necessity for giving up the policy of *non possumus.* He wrung from his Majesty a reluctant consent to lay his scheme of relief before the Bishops; they proved as hostile as the King himself to a settlement, or any attempt thereat.

The month of January arrived, and apparently no progress had been made. The Duke was fighting almost single-handed, for he had lost his Canningite colleagues in the Cabinet—the great advocates of concession; Anglesey had been recalled from Ireland, and Peel only held office provisionally. Still the Duke worked incessantly with the King.

"I make it a rule," he told Charles Greville, "never to interrupt him, and when by turning the conversation he tries to get rid of a subject in the way of business that he does not like, I let him talk himself out, and then quietly put before him the matter in question, so that he cannot escape from it."

At last Peel put his shoulder to the wheel.

"Being convinced that the Catholic question must be settled and without delay: being resolved that no act of mine should obstruct or retard its settlement; impressed with the strongest feelings of attachment to the Duke of Wellington, of admiration of his upright conduct and intentions as Prime Minister, of deep interest in the success of an undertaking on which he had entered from the purest motives and from the highest sense of public duty; I determined not to insist on retirement from

* *Civil Despatches,* v. 453.

Æt. 59. office, but to make to the Duke the voluntary offer of that official co-operation which he scrupled, from the influence of kind and considerate feelings, to require from me." *

Parliament was to meet on 6th February; on 12th January Mr. Peel drew up a memorandum to the King, strongly setting forth the reasons which had convinced him that the time had come when the barrier should be removed which prevented the Cabinet from considering the Catholic question.†

Peel assents to emancipation, and the King gives way. The poor King's last support had broken down; Peel— "Orange" Peel as the staunchness of his Protestant convictions had caused him to be named—had deserted the cause; the Duke of Cumberland, luckily for the public peace, was abroad; his Majesty had no one but the Bishops to help him against his masterful servants—even among the Bishops, Winchester was found advocating concession,‡ and the King succumbed. On 1st February he signed the draft of the Speech from the Throne, in which, after asking Parliament for additional powers for the repression of disorder in Ireland, he was made to say—

'His Majesty recommends . . . that you should take into your deliberate consideration the whole condition of Ireland, and that you should review the laws which impose disabilities on his Majesty's Roman Catholic subjects."

The bitterness of surrender was mitigated only by the mention of concurrent measures to disfranchise the Irish forty-shilling freeholder, and to regulate the assumption of ecclesiastical titles by Roman Catholics.

This must be regarded as the greatest of Wellington's acts as a Minister. No other man in England could have turned King George from the one principle to which he clung with all the intensity of his nature—from the one conviction he held from conscientious scruples. Well might Charles

* *Peel Letters*, ii. 79.    † *Civil Despatches*, v. 436–440.    ‡ *Ibid.*, 324.

Greville pronounce that the Duke was in a higher position ANN. 1829.
than any subject had touched in modern times.

> " He treats the King as an equal, and the King stands entirely
> in awe of him. . . . Whatever he may be, he is at this moment one
> of the most powerful Ministers this country has ever seen.   The
> greatest Ministers have been compelled to bow to the King, or
> the aristocracy, or the Commons, but he commands them all."

It needed all the strength of this ascendency to stand the
storm which arose on the announcement of the Government
programme.   The Tories were furious at what they denounced
as their betrayal ; all over the country the stout Protestant
feeling was in arms.   Peel pressed the Irish Coercion Bill
through all its stages, the Opposition assenting on the faith
of the Relief Bill which was to follow, and then gave his
constituents an opportunity of pronouncing on his conduct
by vacating his seat for Oxford.   He was defeated at the Peel's
poll by 755 votes to 609, and was driven to seek refuge in defeat at<br>Oxford.
the small rotten borough of Westbury, where he escaped
another reverse only because his Protestant opponent came
late upon the field.   The Duke of Beaufort and Lord Westmorland both evinced their disapproval of the new departure
by declining the office of Lord Privy Seal ; Sir  Charles
Wetherell, the Attorney-General, refused to draft the bill,
or to be any party to legislation of which his conscience
disapproved, but was permitted, for the nonce, to retain office.

In the middle of February the Duke of Cumberland returned to England.   Wellington, foreseeing unmixed mischief
from his presence at the King's ear, had earnestly counselled
him to stay away.   " Your Royal Highness has been already
so much mixed up in discussions on the Roman Catholic
question that you cannot avoid interfering." *   The remonstrance was in vain, and, personal difference arising, all
intercourse shortly ceased between the King's brother and
the Prime Minister.

* Civil Despatches, v. 483.

ÆT. 59.
On 3rd March Peel gave notice that on the 8th he would make known what the Government proposed in regard to the clause in the King's Speech referring to the removal of disabilities. Next morning his Majesty sent for the Duke, Lord Lyndhurst, and Mr. Peel to Windsor, and desired an explanation of the proposed measure. The Duke of Cumberland had been diligent with his Majesty, had persuaded him that the Tories were strong enough to form a Protestant administration by themselves, and that nothing ought to induce him to violate his coronation oath by consenting to concessions to Roman Catholics. The interview between King George and his Ministers was a most distressing one. Peel, being in charge of the bill, proceeded to explain it to the King, who interrupted him by constant digressions upon irrelevant subjects, and was as often brought back to the point by the Duke. When they arrived at the clauses framed to repeal the transubstantiation test and to modify the oath of supremacy, the King, loudly protesting that he had been misled and deceived,* refused to give the Royal assent to such a measure, and asked Peel how he intended to act in the House of Commons under such circumstances. Peel replied that he should announce on the morrow his regret that it had been taken out of his power to bring forward the promised Relief Bill in his official capacity, as he had no longer the honour of being his Majesty's Minister. The Duke and Lord Lyndhurst likewise made their resignations, and the King closed the interview, which had lasted five hours and a half, by dismissing his Ministers with a kiss on each cheek.

*The King changes his mind.*

The Prime Minister, the Lord Chancellor, and the Home Secretary then returned to London out of office. That night there was a Cabinet dinner at Lord Bathurst's, where, of course, the situation was closely discussed. All concluded that the Government was out, except the Duke.

"Don't be afraid," said he; "before to-morrow morning

* *Salisbury MSS.*

depend upon it I shall hear from the King again." * The Ann. 1829.
words were scarcely spoken before the Duke was summoned The King
home to receive a letter from the King. withdraws
his assent.

" Windsor Castle, Wednesday evening,<br>
" 8 o'clock, 4th March, 1829.

"My dear Friend,—As I find the country would be left without an administration, I have decided to yield my opinion to *that*
which is considered by the Cabinet to be for the immediate
interests of the country. Under these circumstances you have
my consent to proceed as you propose with the measure. God
knows what pain it costs me to write these words.

" G. R."

*The Duke of Wellington to the King.*

" London, 4th March, 1829, at midnight.

"I have just received your Majesty's most gracious letter of
8 p.m., and I assure your Majesty that I sincerely lament the
necessity which exists for urging your Majesty to sanction
measures the adoption of which appears to occasion your Majesty so
much pain. Mr. Peel will proceed with the Bills to-morrow, in the
full confidence and with the full understanding that your Majesty's
servants have your sanction and support, and that your Majesty
will go through with us. I entreat your Majesty to give your
gracious approbation to my letter of the 2nd instant, containing
the Minute of Cabinet; or to inform me if my understanding of
your Majesty's letter of this afternoon is not correct. Which is
humbly submitted, etc.

" Wellington."

*The King to the Duke of Wellington.*

" Windsor Castle, Thursday morning, quarter-past 7,<br>
" from my bed, 5th March, 1829.

"My dear Friend,—I am awakened by the messenger with
your letter, and as I know that you are much pressed for time,
I send him off again immediately. *You have put the right construction upon the meaning of my letter of last evening ;* but, at the

* *Salisbury MSS.*

Æt. 50.     same time, I cannot disguise from you that my feelings of distress
in consequence are such as I do scarcely know how to support
myself under them.

"G. R."

The Bill before Parliament.    The Emancipation Bill went forward with the hearty
support of the Opposition. Brougham agreed to the con-
current disfranchisement of the forty-shilling freeholder, "as
the price, as the high price, as the all but extravagant price,
of this inestimable good. That price, to obtain that good,
he, for one, would most willingly pay." The first reading
was carried by 348 votes to 160, the minority consisting of
the irreconcilable Tories. Among them were two members
of the Government, the Attorney-General and Lord Lowther.
The latter was the son of Lord Lonsdale—the "cat-o'-nine-
tails," so named because he returned nine members to Parliament, obedient to himself. The Prime Minister, equally
unwilling to forfeit irrevocably Lord Lonsdale's support, and
to bring about by-elections at such a critical time, allowed
his recalcitrant subordinates to retain office; but on the
second reading Sir Charles Wetherell made such a violent
attack upon his colleagues that a few days later the Duke
dismissed him from office.* Greville gives currency to the
report that Wetherell was drunk when he made this speech.
"When he speaks, he unbuttons his braces, and in his
vehement action his breeches fall down and his waistcoat
runs up, so that there is a great interregnum." The Speaker
observed afterwards that Wetherell's only lucid interval was
between his waistcoat and breeches.

In the Commons, however, despite Wetherell's escapade
and the stiffness of the Old Tories, the Emancipation Bill
was in the house of its friends; the real ordeal awaited it in
the other Chamber. Macaulay, discussing its prospects there
with Lord Clarendon, speculated how the Duke would explain
his altered opinions and justify the bill. "Oh, that will be
simple enough," replied Clarendon. "He'll say, 'My lords!

* *Civil Despatches,* v. 547.

Attention!  Right about face!  Quick march!' and the Ann. 1829.
thing will be done."

My lords, as the event proved, obeyed the command with
surprising alacrity, but not before an unpleasant incident
took place, characteristic of the times.   On 14th March a *The Duke's*
letter appeared in the *Standard* newspaper signed "Win- *duel with Lord Win-*
chilsea and Nottingham," referring to the King's College of *chilsea.*
London, an institution which he and other supporters of the
Church of England had founded in 1828 in the intention of
establishing an educational counterpoise to the freethinking
and radical influence of the London University.

"I was one of those who at first thought the proposed plan
might be practicable, and prove an antidote to the principles of
the London University.  I was not, however, very sanguine in
my expectations, seeing many difficulties likely to arise in the
execution of the suggested arrangement, and I confess that I felt
rather doubtful of the sincerity of the motives of some of the
prime movers in this undertaking, when I considered that the
noble Duke at the head of his Majesty's Government had been
induced on this occasion to assume a new character, and to step
forward as the public advocate of religion and morality.  Late
political events have convinced me that the whole transaction
was intended as a blind to the Protestant and High Church party;
that the noble Duke, who had for some time previous to the
period determined upon breaking in upon the Constitution of
1688, might the more effectually, under the cloak of some outward
show of zeal for the Protestant religion, carry on his insidious
designs for the infringement of our liberties, and the introduction
of Popery in every department of the State."

The Duke's attention having been called to this letter, the
following correspondence ensued :—

*The Duke of Wellington to the Earl of Winchilsea.*

"London, 16th March, 1829.

"My Lord,—I have just perused in the *Standard* newspaper of this day, a letter addressed to Henry Nelson Coleridge,

Esq., dated Eastwell Park, March 14th, 1829, signed *Winchilsea and Nottingham;* and I shall be very much obliged to your Lordship if you will let me know whether that letter was written by you and published by your authority.

"I have the honour to be, etc.,

" WELLINGTON."

### *The Earl of Winchilsea to the Duke of Wellington.*

" Eastwell Park, Ashford, 18th March, 1829.

" MY LORD,—I have the honour to acknowledge the receipt of your Grace's letter of the 16th instant, and I beg to inform you that the letter addressed to H. N. Coleridge, Esq., was inserted in the *Standard* by my authority.    As I had publicly given my approbation and sanction to the establishment of King's College, London, last year, by becoming a subscriber to it, I thought it incumbent upon me in withdrawing my name, also publicly to state my reasons for so doing.

" I have the honour to be, etc.,

" WINCHILSEA AND NOTTINGHAM."

### *The Duke of Wellington to the Earl of Winchilsea.*

" London, 19th March, 1829.

" MY LORD,—I have had the honour of receiving your Lordship's letter of the 18th instant.    Your Lordship is certainly the best judge of the mode to be adopted in withdrawing your name from the list of the subscribers to King's College.    In doing so, however, it does not appear necessary to impute to me, in no measured terms, disgraceful and criminal motives for my conduct in the part which I took in the establishment of the college. No man has a right, whether in public or private, by speech, in writing, or in print, to insult another by attributing to him motives for his conduct, public or private, which disgrace or criminate him.    If a gentleman commits such an act indiscreetly in the heat of debate, or in a moment of party violence, he is always ready to make reparation to him whom he may thus have injured.    I am convinced your Lordship will, upon reflection, be anxious to relieve yourself from the pain of having thus insulted Ann. 1829. a man who never injured or offended you.

"I have the honour to be, etc.,

" WELLINGTON."

The last letter was carried by Sir Henry Hardinge to Lord Winchilsea, with instructions to demand an apology. This Lord Winchilsea declined, though he offered to express regret for having mistaken the Duke's motives, provided the Duke would declare that when he presided at the meeting for the establishment of King's College, he had not in contemplation a measure of Roman Catholic relief. He appointed Lord Falmouth to conduct further communications with Sir Henry Hardinge acting for the Duke. The Duke, however, wrote once more to Lord Winchilsea.

" London, 20 March, 1829, 6½ p.m.

"MY LORD,—Sir Henry Hardinge has communicated to me a memorandum signed by your Lordship, dated 1 p.m., and a note from Lord Falmouth dated 3 p.m.

"Since the insult, unprovoked on my part, and not denied by your Lordship, I have done everything in my power to induce your Lordship to make me reparation ;—but in vain. Instead of apologising for your own conduct, your Lordship has called upon me to explain mine. The question for me now to decide is this. Is a gentleman who happens to be the King's Minister to submit to be insulted by any gentleman who thinks proper to attribute to him disgraceful or criminal motives as an individual? I cannot doubt of the decision which I ought to make on this question. Your Lordship is alone responsible for the consequences.

"I now call upon your Lordship to give me that satisfaction for your conduct which a gentleman has a right to require, and which a gentleman never refuses to give.

" I have the honour, etc.,

" WELLINGTON."

A meeting having been arranged to take place the following morning in Battersea Fields,* Hardinge desired Dr.

---

* Not at Wimbledon, as Charles Greville has it, vol. i. p. 192.

Hume to be in attendance. The good man only knew that it was an affair of honour between gentlemen. In the interesting report of the circumstances which he drew up for the Duchess of Wellington, he has given an amusing description of his dismay when the Duke himself rode up with Hardinge.

"Well, doctor," said the Duke, laughing, "I dare say you little expected it was I who wanted you to be here."

"Indeed, my lord," replied the doctor, in great agitation, "you certainly are the last person I should have expected here."

"Ah, perhaps so," returned the Duke; "but it was impossible to avoid it; you will see by-and-by that I had no alternative, and could not have done otherwise."

The Duke, strange to say, had no duelling pistols; still more strangely, it was the doctor who produced a pair for his use, and afterwards loaded them, Hardinge having lost an arm at the battle of Ligny. Lords Winchilsea and Falmouth arrived late; their coachman having driven them to Putney Bridge instead of Battersea Bridge.

The five gentlemen walked across the first field to the fence on the other side, where, perceiving some people at work, they crossed a ditch into a second field.

"Now then, Hardinge," said the Duke, as soon as his opponent was on the ground, "look sharp and step out the ground. I have no time to waste. Damn it!" he continued, "don't stick him up so near the ditch. If I hit him he will tumble in." *

The gentlemen having taken their places, Hardinge advanced halfway between them, and summoned Lord Winchilsea and Lord Falmouth to listen to his protest against pushing matters any further, and a discussion ensued which certainly seems inconsistent with the traditional punctilio observed on such occasions. Hardinge represented the Duke of

---

\* Not in Dr. Hume's narrative, though he mentions the ditch, but told by him to the late Admiral Sir G. Seymour. The exact spot is supposed to have been in the hollow now filled by the Ladies' Pond.

Wellington, who was the challenger, and surely remonstrance ANN. 1829. at this stage on his part was not a little anomalous. However, it led to nothing; and Sir Henry, pointing to some people who had collected at the end of the field and were viewing the proceedings with curiosity, said, "We had better take our ground. The sooner this affair is over the better."

The seconds then stepped back: Lord Falmouth asked Sir Henry to give the signal, who, after a few seconds, called out, "Gentlemen, are you ready—Fire!"

The Duke levelled his pistol at once, but seeing that Lord Winchilsea did not move, seemed to hesitate for a moment, and then purposely fired wide of him.* Lord Winchilsea, smiling, then raised his arm and fired in the air. The Duke stood on his ground, but Lord Winchilsea and Lord Falmouth came towards Hardinge, and Falmouth said that his principal, having received the Duke's fire, was now in a position to make the reparation required. He then took a paper from his pocket and began reading it. The Duke, having drawn nearer, exclaimed in a low voice, "This won't do; it's no apology." Sir Henry then took the paper, walked aside with the Duke, and returned presently, saying, "My Lord Falmouth, it is needless to prolong this discussion. Unless the word *apology* is inserted, we must resume our ground." Further consultation took place, which ended in Lord Falmouth inserting in pencil the words "in apology" in the expression of regret already tendered, which was accepted as satisfactory, and the gentlemen exchanged formal salutes. Lord Falmouth, who had been in much agitation throughout the affair, then began to give to the Duke an explanation of his conduct, saying that he had always told Lord Winchilsea he was completely in the wrong.

"My Lord Falmouth," said the Duke, interrupting him,

---

* *Brialmont*, iii. 361. It ought to be recorded that Lord Winchilsea had written to Lord Falmouth overnight to say that it was his determination not to fire at the Duke, and that after the first fire he should offer the expression of regret which he would then be ready to make (*Civil Despatches*, v. 539, note).

"I have nothing to do with these matters." Then, touching the brim of his hat with two fingers, he added, "Good morning, my Lord Winchilsea; good morning, my Lord Falmouth," mounted his horse, and rode off with Sir Henry Hardinge, leaving Dr. Hume to pack up the pistols.

The Duke's justification of himself.

The affair was over with less mischief than might have ensued, a curious interlude in the hurricane of wordy war with which the country was torn; but no notice of it, however brief, would be complete without mention of the justification which the Duke offered to persons who took him to task for his conduct in it. A long lecture from Jeremy Bentham, beginning "Ill-advised Man!" and calling on him to stand up in his place in the House of Lords, confess his error, declare his repentance and his resolve never under any provocation again to give or receive a challenge, is simply minuted "Compliments. The Duke has received his letter." But in reply to a remonstrance from the Duke of Buckingham he entered into full explanation.

" London, 21st April, 1829.

"MY DEAR DUKE,—I am very much obliged to you for your letter of the 6th, which I received this morning. The truth is that the duel with Lord Winchilsea was as much part of the Roman Catholic question, and it was as necessary to undertake it and carry it to the extremity to which I did carry it, as it was to do everything else which I did do to attain the object which I had in view. I was living for some time in an atmosphere of calumny. I could do nothing that was not misrepresented as having some base purpose in view. If my physician called upon me, it was for treasonable purposes. If I said a word, whether in Parliament or elsewhere, it was misrepresented for the purpose of fixing upon me some gross delusion or falsehood. Even my conversations with the King were repeated, misrepresented, and commented upon; and all for the purpose of shaking the credit which the public were inclined to give to what I said. The courts of justice were shut, and not to open till May. I knew that the Bill must pass or be lost before the 15th of April. In this state

of things Lord Winchilsea published his furious letter. I imme- ANN. 1829.
diately perceived the advantage it gave me; and I determined
to act upon it in such a tone as would certainly put me in the
right. Not only was I successful in the execution of my project,
but the project itself produced the effect which I looked for and
intended that it should produce. The atmosphere of calumny
in which I had been for some time living cleared away. The
system of calumny was discontinued. Men were ashamed of
repeating what had been told to them; and I have reason to
believe, moreover, that intentions not short of criminal were
given up in consequence of remonstrances from some of the most
prudent of the party, who came forward in consequence of the
duel. I am afraid that the event itself shocked many good men.
But I am certain that the public interests at the moment required
that I should do what I did. Everything is now quiet; and in
Ireland we have full reason to be satisfied. We must, however,
lose no time in doing everything else that is possible to promote
the prosperity of that country." *

The Relief Bill came before the Lords on 31st March. The Relief
The most practised politicians could form no estimate of its Bill in the Lords.
prospects. The Princes were divided; the Bishops were
divided; the King made no secret of his hopes that the
measure would be thrown out, and he was bombarded by
innumerable petitions from Protestants in the country.
The speech of the Duke of Clarence, the heir presumptive
to the throne, had been strongly in favour of the bill, and the
Duke of Cumberland told the King that it was believed outside to represent his Majesty's real feelings. This made the
King very angry; in private audiences, to which he admitted
the heads of the Protestant party, he constantly represented
himself as having been misled and forced into measures
for relief of the Catholics, and he even went so far as to
write a letter to that effect to Lord Eldon, with a request
that it should not be published till after his (the King's)
death.†

* *Civil Despatches,* v. 585.        † *Salisbury MSS.*

" If I had known in January, 1828," wrote the Duke a few months later to Sir W. Knighton, "one tithe of what I do now and of what I discovered in one month after I was in office, I should never have been the King's Minister, and should have avoided loads of misery! However, I trust that God Almighty will soon determine that I have been sufficiently punished for my sins, and will relieve me from the unhappy lot which has befallen me. I believe there never was a man suffered so much ; and for so little purpose." *

The King told the Duke that he might have his way so far as passing the Emancipation Bill through Parliament, but that the Royal Assent would be withheld. This the Duke plainly told the King would be a dishonourable proceeding, both to Ministers and to the Opposition, seeing that the Coercion Bill had been allowed to pass only on the faith of the Emancipation Bill to follow. The King had no alternative but to fulfil his pledge or to find new Ministers, which, as even the Duke of Cumberland admitted, " could not be done in a few hours." †

*The Emancipation Bill in the Lords.* The Emancipation Bill came before the Lords for second reading on 2nd April; the division took place after three days' debate, in which Lord Eldon and the Archbishop of Canterbury led the opposition. The result justified Lord Clarendon's estimate of their lordships' discipline : the second reading was carried by a majority of 105—217 votes to 112. Out of twenty-nine Bishops voting, ten supported the bill. On 10th April the bill passed the third reading in the Lords ; it was taken down to Windsor on the 11th, returned on the 13th with the Royal Assent ; Parliament adjourned for the Easter holidays on the 16th, reassembled on the 28th, on which day, for the first time since the Revolution, Roman Catholic peers took the oaths and their seats in the House of Lords.

* *Civil Despatches,* vi. 294.  † *Ibid.*

# CHAPTER VIII.

## THE EVE OF REFORM.

### 1830–1831.

PERSONALLY, as well as politically, the Duke had to pay a heavy penalty for dealing with the Roman Catholic claims. Some of his oldest associates and political supporters ranged themselves against him; his Government was carried on by means of the precarious support of the Whigs; the solid earth seemed to have failed beneath the feet of the Old Tories when their champions, Wellington and Peel, turned aside from the course they had steered for so many years. Regarding these men merely as supporters, the Duke may be supposed to have endured the parting without

The Duke's position after the Emancipation Act.

Æt. 60. great pain. It was the cost reckoned in advance of carrying
on the King's Government in the only possible way. "The
party!" exclaimed he to Lady Salisbury when, on a later
occasion, she expressed apprehension of a split in the party,
"the party! What is the meaning of a party if they don't
follow their leaders? Damn 'em! let 'em go!" *

In respect, however, to some old comrades and personal
friends his feelings must have been acute, though it was
never his way to allow them outward expression. Lord
Anglesey, for instance, who, as Lord Uxbridge, had handled
the cavalry at Waterloo so ably, so gallantly, and with
such splendid effect, complained bitterly of his treatment. He
had been removed from the Lord Lieutenancy of Ireland for
undue encouragement to the Roman Catholic agitation; fifteen
days later the Government produced a measure conceding
the very object of that agitation. One cannot but sympathise
with his indignation; yet the Duke could not overlook
Anglesey's breach of duty in not administering the law as it
stood, instead of anticipating the proximate change therein.
The Duke cared nothing for popularity; he knew well that if
he had resisted the Roman Catholic claims, to quote his own
words, "he might have made himself the most popular
Minister that ever presided over the councils of a sovereign."
But genuinely as he despised the incense of the masses, he
was penetrated with a sense of duty in governing them justly
and temperately, and, having made up his mind that concession was just and for the advantage of the people, he
neither shrank from the cost nor complained at having to
pay it.

There was little at first to recompense Ministers for the
effort and sacrifice involved in the emancipation of Roman
Catholics. In Ireland the effect of conciliation was neutralised
by the discontent arising out of severe agricultural depression;
it was shorn of its grace by the refusal of the House of
Commons, on technical grounds, to allow O'Connell to take

* *Salisbury MSS.*, 1838.

his seat for Clare;* the small freeholders were sore at being Ann. 1830. disfranchised, the Protestants at being robbed of their supremacy. The practice of absenteeism became more general. From his earliest acquaintance with Irish politics Wellington had never ceased to deplore the effects of this evil; as head of the Government he was watchful in his endeavours to stem it.

*The Duke of Wellington to the Duke of Northumberland.*

"April, 1830.

" . . . If we cannot enforce residence in Ireland we must at least endeavour to encourage it, and this can be done only by prevailing upon the King to adhere to the rule of granting Irish offices, honours and distinctions only to those resident in that country. I have invariably adhered to this rule."† . . .

"7th July.

"I confess that the annually recurring starvation in Ireland for a period differing, according to the goodness or badness of the season, from one week to three months, gives me more uneasiness than any other evil existing in the United Kingdom. . . . It occurs every year for that period of time that elapses between the final consumption of one year's crop of potatoes, and the coming of the crop of the following year, and it is long or short according as the previous season has been bad or good. Now, when this misfortune occurs, there is no relief or mitigation, excepting a recourse to publick money. The proprietors of the country, those who ought to think for the people, to foresee this misfortune, and to provide beforehand a remedy for it, are amusing themselves in the clubs in London, in Cheltenham, or Bath, or on the Continent, and the Government are made responsible for the evil, and they must find the remedy for it where they can—anywhere excepting in the pockets of the Irish gentlemen. Then, if they give publick money to provide a remedy for this distress, it is applied to all purposes excepting

* Relief under the Act was limited to those Roman Catholic members who should be returned after it had become law.

† *Apsley House MSS.*

the one for which it is given ; and most particularly to that one, viz. the payment of the arrears of an exorbitant rent. . . . You may rely upon it that you have judged correctly in refraining from giving the publick money to relieve the existing distress. The Irish gentlemen of all ranks must be made to feel, or we shall never have a permanent remedy." *

In Great Britain, also, distress prevailed in many industries: at Rochdale, Manchester, Bethnal Green, and elsewhere there were formidable riots, and in agricultural districts wages sank to starvation level and poor rates were mounting to an alarming extent. Country gentlemen instinctively relied on the Tories to help them, for the Government was still Tory in name : their expectation was dashed when Parliament met on 4th February, 1830, by the cold comfort contained in the Speech which Ministers prepared for the King.

" It would be most gratifying to the paternal feelings of his Majesty to be enabled to propose measures calculated to relieve the difficulties of any portion of his subjects, and at the same time compatible with the general and permanent interests of his people. It is from a deep solicitude for these interests that his Majesty is impressed with the necessity of acting with extreme caution in reference to this important subject. His Majesty feels assured that you will concur with him in assigning due weight to the effect of unfavourable seasons, and to the operation of other causes which are beyond the reach of legislative control or remedy."

The resentment stirred by this chilly philosophical lecture took an unusual form. Fifteen years had passed since any amendment had been moved in Parliament upon the Speech from the Throne. In the Lords Lord Stanhope, in the Commons Mr. Knatchbull, Tory member for Kent, now moved amendments. The first was easily resisted by the help of the Whig peers; but the second was nearly fatal to the Duke's

* *Civil Despatches,* vii. 111.

administration. The Government Whips had made up their books for defeat, which was only averted by the sudden and unexpected accession of Lord Howick, son of Lord Grey, who, chiefly out of dislike of Brougham, carried with him Hume and the Radicals into the Ministerial lobby. Matters mended for a while after this escape, but the session was marked by the rise of a formidable financial critic in the person of Sir James Graham, who, an industrious student of Adam Smith's writings and an able exponent of economical principles, induced the Government to undertake a revision of salaries, establishments, and pensions with the object of retrenchment in expenditure. The result was that although the national defences were already, in the Duke of Wellington's opinion,* in a dangerously weakened condition, half a million was pared off the army estimates, and another half million off the estimates for the navy, ordnance, and miscellaneous service. The Government, however, in proposing to abolish some sinecures, thought it incumbent on them to provide pensions for those thrown out of office. Lord Bathurst drew a salary of nearly £4,000 a year as Teller of the Exchequer; Lord First de-Melville one of nearly £3,000 a year as Keeper of the Privy feat of the Seal in Scotland. Neither office entailed any work, nor was ment. it proposed to abolish either of them, yet when it *was* decided to abolish the office of Commissioner of the Navy, held by Lord Melville's son, and that of Commissioner of the Victualling Department, held by Lord Bathurst's son, the Treasury proposed that they should receive respectively pensions of £500 and £400 a year for life. Each official had only held his appointment for less than four years. This was too strong for the stomach even of an unreformed Parliament, and the votes were refused, against the Government, by a majority of sixteen.

The next defeat sustained by the Government, in resisting Second the introduction of a bill to admit Jews to Parliament, defeat of the Go-

* See his long and elaborate memorandum to Lord Goderich in 1827 (*Civil* vernment. *Despatches*, iv. 106).

Æт. 60. revealed to Wellington yet more clearly the disaffection of his old supporters. Peel was away at Drayton, attending his father's death-bed.

### The Duke of Wellington to the Right Hon. Robert Peel.

" London, 6th April, 1830.

"Goulburn will have written you an account of the disaster last night. It came upon me quite unexpected. As far as I could form a judgment from what I heard from others, as well as from what about sixty members of Parliament who dined with me on Saturday and Sunday said, I was inclined to think that we could not have carried the measure if we had wished it. It appears, however, not only that there are many of our friends in favour of it, but that, as usual, many, pretending that they did not like to oppose a measure for which they should afterwards be called upon to vote, etc., stayed away." *

The Ministry remained in office partly by grace of the Opposition and partly because of its disorganisation. When Tierney, the nominal leader of the Whigs in the House of Commons, died in January, 1830, the party, distrusting the more brilliant Brougham, chose Lord Althorpe to act at their head, who set to work in businesslike fashion to organise his forces. The state of the King's health, however, had the effect of protecting Ministers from a systematic attack.

The Duke's relations with George IV. The Duke of Wellington had obtained a great ascendency over George IV., who was by no means deficient in natural ability, though it was obscured and rendered capricious by his irregular habits of life. He could not fail to value the sterling qualities and unvarying sincerity of his servant. During the negociations for Canning's return to the Cabinet in 1822, in which the Duke took the foremost part, the King wrote to Lord Liverpool from Scotland, agreeing not to make up his mind about Canning till he saw his Ministers, but added in a postscript, "Upon no account delay a certain

* *Peel Letters.* ii. 145.

gentleman's departure for India," alluding to Canning's appointment as Governor-General. Lord Liverpool read this letter to his colleagues, suppressing the postscript. The other Ministers threatened to resign if Canning were not admitted.

" No," said the Duke, " we will not resign ; if possible, we will persuade the King to take Canning ; if not, we will do the best we can."

When the King heard this, he said to the Duke, " You are the only one who has treated me like a gentleman. I will follow your advice." *

The King, however, was always subject to the influence of a steadier will than his own ; intercourse with Canning had worked a great change on his feelings towards the Duke, which were greatly, and not unreasonably, embittered by the Duke's behaviour about the command of the army. Then came the Roman Catholic question, bringing on the scene the Duke of Cumberland, whose efforts to destroy the Duke of Wellington's influence were unceasing.† It has been shown above how far they were successful, but in his last illness King George conceived a dislike to the Duke of Cumberland, and it was with difficulty that Wellington persuaded his Majesty to see his brother. Unhappy King ! his last days were distraught with suspicion, and disquieted by considerations which one would fain dissociate from a death-bed. Wellington was witness of some strange incidents in the

---

* *Salisbury MSS.*

† In justice to the Duke of Cumberland it must be said that his motives in resisting the Duke were entirely founded on his own objections to Catholic emancipation. Writing to Colonel Cooke when the Duke first formed his administration, he said, "I look upon it as a most fortunate event for the country that His Majesty has made choice of the Duke of Wellington for the place of Premier ; for, if you remember, when I had the pleasure of seeing you here [Berlin] last summer, I then ventured to say that had I been in England this time last year, when that calamity befell our country of Lord Liverpool's illness, I would have exerted every possible means to have persuaded the Duke then to have accepted his present situation, which, depend upon it, *he* is completely able to fill ; for though not so *eloquent* as Mr. Canning, still, believe me, he is in everything else his *superior* " (*Civil Despatches,* iv. 262).

closing scenes.* It became necessary, as the King grew weaker, to obtain an Act of Parliament authorising his Majesty to use a stamp, instead of affixing the sign manual to papers submitted by his Ministers. The Duke went down to Windsor to propose this to the King, who said he was too ill to receive him. Sir Henry Halford then walked on the terrace for a while with the Duke. The King, hearing they were together, called his secretary, Sir William Knighton, and said—

"Go and see what that little snivelling fellow my physician has to say to my Prime Minister; find out, and bring me word. Mind you tell me the truth!"

Service was read every morning during these last weeks in the King's bedchamber, Lady C—— being present with others, and it was his Majesty's extraordinary fancy to pronounce the benediction himself at the close, as head of the Church of England. He sent word to Lady C—— by Sir William Knighton that he intended to leave her everything he had. When Sir William returned, "Well," said the King, "how did she receive it?"

"She was very much affected, sir," answered Knighton, "and burst into tears."

"Oh, she did, did she," was the King's reply; but although he lived six weeks longer, and although Lady C—— took care that pen and ink should always be at his bedside, the promised will was never made. The Duke of Wellington, who was very frequently at Windsor during his Majesty's illness, took every precaution that the will should not be executed.

Often it has been made the reproach of modern society that so much of its morality is conventional, but it requires an effort to realise that there was a good deal of conventional immorality also previous to the present reign. Puritan austerity never prevailed to purge continental courts and society to the extent it did in England and Scotland; with the Hanoverian dynasty there was imported a code and

* *Salisbury MSS.*

practice which European subjects had grown accustomed to accept as characteristic of monarchy. The great middle class in Britain continued to treat private irregularity as something disreputable, and the example of a pure domestic life set by George III. did much to endear that Sovereign to his people. Unfortunately the evil tradition was revived in the person of his son, who, during two-thirds of his father's long reign, maintained a rival Court according to the old and worst pattern. Royal licentiousness was not only winked at and condoned; receiving a kind of parliamentary sanction by the application of public money to the payment of the Prince Regent's debts, it assumed a semi-official character. Thus it had come to pass in his latter days that, although reduced by disease to a condition in which the orderly, quiet regimen of an invalid would have been natural and easy to George IV., he considered it inconsistent with his credit to be without a chief *liaison*, and scarcely less so to be without a rival. At first he professed to be jealous of Lord Ponsonby, but during his last illness he confided to the Duke of Wellington that his brother Cumberland was supplanting him in Lady C——'s affections. The King often complained, also, to the Duke about Lady C——'s covetousness; "but," said he, "at my age and with my infirmities it is not worth looking out for another."

Wellington's own morality in certain respects was far from rigid; but self-respect—pride, perhaps, were a fitter definition —made him keep his own foibles secret, and caused him to abhor cynical profligacy in others. George IV.'s habits were a severe trial to the Duke, though he admitted that his Majesty was often brilliantly witty in conversation. Of George III. he said to Lady Salisbury that he was the best The Duke's king England ever had, and understood kingcraft the most opinion of George III. thoroughly—a far superior man in real ability to his son, and George IV. though he had not the same quickness and talent. However, he had no scruple in throwing over his friends or his instruments whenever it suited his purpose. But Wellington

ÆT. 61. passed a very different and far severer judgment upon George IV., in terms which that King's harshest censors have scarcely exceeded. It avails not to repeat them, spoken as they were under the seal of intimate friendship; yet without a knowledge that they *were* spoken—that this judgment *was* pronounced—no man could rightly understand the nature of Wellington's loyalty to the Crown. Mistrusting the man and detesting his habits, the Duke never failed in duty to the monarch. Loyalty, esteem, and personal affection have gone hand-in-hand so long in this country, that no public man now living has ever been called upon to exercise the first without the support of the other sentiments. Statesmen are trained, or ought to be trained, to dissociate the Crown from the personal attributes of its wearer; yet in a period when thrones were shaking and institutions crumbling away all over Europe, the unpopularity of George IV. added no small burden to the responsibilities of his Ministers.

Death of George IV. The King's last moments were not without dignity. Waking shortly before three on the morning of 26th June, he complained of faintness, and his attendant physician, Sir Wathen Waller, prepared some sal volatile and water. His Majesty could not drink it, and Sir Henry Halford was sent for; but before he entered the room, the King pressed Sir Wathen's hands, saying, in a strong voice, "My boy, this is death." He never spoke again, but peacefully expired a few minutes later.

With the Duke of Clarence, who succeeded to the throne as William IV., Wellington had passed through some unpleasant experience, having had, as head of the King's Government, first to reprimand him sharply for the arbitrary exercise of his office of Lord High Admiral, and then to remove him from office altogether. The Duke, therefore, could scarcely expect that he should retain his Majesty's confidence; but King William was gifted with good temper, and acted with commendable dignity on assuming the Crown. Bygones with him were bygones; he continued his late brother's Ministers in office, and the Duke found him to be

Relations of the Duke with William IV.

a monarch far more worthy of confidence than George IV. Ann. 1830.
Moreover, William had done nothing to earn a share of the
late King's unpopularity; indeed, as a sailor he enjoyed that
kindly favour which the English people have always shown
to those who go down to the sea in ships. All this was well,
for the times were entering upon a troubled phase. A cyclone
of revolution was raging almost within sound of our shores. In
Paris, the attempt of Charles X. and his Minister Polignac ended
in the revolution of July, the abdication of the King on
2nd August, and the proclamation of Louis Philippe by the Revolu-
Provisional Government on the 7th. In Belgium, the union France and
with Holland imposed on the Belgians by the Congress of Belgium.
Vienna had never been a comfortable one. The affinities
of the Belgians were far more French than Dutch, and scenes
as violent as those in Paris began to be enacted in Brussels
on 25th August. All the chief towns in Belgium demanded
the dissolution of the union; the Prince of Orange, endeavouring to take possession of Brussels, was compelled
after four days of street fighting to withdraw his forces to
Antwerp. The King of Holland appealed to France and the
Allies; a conference of the representatives of the Great
Powers, held in London on 4th November, decreed an armistice
and the withdrawal of all Dutch troops from Belgium, and
the Belgian people obtained their independence.

In these disturbances the Duke of Wellington's efforts
were consistently directed to the maintenance of constituted
authority. Canning had created a popular interest in British
foreign policy which it had never possessed before, by imparting thereto a novel character sympathetic with the
general revolt against autocracy, a revolt to which Wellington, though a constitutional Minister and faithful to the
British constitution as he knew it, would lend no assistance.
Liberal institutions, even in the limited sense of pre-reform
days, were well enough for Englishmen, but he disbelieved
in their safety for Continental nations. Canning had exerted
himself to obtain good terms for the Greeks, and had inspired

many of his countrymen with a generous sympathy for that race with all its noble associations: Wellington, on the contrary, disapproved of Canning's Greek policy;* the dominant note of his own was the same which, to this day, jars so discordantly on Liberal ears, and was concisely expressed in one of his Cabinet memoranda in November, 1830. "The policy of the British Government has invariably been to prevent the overthrow of the Turkish Power in Europe, and the substitution for it of a Russian Power or a Power under Russian influence at Constantinople." †

The Duke had been the principal figure in the group which rearranged the map of Europe in 1815; he had been the chief agent in making such a rearrangement possible, and was not disposed to have any hand in disturbing it out of consideration for national or social aspirations; Legitimists and Conservatives all over the Continent drew courage from

Beginning of the Duke's un- popularity. his position as Minister of England. For the same reason, even before the first tremours of the great convulsion of Reform made themselves felt, the popular party in Britain had been gradually learning to look upon him as their implacable foe. Lord Durham, who owed his peerage to Wellington's confirmation of Goderich's recommendation,‡ wrote to Brougham about the "odious, insulting, aide-de-campish, incapable dictatorship," and the struggles for freedom in foreign nations communicated an impulse to discontent and desire for change in the British and Irish constituencies, which augured ill for the prospects of the Government in the elections. Added to all this was the

---

* "It may be safely said by anybody that I did not approve of the Treaty (of Adrianople). The truth is that I did everything I could to prevail upon Mr. Canning not to enter into the Treaty; and he certainly negociated it, as far as the negociations went before the illness and secession of Lord Liverpool, without the knowledge of any of his colleagues except myself. But they and we all are highly blamable for having suffered the negociation to move at all after we had, and particularly I had, a knowledge of it" (Letter to Dean Philpotts: *Civil Despatches*, vii. 170).

† *Civil Despatches*, vii. 335.          ‡ *Ibid.*, iv. 188.

prevailing distress, arising, not as in 1816, 1819, and 1822 A.D. 1830.
from the dearness of breadstuffs, but from their relative
cheapness, which caused farmers to cut down wages, and
to the substitution of machinery for hand labour.

The Duke was fully aware of the weakness of his position, The Duke
and the necessity for reinforcing it by inducing the Canning- proposes to resign.
ites to re-enter the Cabinet; but he could not bring himself
to invite them back himself.

"I think we could get on in the House of Lords," he wrote to
Peel on 30th June; "the question is, what is to be done in the
House of Commons? I have as little feeling of political
animosity as any man, but I don't think that I personally could
or ought to sit in a Cabinet again as First Lord of the Treasury
with Mr. Huskisson,[*] Lord Palmerston, or Mr. Charles Grant.
In considering this matter you and I must not look to what is
personal to ourselves, but what is necessary for the King's service,
and we must make sacrifices to provide for its security. I have
long been of opinion that it is desirable that the power of the
Government should be concentrated in one hand, and that hand
that of the leader of the House of Commons. The affairs of the
country cannot now be otherwise conducted with advantage, and
I know of no person so capable of conducting them as yourself.
I would earnestly urge, therefore, that I should take the
opportunity of the King's death to retire from office; that you
should undertake the Government as First Lord of the Treasury
and Chancellor of the Exchequer, forming your Government as
you may think proper, in the several offices. I would support or
serve any Government that you might form."[†]

The weakness of the Government became more apparent
after the elections. The Tories, indeed, came back from the
country in a majority; but the Old Tories had learnt to
distrust Wellington and Peel, and were almost more hostile

---

[*] Six weeks later Mr. Huskisson was killed in the presence of the Duke and
Sir Robert Peel at the opening of the Liverpool and Manchester Railway. He
had left his seat in the train to shake hands with the Duke, and in returning to
it, tripped and fell before a passing engine.

[†] *Civil Despatches*, vii. 108.

than the Whigs. Affairs on the Continent had given a
notable impetus to the demand for parliamentary reform and
an extension of the franchise. The Birmingham Political
Union had taken its rise out of a gathering early in 1830
of a few persons who desired to repeal the Act of 1819,
which established cash payments. Under the leadership of
Mr. Attwood, whom Huskisson denounced as an agitator
scarcely less formidable than O'Connell, this organisation
acquired power and activity in an amazingly short space of
time. It requires an effort to remember that under the
constitution which gave two members to a corrupt little
village like Penryn, and representation to many other places
equally insignificant, Birmingham and Manchester, the chief
centres of industrial activity in the country, were still un-
represented in Parliament. As the first step, then, towards
obtaining their desires in regard to the currency, these
gentlemen turned their efforts to creating a demand for
equitable representation. The agitation—a perfectly constitutional one—spread like a prairie fire. Political unions on
similar lines sprang into existence all over the kingdom; it
was obvious to Wellington that in order to resist the movement, to which he had no intention of yielding, he must
strengthen his Ministry.

It was not so obvious to the Whigs and the public that
the Minister who had carried Roman Catholic emancipation
would prove inflexible about Reform; accordingly, Mr.
Arbuthnot became the bearer of important overtures from
the Opposition to the Government. Already, in July, Wellington had overcome his dislike of the Canningites so far
as to sound Melbourne and Palmerston upon the feasibility
of *rapprochement*, but had received no encouragement.*

* "The Duke told me," wrote Lady Salisbury in her journal, 22nd October,
1832, " that he had never regretted but one of the steps he took previous to leaving
office in 1830, which was—making an overture to Lord Palmerston to join him
with the Canningites. Peel insisted upon it, saying that otherwise he could
not go on in the House of Commons, and the Duke saw Lord Palmerston, but

Now, with the result of the general election before them, A.N. 1830. it was the other side who reopened negociations. Mr. Littleton * came to Arbuthnot on 1st November, and assured him that all that was necessary to secure the adhesion of Palmerston, Stanley,† Graham, and Grant was a satisfactory understanding on five points, namely, the Civil List, the Regency (in the event of King William's demise), the China trade, Parliamentary Reform, and the abolition of pluralities.

"Upon the subject of Parliamentary Reform the whole difficulty would turn. He (Mr. Littleton) could hardly suppose that the Duke of Wellington was not aware that the general sense of the country was now in favour of a moderate Reform, and he knew that strength to the Government could be obtained by consenting to Lord J. Russell's plan, or even to the giving members now to the three great towns, and hereafter to other great towns, whenever there should be such proof of corruption as would cause the disfranchisement of some borough. . . . In conclusion, he informed me," continues Arbuthnot, "that he had been commissioned by Lady Stafford to say to the Duke of Wellington that unless a moderate Parliamentary Reform was intended by the Government, Lord Stafford and all belonging to him must go into opposition." †

The above is an extract from Arbuthnot's letter to Peel, who must have shown it to Wellington, and taken counsel with him upon it; yet is there not the slightest reference to these friendly overtures in the correspondence of either statesman. On the very next day, the door held open so amicably, so The Duke reasonably, was violently slammed in the face of the friendly puts down his foot.

---

found his expectations were too high to be complied with. He not only proposed to bring in Melbourne and the Grants, but also Lord Grey and the Whigs; his expression was that there should be a considerable change both of measures and men " (*Salisbury MSS.*).

* Created Baron Hatherton in 1835; married a natural daughter of Richard, Marquess Wellesley.

† Afterwards 14th Earl of Derby, the "Rupert of debate."

‡ *Peel Letters*, ii. 103.

section of the Opposition by the Duke himself. The Speech from the Throne was under discussion in the House of Lords: it contained an ominous reference to the revolution in Belgium, and indicated that Great Britain probably would have to interfere to defend the Netherlands monarchy by force of arms.

"You see," said Lord Grey, leader of the Opposition in the Lords, "the danger around you: the storm is on the horizon, but the hurricane approaches. Begin, then, at once to strengthen your houses, to secure your windows, and to make fast your doors. The mode in which this must be done, my lords, is by securing the affections of your fellow-subjects, and — I will pronounce the word—by reforming Parliament."

The Duke could never compare with Grey in eloquence, nobody expected it of him; yet in statecraft there were many, especially in that assembly, who assigned to him a high place. Their hearts were chilled by the concluding sentences of his reply—those in which he dealt with his opponents.

"The noble earl has been candid enough to acknowledge that he is not prepared with any measure of reform, and I can have no scruple in saying that his Majesty's Government is as totally unprepared with any plan as the noble lord. Nay, I, on my own part, will go further and say that I have never read or heard of any measure up to the present moment which can in any degree satisfy my mind that the state of the representation can be improved, or be rendered more satisfactory than at the present moment. . . . I do not hesitate to declare unequivocally what my sentiments are. I am fully convinced that the country already possesses a legislature which answers all the purposes of good legislation. . . . I will go further and say that the legislature and the system of representation possesses the full and entire confidence of the country. . . . I will go still further and say that if at the present moment I had imposed on me the duty of forming a legislature for any country, and particularly for a country like this, in possession of great property of various descriptions, I do not mean to assert that I could form such a legislature as you possess now, for the nature of man is incapable

of reaching such excellence at once; but my great endeavour Ann. 1830.
would be to form some description of legislature which would
produce the same results. . . . I am not only not prepared to
bring in any measure of the description alluded to by the noble
lord, but I will at once declare that, as far as I am concerned,
as long as I hold any station in the Government of the country,
I shall always feel it my duty to resist such measures when
proposed by others."

The Duke's vehemence was owing, no doubt, in some
measure to his indignation at a taunt thrown out by Lord
Grey that he had been intimidated into concession to the
Roman Catholics.

" I really do not see the advantage of repeating against me
the reproach of my having given way upon the Catholic question
from motives of fear. I deny that I have been influenced, even in
the very slightest degree, by any such motive. I gave way, if it
can be termed giving way, solely because the interests of the
country required it. I urged the question upon the views of policy,
and expediency, and justice, upon these grounds I now justify the
measure, and upon these grounds I shall ever defend my conduct."

" I have not said too much, have I ? " asked the Duke of
Lord Aberdeen as he sat down.
" You'll hear of it ! " was the brief but pregnant reply.
Having pronounced his challenge the Duke flinched not The
from the conflict. With prompt military instinct he drew gauntlet
up a plan for the defence of Apsley House,* and directed thrown.
effective measures for putting down meetings which he
regarded as seditious; that they assumed a seditious character under the menace of repression was inevitable, but
neither Lyndhurst nor Peel seem to have possessed greater
prescience than the Duke of the force and justice of the
movement. They apprehended violence, indeed, and by a
strange fatality the first act of the Ministry, denounced by
Lord Wellesley, now amongst the severest critics of his

* *Civil Despatches,* vii. 354.

brother's administration, as "the boldest act of cowardice he had ever heard of," gave encouragement to lawlessness. The King and Queen had accepted the invitation of the Lord Mayor-elect to the annual banquet on 9th November. On Saturday the 7th the Lord Mayor-elect wrote to Wellington advising him to come with a strong escort: a Cabinet was immediately summoned to deliberate on this letter, and adopted the Duke's advice that the royal visit to the City should be postponed. Something like a panic was the result; the funds had already dropped 4 per cent. since the Duke's speech in the Lords; they fell further 3 per cent. on the morning of Lord Mayor's Day. In the end the disturbances in the metropolis proved so trifling that Ministers had to stand ridicule, more deadly to an administration than any hatred, for their unfounded apprehensions. The fate of the Government was imminent, but it was winged from an unexpected quarter. Brougham had given notice of a motion for Reform on 16th November, and the Whips on each side were diligent marshalling forces for a full-dress debate; but on the 15th a division, taken on an amendment moved by Sir Henry Parnell, an Irish member, on the Civil List, was carried against the Government by a majority of 29. Had the Duke been never so anxious to retain office he could not have done so in face of this defeat. It was no snap division—the numbers were 233 to 204; Radicals, Canningites, and Tories, even the Duke's own nephew, Wellesley Pole, voted in the majority.

*The Duke of Wellington to the Duke of Northumberland.*

"London, 16th November, 1830.

"MY DEAR DUKE,—After the decision in the House of Commons last night, which unequivocally shows the indisposition of the House towards the existing Government, you will not be surprised that we should have determined to retire from the King's service. . . . The King has, from the moment of his accession to this moment, conducted himself towards his Government in the most admirable manner; and the only regret I feel

is that I am under the necessity of quitting his service in times ANN. 1830.
of such difficulty abroad as well as at home."

The Duke quitted office in the dusk of discredit and under Resigna-
the chill disapproval of all parties. tion of<br>Ministers.

"The effect produced by this declaration exceeds anything I ever saw, and has at once destroyed what little popularity the Duke had left, and lowered him in public estimation so much that, when he does go out of office, as most assuredly he must, he will leave it without any of the dignity and credit which might have accompanied his retirement." *

His old followers stood aloof, alienated by what they resented as their betrayal on the Roman Catholic question; he disdained to attract new ones by adopting the natural consequence of his first act of reform, in taking up and dealing with the demand for extended electoral rights and in purging the electoral system, as he was ready to do a few months afterwards, when, late in time, he came to recognise the inevitable.

The most painful consequence arising immediately out of this crisis as regarding the Duke of Wellington was the estrangement which it brought about between him and the ablest and faithfullest of his colleagues, Sir Robert Peel.

"There's that fellow in the House of Commons," quoth the Duke to Lady Salisbury; "one can't go on without him; but he is so vacillating and crotchetty that there's no getting on with him. I did pretty well with him when we were in office, but I can't manage him now at all. He is a wonderful fellow—has a most correct judgment—talents almost equal to those of Pitt, but he spoils all by his timidity and indecision." †

As to the coldness of some of his other friends, the Duke professed absolute indifference.

"There is nobody," he wrote to Lady Salisbury, "who cares so little as I do for an embarrassment such as you describe. I meet

---

* *Greville*, part i. vol. ii. p. 53.     † *Salisbury MSS.*, 1831.

with it every day, and I proceed as if there were no such embarrassment, and no such persons existing as those who do not speak to me. The truth is that when people differ with me in politics they think proper not to speak to me or to observe towards me the common forms of society. They are then very angry and very awkward because I don't care one pin, and do not put myself out of the way either to alter my relations with them, or to render those relations less embarrassing to them. . . . I have sent a song for Lady Catherine Grimston. This is not *the* song, for which I have written; but I send it in order to prove to her that I have not forgotten my promise." *

**Lord Grey forms a Ministry.** The King having laid his commands on Lord Grey, a new Cabinet was formed on a comprehensive basis, including the Duke of Richmond, Lords Goderich and Palmerston from the Conservative ranks, Lords Lansdowne and Holland from the Whigs, and Lord Durham and Sir James Graham from the Radicals. Brougham was muzzled by raising him to the woolsack with the title of Lord Brougham and Vaux—*vox et præterea nihil*, as the wits had it.

**The First Reform Bill.** It is unnecessary to dwell in detail upon the successive bills introduced by the Government in fulfilment of their pledges of reform. The Tories, whose votes had expelled the last Ministry, listened with wry faces as Lord John Russell expounded the sweeping provision of the bill introduced on 21st March, 1831. The bill passed second reading by a majority of a single vote; but Ministers, defeated by 8 votes on a motion upon going into Committee upon it, sustained a second defeat the following night, when the House of Commons refused by 164 votes to 142 to grant supply, and requested his Majesty to dissolve Parliament.

They did more. They induced the King to come to the House of Lords in person, and to deliver a speech from the Throne explaining that he dissolved Parliament "for the purpose of ascertaining the sense of my people in the way in which it may be most constitutionally and authentically

* *Salisbury MSS.*, 9th December, 1832.

expressed, on the expediency of making such changes in the Ann. 1831.
representation as circumstances may seem to require."

Great was the Duke of Wellington's disgust at what he
considered the King's act of desertion; but his attention was
withdrawn from public affairs at this juncture, and from the
frantic jubilation which convulsed the nation at the announcement that Parliament was to be dissolved, by an event in his
own household. The mob in London decreed a general Apsley House
illumination of London to take place on the night of 27th assaulted
April, and proceeded to enforce their will by breaking the by the Reform
windows of Tory peers and others who declined to comply. mob.
Apsley House, a conspicuous feature in one of the main
thoroughfares, stood dark and still without a sign of rejoicing:
it was not to be expected that its proud owner would stoop to
gain security by simulating sympathy which he did not feel,
and volleys of stones began to crash through the windows.
Some of the new police * were on duty on the spot, all too
few and feeble to interfere by force; but force was not
required. An English mob is seldom unkindly or cruel; the
police managed to inform the leaders that the Duchess of
Wellington had died two days before, and that her body lay
at that moment within the house. Immediately the crowd
desisted from their mischief, moving off to smash Lord
Londonderry's windows in Park Lane.

The Duke was with his wife when she died. Their Death of the
married life leaves little matter for mention. It had not Duchess of
been unhappy, but it had been very far from ideal. Warmly Welling-ton.
affectionate, as Maria Edgeworth delighted to testify, and
worshipping her husband to the end, the Duchess had not the
mental qualities on which that husband could rely for light
in perplexity or support in stress of action. A more serious
defect was her want of tact, a gift which often serves women

---

* There never was a more thoroughly popular force than the London Police
has become, yet the names "Bobby" and "Peeler" are not unfamiliar even at
this day, reminding us of the dislike and ridicule attached to the creation of
Sir Robert Peel.

ÆT. 61. in place of higher attributes. If there was one thing for
which the Duke had more aversion than another it was being
"shown off;" yet the Duchess never learnt to avoid it, and
delighted in drawing attention to his great qualities and
achievements. They formed a couple wholly unsuited to
each other, and it avails not to scrutinise or criticise their
relations more closely. It would be idle to pretend that the
parting brought deep grief to the Duke; it is not so referred
to in any of his correspondence; indeed, there never was a
wife, in her death as in her life, of whom her husband made
such rare mention in his letters. To Lady Salisbury, indeed,
who, with the exception, perhaps, of the Arbuthnots, was at
this time and continued to be till her death his most intimate
correspondent and confidante, the Duke did impart a very
frank explanation of his infelicitous experience of married
life; of the Duchess's extravagance, of her insincerity towards
himself about the amount of her debts, about her flightiness
and injudicious treatment of her sons; and these observations
are preserved in Lady Salisbury's journal.* But they were
spoken several years after the Duchess's death; during her
life the Duke never mentioned or treated her but with
respect, and it would serve no good purpose to resuscitate
slumbering *griefs*. Wellington's life, with all its stir and
unceasing activity, was a lone one; his sense of having missed
something in the lottery of marriage is revealed by a casual
remark in one of his conversations. Lady Salisbury asked
him whether Lady Peel had any influence over Sir Robert.

"No," he replied; "she is not a clever woman: Peel had
no wish to marry a clever woman."

"It is very curious," remarked Lady Salisbury, "that a
man of ability should not care to have a wife capable of
entering into subjects in which he takes an interest."

"Aye," said the Duke, "and of anticipating one's meaning;
that is what a clever woman does—she sees what you
mean." †

* *Salisbury MSS.*, 1837.          † *Ibid.*, 1834.

# CHAPTER IX.

## THE BATTLE OF REFORM.

### 1831–1834.

IN no uncertain tone came the reply of the constituencies to the appeal of a general election. Lord John Russell introduced his Second Reform Bill to the new Parliament on 24th June: on 8th July it received a second reading by a majority of 136 votes; and on 22nd September, after the Coronation of King William had taken place * on the 8th, it was laid before the House of Lords. The Duke felt no doubts as to the course he should pursue as leader of the Opposition in the Upper Chamber.

* William IV. was the first English king crowned in trousers;!

ÆT. 62.    "I shall certainly vote," he wrote to Mr. Gleig, "against the second reading of the bill, and shall do everything in my power to prevail upon the largest possible number of Peers to do the same, and throw it out if I can. I am convinced that any Reform of Parliament upon the principle of this bill will destroy this great country. No evil can arise from the rejection of the bill at all equal to that which will arise from carrying it." *

In opposing the bill in the memorable debate of 3rd October, the Duke took his chief stand on the constitutional objection to the course pursued by Ministers of appealing to the country, not on a general principle—for the principle of reform had been affirmed by the late House of Commons—but on the question of a particular plan of reform.

"I charge the noble lords with having excited the spirit which existed in the country at the period of the last general election; and with having been the cause of the unconstitutional practice, hitherto unknown, of electing delegates for a particular purpose to Parliament—delegates to obey the daily instructions of their constituents, and to be cashiered if they should disobey them. . . . This is an evil of which the country will long feel the consequences, whatever may be the result of these discussions."

He persisted in regarding all reform as an attack on the constitution, and not as an attempt to amend and develop it.

"My noble friend (the Earl of Harrowby) regretted that I should have made the statement I did make to your lordships of the character and conduct of Parliament. My lords, I beg my noble friend to recollect that, when I spoke of Parliament, I spoke as the King's Minister, and that it is the duty of the King's Minister to support the institutions of the country: it had never, when I was in office, been the practice for the King's Ministers to give up the institutions of the country and abandon them the moment they were attacked."

The division took place at six o'clock on the morning of 8th

* *Civil Despatches*, vii. 473.

October. By 199 votes to 158 the peers threw out the bill,
and the country was immediately convulsed from end to end
by an agitation of terrible violence. Macaulay's words—" I
know only two ways in which societies can be governed—by
public opinion and by the sword "—had not been spoken
many days before the reality of the alternative they described
was being realised. The history of 1831–32 contains ample
evidence that anarchy, triumphant in Bristol, in Nottingham,
and in many places in the north, was no more than matched
in others by the armed forces of the Crown. The miserable
condition of the country was intensified by the appearance of
a novel disorder—the cholera, which, breaking out in London
in February, 1832, is believed to have carried off 50,000
victims in the United Kingdom before the end of the year.

Wellington continued blind to the genuine force and depth
of the cry for Reform; he suspected it to be partly manufactured by collusion between the Cabinet and the political
unions at Birmingham and elsewhere. "You forget," he
wrote to Lord Wharncliffe, "that the King and his Government have been apparently in a combination with the mob
for the destruction of property."* He believed that the true
sense of the country was opposed to Reform.

"I am quite certain," he wrote in another letter to Lord
Wharncliffe, "that I am well informed that the gentlemen and
better description of yeomanry and others possessing property
in this intelligent and opulent county (Kent), and in Hampshire,
are against these measures. I believe I could name as many as
a dozen others in this part of England. If I am not misinformed,
there is no small reaction in Scotland; and in Ireland the
Protestants are to a man against any change."

Fallacious as was the interpretation he put upon the signs
of the times, still more so, though more pardonably, was the
Duke's forecast of the future.

* *Civil Despatches,* viii. 99.

"If we take the bill or even give improvements of it, as I understand it, you may rely upon it that neither Lord Grey nor any nobleman of his order, nor any gentleman of his caste, will govern the country six weeks after the Reformed Parliament will meet, and that the race of English gentlemen will not last long afterwards. That is my sincere opinion, founded upon what I see here and have seen elsewhere, and I earnestly recommend it to your attention." *

With truer prescience Lord Wharncliffe and Lord Harrowby were negociating with Lord Grey for a compromise. The initiative had been with Lord Grey, but there were many Conservative peers—" Waverers " they were called—anxious to anticipate the irresistible and avoid further collision. Long, patiently, and eloquently Lord Wharncliffe laboured to prevail on the Duke to listen to reason ; his letters are truly statesmanlike and deserve careful perusal,† but his efforts were in vain. The Duke remained obdurate.

"I don't believe," he admitted on 3rd February, 1832, "that we can go on without some Parliamentary Reform ; but the passion for Reform, and particularly for *the bill*, no longer rages, whatever may have passed at the meetings in the autumn : the fashion is gone by ; and I firmly believe that when the bill passes, if ever it should pass, it will be to be forced upon the country. But as for civil war or any confusion being caused by another rejection of the bill, I'll answer for it that there will be no such thing if this Government, or any Government, will only perform the duty of discountenancing it." ‡

" Lord Wharncliffe's communications with the Government are at an end," he wrote to Lord Londonderry. " Why, or what passed, I know not. But I conclude that he found the Radical party too strong for him. You may rely on it that I neither have nor shall have any communication with the Government,

---

* *Civil Despatches*, viii. 110.
† *Ibid.*, viii. 92, 104, 110, 173, 210. et passim.
‡ *Ibid.*, viii. 206.

excepting in the way of advice in Parliament or through the A<small>NN.</small> 1831. King." *

Earlier in the year Lord Salisbury had written to consult the Duke about the course he should pursue in prospect of a meeting of Whigs and moderate Reformers about to be held in Hertford. He himself was disposed to attend the meeting and negociate with them.

"I should not like, however, to be the first to adopt the course I have suggested without your concurrence, for fear, if the example is followed, it should embarrass you or your party." †

The Duke's reply was the reverse of favourable to compromise.

"All reform is in my opinion bad and dangerous, and every reform would end by being Radical. I should think that a question of universal suffrage being carried against you at Hertford would not look well." ‡

Parliament, prorogued on 20th October, met again on 6th December. On the 12th Lord John Russell introduced his Third Reform Bill. It passed second reading by a majority of two to one. After an ordeal of twenty-two sittings in Committee, it left the House of Commons on 23rd March, and came before the Lords on the 26th. Early in the autumn the King had been urged by Brougham, Durham, and Graham to exercise his prerogative in the creation of enough peers to ensure the safety of the measure. His Majesty, though desiring a settlement of the great question, was averse from taking that course; so were the Government leaders in both Houses; indeed, Lord Grey's dislike to any scheme of swamping the Lords had been the origin of his overtures for a compromise with the Opposition. But when the overtures failed, Grey reluctantly fell back on the exercise of the prerogative, and the King gave his assent. The intention

The Third Reform Bill.

* *Civil Despatches,* viii. 119.     † *Salisbury MSS.,* January. 1831.     ‡ *Ibid.*

ÆT. 62.

Read a
second
time in the
Lords.

was suffered to get wind; the Waverers, anxious to save their order from the indignity which menaced it, assured the Government, through Lords Wharncliffe and Harrowby, that they would vote for the second reading, which was carried on 6th April by a majority of nine.

The Waverers had saved the measure, but by such a slender margin that Ministers could entertain no hopes of their fledgling bill surviving the perils of Committee. The result

Ministers
defeated in
Com-
mittee.

justified their worst apprehensions. On the first evening after the Easter recess, the Government was beaten on Lord Lyndhurst's motion to postpone the clauses disfranchising the small boroughs. On 8th May the Cabinet advised the King to create enough peers (fifty, according to Greville, who was Clerk of the Council; sixty or eighty, according to Brougham, who was in the Cabinet) "as might ensure the success of the bill in all its essential principles." His Majesty, whose favour towards the measure had cooled since the second reading, refused to act on the advice of his Ministers, who forthwith resigned on the 9th, and then, if it may be permitted to use a homely Scots expression, "the kail was in the reek" with a vengeance. The King sent for Lord Lyndhurst, who advised him to send for a Minister who should be prepared for a moderate measure of Reform. The King, however, considered his honour pledged to an extensive measure, and Lyndhurst, assenting, conveyed his Majesty's

The Duke
undertakes
to form a
Govern-
ment.

pleasure to the Duke of Wellington. Now, the Duke, at each successive stage in the fight for Reform, had pledged himself more deeply and vehemently against it; and, lest there should be any doubt of his sentiments, he reiterated his objection in the following remarkable letter :—

*The Duke of Wellington to Lord Lyndhurst.*

"10th May, 1832, 10 p.m.

"I shall be very much concerned indeed if we cannot at least make an effort to enable the King to shake off the trammels of

his tyrannical Minister. I am perfectly ready to do whatever his ANN. 1832.
Majesty may command me. I am as much averse to the Reform
as ever I was. No embarrassment of that kind, no private
consideration, shall prevent me from making every effort to serve
the King." *

He was "as much averse to the Reform as ever he was,"
yet to save the Peers from the indignity of being swamped and
to carry on the King's Government, he was able to sink his
own convictions, swallow his repeated declarations, and take
office on the understanding that he would carry an *extensive*
measure of Reform. The undertaking failed, as one is forced
to admit it deserved to fail. The Duke first approached Sir
Robert Peel.

"I foresee," wrote Sir Robert to Croker, "that a Bill of
Reform, including everything that is really important and really
dangerous in the present Bill, must pass. For me individually
to take the conduct of such a Bill, to assume the responsibility
of the consequences, which I have predicted as the inevitable
result of such a Bill, would be, in my opinion, personal degradation
to myself. . . . I look beyond the exigency and peril of the
present moment, and I do believe that one of the greatest
calamities that could befal the country would be the utter want
of confidence in the declarations of public men which must follow
the adoption of the Bill of Reform by me as a Minister of the
Crown. It is *not* a repetition of the Catholic question. I was
then in office. I had advised the concession as a Minister. I
should now assume office for the purpose of carrying the measure
to which up to the last moment I have been inveterately
opposed." †

Notwithstanding his own feelings on the subject, Peel paid
a tribute afterwards in the House of Commons to the integrity
of the Duke's motives.

"It was precisely on the same grounds, a sense of personal
honour, that I could not take office to carry on the Reform Bill.

* *Civil Despatches*, viii. 304.        † *Peel Letters*, ii. 205.

These opinions separated me from some noble friends of mine, who did not feel themselves placed in the same situation. I regret that separation, even though it be temporary, particularly the separation from that man whom I chiefly honour; and I am anxious to declare that even that separation has only raised him in my esteem." *

Foiled in obtaining Peel to lead the House of Commons, the Duke next tried Baring, who declined on the score of health, though he afterwards accepted office without the leadership. The Speaker, Mr. Manners Sutton, was Wellington's next hope, whose reply was friendly, but not reassuring. "If *no other* arrangement *can* be made, I must give way, though with fear and trembling."† It soon became evident that the Duke had attempted the impossible in undertaking to form a Tory Government with an Opposition of nearly two to one in the House of Commons. Better for his reputation had he never set hand to the task. On Monday, 14th May, Sir Robert Inglis declared in the House of Commons that he knew no difference between a code of public and private morals, and deplored the Duke's conduct in taking up a measure which on every previous occasion he had vehemently reprobated. Inglis spoke with the greater effect because of the evident pain he suffered in condemning his own leaders.

Peel at once declared the speech to be decisive against any attempt to form a Reform Government out of the anti-Reform party. The House rose at shortly before midnight, when the Speaker took Peel, Hardinge, and Croker in his carriage to Apsley House, where they were joined by Baring. An earnest consultation was held, lasting till nearly three in the morning, as to the course to be taken to save the King from being forced to create peers. At last, on Sir Robert Peel's motion, it was agreed that the Duke should inform the King that to form a Tory administration, pledged to extensive reform, was impossible, and that to save his Majesty's personal honour in

---

* *Peel Letters,* ii. 207.    † *Civil Despatches,* viii. 315.

the matter of creating peers, the Duke would abstain, so far
as he was concerned, from opposing the bill in the House of
Lords." * At nine o'clock the Duke went to Lord Lyndhurst
and informed him that he was going to the King to throw up
his commission. When he was gone, Lyndhurst said to his
wife, "I wish I had prevailed on him to consult with his
party first. I will go after him and detain him."

"You had better start at once," said Lady Lyndhurst, "or
he will be gone."

"Plenty of time," replied Lyndhurst; "he must go home
first, and he has to breakfast."

But when Lord Lyndhurst arrived at Apsley House the
Duke was gone. Following him to St. James' Palace, he found
that he had just been admitted to audience with the King,
and the fate of the Tory Ministry was sealed. Lord Lyndhurst
was admitted, however, and was present with the Duke while
his Majesty, with perfect composure, wrote his letter to Lord
Grey, after which he began to talk about trifling and indifferent
matters.†

From their places in the House of Lords the Duke and
Lord Lyndhurst on 17th May made explanatory statements,
and quitted the House, followed by a large number of Tory
peers, thus silently protesting against the measure which
they had decided to oppose actively no longer.

How Lord Grey's Whig Ministry came in and carried their
bill is part of the public history of the country; it is a
page which the biographer of Wellington is fain to turn
quickly, for the Duke's action at this crisis is the part of
his conduct one dwells on with least admiration. His own
defence of it comes nearer to casuistry than anything to
which he ever lent himself before or afterwards, and contrasts
ill with Peel's *meâ virtute me involvo.*

"I think that the mistake made by my friends is this: First,
in not estimating the extent of the advantage of taking the King

---

* *Croker.* ii. 167.        † *Salisbury MSS.,* 1832.

out of the hands of the Radicals *—that is, in reality, of giving the country the benefit of some Government ; secondly, in not estimating the further advantage of diminishing the mischief of the Reform Bill, and particularly that of the Scotch Bill.   In my opinion the advantage first mentioned more than compensates for all that would have been lost by our having anything to say to the Reform Bill." †

Yet on the very next day, 22nd May, the Duke was writing to Lord Eldon—

"I have always considered the Reform Bill as fatal to the Constitution of this country.   It was a matter of indifference whether the House of Peers should be first destroyed by the creation of Peers to carry the bill, or should fall with the other institutions of the country." ‡

*The Duke's great unpopularity.* The gloomy anticipations entertained by the Duke were deepened, and to some extent justified, by the attitude of the people towards himself.   From the pinnacle of fame and popularity he had been lowered to the depth of odium. Coarse reproach and bloodthirsty menace were yelled at him from the very throats which, only a few years before, had ached with unceasing cheers.   His matchless services to King and Country were forgotten : for many months he had continued to receive warnings of the danger in which he went of his life ; warnings which he put aside lightly enough, although causing the ground-floor windows of Apsley House to be protected by iron shutters, organising a complete system of domestic defence, and, when travelling, carrying loaded firearms in his carriage.

*The Duke of Wellington to the Countess of Jersey.*

"London, October 13, 1831.

"MY DEAR LADY JERSEY,—My House having been surrounded by a Mob all day yesterday, I don't think that I should have

* A sentiment which, after the lapse of a generation, Lord Derby expressed more bluntly in regard to his own and Disraeli's Reform Bill—that "it had dished the Whigs."

† *Civil Despatches*, viii. 340.　　　　　‡ *Ibid.*, 341.

acted very discreetly if I had gone out and had led it to yours, nor would my visit have been very agreeable to you under the circumstances. I knew that you dined out yesterday. I concluded that you would be out in the Evening. It is really quite impossible for me to fix a time to go out to see you. My House is constantly surrounded. It is so at this moment. I am followed wherever I go, and there a Mob collects. . . . Believe me ever yours,

" W<sup>n</sup> " *

Ann. 1832.

Matters did not mend even when the bill had become law.† On 18th June, the seventeenth anniversary of Waterloo, the Duke was riding back from a visit to the Mint, when he was set upon by a yelling mob who followed him from the Tower through the Minories to Fenchurch Street, where attempts were made to drag him from his horse. Against this danger he was protected by a couple of old soldiers who kept close to his stirrups, and faced about each time the pressure of the crowd brought the Duke to a halt. In Holborn the blackguards began to throw stones and dirt, but now two policemen ranged themselves one on each side of the horse's head, and the Duke, turning down Chancery Lane, rode to the chambers of his quondam Attorney-General, Sir Charles Wetherell. The gate of New Square having been closed behind him, and the mob thus kept at bay, the Duke, followed by his groom, quietly rode out into Lincoln's Inn Fields, and so home to Apsley House.

Mobbed and insulted in the City.

How many street scenes must have passed through Arthur Wellesley's memory during this strange ride! Alleys, bulwarked and barricaded with corpses in sunburnt Seringapatam—drunken heroes firing ball cartridge unsteadily in his honour in the square of blood-steeped Badajos—flowers and waving scarves and *vivas* in Salamanca and Madrid—steady tramp of his own columns streaming into prostrate Paris—was this to be the end of it all—a scuffle—a rush—a well-aimed brick—the fresh cheek blenched, white hair

---

* Original at Middleton Park.
† It received the Royal Assent on 7th June, 1832.

Æт. 63. dabbled in blood, the light of those brave old eyes quenched
for ever? Or (for on his own life he bestowed no second
thought) did not this mad tumult, this orgy of ingratitude,
betoken the whelming of his country in that hopeless, aimless
anarchy he had striven so stoutly to ward from her shores?
He believed it had all come to this. In countless letters
he pronounces the conviction that King, Lords, and Commons
had been hoodwinked into a conspiracy which should destroy
the Constitution, and that social order must soon cease for
ever.

*The Duke of Wellington to H.R.H. the Duke of Cumberland.*

" Apethorpe, January 1, 1833.

". . . We are in a most critical situation. The Conservative
Party have a Majority in the House of Lords. The Royal Mind
will be with them. The Royal Authority, the Administration,
the Majority of the H. of Commons, and the decided sense of
the County against them; at the same time we know now to
a certainty that the Conservative Party consists of the infinite
Majority of the landed Proprietors and the great Commercial
and Manufacturing Capitalists throughout the three Kingdoms.
We must be very cautious in our Measures. A false step might
do the greatest injury to the Institutions and Interests of all
descriptions which it is our duty as well as our object and our
Inclination to support and maintain. We must never forget that
in times of Revolution such as those we have the misfortune of
witnessing the passions of individuals have an Influence upon
publick Affairs which in ordinary times they have not, and that
it is the duty of those who wish to preserve what exists, not to
dispute those passions unnecessarily, at the same time that they
steadily persevere in their course, making no compromise of
Principle or of any Interest.

"I think it very improbable that there will be any desire on
the part of those who have the Power of the County in their
hands to share it with their Rivals and those who entertain opinions
so different from their own. I think that they are much more
likely to find themselves under the necessity of making further

concessions to the Democratick party, and of forming a closer Union with the Radicals. It is my opinion that that is the tendency of the Policy of the day, and in my view of the situation of the County the Chances of the junction of the Whigs with the Radicals greatly increase the difficulties and embarrass all our proceedings." *

There was not much material for hope even when the newly enfranchised began to exercise their rights. While the elections were in progress, Lord Stanhope's tenantry, indeed, drew the Duke's carriage with music into Chevening Park, but a band of miscreants waylaid him with volleys of stones between that place and Wildernesse.† The Duke could not pass unnoticed anywhere, but it was always uncertain at this stormy period whether the recognition would take the form of hoots or hurrahs.

"On Friday," he wrote to Lady Salisbury as late as 18th December, "I was hooted returning from hunting through Aldermarten. Luckily I am accustomed to it, and I rode through the town as quietly as I did through London. I was alone, having sent away my groom to look for my curricle." ‡

The Duke's eldest son, the Marquess of Douro, had offered himself as candidate for Hampshire, and encountered the full displeasure of the new electorate. At no time between the Duke and his son did there exist much easy confidence; the Duke was stern in judgment and prompt to pronounce it— the Marquess reserved, with the sensitive consciousness of inferior abilities.

" I regret that Douro resigned before he had polled his last man; § and I think those who are contesting other counties at this very moment have some reason to complain of his being in

---

* *Apsley House MSS.*, 1833.

† *Stanhope*, 177.

‡ *Salisbury MSS.*

§ Under the new Act the poll was kept open two days only, instead of fourteen as heretofore.

such a hurry to retire. He did so without consulting me; although he determined on the measure at Basingstoke; eight miles from hence. But we cannot always expect to find wise heads on young shoulders. This is certain: he could not have carried the election." *

**The Duke's action in Opposition.** However little hope the Duke was able to discern for the monarchy in the future, he perceived that there was a clear duty for the Opposition in the Lords, and for the Duke to perceive a duty meant that he did his best to perform it. He was never of the opinion expressed by a statesman of more recent times,† that the chief duty of an opposition was to oppose, and he encountered much difficulty in restraining the activity of his peers and moderating their animosity against all the proposals of Lord Grey's Government.

### The Duke of Wellington to the Earl of Aberdeen.

" Stratfieldsaye, 18th January, 1833.

"I have received your letter and I confess that I find great difficulty in answering it. I have never relished, as you know, the seeking opportunities to carp at and oppose the measures of the Government; the whole course of my life has been different. I dislike such conduct at present more than I did heretofore. In truth we do not know what sort of Constitution we have got—whether a Monarchy or a Republick, or that best (?) of Republicks—la Democratie Royale ! . . . The principal field of battle of the campaign will be Ireland ; and if they are at all fair upon that subject we must support them. . . . I consider Lord Grey's Government as the last prop of the Monarchy, however bad it is and however unworthy of Confidence. After him comes Lord ( ? ) ‡ probably, and chaos ! It will not be wise for us to endeavour to break down Lord Grey, without knowing what is to follow him. . . . The course, then, which I would recommend on the whole is one of attentive observation rather than of action . . . that we should not oppose and bring our

* *Salisbury MSS.*               † Lord Randolph Churchill.
‡ Illegible in original.

opposition to a division, excepting in a case of paramount Ann. 1833. importance essential to the best interests of the country." *

He was not solicitous for the attendance of the Old Tories, with the Duke of Cumberland at their head, in the House of Lords.

### To the Marquess of Londonderry.

" Stratfieldsaye, March 7, 1833.

" I do not see any prospect of the Necessity for an attendance in the House of Lords.  In truth the Revolution is effected. . . . Property, and the House of Lords in particular have lost their political Influence.  Any Deliberative body composed of Men of Cultivation, of Habits of Business and of Talent may by their Discussions have a moral (influence) in Society and over the Legislature and the Mob.  But their Discussions must be opportune ; and those of the House of Lords in Particular, which still possesses a Legislative Power, but no political Influence, ought to be very cautiously managed.

"I have been here generally amusing myself with the Foxhounds." †

### To Lord Roden.

" Stratfieldsaye, March 13, 1833.

". . . There is no man who dislikes more than I do the principles and the policy of the existing administration ; or is more opposed to their course of action.  But I cannot shut my eyes to the state in which parliament and the country are.  That there is no power in it excepting to do mischief ; and I cannot wish to remove from office men who profess at least to have good intentions in order to place the power in the hands of those who have not the grace even to make such professions. . . . I wish therefore, as far at least as I am personally concerned, to afford no ground for the charge of ' Faction.'  Other noble Lords may entertain a different opinion.  But I confess that it appears to me that it behoves those who possess large properties and who must feel that the political influence over the councils of the

* *Apsley House MSS.*, 1833.      † Original at Wynyard Park.

ÆT. 64 country is in the hands of those who possess nothing, to consider well the course which they ought to follow particularly in the House of Lords." *

*To the Marquess of Londonderry.*

" London, June 6, 1833.

". . . We must consider of the real situation of the Country; and of that which is best to be done to save our Properties from Destruction. As for Office or Power, both are out of the Question." †

*To H.R.H. the Duke of Cumberland.*

" Walmer Castle, October 1st, 1833.

". . . I must say I have always felt myself in a very awkward, and I must add false Position in opposition to the King's Government. I am connected with the Government in many ways; scarcely a day passes on which I am not under the Necessity of communicating with them on some subject or other. I have been in office and have served the King throughout my life; and I know all the Difficulties in which the Government are placed. . . . I cannot enter upon an opposition to Government without knowing what it is I am to oppose, and with a view to impede their course by increased difficulties. I would diminish those difficulties if I could. Neither could I oppose the Gov! with the view to break up the Administration and form a new one. Nobody has a worse opinion of, or less Confidence in, the Existing Ministers than I have. Under their Guidance we have been on the Road to Ruin, we have made some Progress already, and we shall certainly make more. But for the sake of the King and his Family, as well as the Country, I cannot take upon myself the Responsibility of breaking up the Gov! without knowing how or for whom another is to be formed, whether it can be supported— whether it can even claim support: and what the King thinks and wishes. Since the year 1830 I have foreseen and lamented the state of things to which we were coming. But I confess that I cannot see the Remedy in the formation of what is called

* *Apsley House MSS.* † Original at Wynyard Park.

a determined and active opposition to the King's Government, especially in the House of Lords." *    Axx. 1833.

The Duke, oppressed though he was by the conviction that The Duke
ruin had descended on his country, resumed the ordinary in the hunting-
avocations and amusements of an English country gentleman, field.
dividing his time between Strathfieldsaye and Walmer Castle.
Always a warm supporter of the chase, he subscribed liberally
to the Vine and the Bramshill hounds in his own neighbourhood,† and attended their meets as often as he possibly could.
"Nim South," a writer in the *New Sporting Magazine*, has
left some interesting notes of the Duke's appearance and performance in the field, having apparently been as unfavourably
impressed by the one as by the other. He tells how one wet
day in 1831 he was waiting for Sir John Cope's hounds at
Hartley Row Gate, when he perceived a red coat approaching
through the drizzle. As the new-comer drew near, "Nim
South" took stock of his attire, which included a scarlet
frock coat, a lilac silk waistcoat, kid gloves, a pair of fustian
trousers strapped tightly down over a pair of Wellington
boots! "And certainly they were Wellingtons in every
sense of the word, for the wearer was neither more nor less
than the illustrious Arthur himself."

"We had," says Nim, "just the sort of day's sport to please
a man like the Duke of Wellington, who, though mighty in the
field of war, cuts no great figure in the hunting-field. Indeed, to
do him all due justice, I have seldom seen a man with less idea
of riding than he has. His seat is unsightly in the extreme, and
few men get more falls in the course of the year than his Grace.
Nevertheless he seemed to enjoy the thing amazingly, and what
with leading over occasionally and his groom's assistance, he did
very well."

The Duke gave much attention also to the improvement
and management of his estate of Strathfieldsaye, spending

* *Apsley House MSS.*
† At one time his subscription to the Vine was £400 a year.

Æт. 64.

liberally on the land and laying by all the surplus rents for
his successors, who he knew would not enjoy all the sources
of emolument which he did. He also spent much of his time
at Walmer Castle, his official residence as Warden of the
Cinque Ports, an office which he by no means regarded as
a sinecure.

### Lord Mahon to the Countess of Jersey.

"2nd October, 1833.

"Yesterday I dined at Walmer Castle. The Duke is in
amazing force. We were to meet their R! Highnesses of
Cumberland, and sat waiting for them from seven till a quarter
to nine. . . . Some country neighbours, being little used to late
hours, appeared half dead at the delay." *

Corre-
spondence
with
Bishop
Philpotts.

A correspondence between the Duke and Dr. Philpotts,
Bishop of Exeter, took place about this period, throwing some
interesting light on the view the Duke took of the obligation
of church-going.

"Let me beseech your attention to one particular," wrote the
prelate, "in which you may do honour to God, and, by His grace,
much spiritual good to men—I mean, by regularly attending His
public service; by showing before the world that you *glory* in
being the servant of God; by setting an example, the value of
which will be proportioned to the greatness of your earthly
renown." †

The Duke took the Bishop's long lecture very meekly,
recognising that his admonitor was only discharging the duty
of his office.

### The Duke of Wellington to the Lord Bishop of Exeter.

"London, 6th January, 1832.

"MY DEAR LORD BISHOP,—I am very grateful for your letter.
It is highly creditable to your Lordship, and most suitable for
you to write it in these times to any individual, more particularly

* Original at Middleton Park.　　† *Civil Despatches*, viii. 146.

to me, afflicted with sickness as I have been. . . . What I am particularly anxious to remove from your mind is the notion that I am a person without any sense of religion. If I am so, I am unpardonable ; as I have had opportunities to acquire, and have acquired, a good deal of knowledge on the subject. I don't make much show or boast on any subject. I never have done so. The consequence is that, in these days of boasting, I have been set down from time to time as the most ignorant and least qualified public man of my time, and this even upon professional matters, upon which it might be imagined that from the commencement of my career I had been sufficiently tried. Then in private life I have been accused of every vice and enormity ; and when those who live with me, and know every action of my life and every thought, testify that such charges are groundless, the charge is then brought, 'Oh, he is a man without religion.' As I said before, I am not ostentatious about anything. I am not a ' Bible Society man ' upon principle, and I make no ostentatious display either of charity or of other Christian virtues, though I believe that, besides enormous sums given to hundreds and thousands who have positive claims upon me, there is not a charity of any description within my reach to which I am not a contributor, although I am convinced, and indeed know, that many of them are gross jobs.

"The next objection is ' He does not go to church ! ' Whenever or wherever my presence at church can operate as an example, I do go. I never am absent from divine service at Walmer or when I am in Hampshire, or in any place in the country where my presence or absence could be observed. But it must be recollected that some ten years ago I met with an accident which affected my hearing, and, in point of fact, I never hear more than what I know by heart of the Church service, and never one word of the sermon. Then observe that during at least eight months of the year I should have to sit for two hours every week uncovered in a cold church : this would certainly have the effect of depriving me of my sense of hearing altogether. For some time I did attend divine service early in the morning at St. James's, which lasted only an hour ; but I found it too cold for me, and it is true that I do not attend divine service in any parish in London. But excepting that duty, which I never fail to perform in the country, I don't know of any that I leave unperformed. There is room for amendment in every man, in me as well as in others; and there is nothing better calculated to inspire such amendment than such a letter as that from your Lordship. In answering it as I have done, I hope you will believe that I don't reject the advice. On the contrary I thank you for it; and I assure you that it will not be thrown away upon me. But if you have believed what you have read and heard of me, I must tell you that these reports do not do me justice." [*]

Of the extraordinary energy shown by the Duke of Wellington in private correspondence many examples might be quoted, although he was very scrupulous in destroying during his life almost all the letters he received of an exclusively private nature, especially those from ladies. A few instances may suffice to show the prodigious fluency of his pen at this period.

Mr. Croker having sent him, in September, 1833, a number of pamphlets on foreign affairs with a request for his criticism, the Duke sat down at Walmer Castle and replied on sixty sides of large letter-paper! [†]

**The Duke's letters to Miss J.** The Duke's correspondence with Miss J. has been published; [‡] certainly, if they may be taken as genuine, and their authenticity has not been seriously called in question, [§] these letters must take rank among the most extraordinary littlenesses of great men. Miss J., it is stated, was the daughter of English parents of the class of smaller gentry, fashionably educated, possessed of great beauty, highly emo-

---

[*] *Civil Despatches*, viii. 147.

[†] The draft of this document at Apsley House is not, as is usual, in his own handwriting, but in a small, close feminine hand. Had he written it himself it would have covered one hundred and twenty pages.

[‡] *The Letters of the Duke of Wellington to Miss J.*, 1834–1851. London, 1890.

[§] Lady de Ros was of opinion that the first two or three of the series were genuine, and the rest fictitious. It is, of course, exceedingly suspicious that the originals have never been submitted to inspection; nevertheless, the imitation—if imitation it be—of the Duke's style is very close.

tional, and a religious zealot. Having succeeded in making a convert of a convicted murderer, and persuaded him to make full confession before he was taken to the gallows, she conceived that she had a mission to arouse the most prominent public characters to a sense of their sinfulness, and selected the Duke of Wellington as the first subject, without even knowing that he was the conqueror of Napoleon. She wrote to him on 15th January, 1834, and received an answer by return of post, the beginning of a correspondence which, alternating with interviews, lasted till a few months before the Duke's death in 1852. Miss J.'s letters are full of religious fervour, earnest exhortations to seek salvation, and feminine resentment of the slightest want of ceremony in addressing her. Thus on one occasion she took deep offence because the Duke took to sealing his letters with a plain seal instead of with his coat of arms.

"I take this opportunity," she writes in 1835, "of making two enquiries respecting which my mind is not at all satisfied. The first is: Why am I to receive a change of style in the appearance of your letters with regard to the Seal thereof? and the next, *called forth thereby: Why* you *ever* ceased to sign your *Name* at the conclusion of your letters. If either of these changes sprang from disrespect or want of confidence in my integrity, confidence, Christianity and friendship, I shall without hesitation or delay return Your Grace every letter I have in my possession, as in *that* case they will cease to have any value in *my* estimation. I will also beg to decline all further intercourse, knowing that the sincerity and purity of my friendship merits both consideration and respect."

The Duke's answer to this effusion may be given as an example of the style of his share in the correspondence.

"Strathfieldsaye,* September 17, 1835.

"MY DEAR MISS J.,—I always understood that the important parts of a Letter were its Contents. I never much considered

* Having never seen the originals of these letters, I can pronounce no opinion as to their authenticity. If, however, the printer has faithfully followed the

the Signature, provided I knew the handwriting; or the Seal, provided it effectually closed the letter. When I write to a Person with whom I am intimate,* who knows my handwriting, I generally sign my Initials. I don't always seal my own Letters; they are sometimes sealed by a Secretary, oftener by myself. In any Case, as there are generally very many to be sealed, and the Seal frequently becomes heated, it is necessary to change it; and by accident I may have sealed a Letter to you with a blank Seal. But it is very extraordinary if it is so, as I don't believe I have such a thing! You will find this Letter however signed and sealed in what you deem the most respectful manner. And if I should write to you any more, I will take care that they shall be properly signed and sealed to your Satisfaction. I am very glad to learn that you intend to send back all the letters I ever wrote to you. I told you heretofore that I thought you had better burn them all. But if you think proper to send them in a parcel to my House, I will save you the trouble of committing them to the flames.

"Believe me, Ever Yours most sincerely,

"WELLINGTON."

And this sort of twaddle went on for the space of seventeen years, for it was all twaddle except the fervid and fanatical exhortations on the lady's part. They were perpetually quarrelling, and as often making it up, till, in the later years, the correspondence became more material, and the question of pecuniary assistance came on the carpet. No more tiresome or futile intercourse can be imagined for a man of affairs constantly occupied in the discharge of the highest functions of a subject. The whole episode of Miss J.—assuming it to be genuine—is a curious psychological puzzle; the religious lectures and discussions one would have said were of the very kind to bore the Duke, whose religion was of a somewhat conventional type; to account for his having been at the

text, the spelling of this name suggests that they came from another hand than the Duke's, who always wrote "Stratfieldsaye."

* He had not seen her a dozen times.

pains to indite three hundred and ninety epistles to Miss
J., one is thrown upon the conclusion that, although there is
a total absence of amatory expressions, he found recreation
in intercourse with a pretty young woman of unconventional
ways.

Even this is barely comprehensible when regard is had to
the volume of the Duke's daily correspondence.

"The Duke," wrote Lady Salisbury in 1837, "complained to
me terribly of the incessant persecution of notes and letters on
all subjects from everybody—told me he had written fifty notes
or letters that morning, although he had a secretary, an assistant
and a librarian. 'I declare that I dread going into my own
house, from the heaps of letters that are ready to receive me
there. The other morning I had a visit from a man who had
made repeated applications to see me on business of importance—
a baronet—who has published a pamphlet or two. The interview
began with high-flown compliments on his side, which I soon put
an end to by saying, 'We did not meet to make compliments. You
stated that you had something to say to me.'

"'Yes, my lord,' said the baronet, 'I have a question to put.
I wish to ascertain whether, if your Grace were to return to office,
you would support principles of moderate reform.'

"'That is your question, is it?'

"'Yes, my lord.'

"'Then allow me to put a question in return—what right have
you to ask me?'" *

It was not with ladies alone, however, that the Duke was
ready to correspond. Postcards, in which the late Mr.
Gladstone was so amazingly fecund, were not at his disposal;
but it is no exaggeration to say that he used up hundred-
weights of gilt-edged letter and note-paper in replies on the
most trivial subjects, the drafts being duly retained, endorsed,
and filed, usually, as in the following case, *in his own
handwriting*. Some unknown quack had sent him a box
of salves; he replied as follows :—

* *Salisbury MSS.*, 1837.

                                        " Stratfieldsaye, 26th January, 1839.

"Sir,—I have received your letter and the box of salves, etc., which you have sent me. This last will be returned to you by the coach of Monday. I beg you to accept my best thanks for your attention. I think that you and I have some reason to complain of the Editors of Newspapers. One of them thought proper to publish an account of me, that I was affected by a Rigidity of the Muscles of the Face. You have decided that the disorder must be the *Tic douloureux*, for which you send me your Salves as a remedy. I have no disorder in my face. I am affected by the Lumbago or Rheumatism in my Loins, shoulders, neck, and back, a disorder to which many are liable who have passed days and nights exposed to the Weather in bad Climates. I am attended by the best medical Advisers in England, and I must attend to their advice. I cannot make use of Salves sent to me by a Gentleman however respectable of whom I know nothing, and who knows nothing of the Case excepting what he reads in the Newspapers." *

A few more characteristic illustrations may be taken almost at random from the pyramids of manuscripts at Apsley House, where, gazing upon the high desk at which the Duke used to work, one is staggered at the evidence of energy sufficient to drive the quill over so many acres of harsh, rough paper, and to retain autograph drafts of the most trivial communications. It is well, however, to bear in mind the warning contained in one of these letters.

*To Lord Mahon.*

                                        " September 18th, 1836.
"You are quite right to avoid to publish what you may learn in your Private Correspondence or Private Conversation with anybody. We converse loosely ; we may say nothing that we do not think, or know to be true. But if I was to think that every Word I ever say or write was to be brought before the Publick, I should hesitate before I dared to write or talk at all ;

* *Apsley House MSS.*

and I should take care so to explain myself as that I could not Ann. 1833.
be misunderstood."

*To a Clergyman who deplored Roman Catholic Emancipation.*

"Walmer Castle, 29 September, 1839.

" F.M. the Duke of Wellington presents his compliments to
Mr. Anderson. Everybody has a right to write to the Duke
what he pleases ; the Duke hopes that he will be permitted to
answer or not as he pleases. Mr. Anderson has thought fit to
attribute to one cause the state in which the country is at
present. The Duke, who is an actor in the affairs of the Day,
would attribute these unfortunate circumstances to the conduct
of a powerful Party, of which, if the Duke is not mistaken,
Mr. Anderson is one, to the course which this party followed
subsequently to the almost unanimous adoption by Parliament
of the measure to which Mr. Anderson has referred, and most
particularly to the course which many belonging to the same
party followed in the course of the years 1830, 1831, and 1832.
This is the answer which the Duke has to give to Mr. Anderson :
he had better write to somebody else. Before Mr. Anderson
refers to the authority of Scripture in relation to the Acts for
Catholick Emancipation in correspondence with others, the Duke
would recommend to him to peruse the Acts of Parliament
establishing the Reformation of the Church of England in
England and Ireland. He will judge for himself whether these
in any manner affected the civil privileges of Roman Catholicks ;
whether such privileges were affected till the enactment of the
Corporation and Test Acts in the reign of Charles II. ; whether
the authors of these Acts, the founders of the Church and its
doctrines, left for two centuries in existence and in exercise
privileges forbidden by the word of God."

*Ordering a Pair of Post-horses.*

"Stratfieldsaye, November 24, 1846.

" F.M. the Duke of Wellington presents his compliments to
the Landlord of the Norfolk Arms Inn. The Duke has been
invited to Arundel Castle during the period of the visit of H.M.

the Queen to His Grace the Duke of Norfolk. He will arrive at Arundel by the Rail Road on Tuesday the 1st of December by the train which will quit the Station London Bridge at eleven a.m. and reach the Station Arundel at 1.39. He will bring his Carriage with him, and he requests the Landlord of the Norfolk Arms Inn to give orders, and if necessary to take Measures, that he may find a pair of Horses at the Arundel Station at half-past one on Tuesday the 1st of December, to draw his Carriage from thence to the Castle.

"The Duke will have with him two Saddle Horses, and he requests the Landlord of the Norfolk Arms Inn to give orders that Stabling may be ready for them at the Norfolk Arms if possible; if not, in the Town in the immediate Neighbourhood.

" If the Landlord of the Norfolk Arms Inn should have occasion to write to the Duke of Wellington, it is requested that he will address the letter to Piccadilly, London."

> *Endorsed*—"To the Landlord of the Norfolk Arms Inn, Arundel, desiring him to have a pair of horses to take the Carriage to the Castle." *

*To one who asked the Duke for a Certificate of Respectability.*

" London, July 21, 1847.

" F.M. the Duke of Wellington presents his compliments to Mr. Oliver. He declares distinctly that he knows nothing of Mr. Edward Oliver, and that he is astonished at the *Insolence* of any person requiring him to certify to Messrs. Coutts and Co., or any other person, that of which the person who makes the requisition must know that the Duke has no personal knowledge."

*To a Washerwoman.*

" London, September 1, 1848.

"The Duke of Wellington presents his compliments to Mrs. Herrick. His son, the Marquis of Douro, is a housekeeper in Belgrave Street. He is not responsible for the payment of his

---

* The whole of this, including the endorsement, is in the Duke's own hand.

washing bills, even to the wife of a soldier. It appears to the <small>ANN. 1833.</small> Duke that the regular mode of proceeding would be to apply to the debtor himself, and, if payment should be refused or omitted, to enforce the same by all means sanctioned by law. This would be a regular mode of proceeding. That adopted is *impertinent*, in the real and not offensive meaning of that word."

### To a Lady who sent a Box to Apsley House.

" Walmer Castle, 3rd November, 1849.

" Field Marshal the Duke of Wellingon presents his compliments to Miss Jane Fyffe. He has this morning received in a deal box her letter of 3rd October. He has long been under the necessity of preventing his house being made the deposit of all the trash that is manufactured or made up. Giving money is one thing—receiving into his house all the trash made up is quite a different one ! To the latter he will not submit. He invariably returns everything sent to his house without his previous permission, if he can discover the mode of doing so. But there is no direct communication between this place and Edinburgh. The deal case was brought down here from the Duke's house in London, the Duke is ignorant in what manner. He desires Miss —— to inform him in what manner it is to be returned to Edinburgh. He gives notice that if he does not receive an answer by return of post, the box and its contents will be thrown into the fire. He will not allow things to be sent to his house without his previous consent."

In his later years the Duke had a variety of forms of refusal lithographed in facsimile from his own handwriting, for such purposes as declining invitations to dinners and parties, declining to give orders to the gallery of the House of Lords or to send an autograph signature, and, especially, explaining the limitation of his patronage as Commander-in-chief.

In his last years his handwriting became almost illegible ; so much so that in 1852, when Lord Derby, then in office,

received a letter from the Duke which no one in Downing
Street could decipher, he sent his private secretary, Colonel
Talbot, to ask the Duke to explain his own letter.  The
Duke took it, looked at it, and, handing it back to Colonel
Talbot, observed with a smile, " It was my business to write
that letter, but it is *your* duty to read it ! "

Returning to the year 1833—for the ordinary incidents and
social obligations of political life the Duke at this time felt a
strong disinclination, all the more marked because he was
usually so conscientious in meeting them.

### The Duke of Wellington to the Marchioness of Salisbury.

" S.S.. March 28th, 1833.

" MY DEAR LADY SALISBURY,—I have received your note about
dining with the Lord Mayor, which is a ceremony which I confess
that I am anxious to avoid unless you wish it very much.   I
wish to avoid for three reasons.  First, I think that all in the
City, Conservatives * as well as the others, behaved most shame-
fully to me in the year 1830 on the occasion of the King's
intended visit to the City.  I then determined that I would not
go again either to the Mansion House or to dine at the Guildhall.
Secondly, I am very anxious to avoid to meet the Ministers anywhere ; but particularly in the City at the Lord Mayor's, where
they must be toasted, applauded, etc., etc.  Thirdly, it is not
quite clear to me that if the Ministers knew, as they must, that
I intended to be present, they would not favour me by having
a mob ready to receive me on arriving at, or going away from,
the Mansion House, as Mr. Canning's Government had on one
occasion that I attended a dinner given by the East India
Company when he was present.  My own inclination, therefore,
would induce me not to go." †

It is rather lamentable to find the Duke entertaining
suspicion that English Ministers and gentlemen would stoop

* The earliest example which I have noted of the use by the Duke of the
modern term for what remained of the Tory party.
† *Salisbury MSS.*

to wrest the Lord Mayor's hospitality into the occasion for a ANN. 1834. hostile demonstration against a political opponent, but this was not the only symptom of how much his spirit had been embittered and his judgment warped by resentment against the authors of the legislative revolution. Unhappily, he allowed his resentment to extend to some who deserved censure from him least of all.

Early in 1834 the Chancellorship of the University of Estrange-ment be-tween the Duke and Sir R. Peel. Oxford became vacant through the death of Lord Grenville, and the Conservatives of the University approached the Duke with the view of inducing him to consent to be put in nomination. He told them that he "knew no more of Greek and Latin than an Eton boy in the remove; that these facts were perfectly well known, and that he must be considered incapable and unfit," * and he urged them to look elsewhere, naming the Duke of Beaufort and the Lords Bathurst, Mansfield, Sidmouth, and Talbot. Yielding, however, to the urgent pressure of his proposers, the Duke consented to be put forward, considering himself "in all instances of this kind an instrument to be used by the public." † Meanwhile another party in Convocation had invited Sir Robert Peel to allow his nomination, and Mr. Hayward Cox wrote to the Duke suggesting that it would be a gracious act if he were to withdraw in favour of his colleague, who, by his conscientious action at the time of the Roman Catholic legislation, had lost his seat for the University. The Duke replied, declining to withdraw on the ground that the appeal had come too late, and that it would be unfair to the gentlemen who, at his request, had first reconsidered, and then repeated, their invitation to himself.

Accordingly, the Duke was installed as Chancellor of the University on 10th June. With Croker, who accompanied him, he stipulated for an avoidance of display.

---

* *Apsley House MSS.*      † *Ibid.*

"I intend to send a footman and coachman and horses to Oxford; but as for a magnificent entry, etc., I must enter that city as I have always entered that and others—as an individual." [*]

"I could not make the Duke," Croker wrote to his wife, "take off his hat to any one, not even the ladies; he kept saluting like a soldier. I, however, made him show himself occasionally, and take notice here and there; but he is a sad hand at popularity hunting. . . . Mr. Arnould repeated some very good verses on the Hospice of St. Bernard; and, after alluding to Buonaparte's passage of the Alps, and praising his genius, etc., and recounting all his triumphs, he suddenly apostrophised the Duke, and said something equivalent to—'invincible till he met *you!*' At that word began a scene of enthusiasm such as I never saw; some people appeared to me to go out of their senses—literally to go mad. The whole assembly started up, and the ladies and grave semicircle of doctors became as much excited as the boys in the gallery and the men in the pit. Such peals of shouts I never heard; such waving of hats, handkerchiefs and caps I never saw; such extravagant clapping and stamping so that at last the air became clouded with dust. During all this the Duke sat like a statue; at last he took some notice, took off his cap lightly, and pointed to the reciter to go on; but this only increased the enthusiasm, and at last it ended only from the exhaustion of our animal powers." [†]

Now it may easily be believed how little the Duke, loaded already with all the honours which human ingenuity has devised to indicate human gratitude, coveted for himself the honorary office of Chancellor; nevertheless, Peel was deeply hurt that the Duke, in suggesting the names of others, should not have mentioned him as one who had deserved well of the University.[‡] He was not aware, as appears from an unpublished letter from the Duke to Lord Aberdeen, that the Duke "had done everything in his power to prevail

---

[*] *Croker*, ii. 225.　　　　　　　　[†] *Ibid.*, 228.

[‡] Peel was afterwards informed by Sir Henry Hardinge that the Duke "had been urging Mr. Wintle to force the office upon you (Peel) by a junction of all parties;" but the Duke was informed that a peer was indispensable.

on them to take Sir Robert Peel," * but in vain. Peel ANN. 1834. therefore withdrew, and the Duke was unanimously elected. Such a trifle as this would never have disturbed the intercourse of men who were on confidential terms, but such, unhappily, no longer prevailed between the two leaders of the Opposition.

"Peel complains," wrote Lady Salisbury in her journal, "that he has asked the Duke three years running to Drayton, but he has never been asked to Strathfieldsaye. There certainly never were two men less fitted to go on well together in the intercourse of private life. The only way to deal with the Duke is by perfect openness and candour, and Peel is always stiff, reserved, and unfathomable." †

"Why won't you go to Drayton ?" asked Lady Salisbury.

"Ah, that is the way!" returned the Duke. "Why does the Duke not do this, and why does the Duke not do that ? It is very hard if the Duke is to be the only man who may not do as he likes." ‡

On another occasion Lady Salisbury, after listening to some complaint by the Duke about Peel's tiresome ways, remarked, "Never mind; he is a thoroughly honest man and devoted to you."

"In the first position, you are quite right," replied the Duke—"he *is* thoroughly honest. I never saw a man who adhered more invariably to truth on all occasions. As to the second, I have my doubts of that." §

It was one of the Duke's peculiarities that he was very slow—unconquerably slow—to change an opinion he had once formed. It was the work of years to convince him that he had been mistaken in his original belief that Peel disliked him. On 1st May, 1834, they met at dinner at Mr.

* *Apsley House MSS.*  † *Salisbury MSS.*, 1836.
‡ *Ibid.*  § *Ibid.*

Arbuthnot's, and their host was so struck by the absence of the old cordiality between them, and so apprehensive that an open rupture was imminent, that he wrote to express his anxiety to Lord Aberdeen, as the only man able to set matters right.

> "I know not which of the two is in fault. Perhaps there is no fault on either side, merely misconception. . . . The Duke, I know, imagines that Peel does not like him. In this I am sure he is in error. If there is one subject upon which, when I was seeing Peel daily, he spoke to me more than upon all others, it was in praise and admiration of the Duke. . . . It seems therefore to me that the one thing wanted is that they should understand each other." *

Now, Lord Aberdeen was equally friends with the Duke and Sir Robert, and it is significant that, instead of going straight to the Duke, who was in the habit of grumbling to him confidentially about Peel, he forwarded Arbuthnot's letter to Peel. The fact is that the Duke was rather an impracticable person in delicate negociations; he was so impatient of any want—not of sincerity, for he always gave Peel the utmost credit for absolute truthfulness—but of frankness of manner and directness of expression, that his friends found it difficult to induce him to use those little attentions and considerations which do so much to make intercourse run smoothly. Aberdeen found that chief among two or three other causes for Peel's soreness was the remembrance of Wellington's words when, in 1832, he had been explaining to the Lords his action and motives in endeavouring to form a Ministry which Peel had refused to join. They certainly were barbed expressions, and it is not surprising that they rankled in a spirit so sensitive as Peel's.

> "For myself, my Lords, I cannot help feeling that if I had been capable of refusing my assistance to his Majesty, if I had

* *Peel Letters,* ii. 232.

been capable of saying to his Majesty—'I cannot assist you in this affair,' I do not think, my Lords, that I could have shown my face in the streets for shame of having done it, for shame of having abandoned my Sovereign under such distressing circumstances. I have indeed the misfortune of differing from friends of mine upon this subject, but I cannot regret the steps I have taken."

The faithful Arbuthnot did not relax his efforts to bring about a reconciliation. He was determined to remove the misunderstanding between these men, not only from the deep admiration and affection in which he held them, but because he looked upon them as essential to the welfare of the country. The Ministry was crumbling to pieces ; were it to fall, it were lamentable that there should exist anything short of the fullest confidence between Wellington and Peel. To Peel, therefore, Arbuthnot wrote on 12th May—

"The Duke told me yesterday that he had met Hardinge, and that he said to him that things were in that state which might make it necessary for you to make up your mind at a moment's warning what course you would pursue. I don't think he said much more . . . except that the Minister must be in the House of Commons. . . . Supposing that the King had to form a new Government, I should hope that he would send for you and the Duke at the same time. The Duke would represent the absolute necessity of having the Minister in the House of Commons, and he would exert himself most strenuously in aiding you to form a Government. It would then be settled between you what share in it he was to take ; but I know that his object is the Horse Guards." *

The misunderstanding and coldness, however, were not so easily removed. It endured for years, despite the closer relations into which political changes brought the Duke and Sir Robert, and although Arbuthnot, Croker, Lady Salisbury,

* *Peel Letters*, ii. 240.

**Æt. 64.** and other friends used their best offices to put matters on a more comfortable footing. Complete reconciliation—*redintegratio amoris*—did indeed come at last, but not before the end of both these great lives was at hand.

**The Duke's difficulties with his party.** The Duke's efforts during 1834 were chiefly directed to restraining the indiscretions of his own party. "I understand," he wrote to Lord Aberdeen before the opening of the session, "that our zealous friends are very unreasonable, and I shall have some trouble with them." * Writing on the same day to the Duke of Buckingham, one of these "zealous friends," he indulged in a little jeremiad on the times.

"The truth is that all government in this country is impossible under existing circumstances. I don't care whether it is called monarchy, oligarchy, aristocracy, democracy, or what they please, the government of the country, the protection of the lives, privileges, and properties of its subjects and the regulation of the thousand matters which require regulation in an advanced and artificial state of society, are impracticable as long as such a deliberative assembly exists as the House of Commons, with all the powers and privileges which it has amassed in the course of the last two hundred years." †

It was with Lord Aberdeen that the Duke took closest counsel in leading the Opposition in the Lords. Church reform was in the air, and Ministers were being urged to take it up, without, however, showing much inclination for the task.

*The Duke of Wellington to the Earl of Aberdeen.*

"17th January, 1834.

". . . There is a good deal of alarm about the Church, principally among the dignified clergy, and the politicians of the world. My friends the country gentlemen don't seem to me to think much about that or anything else excepting their homes and foxes." ‡

* *Apsley House MSS.*, 1834.    † *Ibid.*    ‡ *Apsley House MSS.*

*The same to Lord Roden.*

"17th January, 1834.

"It is impossible for me to tell what will be the course of events in Parliament. From the moment that the word 'Reform' was mentioned in Parliament I never doubted of the consequences which must follow from it. We have not half done with them yet. My opinion has been invariably that we ought to descend from our high station by the most gradual road, in order to avoid any great shock to our complicated Machine, and that we might each of us take our Station in the new system according to which it has pleased Gentlemen to be governed. I therefore have done and will do all that I can to prevent any sudden or general mischief. People are telling me every day that noblemen and gentlemen like to be consulted, and to know the opinion of each other. I thought that I could not adopt a better mode of consulting than to invite to dine with me on the day preceding the Meeting of Parliament every Nobleman in the habit of speaking in the House of Lords, or whose opinion was likely to have weight with others. I have invited as many as fifty; from some I am sorry to say I have not received very civil answers. Many have not answered at all; some have excused themselves for not attending; very few have said that they will attend. I confess that I should find it difficult to give a Reason for having sent these invitations. If a meeting was desirable, those who should wish it might have met at a club, or at the house of any other noble lord." *

"I am persuaded," wrote Charles Greville in his journal, "that the Duke deludes himself with some extraordinary false reasoning, and that the habits of intense volition, jumbled up with party prejudices, old association, and exposure to never-ceasing flattery, have produced the remarkable result we see in his conduct. Notwithstanding the enormous blunders he has committed, and his numerous and flagrant inconsistencies, he has never lost confidence in himself, and,

* *Aspley House MSS.*

.Ær. 65 what is more curious, has contrived to retain that of a host of followers." *

Death of Mrs. Arbuthnot. The political convulsion anticipated as immediate by the Duke and Mr. Arbuthnot was postponed for a few months, and before it came about the Duke was fated to sustain a severe loss in the death of Mrs. Arbuthnot, one of his few intimate friends. Gossips loved to point an inquisitive finger at this friendship, which began when the Arbuthnots were in Paris after the peace of 1815; and, in whatever degree of indiscretion the acquaintance may have had its rise, it had ripened with years into a friendship very dear to the Duke. He was at Hatfield when the news came, and Lady Salisbury has described the scene in her journal.

*August 2nd*, 1834.—"Lord S. came down with Lds. Ellenborough and Rosslyn, the Clanwilliams and the G. Somersets. They had a splendid division last night in the Lords on the Admission of Dissenters Bill—majority 102—greater than any division of the Opposition in this century. At least this, I trust, will put swamping the H. of Peers out of the question. The Duke came down to dinner in high spirits. He told us Mrs. Arbuthnot had been ill at Woodford with an attack of the nature of cholera—but was better. I had just gone to bed, with the other ladies, when an express arrived to the D. with the intelligence of Mrs. Arbuthnot's death. He threw himself in the greatest agitation on the sofa, as Ld. S. told me, and the letter on the floor; and then rose and walked a few minutes about the room, almost sobbing, after which he retired. In the morning Lord S. got a note from him, saying he must go to Mr. Arbuthnot; he left for Woodford about half-past eight on Sunday morning. It is a dreadful loss to him; for whether there is any foundation or not for the stories usually believed about the early part of their *liaison*, she was certainly *now* become to him no more than a tried and valued friend, to whom he was sincerely attached. Her house was his home; and with all his glory and greatness, *he never had a home*. His nature is domestic,

* *Greville*, 2nd series, iii. 173.

MRS. ARBUTHNOT.

(From a Miniature at Apsley House.)

[Vol. ii. p. 296.

and, as he advances in years, some female society and some Ann. 1834.
fireside to which he can always resort become necessary to
him." *

Mr. Arbuthnot, who was slightly older than the Duke,
shortly after he became a widower, was induced to make his
London residence in Apsley House, and the friendship between
these two men continued without change or abatement, till
it was severed by Mr. Arbuthnot's death in 1850.

* *Salisbury MSS.*, 1834.

# CHAPTER X.

## AFTER THE STORM.

### 1834–1839.

Gloomy apprehensions of the Tories.

THE old order was changing fast; in the Duke of Wellington's opinion it was passing away altogether. His apprehensions continued of the gloomiest.

"I think," said he to Lady Salisbury, "that persons of property ANN. 1834. in this country are coming to their senses; but while the Reform Act is in force they have no influence. Formerly there were certain places given up to the democratic interest, and it was very proper, in a constitution like ours, that there should be such; the rest were in the hands of the property of the country. But the Act has brought home democracy to every man's door. I doubt whether, even if the Reform Act were repealed,* the country could again enjoy its ancient constitution without further changes. The House of Commons has of late swallowed up all the power of the State; the rotten boroughs moderated this power by the infusion of aristocratic influence; to restore them would be impossible. It remains to be considered in what manner to re-establish the ancient balance, whether by giving to the House of Lords more power by controlling the money bills and so on, or by giving the King a real and effectual veto. If there were a revolution in this country, it must end by a military dictator; I am too old, but there would be one." †

The Duke was not alone in anticipating a violent revolution; his apprehensions were shared by some of the Whigs. On hearing that the Duke of Bedford had declared that, in his opinion, the choice lay between despotism and anarchy, the Duke remarked, " I can tell Johnny Bedford that if we have anarchy, I'll have Woburn!" ‡

Bitterly as he disapproved of Lord Grey's policy, still his Cabinet was the King's Government, and Wellington could not be induced by Buckingham, Londonderry, and the other Tory *frondeurs* to offer any factious opposition to their measures. Least of all was he disposed to take issue with them upon the new Poor Law.

* It is a singular thing that, as shown by many expressions in the Duke's letters at this time, he contemplated partial repeal of the Reform Act as a possible and desirable thing.

† *Salisbury MSS.*, 1834.

‡ *Ibid.*

*The Duke of Wellington to the Marquess of Londonderry.*

"17 June, 1834.

"MY DEAR CHARLES,— . . . In the last session of Parliament
I fought *several fair stand-up fights* throughout the Dog Days
and till the end of August, with the support of not more than
a dozen Peers; upon questions of the greatest Publick and personal
interest, even to the Duke of Buckingham himself; but I do not
recollect that I had the Advantage of the Duke's support on any
one of these occasions. . . . I decline to make the Poor Law
Bill a Party Question, or to oppose any provision in it of which,
when I see it, I shall approve. . . . I do not choose to be the
Person to excite a quarrel between the two Houses of Parl!
This quarrel will occur in its Time; and the House of Lords will
probably be overwhelmed. But it shall not be owing to any action
of mine."

"London, June 19, 1834.

"If I am to carry on a Warfare with the D. of Buckingham
by Letter, he must write Legibly. I can scarcely read one Word
of his Letter. Indeed not one Word beyond the first Page.

"In answer to that Page I assert that I was left almost alone
to fight the Battle in the House of Lords in the last Session of
Parl! We consequently lost many Questions. . . . To talk of my
being Leader of a Party or anything but the Slave of a Party, or
in other Words the Person whom any other may *bore* with his
Letters or his Visits upon publick Subjects, when he pleases, is
just what I call *Stuff*." *

During the summer of 1834 Lord Grey's Ministry staggered
on under increasing difficulties. Their popularity out-of-
doors suffered from the disappointment of those who had
imagined that all kinds of benefits would immediately flow
from the establishment of a people's Parliament. They were
at issue among themselves on the proposals for dealing with
the revenues of the Irish Church, which brought about in
May the resignation of the Duke of Richmond, Lord Ripon,

* Originals at Wynyard Park.

Sir James Graham, and Mr. Stanley.*     Grey himself was Ann. 1834.
only restrained from retiring at the same time by the remonstrance of Brougham ; he did resign in July, and was succeeded as Prime Minister by Lord Melbourne, Parliament being prorogued at the same time.

Lord Melbourne accepted office, relying chiefly on Lord Althorpe's influence as leader of the House of Commons ;† but on the death of his father, Earl Spencer, on 10th November, Althorpe went to the House of Lords, and Lord Melbourne, feeling that the position was seriously modified, asked the King whether it was his pleasure that he "should attempt to make such fresh arrangements as might enable his Majesty's present servants to continue to conduct the affairs of the country ; or whether his Majesty deems it advisable to adopt any other course." It has usually been understood that the King dismissed his Ministers on this occasion by the exercise of his prerogative,‡ but the above extract from Lord Melbourne's letter to the King on 12th November shows that, technically, he placed his resignation in his Majesty's hands. In his reply the King replied that, looking to the effect on the strength of Ministers of the withdrawal of Lord Althorpe from the House of Commons, and also to the division of opinion in the Cabinet on the question of the Irish Church, "he did not think he would be acting fairly or honourably by his Lordship if he called upon him for the continuance of his services in a position of which the tenure appeared to the King so precarious." The dismissal by the King of his Ministers, for such it was in effect,§ gave rise to a situation wholly without parallel. Melbourne, after

*Marginal note:* Fall of the Melbourne Ministry.

---

\* Became Lord Stanley on the death of his grandfather, the twelfth Earl of Derby, 21st October, 1834.

† See Melbourne's letter to the King (*Peel Letters*, ii. 253).

‡ Brougham industriously circulated the unfounded report that the Ministry had been dismissed as the result of an intrigue between the Tories and the Queen.

§ And so the King believed it to be, avowing it as "his own immediate and exclusive act" in a subsequent letter to Sir Robert Peel (*Peel Letters*, ii. 288).

Æt. 65.

The King sends for the Duke.

a personal interview with his Majesty at Brighton, offered to convey to the Duke of Wellington his Majesty's commands, and actually waited while Sir Herbert Taylor wrote the letter.* The Duke was just starting from Strathfieldsaye for hunting on 15th November, when the King's letter was brought to him. He started at once for Brighton, arriving there late at night. He told the King that the House of Commons was the chief difficulty in the way of a Tory Government, that the head of the Government ought to be in the House of Commons, and he recommended his Majesty to name Peel as First Minister. Peel was absent in Italy, and the Duke undertook to conduct the Government till he should return, filling up no offices so as to leave Peel an entirely free hand when he came home. The King, greatly incensed with the reports circulated in the press by Brougham, and eager to get rid of his old Ministers at once, appointed

The Duke administers all the chief offices.

Wellington First Lord of the Treasury, and committed to him in addition the seals of the Home, Foreign, and Colonial Offices. The Duke wrote a letter of four lines to Lord Brougham, stating that "he had his Majesty's commands to request him to deliver up the Seal on Friday next at 2 o'clock." Brougham replied on four sides of *letter* paper, after perusing which the Duke remained in doubt whether he meant to give up the seal or not—an incident very characteristic of both men.†

The Whigs and the Whig press affected great indignation at this concentration of offices and patronage in the hands of one subject; they declared it to be unconstitutional; but the cloud of unpopularity had passed away from the hero of Waterloo; nobody suspected the Duke of serving his private interests at this juncture; his character was far too simple and downright to admit of the faintest imputation on that

---

* *Croker*, ii. 224.

† *Salisbury MSS.*, 1834. I have been able to verify the exactness of this statement. The originals of these letters are at Apsley House, and exactly correspond in dimensions to those quoted by Lady Salisbury.

score; people were proud of the veteran who rode from door
to door, methodically discharging the routine business of four
public departments, "worked as no post-horse at Hounslow
ever was," as he expressed it himself.

"It was really a moment worth living for," wrote Lady
Salisbury in her journal, "to see that great man once more where
he ought to be, appreciated as he deserves by his King, and at
the head of this great country—if it does but last! But one
must not embitter such moments by thoughts like these." *

King William was in great glee at having got rid of the
Whigs, and urged on Wellington to anticipate Peel's return
by filling up the offices. But the Duke was firm.

"The King," he wrote to Lord Melville on 23rd November,
"is in great spirits, but he is, thank God between ourselves!
gone out of town; he is becoming a little in a hurry, and I am
afraid that I should not have kept him quiet." †

The King's summons reached Peel at a ball in Rome on
25th November; he reached London on 9th December, having,
as he afterwards noted, taken exactly the same time over the
journey as the Emperor Hadrian did. His first act after
assuming the office of Prime Minister was to invite Lord
Stanley to take office in the new Ministry. This was in
accordance with Wellington's suggestion, who had included
the names of Stanley and Graham in a list of Ministers which
he had forwarded to Italy for Peel's consideration, expressing
doubts at the same time whether they would accept office.
The Duke had convinced himself that the party must move
with the times.

"I think that you will find the Tories, my Lords in particular,
very well disposed to go all reasonable lengths in the way of
reform of institutions. . . . I have been astonished at their being
so docile." ‡

Stanley declined office on the ground that, however possible
it might be for him to serve with Peel, the circumstance that

ANN. 1834.

Lord
Stanley
declines
office.

* *Salisbury MSS.*, 1834.        † *Apsley House MSS.*        ‡ *Ibid.*

ÆT. 65. the Duke of Wellington was the person who received the first mark of the King's confidence "must stamp upon the Administration about to be formed the impress of his name and principles." Lord Stanley was mistaken in supposing that the Duke had any ulterior views about the conduct of the Government. Misunderstandings between him and Peel there certainly had been and were to be, but nothing can have been more complete than the Duke's loyal deference to Peel, and his resolve that the Administration should be Peel's and no other.

"It is impossible," wrote Mr. Dawson to Sir Robert before his return to England, "to praise too highly the delicate chivalry of the Duke towards you. I dined with him on Wednesday, and he told me that he should take no step, that he should not utter an opinion until your arrival; that he looked upon you as the only man to steer the country through its difficulties; that he occupied his present position solely to resign it in the fullest way to you; and that on your arrival you should not find one single thing done to fetter your judgment." *

Indeed, the Duke's action in this crisis—his perfect loyalty to the absent Peel and his discretion in recognising the limitations of his own power, as shown by his failure to form a Ministry in 1832—affords one of the best features in his whole political career.

That Stanley and his friends, representing the moderate Reformers or Liberal-Conservatives, should hold aloof was a keen disappointment to Peel. "It will be the Duke's old Cabinet over again," he said querulously to Mr. Croker; † and so it was in effect, with Lyndhurst on the Woolsack, Aberdeen at the Colonial Office, Goulbourne Home Secretary, and Hardinge Chief Secretary for Ireland.

Peel's first Cabinet. Lord Stanley's apprehensions, however, that the policy of the new Cabinet would be high-and-dry Tory, were soon dispelled by a manifesto issued by Peel, with the approval of

* *Peel Letters,* ii. 260.        † *Croker,* ii. 249.

THE RIGHT HON. SIR ROBERT PEEL, BART., M.P.

*From a painting by Sir Thomas Lawrence*

Vol. II, p. 367.

his colleagues,* to the electors of Tamworth, in which the Anx. 1835.
Reform Act was referred to as " a final and irrevocable settlement of a great constitutional question," and a programme of
economy, of deliberate and dispassionate reform of every
institution which stood in need of it, and of steady redress of
grievances. Immediately upon this Parliament was dissolved ;
but although the Ministerialists, who could only reckon 150
votes in the first reformed Parliament, came back greatly
reinforced, they still formed but a minority of the House of
Commons.

A characteristic letter from Benjamin Disraeli explained to
the Duke his view of the causes for his defeat in the contest
for High Wycombe.

" I have fought our battle and I have lost it by a majority of
fourteen. . . . Had Lord Carrington exerted himself even in
the slightest degree in my favour, I must have been returned.
But he certainly maintained a *neutrality*—a neutrality so strict
that it amounted to a blockade. . . . Grey made a violent anti-
ministerial speech, and I annihilated him in my reply ; but what
use is annihilating men out of the House of Commons ? . . . I
am now a cipher ; but if the devotion of my energies to your
cause, IN and OUT, can ever avail you, your Grace may count
upon me, who seeks no greater satisfaction than that of serving
a really great man." †

The life of the Ministry was short and troubled. Beaten
on the election of a Speaker and again on the Address, Peel
persevered ‡ until he had sustained six defeats in the

* Mr. Walpole speaks of the Tamworth manifesto as if it had been a
disagreeable surprise to the Tory Cabinet (*History of England*, iii. 281). We
have, however, Peel's own assurance that he submitted the draft to his colleagues.
and that it had their approval (*Peel Memoirs*, ii. 58).

† *Apsley House MSS.*

‡ The Duke strongly urged Peel not to give up. "I should not be your
friend," he wrote, " if I did not advise you and entreat you not to give up till
your retaining your position becomes wholly impossible. A week more or less
cannot signify much either way, in any view whatever, excepting to your high

ÆT. 65.

Defeat and resignation of Ministers.

Commons, the last of which happened in April, when Ministers were in a minority of 27 on Lord John Russell's resolution for dealing with the surplus revenues of the Irish Church. While the debate was in progress the Duke was entertaining the Austrian Ambassador at dinner at Apsley House. Lord Lyndhurst offered to send early information of the result of the division.

"I am quite satisfied," said the Duke, "to have it when the newspapers come in at ten o'clock. If I could do any good by having it earlier, I would; but as I can't, I'd just as soon wait."

"You always take things coolly," interposed Lady Salisbury. "I suppose you never lie awake with anxiety?"

"No," replied the Duke, "I don't like lying awake; it does no good. I make a point never to lie awake." [*]

The first attempt at a Conservative Administration had failed, but Conservatism, as expounded by Peel, had commanded such wide sympathy that thoughtful people began to recognise in it the policy of the future. Only among the Old Tories was there rending of garments. In the Duke of Wellington, despite his abandonment of them on Roman Catholic Relief and, ineffectively, on Reform, they had still recognised their brightest hopes of resisting further changes, though they never regarded him as a good "party man," but now the Duke had gone in scot and lot with the new-fangled Conservatism.

The Duke's relations with his party.

"The Duke," notes Lady Salisbury, "has certainly a nervous horror of the annoyances he endures from the ultra-Tories; far greater than any he feels of the Radicals. . . . He told me he was convinced we should soon see a new party formed in the House of Lords, consisting of Lords Brougham and Londonderry and the Duke of Buckingham." [†]

character, and to the contentment of those who have supported you; and I earnestly recommend you to bear with the evils of your position, till the conviction will be general that you cannot longer maintain it."

[*] *Salisbury MSS.*, 1833.　　　　　　[†] *Ibid.*

There was a wild project of overthrowing the Government ANN. 1835.
by an adverse motion in the House of Lords which elicited
from the Duke the following memorandum addressed to the
Duke of Cumberland, the Duke of Buckingham, and the
Marquess of Londonderry :—

"May 5, 1835.

". . . The House of Lords is now in a position very different
from that in which it stood previous to the Reform Bill. The
effect of that measure has been to exclude the influence of the
Crown, of the members of the H. of Lords, and of property in
general in the Election of Members of the H. of Commons. . . .
The consequence is that the H. of Lords have no influence over
the proceedings of the Government, or of the H. of Commons.
Indeed, in the last, the influence of the House of Lords is
considered very much in the same light as the influence of the
Master is over his emancipated slaves. It is sufficient for the
H. of Lords to approve of and recommend a measure to induce
the H. of Commons to reject it. But . . . it must be observed
that the H. of Lords still possesses constitutionally great power
over the Legislature of the Country ; in the exercise of which
it will be supported by the Country, and which it ought to
exercise with diligence, with wisdom, and discretion. It must
not be supposed, however, that this power will be left in the
hands of the Peers, or that they will be allowed to exercise it
with independence (in other words, that they will not be
swamped) if they exercise it lightly and without deliberation,
or if they should render their House contemptible by interfering
in discussions in the H. of Commons and in measures not in
a legislative form, and not regularly before them, or in the
details of the administration of the Gov!, over which it must
be obvious that they can have no control, as they have none over
the Finances of the State. I recommend these few observations
to the attention of the Duke of Cumberland, the Duke of
Buckingham, and the Marquis of Londonderry. I cannot hope
that they will induce them to alter their course. They contain
the reasons for my own.

" W." *

* Original at Wynyard Park.

Æт. 66.

Rapproche-
ment be-
tween Can-
ningites
and Peel-
ites.

Municipal
Corpora-
tious Bill.

The estrangement of the Old Tories was balanced by a decided *rapprochement* between the Canningites—the Liberal-Conservatives under Stanley—and the regular Opposition—the Peelites as they may be called by anticipation—under Peel and Wellington. The principal measure before Parliament in 1835 was one dealing with the reform of municipal corporations, a subject which roused passions almost as intense and apprehensions almost as gloomy as those excited by parliamentary reform. The Duke, despite the advance in his views which had so much dismayed the Old Tories, detected grave dangers in the proposals of the Government.

"The worst of the Corporation Bill," said he, "is that it will form a little republic in every town, possessing the power of raising money. In case of anything like a civil war, these would be very formidable instruments in the hands of the democratic party. Charles I. was ruined by the money levied by the City of London." *

It almost seems as if it required familiarity with the steam engine, not yet universally known, to awaken the minds of the most practised and thoughtful politicians to the beneficent action of the safety-valve. The Duke, even after the reassuring result of the second general election under the Reform Act, could discern security to the State and its institutions only in centralisation of power and political action. Peel was gifted with greater prescience. He had hung back at a time when Wellington was prepared to go forward in the path of reform, but once entered upon, he saw that the path must be followed. He had assisted the Corporation Bill in the Commons, confining his opposition to certain important points; but his influence over its fate ceased with its entry into the House of Lords, and, led by Lyndhurst, the Tories played sad havoc with its provisions, and a collision between the two houses seemed inevitable. A compromise, however, was effected in September, the Duke

* *Salisbury MSS.*, 1835.

cordially co-operating with Peel to save the measure of which, privately, he entertained so much disapprobation.

Nevertheless the friends of both leaders were distressed to perceive a return of that estrangement between them, which had prevailed before the formation of the Administration of 1834. When the Duke asked Peel's advice about the best means of dealing with the Corporation Bill in the Lords, Peel drily replied that "the Lords must do as they pleased," and left London without giving notice to the Duke of his intentions.* Indeed, communications entirely ceased between the two colleagues, although Sir Robert continued to express his views on the Bill to Hardinge and others. The Duke was deeply offended and hurt, and it was chiefly the incessant good offices of Lady Salisbury with the Duke and those of Mr. Arbuthnot with Peel, through Sir Henry Hardinge, that a good understanding was eventually restored, never again to be seriously shaken. *[margin: Renewed coldness between the Duke and Peel.]*

"I could not help," wrote Lady Salisbury, "expressing to Sir Henry Hardinge my concern and disappointment at Peel's conduct, which must end in utter ruin to the Monarchy; and I particularly urged Sir Henry to induce Peel, if possible, to alter his *manière d'être* with the Duke, and treat him with more confidence and cordiality. 'The truth is,' said Sir Henry, 'that Peel has no respect for any man's opinion but the Duke's, for whom he has the highest possible veneration. . . . When one speaks to him, he meets one with such a flow of words, and such knock-me-down arguments, it is impossible to reply. When he knows his opinions are contrary to those of the Duke, he avoids coming into collision with him, and will not enter into the subject personally, but transmits it through a third person. That is the reason of his apparent reserve : it is a mixture of habitual reverence for the Duke and obstinacy and *mauvaise honte.*'

"Next day the Duke came to me. I repeated to him what Sir Henry had told me of Peel's high respect for him and dislike

---

* *Salisbury MSS.*, 1835.

of coming into direct collision with his opinions. He listened
with great attention, and made no answer." *

Neither Wellington nor Peel were deficient in common
sense; the representations of their friends had a more felicitous
effect than sometimes rewards the exertions of the best-
intentioned persons, and by the beginning of 1836 the friendly
relations of country gentlemen were restored between them.

"I shall certainly be at Drayton on Wednesday," wrote the
Duke to Sir Robert on 18th January, 1836. "I will send
Jonathan down to-morrow, and I will bring my red coat, and be
prepared to do whatever you please. In respect to business, the
few words that passed between us already show that we are of
the same opinion as to the course to be pursued in Parliament." †

The Duke wrote to Lady Salisbury after this visit—

"Upon the whole, between ourselves, I think him (Peel) disposed to act more rationally than I have ever known him before.
I conducted myself towards him as I always have done; with
unaffected good temper and cordiality." ‡

And thus ended a disagreement between two men whose
concord was of so great importance to their country at a time
when the classes and masses were settling, not without friction
which might have engendered conflagration, into new relations
with each other. It is agreeable to read the close and constant
correspondence which arose out of their joint conduct of the
opposition; there was now no longer any frigid "The Lords
must do as they please," nor testy references by the Duke to
the vacillation of "that fellow in the House of Commons;" but
close co-operation in restraining, on the one hand, the extreme
members of their own party, and resisting resolutely the most
objectionable measures of the other.

* *Salisbury MSS.*, 1835.        † *Peel Letters*, ii. 321.
‡ *Salisbury MSS.*, 1836.

Lord Melbourne's Ministry was placed between a vigilant Aɴɴ. 1837. Opposition and an unruly Radical "tail."

### The Duke of Wellington to Sir Robert Peel.

" 23rd March, 1837.

" . . . Is not the probable resignation of the Government the great question of the day? It is obvious that they are surrounded by difficulties, abroad and at home, in colonies and everywhere. . . . Their resignation is a great misfortune, but I cannot doubt that it will take place. How does the expectation of this event affect the question under consideration? It is very desirable that the public should understand clearly what the difference of opinion between the two parties is—that you are determined to uphold the Protestant religion, the Church of England in Ireland as well as in England; that you are determined to maintain the independence of the House of Lords. I think that a debate upon the third reading might bring out these points very forcibly, and that men might be induced to look a little further than the mere question of the municipal administration of towns which are bankrupt in property. I shall be satisfied with whatever course you may decide upon. I may have a little more or less facility by your adopting one or the other; but in the consideration of the great interests involved in the decision, such trifles must be laid out of the question." *

The "great misfortune" was averted by an unforeseen event. Chief among Lord Melbourne's difficulties was the intense dislike which the King had conceived against, and took no pains to conceal from, his Whig servants. On 20th June took place what Spencer Walpole unkindly terms the most important political circumstance in the life of William IV., namely, his death. With the new monarch Melbourne at once found himself on a very different footing, both personally and politically; for the Princess Victoria was fond of Lord Melbourne as a friend, and had been sedulously educated in

*Death of William IV.*

* *Peel Letters,* ii. 342.

Æt. 68.

The
Duke's
opinion of
Queen
Victoria.

Whig principles by her mother, the Duchess of Kent. It is curious to note, considering what the Duke's relations with his Queen became in after years, that almost the first public act of her Majesty met with his disapproval. A royal review was to be held in July, at which the young Queen made up her mind to appear on horseback, in spite of the remonstrance of her Ministers. Somebody to whom the Duke imparted, bluntly enough, his objection to what he regarded as a piece of theatrical display, conveyed what he said straight to her Majesty, but this did not in the least affect her resolve. The Duke had misgivings about the Queen's horsemanship, which proved to be groundless. "Much better come in her carriage," he said grimly to Lady Salisbury. "I would not wish a better subject for a caricature than this young Queen, alone, without any woman to attend her, without the brilliant cortège of young men and ladies as ought to appear in a scene of that kind, and surrounded only by such youths as Lord Hill and me, Lord Albemarle and the Duke of Argyll! And if it rains and she gets wet, or if any other *contretemps* happens, what is to be done? All these things sound very little, but they must be considered in a display of that sort. As to the soldiers, I know *them*; they won't care about it one sixpence.* It is a childish fancy, because she has read of Queen Elizabeth at Tilbury Fort; but *then* there was threat of foreign invasion, which was an occasion calling for display; what occasion is there now?" †

Much occasion, as the Duke himself lived to realise. The nation was just awaking to political life. This act of the Queen was the first in a long series of gracious appearances which were to endear her to her people in a degree never attained by any preceding British monarch—the initial step in a reign, of which the character has done more than all the precautions of politicians to avert the dangers which the

* Either the Duke was mistaken, or the British soldier has changed his character in the last sixty years.

† *Salisbury MSS.*, 1837.

Duke foresaw, and which undoubtedly were impending over Ann. 1837. the ancient institutions of the country.*

Lord Melbourne's moderation and the irritation it occasioned among his Radical followers, not unnaturally suggested the expediency of a coalition between parties. The Duke recognised no merit in the idea.

*The Duke of Wellington to Lady Burghersh.*

" Walmer Castle, 31st August, 1837.

" There is nearly an equality of Members in Parliament, which renders the House of Commons a Curiosity as a deliberative assembly; and the management of which by what is called Government must be found hereafter, as it has been lately, impracticable. Then comes your Gentleman from the moon who says you must have a fusion—a junction—a Coalition of Parties. That is the remedy. He may give it what name he pleases; it *will be a Coalition !* will be so called, and detested accordingly ! This difficulty would be sufficient. But is there no other ? Since the great coalition of 1782-3 we have had others. The great whig Leaders joined Mr. Pitt in 1794 in support of his Anti-Revolutionary Policy in the French war. They had supported him long before they coalesced with him in Government. He was strong, and did not depend on their Support. Mr. Canning made a sort of Coalition with the Whigs and he died ; but if he had lived, he could not have gone on. The truth is that *Coalitions* have a bad name ! Everybody on all sides must be against them, that does not profit by them : excepting the very small numbers indeed who sometimes think of the *Interêt de la Chose !* But it is said that after my declaration there can be no difference of opinion. My declaration was neither more nor less than the application to a particular set of Questions of the Principle on which I have been acting for years. But there is a great distance between my declaration and a general concurrence

---

* Nor of this country alone. It was wisely observed by Lord Rosebery on a recent occasion (1899) that the example of Queen Victoria as a constitutional ruler has had an influence far beyond these shores in reconciling European nations to monarchy as a form of government.

Æт. 68.

of opinions, much more a Coalition founded upon the existence of such agreement. It is my opinion that the only chance that any Government has in England in these times is to take a very moderate course ; and to take its chance of support from the moderate men of all sides, if there are any such." *

**The Duke's political faith.**

The above letter, were there no other testimony in existence, were sufficient refutation of the prevalent idea that the Duke was a cut-and-dried Tory. The truth is that, while he welcomed some reforms, such as Roman Catholic Emancipation, he hated and dreaded others, such as parliamentary reform and the abolition of the corn laws, and only yielded when he recognised, as the bulk of his party did not, that the forces behind them were irresistible, and, if longer resisted, would, by the accumulation of energy, sweep away a great deal that might and ought to be preserved. He has been denounced by Reformers as an impracticable Tory—by Tories as a mere Opportunist. In fact, he was neither. An Opportunist is one who will adopt the policy of the majority of the moment, in order to keep his party or himself in power. The Duke had no party, and was absolutely indifferent to and independent of office. But he was strongly convinced that the security of Crown and country were involved in keeping the Radicals out of office, and, in order to do that, he was prepared to accept and even to promote—he did accept and promote—measures which as a Tory he detested. He was a Possiblist—if a new term may be coined—rather that an Opportunist, prepared to resist change as long as possible, but to give way rather than throw the power into the hands of those who, he honestly believed, would wreck the realm.

**Impatient Tories.**

The Opposition, acting under the direction of Peel and Wellington, who now understood and respected each other thoroughly, preserved an attitude of forbearance to the Government which was not entirely to the taste of all the

---

* *Apsley House MSS.*

party. Lord Wilton having written to complain of Sir Ann. 1838.
Robert Peel's lukewarmness, the Duke replied—

"31st October, 1837.

" I do not like to interfere in the affairs of the House of
Commons, first, because I have nothing to say to them, and next
because I really do not understand them. Old men ought not to
chatter of things that they don't understand any more than
*charming women!* . . . I generally find that without much communication of any sort, Sir Robert Peel and I find ourselves
pretty nearly on the same ground." *

During the winter the Tory rank and file grew still more
impatient. Many friends, personal and political, beset the
Duke with appeals to attack the Government, but he never
varied the spirit of his reply.

*The Duke of Wellington to Lord Redesdale.*

" January 28th, 1838.

". . . I daresay that I am in the wrong. There is nobody
who dislikes, so much as I do, and who knows so little of Party
Management. I hate it ; because in my opinion it is the cause
of all that we are suffering at present. It destroyed the Parliament of 1830. It caused the Reform Bill. It prevented the
Alteration of the Reform Bill in the House of Lords in the Year
1832 and the formation of the Parliament in May of that Year.
It had nothing to say to the Events of 1834. It destroyed the
Parliament formed by those Events. That which I cannot and
will not do is to become a Party to any vote which is to involve
the Honor of the Country or that of the House of which I am a
Member. But I have no objection to others doing what they
please. I am afraid that my opinions are very displeasing to many ;
as well Members of our House as out of doors—I am sorry for
it ; but if I am to act it must be according to my own opinions." †

* *Apsley House MSS.*
† *Ibid.* The drafts of these and innumerable other letters are usually in
the Duke's own handwriting.

*The same to Mr. Arbuthnot.*

" 15th February, 1838.

" If I was to decide for myself I should say don't engage in a vote which is to turn out the existing Government. . . . Let us avoid to involve the country in the difficulty of having no Government at all, in order to get out of the difficulty of having a very weak one. To this you answer, Let Peel dissolve the Parliament. I doubt the measure having the effect of giving him a majority to enable him to carry on the Government. We can't carry on a Government with a working majority of 30, as the existing Government do. Our people will not attend to support us. All theirs attend to support them in Government and will attend to oppose us in Government. But there is an element in this case which is a novelty since the year 1831—that is the objection to change on the part of the Queen. I dined yesterday at the Palace, and passed there the evening. Lord Melbourne was there. I sat on her right, he on her left, at dinner. I entertain no doubt that her Majesty is quite satisfied with him. My opinion is that she does nothing without consulting him, even upon the time of quitting the table after dinner and retiring to bed at night. I must say that if the adoption of a course in Parliament which is to break up the existing Government is doubtful, supposing the Queen to be favourable to our views, or at least neutral, the circumstances are still more complicated if we are not only to force ourselves upon the House of Commons and the publick, but likewise upon the Queen herself. . . . I have always been and always shall be in front of the Battle. I cannot hold back. But it is a little too much for Noblemen and Honble. Gentlemen to call upon Sir Robert Peel and me to put ourselves at their Head to carry into Execution a course of policy of which we disapprove and see the danger; trusting to their support; when we have found in this very Session that we cannot rely upon their support in any opinion of ours; or upon any Measure whatever." *

The Canadian rebellion. In truth, the Government were experiencing plenty of difficulties within their own camp. The first announcement

* *Apsley House MSS.*

by Ministers on the meeting of Parliament on 16th January, ᴀɴɴ. 1838.
1838, had reference to the provinces of Upper and Lower
Canada, which had been in active rebellion for several months.
The Government had determined to suspend the constitution
of Lower Canada, and to invest Lord Durham with almost
plenary powers to restore the authority of the Crown. The
Radicals vehemently opposed this proposal, which was
objectionable also from a Conservative point of view; but
Peel agreed with Wellington that it would never do to join
the Radicals in an attack on the Government. There was
perfect harmony between the Opposition leaders of the two
Houses on this question, and Lord Stanley entirely concurred
with them. Stanley wrote to Peel, exceedingly indignant
with Brougham, who, ever since his exclusion from office
in 1835, had been a thorn in the flank of the Administration.
Brougham had written to Stanley—

"I am in wonderment at the extreme self-denial of your Conservatives. I thought I had opened the door of the closet for
them, and put the Government in a fire that would destroy them,
when the Duke steps forward and shuts the door in his own face,
and protects them from my battery. I must say he was their
only defender, and that he has never helped them since; but
a Government has ninety-nine lives if its adversaries help it as
soon as it is in peril."

Far different was Wellington's conception of the duty of
a loyal Opposition. Although opposed in party to Lord
Melbourne, he appreciated the advantage of having at the
head of the Government a statesman who was accustomed
to meet all proposals for reform by the chilling inquiry—
"Why not leave it alone?"

*The Duke of Wellington to Sir Robert Peel.*

" London, 22nd February, 1838.

" I concur in opinion with Lord Stanley that you may be
forced to a vote upon Sir W. Molesworth's resolution, whatever

may be the course that you will take. If that resolution should be carried, the Administration must go, and you will have to consider whether you will or will not undertake the Government. . . . I am certain that the greatest evil that can befall the country is to have the Conservative party forced upon the Queen at the present moment. . . . Do what you may your Conservative Government, however Liberal, will not be supported by the adherents of Lord Melbourne. Then observe how we shall stand. We have a rebellion in Canada, which must occupy our whole force for the next two years— or more if the United States should think proper to avail themselves of that opportunity of settling boundaries, Texas, Mexico, etc.*—leaving not troops in sufficient numbers for the peace establishment anywhere. Suppose that O'Connell should, as he has threatened, avail himself of that opportunity to agitate repeal. What does he mean by agitating Repeal? Not repeal of the 40th George III. (the Act of Union). He means to agitate non-payment of rents, as he has agitated non-payment of tithe, and to force others to repeal the law. Have we the means of enforcing good order in Ireland? Would Parliament grant us the means, or enable us to use them? These are the obvious questions of the day. There are hundreds of others which a Conservative Government could not even look at. Would it be fair to force ourselves on the Queen and the country under these circumstances?" †

Peel was not so sure as the Duke about the expediency of supporting Ministers. He laid stress on the importance of keeping the Conservative party together, which he considered would be difficult if it was called on to defend Ministers against their own people.‡ In the end the expedient was adopted of framing to Molesworth's motion an amendment which the Radicals could not support, thereby affording to the Government a loophole of escape from a vote

---

* This seemed probable at the time, owing to the action of armed bodies of American "sympathisers;" but the United States Government acted in a most friendly manner, and interfered to prevent hostilities on the part of their own people.

† *Peel Letters*, ii. 364.                ‡ *Ibid.*, 365.

of censure. The Government Bill suspending the constitu-tion of Canada having passed the House of Commons, met with vigorous opposition from Brougham in the Lords. In the course of the debate thereon the Duke expressed his opinion in terms which have passed into an aphorism—" A great country like this can have no such thing as a small war."

Although Wellington emphatically declined Lord Stanley's invitation to enter upon a general course of concert with the Government,* he freely gave them the benefit of his professional experience, and, at Lord Melbourne's request, prepared an elaborate memorandum on the conduct of operations in Canada.

The rebellion was suppressed by the vigorous action of Sir John Colborne,† but the difficulties of the Government were intensified by the arbitrary action of their Commissioner in Canada, Lord Durham. Although an active and advanced Radical, Durham far exceeded the powers entrusted to him, and violated the law by transporting persons without trial, and sentencing others to death should they venture to show themselves in Canada. His administration was a glaring failure; nevertheless, the honour is his of having given his sanction to the scheme of a constitution for Canada which was ultimately carried into effect in 1840, with the felicitous result to both colony and mother-country which is apparent at this day.

In this year the Duke declined the invitation of the

*Marginal notes:* ANN. 1838. — The Duke's relations with Lord Melbourne.

* *Apsley House MSS.*

† Afterwards Lord Seaton. He commanded the 52nd at Waterloo. Wellington was no unfriendly critic of the performances of his successors in the army. He expressed high admiration of the handling of the forces in Canada, and especially of the "journey of the 88th and 43rd regiments from New Brunswick to Quebec by sledges, which he observed was a great proof of the improvement of regimental system and arrangements within the last twenty-five years. It showed the excellence of the subaltern officers, of their notions of duty, and determination to employ all their energies and resources when called upon for exertion. He considered it to have been a very arduous undertaking and highly creditable to the commanding officers" (*De Ros MS.*).

.Ет. 69. University of Glasgow to allow himself to be nominated as Lord Rector; he reiterated the objections on the score of his want of learning which he had made when the Chancellorship of Oxford University was offered to him, and explained that the circumstances in that case were exceptional.*

Coronation of Queen Victoria. The Queen's Coronation in 1838 brought together a group on which a London crowd gazed with intense interest, and bestowed hearty applause. The representative sent to represent Louis Philippe was the Maréchal Soult, Duc de Dalmatic. Some of the chief features in the rejoicings are well described in Lady Salisbury's journal.

*22nd June.*—"The Duke and Soult met in the music room at the Queen's concert for the first time for many years and shook hands. Soult's appearance is different from what I expected: he is a gentleman-like old man with rather a benevolent cast of countenance, such as I should have expected in William Penn or Washington; tall, and rather stooping, the top of his head bald. . . . The Duke, though the lines on his face are deeper, has a fresher colour and a brighter eye. The Duke is extremely annoyed at Croker having brought out that article in the Quarterly on the battle of Toulouse just at this moment. . . . He had written twice to endeavour to prevent him doing so." †

On the evening of the Coronation Day the Duke gave a ball at Apsley House, which was attended by Soult and the other distinguished foreigners.

"I was amused," wrote Lady Salisbury, "to hear the Duc d'Ossuna complimenting the Duke upon the applause he had met with in the Abbey.

"'Vous avez eu un accueil très flatteur, monseigneur, ce matin.'

"'Oui,' replied the Duke, with the utmost indifference, 'on me reçoit toujours très bien dans ce pays-ci.'

* *Apsley House MSS.*
† The publication of the eleventh (Toulouse) volume of Gurwood's edition of the Wellington Despatches had been purposely postponed by the Duke's instructions to avoid giving offence to Soult.

*Le Maréchal Soult Duc de Dalmatie*

" I think, however, though he always despises *mob* popularity, ANN. 1838. that he was gratified with the applause which came from the most respectable people—judges and privy councillors included —which attended his leaving the Abbey. But a feeling—real and sincere, though almost a romantic one—that the chief attention and homage is on all occasions due to the Sovereign when present (the effect of that extraordinary devotion to the Crown which I never saw approached in any other person) diminished his gratification and even gave him a degree of annoyance. He looked back to see if the Queen was coming with an air of vexation, as if to say, 'This is too much—this belongs of right to her.' . . .

2*nd July.*—"Dined at Lord Londonderry's : the Austrian, Russian, Prussian, and Swedish Ministers, the Duke, Peel, Lyndhursts, etc., in all eight and forty. . . . The first time the Duke has been asked to dine there these three years, but I suppose they have at last seen the folly of their conduct, and he is always ready to be reconciled.

3*rd July.*—"A ball at home. . . . I saw the Duke present Hardinge to Soult—'J'ai l'honneur de vous présenter le chevalier Hardinge qui était avec l'armée quand——'

"'Tout ce qui me vient de votre main,' replied Soult, 'm'est toujours agréable' (to which Lady Salisbury added a malicious note of interrogation).

" The Duke is disinclined to give the foreigners a dinner because Soult must necessarily be among them, and he does not like to ask him to a table covered with trophies won against the French. . . .

6*th July.*—"Soult's ball ; another great mob : he asked everybody who had left their names with him.

10*th July.*—" . . . Went to the House of Lords. . . . Brougham opened the debate (on the orders given to attack Sardinian vessels conveying arms to Don Carlos) with a capital speech. Lord Melbourne's reply weak, or rather no reply at all ; Lord Ripon good ; Lord Minto a wretched speech, in which he laid down the doctrine that such orders would be justified by the Quadruple Treaty. This induced the Duke to abandon his first intention of not supporting Brougham's motion, and to resolve upon dividing—very few of our Peers in the House—messages sent off in all directions to collect them—Lord Redesdale * running to and fro—when up gets Lord Melbourne and throws over Lord Minto and his doctrine entirely. This induces the Duke, who forgets that he is not at the head of troops who can wheel about and retire, to rise again and recommend their Lordships *not* to divide ; after delivering which word of command he retired, followed by Lord Aberdeen, to dine with Soult. The Peers on our side were furious, and though some abstained from voting, a great number, among whom I regret to say was Lord Salisbury, divided in support of Brougham's motion, which was lost by the numbers being even. . . . .There is no doubt the Duke was right in the principle of policy, but in a party view nothing could be more fatal than such a change after the Lords had been summoned from all parts for a division. . . .

13*th July.*—" . . . Lord Salisbury went with the Duke to the City dinner—that City dinner which I have been moving heaven and earth to get the Duke to go to, by having the Beresford dinner put off. And a pretty result it has had ! After a long delay in giving the Duke's health, the Lord Mayor at last gave his and Soult's united ! ! His Grace the Duke of Dalmatia and his Grace the Duke of Wellington ! ! ! Lord Londonderry instantly got up and left the room, observing to those about him that he would not stay to be insulted. Lord Salisbury would have followed him, but that he depended on the Duke, who got up and made an excellent reply in very good taste. But he could not do otherwise than feel the insult, and expressed it to Lord Salisbury on the way home. It was proposed to the Duke to give the French army. ' D—n 'em ! ' he said. ' I'll have nothing to do with 'em but beat 'em.'

*Monday, 16th July.*—" Went early to see the Duke. He is going to have the foreigners to dinner on the 28th, and showed me some vases he intended as ornaments on the table : they are presents from Louis XVIII., and therefore *trophies*, but they have no inscriptions or representations to betray their origin.

28*th July.*—" The Duke's great dinner to the foreigners. . . . We dined in the gallery, altogether about 48. . . . Prince George

---

* Conservative Whip.

of Cambridge sat next me and a delightful neighbour he was. ... Ann. 1839.
Curiously enough, when Soult entered the house, the band
played *Vive Henri Quatre!* ... Soult went away rather early.
There was no taking leave between the Duke and him." *

During this summer a reconciliation, or rather a renewal of Reconcilia-
intercourse, took place between the Duke and Lord Wellesley. Welling-
It is melancholy to reflect on the degree in which these ton and
brothers, once so affectionate and relying so much on each Wellesley.
other, had become estranged, especially when it is remembered
how helpful the elder had been to the younger in his early
days.  It is not easy to discern the exact causes of the
coldness; perhaps it arose as much as anything out of the
appointment of Lord Anglesey as Lord Lieutenant of Ireland
in 1828.  At all events, on 16th May, having received a
message from Lord Wellesley through Lady Wellesley, the
Duke rode down to see him at Fulham.  "There was no
*explanation*, but the brothers met most cordially," † the first
time for several years.

The Government had weathered the rough weather from
the Canadian quarter; it was a far less threatening disturbance
which caused them to founder in the spring of 1839.  The
Ministry was strong in the favour of the Queen; no young
monarch could have been more fortunate in the character of
the chief adviser of the Crown, and her Majesty repaid Lord
Melbourne's services with her affection and confidence.  But
out-of-doors the Government were losing such remnant of
esteem which they had preserved hitherto, and their growing
unpopularity soon found reflection in the action of their
supporters in the House of Commons.  The bill for the
suspension of the constitution of Jamaica, where the House
of Assembly had declared against Imperial control or interference, was carried on 6th May by a majority of only five
votes.  The Ministry resigned, and the Queen at once sent Lord
for the Duke of Wellington, who begged to be excused from Melbourne
resigns.

---

* *Salisbury MSS.*, 1838. † *Ibid.*

forming a Cabinet on account of his advanced age, and recommended her Majesty to send for Sir Robert Peel. The Duke's apprehensions about the difficulty of becoming a Queen's Minister were amusing. "Peel has no manners and I have no small talk." He wished to be in the Cabinet without office, but Peel did not approve of this.

### Mr. Arbuthnot to Sir Robert Peel.

" Apsley House, 8th May, 1839.

" Fortunately I caught the Duke ready dressed and sitting in his room. I repeated to him what you said against his being in the Cabinet only as a Privy Councillor. He said—'Very well ; I am quite ready to have the Foreign Office '—which I had named to him in the way that you wished I should—and added, ' that he had promised the Queen to serve her in any way that would be thought most advisable, and that he would keep his promise.' *

The formation of the Cabinet was not difficult, but it is well known how Peel had to resign his commission when it became a question of filling certain offices which he did not even know existed. He made out a list by the aid of a Red Book of new appointments to all the Household offices, except those below the rank of Lady of the Bedchamber. On this list being submitted to the Queen, she declined to hear of the removal of any of her ladies ; Peel, "unable to recognise any distinction in respect to public appointments provided for by Act of Parliament and instituted for purposes of State, on account of the sex of the parties holding them," † could not yield the point, and, on this curiously trivial difference, the formation of a Ministry broke down, and Lord Melbourne with his colleagues was recalled.

The Duke had completed the allotted tale of threescore

*The Bedchamber difficulty.*

*Lord Melbourne resumes.*

* *Peel Letters.* ii. 391. † *Ibid.*, 406.

and ten years. Except his deafness,\* which was a severe ANN. 1839.
trial to him, and a rheumatic affection of the muscles of the
neck, which was the cause of the stooping head which marred
his military carriage, he had enjoyed a singular immunity
from ailments of all kinds. But he had touched the milestone
which is associated with so many partings; he stood at the
point whence the earthly landscape seems empty and drear;
and now the circle of his intimate friends was about to be
lessened by the loss of one of the most cherished. A few
days after the entry last quoted, Lady Salisbury's journal stops
abruptly. She fell into ill health, which, continuing all winter, Lady
was the occasion of her going to Broadstairs for sea air in the Salisbury's illness.
spring of 1839. On her way thither she stayed some weeks
at Apsley House, and it is touching to note the sedulous care
bestowed by the Duke on arrangements for her comfort. In
July Lady Salisbury was recommended to go to Carlsbad,
the Duke, as Master of the Elder Brethren, placing at
her disposal the Trinity House steam yacht. His anxiety
about the invalid is manifested by frequent letters both to
her and Lord Salisbury, and at the same time he provided
for her amusement a commentary on all the current gossip of
the day. The Duke was still apprehensive about the Queen's
tendency to Whiggism, which he was afraid was being
strengthened by the combined influence of her mother, Lord
Melbourne, and King Leopold of Belgium; although the
Whigs suspected her Majesty of being a Tory at heart.

*June 29.*—" I took my daughter-in-law (Lady Douro) to Court
yesterday. She was much admired by everybody, especially by
the Queen, who was very gracious to me there, as well as at Lady
Westminster's at night.

*September 19.*—" On the day that I arrived at Windsor Castle,
the Queen desired me to ride with her. . . . I rode with her,

---

\* On 14th May, 1838, Lord Melbourne postponed the second reading of
the Poor Law Bill which was down for that day at the Duke's request, because
he was suffering from an access of deafness (*Apsley House MSS.*).

ÆT. 70.

was out two or three hours, was wet to the skin—as wet as if I had been drawn through the river Thames; experienced no inconvenience therefrom; was at a ball at night, and travelled here (Walmer) from Windsor in a day, as well as I ever was. God bless you! Believe me, ever yours most Affectionately,

"W__N__." *

As the autumn went on, the news of Lady Salisbury's health became less favourable; she could write no more, and letters passed only between the two men.

*October 3rd.*—"The Duke and Duchess of Cambridge, with twenty followers and servants, are coming here (Walmer) this day. I am never very partial to the part of Boniface! I am less equal to the performance of it this day than I have ever been." †

Death of
Lady
Salisbury.

Early in October the Salisburys returned to England, and Wellington's letters to his lordship were daily; then they ceased suddenly on 15th October, till, on the 28th, he writes—

"I have not written to you since the fatal Tuesday. I was aware how little of consolation anything I could write could be to you; that you must have been sensible that there was no individual in existence who could have known as well as myself the extent of the loss which you and yours have sustained, and that I sincerely felt for you. It would have been impertinent to write on such topics at such a moment. I write to you, however, in order to continue our old habits; which is the course which I feel convinced the Departed would have wished that we should follow. . . . I entreat you to reflect that you are of an age and in a station which render it necessary that you should exert yourself; that your family require much attention and much exertion from you; that there are important publick questions to which you must attend; and that you cannot give way to the affliction which you so naturally feel." ‡

---

* *Salisbury MSS.*, 1839.        † *Ibid.*        ‡ *Ibid.*

The Duke felt the shock very severely, although he does not seem to have confided his grief to anybody. A few weeks later, on 19th November, he had an alarming seizure at Walmer. On returning from a ride, he sat down to write some letters, and, feeling unwell, caused Dr. M'Arthur to be sent for. Before the doctor could arrive, the Duke's bell rang again; his valet, Kendall, found him speechless, with his jaw dropped, but the Duke signed to him to leave the room. He did so, but, remaining behind the door, heard a heavy fall, and, on entering again, saw his master on the floor. On coming to himself the Duke was both blind and speechless, but he gradually recovered all his faculties, and Lord Mahon, who was the first friend to arrive at his bedside, had the satisfaction of remaining to watch his steady restoration to health. The doctors attributed the attack to the Duke's habits of extreme abstemiousness. On the day of his seizure he had eaten nothing but a morsel of dry bread at breakfast, and a piece of Abernethy biscuit on coming in from his ride, and for some months he had left off wine altogether. On the 22nd he had recovered so as to be able to go to London and attend the Privy Council to which the Queen announced her intended marriage.*

* *Stanhope,* 196-214.

# CHAPTER XI.

## THE CORN LAWS.

### 1840–1846.

**The Queen's betrothal.** WHEN the Queen opened Parliament in person on 16th January, 1840, her speech contained the official announcement of her betrothal to Prince Albert. In the House of Lords it fell to the lot of the Duke of Wellington to take exception to the omission of the word "Protestant" in reference to the Prince. It was inserted upon the Duke's amendment, although Lord Melbourne expressed the opinion that it was superfluous. In the House of Commons more serious difference arose over the Ministerial proposals for the Ann. 1840. marriage. On Lord John Russell moving that £50,000 a year should be provided out of the Consolidated Fund for the Queen's Consort, an amendment reducing the allowance to £30,000 was moved by Colonel Sibthorpe, supported by Peel, the Tory Opposition, and the Radicals, and carried against the Government by a majority of 104. Lord Melbourne pocketed the affront, but the fate of his Ministry was not long deferred.

The Duke showed manifest traces of his severe illness. "He looked better than I expected," noted Greville, "very thin, and his clothes hanging about him, but strong on his legs and his head erect. The great alteration I remarked was in his voice, which was hollow, though not loud, and his utterance, though not indistinct, was very slow. He is certainly now only a ruin." *

The Irish Municipal Corporation Bill and the Bill for uniting the two Canadas proved the occasion of fresh difference between the Duke and Sir Robert Peel. Sir Robert felt that the honour of the party was involved in adhering to that engagement,† but the Duke did not share his view of the obligation, and announced his intention of destroying the measure in the House of Lords. *Renewed coldness between Wellington and Peel.*

In regard to the Union of the two Canadas, Peel had expressed himself strongly in favour of that policy, and he adhered to his opinion. "I cannot expect others, who take a different view of this question, to adopt my opinions, but I adhere to my own, and I cannot undertake any responsibility should views adverse to mine be taken, and prevail." ‡ The Duke as strongly held the view that the union of the two provinces would lead to the separation of Canada from the mother-country, and he determined to use his power with the Lords to prevent it. All intercourse ceased between him and Sir Robert; their friends, especially Sir James Graham,

* *Greville,* 2nd series, i. 103.   † *Peel Letters,* ii. 434.

‡ *Ibid.,* 438.

were apprehensive of a split in the party; Lady Salisbury was no longer on the scene to bring about reconciliation; recourse was had to the patient influence of Arbuthnot.

"It is impossible," wrote Graham to Peel on 9th June, "not to make great allowances for the age and infirmities of the Duke. He probably is aware that life with him is drawing to a close, and is honestly and naturally afraid lest concessions made by him against his judgment should lead to fatal results, which, in the opinion of posterity, might cast a shade over the lustre of his fame." *

Herein Graham misjudged the Duke's motives, though he was right about the infirmities. There never was an actor on the great stage so indifferent about the judgment alike of the contemporary public and of posterity. It is true that he was always at great pains to explain his motives to his colleagues, but for the rest he cared nothing. In this he was a striking contrast to Peel, who desired, and wisely desired, to carry public opinion with him, and was sedulous to leave an elaborate *apologia* in his autobiography. Can anybody imagine Wellington sitting down to write his own memoirs?

### Mr. Arbuthnot to Sir James Graham.

"Apsley House, 13th June, 1840.

"I hope you will not now suppose that I say it from vanity, but in truth I believe that my presence here has been useful. It has been of use to let the Duke know what the leaders thought and wished, and this I have done in our several conversations. He has never actually said that he should take the course which was expected of him, but I have seen his mind turning by degrees to that course, and of this I was so convinced yesterday morning that I wrote to Lord Aberdeen that, in my opinion, he had better not talk to the Duke, as he had said to me that he would, but leave it all now to the workings of his own mind.

* *Peel Letters*, ii. 440.

. . . Rely upon it that the party will not break up. . . . What Ann. 1841.
I have most lamented was that I could not get Peel to call on
the Duke. I could not presume to press it, but I told him that
in my opinion it would have the best effect." *

History, when written, seems to be composed of the acts
of a few public men, upon whom the influence of unobtrusive
individuals is scarcely observed, yet this is often of lasting
effect. Arbuthnot's quiet and discreet pressure gradually led
the Duke away from a course of action whence no amount of
argument or invective could have deterred him. When the
Canada Bill came before the Lords for second reading on 30th
June, Wellington declined to vote for it as "a measure
entirely dangerous to the stability of the Colonial Government," yet he advised the House to allow it to go into
Committee. With even greater inconsistency, which it is
impossible to palliate or explain away, he adduced twenty-
seven reasons against the measure on its third reading on
27th July, but recommended his party to remit it to the
House of Commons for further consideration. The fact is
that this was one of the occasions on which the Duke sank
his private judgment rather than bring about a rupture in the
Conservative party, in the early return to power of which he
believed the security of the monarchy and the welfare of the
country to be involved. Lord Aberdeen told Greville that he
considered that the Duke had never rendered greater service
in his whole life to the public good than he did this session,
by moderating the violence of his own party and keeping
them together. They chafed at the restraint; they vowed
the Duke was in his dotage, but they could not refuse
obedience.†

" I cannot contemplate," wrote Sir James Graham to Arbuthnot on 27th July, "a Conservative Government without the
active aid and co-operation of the Duke of Wellington, and
though he may be dissatisfied with Peel's recent conduct, yet

* *Peel Letters*, ii. 443.         † *Greville*, 2nd series, i. 296.

Æt. 72.

approving his general principles, and acknowledging his integrity
and general worth, he will not, if the necessity should occur,
refuse to act with a body of gentlemen entitled to his confidence
and support in a great crisis of public affairs, on account of a
passing difference, the causes of which are practically at an
end." *

Greville speaks much at this time of the failure of the
Duke's powers. "He is a ruin," says he; yet was the old
spirit still strong within him. A Continental war seemed
imminent in 1840; the King of Prussia commissioned Lord
William Bentinck to ascertain if the Duke would consent to
take command of the German Confederate armies; he replied
that he was as able as ever, and as willing!

Arbuth-
not's good
offices.

Arbuthnot the indefatigable succeeded during the autumn in
finally restoring that cordial intercourse between Wellington
and Peel which moderate Conservatives regarded as indispensable to their continuance as a party. Much of the misunderstanding had been caused by the Duke's increasing
deafness; of this, Arbuthnot succeeded in convincing both
him and Peel, so that on 13th November one finds the Duke
once more writing in the old strain of intimacy to his colleague
about his sailor son William Peel.†

"Encourage him by all means to write down his observations
of the operations of which he is the witness, or in which he is an
actor; and above all to revise them after writing them, and
correct any error into which he may have fallen, leaving on the
face of the paper the error and its correction. This habit will
accustom him to an accurate observation and report of facts;
which are most important, destined as he most likely is to direct
and carry on great operations." ‡

Thus when, in the summer of 1841, repeated defeats of
the Government betokened an approaching crisis, not a cloud

* *Peel Letters*, ii. 445.
† Afterwards Captain Sir William Peel, K.C.B., who commanded the Naval
Brigade in the Crimea.
‡ *Peel Letters*, ii. 452.

remained between the Opposition leaders in the two Houses Ann. 1841. of Parliament.

"The truth is," wrote the Duke to Sir Robert, " that all I desire is to be as useful as possible to the Queen's service—to do anything, to go anywhere, and hold any office, or no office as may be thought most desirable or expedient for the Queen's service by you. . . . I don't desire even to have a voice in deciding upon it." *

Peel moved a vote of no confidence in the Government on 27th May; it was carried by a majority of a single vote, and on 23rd June Parliament was dissolved. The fortune of the polls favoured the Opposition : the Conservatives who went to the country in a minority of thirty, were returned in a majority of seventy-six. It would have been greater but for the imminence of disruption in the Scottish Church, and the refusal of Wellington and Peel to pledge themselves to support the Duke of Argyll's bill dealing with ecclesiastical affairs in Scotland; but it was sufficient, and Peel had no difficulty in forming a Cabinet of fourteen ministers. Wellington entered it without holding a department, and the character of the Administration was marked by Sir James Graham taking the seals of the Home Office and Lord Stanley those of the Foreign Office. The Old Tory party drew consolation from the inclusion of the Duke of Buckingham, although Lord Londonderry's indignation at being left out in the cold and sent as ambassador to Vienna was bitter and freely expressed.† "The Duke," wrote Arbuthnot to Sir Robert Peel, " said at Vienna Metternich would know Lord Londonderry well, and prevent him from doing mischief; and that for his part he would rather have him in the House of Lords without any office, and prepared to do his worst, than see him at the Board of Ordnance; but that you must dispose of him as you thought best." ‡

In the disposal of offices outside the Cabinet, Peel duly

*Marginalia:* Defeat of Ministers and General Election. Peel's second Administration.

* *Peel Letters*, ii. 461.　　　† *Ibid.*, 484.　　　‡ *Ibid.*, 483.

recognised the ability and energy of one, at least, of the most promising of the younger Conservatives, William Ewart Gladstone, who was appointed Vice President of the Board of Trade and Master of the Mint, with the rank of Privy Councillor. His services were soon in request in a matter with which his capacity was peculiarly well fitted to deal. The Conservatives had succeeded to an embarrassing heritage in the accumulated deficits of the five years of Queen Victoria's reign. The deficit for 1841-2 had been £2,334,000 ; that estimated for 1842-3 was £2,470,000 ; but before bringing in his budget, Peel dealt with the Corn Law. Under the law

of 1828, when wheat was quoted at 59s. or 60s. a quarter, a duty of 27s. was exacted on foreign corn, which fell as the price rose until, at the quotation of 73s. a quarter, foreign corn was only taxed at 1s. Peel proposed a 20s. duty upon corn when quoted at 50s. to 51s., to be reduced till the 73s. limit was touched, when the duty was 1s. as before. The Corn Law League scouted this measure as an insignificant relief, and Peel was burnt in effigy as an oppressor of the people ; the country Tories denounced it as not giving enough security to profitable agriculture ; the Duke of Buckingham and Lord Hardwicke resigned office. Lord John Russell moved the rejection of the Bill in favour of a fixed as against a fluctuating duty. Mr. Gladstone led the resistance to Russell's amendment, and, after the rejection of Mr. Villiers's proposal to repeal the Corn Laws altogether, Peel's sliding scale was adopted by the House of Commons ; but it did not help him in dealing with the prospective deficiency. He felt himself at the parting of ways, and he proved not unequal to the momentous decision to be made. He produced the most sensational budget of the century. He had the courage to impose a 7d. Income Tax, which, accustomed as the present generation has become to the weight of the burden, was at that time an unprecedented manner of raising revenue in time of peace. Ireland was exempted from the tax, except her absentee landlords, but was called on to pay an additional 1s.

a gallon on spirits, bringing her on an equality in this respect ANN. 1841.
with Scotland. By these and other subsidiary means he
turned his deficit of £2,470,000 into a surplus of £1,900,000.
So far, though there was much ground for grumbling, there
was none for alarm on the part of the high Tories. But
when he went on to explain the proposed application of his Relaxation
surplus to lowering of duties on seven hundred and fifty out of tariffs.
of twelve hundred articles taxed on import, then the Protectionists indeed beheld Pelion upon Ossa piled against them
—the lowered tariff on imported goods as well as the modified
tax on foreign corn. Would the Duke, once their pride and
fearless champion, stand this? nay—would he actually have
a hand in it? The Duke was to stand this and a great deal
more, as time was to prove; but there was one part of the
financial scheme which pleased him little, namely, the continued reductions in the military and naval establishments
for purposes of economy.*

Many lifelike descriptions have been made by eye-witnesses The Duke's
of the Duke's appearance and habits in Parliament during the appear-
last ten years of his life. The invariable blue frock-coat was Parlia-
relieved by a white neckcloth fastened behind by a large ment.
silver or steel buckle. White trousers for summer wear gave
place to dark cloth in winter; the waistcoat was white in
summer, and buff or some brighter hue in winter. During
the last session of his life, 1851–2, his chest and shoulders
were protected by a short cape of white fur, singularly unlike
ordinary masculine attire, but harmonising admirably with
the Duke's clear complexion and white hair. He generally
rode to and from the House,† but sometimes drove in a four-
wheeled chaise designed by himself. In those days it was
still the privilege of peers to vote by proxy, and of such
proxies as many as sixty were sometimes entrusted to the

* See Appendix H. p. 356.
† "The neat, white-haired old gentleman, whom we have all seen rolling upon
his horse in the Park and Pall Mall—a wonder to all bystanders that he did not
topple over" (*Punch*, vol. ix. 1845).

Duke's disposal, rendering him, had he chosen to be less scrupulous in using his power against the Government of the day, a truly formidable personage in opposition.

The Duke's attention to the business before the House was unflagging. He listened, in spite of his disabling deafness, to every speech from beginning to end, seldom leaving the House before it adjourned. His style in speaking was vehement, but the reverse of fluent, and, like many imperfect orators, he used exaggerated phrases to impress his opinions upon his hearers. His speeches abound in repetitions and contradictions, singularly at variance with the lucidity of at least his military despatches. Sir Walter Scott described his method in debate as "slicing the argument into two or three parts and helping himself to the best." "He usually sits," wrote a contributor to *Fraser's Magazine*, "in a state of abstraction; his arms folded, his head sunk on his breast, his legs stretched out: he seems to be asleep. But, in a very few moments, he shows that he has not been an inattentive observer of the debate. He suddenly starts up, advances (sometimes with faltering steps) to the table, and, without preface or preliminary statement, dashes at once into the real question in dispute." In the Cabinet, Charles Greville, who as Clerk to the Privy Council had good opportunities of observation, notes in 1844 the extraordinary deference paid to the Duke by all his colleagues. Each Minister went to sit next to him before speaking, so that the Duke might hear him; but he adds that the old gentleman was very irritable, and never would alter anything he had written.

The Duke and his early associates.  Most of the Duke's biographers, even his most ardent panegyrists, have reproached him with indifference towards or forgetfulness of his old comrades of campaign, but to do so reveals a want of insight into the exigencies of political life. Had the Duke been merely one of those who

> "Lean'd on the walls and basked before the sun,
> Chiefs who no more in bloody fights engage,
> But wise through time and narrative with age
> In summer days like grasshoppers rejoice "—

had he, at the close of one career, assumed his well-earned Ann. 1841.
leisure instead of entering upon another, not less arduous
than the first—then, indeed, he might have been blamed if he
did not constantly and by preference seek the society of those
officers who had enabled him to achieve such greatness. It
can scarcely be doubted that, left to make his own choice, he
would have indulged his inclination for repose; his letters
abound in proof that, in accepting civil office, he was acting
solely under a cogent sense of duty. It shows remarkable
unfamiliarity with the calls upon one in the higher spheres of
political life, to suppose that a statesman has the disposal
of his own time or the choice of his own associates.

When Mr. W. H. Smith, having been First Lord of the
Admiralty in the last Disraeli Administration, was offered
the Chairmanship of the London and North-Western Railway
in 1881, he asked the advice of his chief. Lord Beaconsfield
replied, "Politics is a jealous mistress," and dissuaded Smith
from accepting the desirable post. However open his lordship's syntax may be to criticism, none who have experience
of the exactions of political life can question the truth of his
sentiment. Every hour in every day must be lived; in office
hours and while Parliament sits the man is a slave; the day's
work over, multitudes of social obligations—literally obligations—sadly interfere equally with the cultivation of private
friendship and the ordinary courtesies of acquaintanceship. No
man ever threw himself more unreservedly into the discharge
of duty than did the Duke; he carried into civil life that
concentration of energy on the matter in hand which had
given him ascendency in military operations. "Exclusiveness
of purpose," said Napoleon, "is the secret of great success
and of great operations;" it was that exclusiveness—that
concentration—which made Wellington seem a hard man,
and drew upon him the unfavourable comments of Greville
upon his inattention and want of affection to his mother and
elder brother. There is nothing so chilling to friendship—
nothing which friends and relatives resent so much—as

Æт. 76. preoccupation; yet preoccupation—the withdrawal of attention from those not engaged in a common pursuit—is
inseparable from great performance.  Larpent noticed this in
Wellington during the Peninsular war.  Writing from the
Pyrenees on 9th August, 1813, he said—

"You ask me if Lord Wellington has recollected —— with
regard.  He seems to have had a great opinion of him, but
scarcely has ever mentioned him to me.  In truth, I think Lord
Wellington has an active, busy mind, always looking to the
future, and is so used to lose a useful man that, as soon as gone,
he seldom thinks more of him.  He would be always, I have no
doubt, ready to serve any one who had been about him who was
gone, or the friend of a deceased friend, but he seems not to
think much about you when once out of the way.  He has too
much of everything and everybody always in his way to think
much of the absent." *

It must ever be so in accordance with the limitations of
human nature.  When the head is incessantly occupied, the
emotions of the heart cannot find expression; and, although
this does not imply that the heart is cold or hard, it was
inevitable that men who had been closely associated with
Wellington previous to 1815 should find their intercourse
with him interrupted, and access to him straitened, after
he set his hand to work in which they had no share.  Not
unnaturally, some of his old friends felt sore, and complained
of the Duke's heartlessness.  Frequent reference occurs in
the Duke's correspondence to the constant drafts on what
might have been, when his party was in opposition, his
leisure.  Thus in 1834, when Colonel Gurwood was editing
the despatches, and the Duke found it difficult to revise the
proofs with punctuality—

"The truth is that there is no impediment to any serious occupation like a house full of company; particularly when part of

* *Larpent.* ii. 48.

the company is a member or members of the Royal family. To some men, more time than twenty-four hours are necessary in a day ; others are under the necessity of what is called *killing time.* But when they require that the first should assist them with their company, the mischief that is done to everything like a serious occupation is immense." *

When Parliament was prorogued on 9th August, 1845, the Peel Administration seemed to be floating on summer waters. No boding clouds betokened the storm that was brewing; the prosperity of the country was advancing; the revenue, if not progressing with the leaps and bounds by which its movement was described in later years, was each year in excess of the expenditure : the evil days of deficit had been thrown behind. Some discontent, indeed, there was in the ministerialist ranks ; Mr. Gladstone had seceded from the Government on account of their Maynooth College policy, and Protectionist *frondeurs* muttered their displeasure at the growing inclination of the Prime Minister to Free Trade. Sometimes the muttering assumed the volume of an angry roar, as when Lord Essex, speaking at St. Albans, denounced the Anti-Corn Law League as "the most cunning, unscrupulous, knavish, pestilent body of men that ever plagued this or any other country." "Every act we have done," Peel had said on Mr. Villiers's motion for the repeal of the Corn Law, "has been an act tending to establish the gradual abatement of purely protective duties." But the movement in Peel's own opinions had been so gradual and unobtrusive, it had found reflection in the minds of so many other public and business men, that no visible schism could be traced in the Conservative phalanx. Not the less surely did a fissure exist, and a convulsion was at hand which was to convert it suddenly into a chasm.

At the very moment when legislators were going off with light hearts to their holiday retreats, news came that a mysterious disease had affected the potato crop in the Isle of

*margin notes:* To Ann. 1845.

Peel's Administration.

The potato disease.

* *Apsley House MSS.*

Wight. Soon after it was found to be prevalent throughout the southern English counties as well as in France and the Low Countries. Now, potatoes had come to be to the Irish countryman what wheat was to the Englishman—far more than oatmeal was to the Scotsman. The destruction of the crop in England might mean ruin to a few hundreds of farmers, in Ireland it would bring millions to the brink of starvation. Before the Cabinet met on the last day of October the disease was rampant in Ireland. Ministers had to grapple with a dilemma caused by the destruction of one-third of the whole crop in that country, and the prospective disappearance of the rest. Peel advised his colleagues that Parliament should be summoned before Christmas, and called on them to decide between the "determined maintenance, modification, and suspension of the Corn Laws." He recommended the last, as following the precedent of 1826, but he was too honest to disguise his doubts, amounting practically to conviction, that, once suspended, it would never be in the power of any Ministry to revive them. Only three of his colleagues, Aberdeen, Graham, and Sidney Herbert, agreed with their chief. The Duke of Wellington was opposed to the policy of opening the ports to corn, but declared his intention of not deserting his chief if he considered the repeal of the Act necessary for his (Peel's) position in Parliament and in the public view.

Lord John Russell's manifesto.    The discussions in the Cabinet continued throughout November; the crisis was rendered more acute by a manifesto addressed by Lord John Russell, hitherto a stout defender of the Corn Laws, to his constituents in the City of London, announcing his conversion to the policy of abolishing the fixed duty on corn, and calling on them to put an end to a "system which had proved to be the blight of commerce and the bane of agriculture." Public interest, excited by this adoption on the part of the leader of the opposition of the whole programme of the Anti-Corn Law League, was intensified by rumours that the Prime Minister had done so also.

In reply to Peel's Cabinet memorandum circulated on Anx. 1845. 26th November, the Duke wrote—

"My only object in public life is to support Sir Robert Peel's administration of the Government for the Queen. A good government for the country is more important than Corn Laws or any other consideration ; and as long as Sir Robert Peel possesses the confidence of the Queen and of the public, and he has strength to perform his duties, his administration of the Government must be supported."

At first Peel believed that Wellington's example would carry the Cabinet; but on 2nd December, when he laid before his colleagues the outlines of his proposals, whereby *Difference* the Corn Duty was to be reduced annually so as to disappear *in the Cabinet.* finally in eight years, Lord Stanley and the Duke of Buccleuch announced their intention of resigning rather than have any hand in such a measure. Two days later, the *Times* announced that Parliament would meet early in January, and that the Government would introduce a measure modifying the Corn Laws, with a view to their repeal. The *Times* was wrong. Sir Robert Peel, his Cabinet maimed by the retirement of two Ministers and, as to the rest, deeply divided in opinion, had made up his mind to *Peel* resign, which he did on the following day, 5th December. *resigns.* On the 6th the Queen sent for Lord John Russell, and the *Times*, on realising its blunder, cast all the blame of the crisis on the obstinacy of the Duke of Wellington! Russell had to reckon with a Conservative Parliament, in which the majority might be expected to be hostile to free trade in corn; but that difficulty was resolved by Peel, who assured the Queen that he intended to support such measures as might be "in general conformity with those which he had advised as a minister." The Duke, as leader of the Opposition in the Lords, might be reckoned upon to take the same course; nevertheless Russell advised the Queen to lay her commands first on those Ministers who had seceded from Peel. This her Majesty did, but Stanley and Buccleuch declined the attempt; Russell resumed his task, and encountered this difficulty in his own party, that, whereas Palmerston would not accept any post except the Foreign Office, Grey would not consent to enter a Cabinet in which that department was entrusted to one in whom he had so little confidence. While these negociations were in progress, the Queen wrote to the Duke on 12th December expressing her strong desire, whatever might be the outcome of the crisis, "to see the Duke of Wellington remain at the head of the Army. The Queen appeals to the Duke's so often proved loyalty and attachment to her person, in asking him to give her this assurance." In reply, the Duke begged the Queen not to press him to retain the command of the army, unless with the entire approval of her responsible advisers.

Peel
resumes
office.
As matters turned out, the difficulty solved itself. Russell having finally abandoned his endeavour to form a Cabinet, the Queen once more sent for Peel and desired him to withdraw his resignation. He did so at once, and, returning to London, summoned his colleagues to meet him at half-past nine in the evening, announced to them his intention of proceeding with such measures in Parliament as he believed to be necessary for the public safety, and left the issue in their hands. What followed is succinctly described in his letter to the Queen.

"There was a dead silence, at length interrupted by Lord Stanley's declaring that he must persevere in resigning; that he thought the Corn Law ought to have been adhered to, and might have been maintained. The Duke of Wellington said he thought the Corn Law was a subordinate consideration. He was delighted when he received Sir Robert Peel's letter that day, announcing that his mind was made up to place his services at your Majesty's disposal. The Duke of Buccleuch behaved admirably—was much agitated, thought new circumstances had arisen—would not then decide on resigning. All the other members of the

Government cordially approved of Sir Robert Peel's determina- A̲ɴɴ.1846. tion not to abandon your Majesty's service." *

The Duke of Buccleuch ultimately withdrew his resignation, and the vacancy caused by Lord Stanley resigning the Colonial Office was filled by the admission of Mr. Gladstone.

The Duke of Wellington was actuated throughout this critical time by the single consideration of the best means of carrying on the Queen's Government, but it was not to be expected that he should not have to defend himself against vehement, and even violent, reproaches from members of his own party.

### J. W. Croker to the Duke of Wellington.

"West Moulsey, 4th January. 1846.

" I firmly believe that the only trust of the country is in your Grace's consistency and firmness ; and I confess I cannot see what right Sir R. Peel can have to drag your Grace through the mire of his own changes of opinion. He may say, with truth and candour, that *his* opinions are changed, but can your Grace say so ? . . . Why prefer *his* character and consistency to *your own* ? *You* marked your dissent to Free Trade quite as strongly as *he* marked his assent. Why are you, and the rest, to forfeit all your pledges in order to help him to keep his *last* ? I intreat, I implore your Grace to reconsider your position as to stirring *one inch* in a course, the end and object of which is avowed and visible to every eye. I was in hopes that your authority might have stopped the movement ; if you too join it, even, as I have said, for one inch, all is lost. . . . Your Grace, if you have read so far with patience, may perhaps say that, if you retire from the Cabinet (not from the Horse Guards), the Government will be broken up, as others must go with you. I hope so—that is the natural and straightforward result—but then you ask, where is a Government to be found ? I reply—let Peel answer *that*. Let him make a Government of those who agree with him in opinion, and not of those who *don't*." †

* *Peel Letters*, iii. 284.        † *Croker*, iii. 50.

The public have long been in possession of the Duke's reply to this appeal,* in which occurs the remarkable sentence—"I am the *retained* servant of the Sovereign of this empire. Nobody can entertain a doubt of this truth, as applied to my professional character. I have invariably, up to the latest moment, acted accordingly." But the Duke had to endure remonstrance from persons whose opinions he respected more highly than Croker's.

"Stratfieldsaye. 4th January, 1846.

"MY DEAR LORD SALISBURY,—I have long thought of writing to you; in truth matter comes upon one so thickly every day, that explanation will be impossible if longer delayed; and I feel that even now it will be difficult to explain to one not an actor in the scene all that has occurred in the last few months. It can be understood only by never losing sight of the different epochs, at which the various events occurred.

"I think that the potatoe disease had occurred, and apprehensions of the consequences were seriously felt, before you quitted Walmer Castle. I never felt those apprehensions; and I believe that your feelings were very much the same! This however was not the feeling of others! In the end of October and beginning of November great apprehensions were entertained of the consequences of this disease, that famine might prevail in Ireland within a year from the time, and that it was necessary without loss of time to consider of the measures which it should be necessary to adopt. As for me, I never doubted of the inconvenience which would be produced in Ireland by the potatoe disease, not from the want of food, because there was abundance of food of other descriptions, the produce of last year's harvest in Ireland, as well as in England and Scotland; and in granaries a supply for more than a year's consumption of all descriptions of grain; but the difficulty founded upon the social habits of nearly the whole of the lower class of the Irish population in raising each for his own family the provisions which it should consume, and paying the rent of the land out of what provisions should be

* It is printed at length in the Croker papers.

raised : and by mortgaging his labour for months or even a year, Ann. 1846. left each of them without food, without money, or the facility of earning it by his labour, already mortgaged, to enable him to buy food in the market, however plentiful it should be ! That which was required for Ireland was the organisation of means to find employment for those in want of food. This, it is true, was likely to be expensive, but still practicable ; and there was nothing which apparently required any augmentation of the quantity of food in the country, excepting possibly in one article —maize—which might have been substituted in some cases for potatoes. The first determination of the Government was to wait and see what the nature and extent of the disease was, to prorogue Parliament till the 16th December, and afterwards to consider of the course to be taken. The Cabinet accordingly met again early in December, but the alarm appeared rather to have increased. It was thought by some that even the measures recommended to be adopted in Ireland with a view to apply a remedy to the peculiar local evil there existing, would occasion additional resistance to the Corn Laws ; that a reconsideration of them would at all events be necessary, and certain relaxation the consequence. The majority of the members of the Cabinet was of a different opinion. But the most influential, particularly in the House of Commons, felt strongly the necessity of making an alteration.

" After several discussions it was found, that the adoption of a plan upon which all should agree was hopeless ; and, after full consideration, it was felt that the most advantageous plan of proceeding for the Queen's service, for Her Majesty personally, and for the landed interests in general, was that the Minister should inform Her Majesty that, finding he could not go into the House of Commons and propose a plan with the consent of his colleagues, he recommended to Her Majesty to consider of the formation of another administration. This communication was made on Saturday the 6th of December, on which day H. M. sent for Lord John Russell. The Ministers attended H. M. Council at Osborne on Wednesday the 10th December and Parliament was further prorogued to the 31st December, and from that day forward H. M. servants continued in office only till a new administration should be formed. Lord John Russell saw H. M. either on Wednesday the 10th or Thursday the 11th, undertook the commission of forming an administration, and continued his efforts to form one till Saturday the 20th, on which day he resigned the commission. I beg you to bear in mind all these dates, as they are important.

"During the interval between the 10th and 20th December those members of the Cabinet who had objected to the plan proposed by the minister were required to state whether they, or any of them, were prepared or disposed to form an administration on the principle of maintaining the corn laws as they are. I, and I believe all, answered that they were not; and I must add that, however much we read and hear of protection, we have never heard of any individual approaching the Queen with the advice that she should form an administration on that principle !

"When Lord John resigned his commission on the 20th December, H. M. sent for Sir Robert Peel, and, before he went, he wrote to me and informed me that if the Queen should desire it he would resume his office; and, even if he stood alone, would, as Her Majesty's minister, enable H. M. to meet her Parliament, rather than that Her Majesty should be reduced to the necessity of taking for her minister a member of the League or those connected with its politics. As soon as I heard of this determination I applauded it; and declared my determination to co-operate in the execution. The question was not then to be considered what the corn law should be, but whether the Queen should have a Government, and I felt then bound to stand by the Sovereign as I had done in 1834. At the same time I saw very clearly that the result of what had happened made a great alteration in the position of the question of the Corn Laws.

"As soon as Lord John Russell undertook on the 10th or 11th December to form an administration for the Queen, he was entitled to demand, and he obtained, a knowledge of the cause of the dissolution of the preceding administration; and he became acquainted with the opinion of Sir Robert Peel and the difference between him and a majority of his Cabinet. Of course then (he knows) that Sir Robert Peel can no longer go into Parliament as the defender of the corn law !

" The members of the Cabinet likewise who differed from Ann. 1846. Sir Robert, previous (to) the 6th and 10th of December—how do they stand ? They must feel that, although with numbers to vote in support of the existing corn law, they cannot reckon upon maintaining it in debate, and they must look to some other system which shall provide for the interests of the land equally with the existing law ; although differing from it in the provisions which it should propose to enact.

" What I desire is, considering what has passed, the dates and facts stated, and the situation in which the Government stands at present—let the great landed proprietors and the landed interest consider well what is proposed to them, and not separate themselves from the Government till they should see, and have considered what it is. I see some of them have already loudly declared against such a course as being the same as locking the stable door after the steed should have been stolen. Be it so ! If they will not adopt that reasonable, manly course, let them agree among themselves to form a Government for the Queen. Let one or more of them solicit an audience of Her Majesty, and solicit Her Majesty to select for her servants men who will maintain at all events the existing corn law ! But let them prepare immediately to produce to Her Majesty the names of the persons to fill the different offices of the State, who will be responsible for carrying on the Government. If not prepared to do that, they must either support the Government of Sir Robert Peel, or be prepared to consider of the measures of one formed under the ——— * of Cobden and Co. ! There can be no other course !

" I entreat you to consider of all these circumstances ; the order of their concurrence ; their dates ; and the peculiar events in operation at the period at which each existed. And I entreat you to exert your influence over those who like yourself are great landed proprietors ; and to take a course upon this occasion which will be worthy of your station, your talents and your patriotism. Don't be in a hurry ; consider maturely what will be submitted for the consideration of Parliament ; it can never be too late for the great landed interest to take its course.

* Illegible in original.

Æt. 76.
But if it is to take any course now excepting that of waiting to see what is proposed, it should be to solicit a commission for the formation of a Government.

> " Believe me ever yours most affectionately,
>
> " WELLINGTON." *

The omens were adverse to the resuscitated Peel Cabinet. In the elections consequent on the redistribution of Government posts, Ministerialists suffered defeat in the southern constituencies at the hands of Protectionist candidates, while **Peel proposes to repeal the Corn Laws.** electors in the north returned Whigs or Radicals. Not the less boldly did Peel face Parliament when it assembled on 22nd January, 1846, and explained the situation as one which could only be relieved by the repeal of the Corn Laws. Then, in truth, the country party knew that impious hands had been laid on the Ark of the Covenant ; mutely they listened to their doom—mutely, because it transcended the power of any of them to confute Peel's well-marshalled arguments, or deny the urgency of the situation created by the failure of potatoes in Ireland—mutely, save for the vehemence of Lord George Bentinck and the virulence of Benjamin Disraeli against "the sublime audacity" of the minister who had just avowed his abandonment of the position entrusted to his defence. Almost mutely, therefore ; but if country gentlemen could not be eloquent they could vote ; it was clear they had the destiny of the Administration in their hands—equally clear that there was no place for mercy in their hearts. The Protectionists organised themselves into what would now be termed a "cave" under the lead of Lord George Bentinck, with Disraeli as his lieutenant.

**The Duke considers his position.** The Duke, in view of the probability of his party being thrust from office, had to consider his position. As Commander-in-chief, he was, as he had told Croker, the "retained servant" of the Crown. To assume the leadership of the Opposition in the House of Lords would be to enter upon

* *Salisbury MSS.*

a contest with the other servants of the Crown. In conver- ANN. 1846.
sation with Lord Stanley, who had been raised to the peerage,
he explained his own situation, and made the remarkable
proposal that Stanley should succeed him as leader of the
Conservative party in the Lords.  It was a remarkable proposal, not because Stanley was not the ablest man for the
task, but because he had seceded from the Cabinet on the very
point of policy which seemed about to be fatal to Peel's
Government.  It was a remarkable proposal, therefore ; as His offer
remarkable as it would have been had Mr. Gladstone, fore- to Lord Stanley.
seeing defeat on his Home Rule Bill in 1886, retired from the
leadership and invited the Marquess of Hartington to take his
place.  A few extracts from correspondence well illustrate
the peculiar situation.

### *Lord Stanley to the Duke of Wellington.*

"18th February, 1846.

". . . We cannot disguise from ourselves that the unfortunate measure now under consideration has, for the time at
least, completely dislocated and shattered the great Conservative
party in both Houses ; and that the sacrifice of your own private
opinion which you and others have made for the purpose of
keeping it together, has failed, as I feared it would, to effect
your object. . . . I think it very doubtful whether even your
great name and influence will induce the Lords to sanction the
Bill. . . . I am obliged to add frankly that I think confidence
has been so shaken in Sir Robert Peel, that in spite of his pre-
eminent abilities and great services, he can never reunite that
party under his guidance.  Nor do I see any one in the House
of Commons of sufficient ability and influence to do so. . . . In
the House of Lords the case is widely different.  There, your
influence and authority are, and must be, paramount ; and much
as many of your followers may regret the course which a sense
of duty has led you to take on this occasion, they still regard
you with undiminished personal respect and attachment, and
will follow no other leader, if any were ill-judged enough to set
himself up in opposition to you. . . . When, with that disregard

of yourself which you have shown throughout your life, you advise that I should now endeavour to rally the Conservative party, I am forced to remind you that in the present state of affairs and feelings, they could only be rallied in opposition to measures of your own Government." *

Lord Stanley then proceeds to explain that, inasmuch as he himself will probably feel it his duty to give his vote against the measure, he wishes to do so in the manner least likely to give him the appearance of putting himself in competition with the Duke, and adds that, in his opinion, the Conservative party can only be reunited as the result of a long period spent in opposition to a Whig administration. In this opinion the Duke concurred, and wrote next day, giving at great length his reasons for feeling unable to continue as leader of the Conservative party in the House of Lords and for desiring to see Lord Stanley in that position. He admits that Peel's influence has been destroyed, and that there is " no chance of its revival."

" That which I look for, therefore, is the holding together in other hands the great and at this moment powerful Conservative party, and this for the sake of the Queen, of the religious and other antient institutions of the country, of its resources, influence and power. . . . It is quite obvious that I am not the person who can pretend to undertake, with any chance of success, to perform this task. It is not easy to account for my being in the situation which I have so long filled in the House of Lords. Its commencement was merely accidental." †

He then recalls how he had succeeded to the position held by Lord Liverpool, but that he felt that his influence, " if it has not already terminated, must terminate in a very short period of time."

" You will see, therefore, that the stage is entirely clear and open for you. . . . For many years, indeed from the year 1830,

---

* *Apsley House MSS.*　　　　　　　† *Ibid.*

when I retired from office, I have endeavoured to manage the ANN. 1846. House of Lords upon the principle on which I conceive that the institution exists in the constitution of the country. . . . I have invariably supported Government in Parliament upon unimportant occasions, and have always exercised my personal influence to prevent the mischief of anything like a difference or division between the two Houses. I am the servant of the Crown and People. I have been paid and rewarded, and I consider myself retained, and that I can't do otherwise than serve as required when I can do so without dishonour. . . . The stage is quite clear for you, and you need not apprehend the consequences of differing in opinion from me when you will enter upon it ; as in truth I have, by my letter to the Queen of 12th of December, put an end to the connection between the Party and me, when the Party will be in opposition to H. M.'s Government. . . . I don't despair of carrying the Bill through. You must be the best judge of the course which you ought to take, and of the course most likely to conciliate the House of Lords. My opinion is that you should advise the House to vote that which would lead most to publick order and would be most beneficial to the immediate interests of the country. But do what you may, it will make no difference to me ; you will always find me aiding and co-operating in the road of good order, conservation and government, and doing everything to establish and maintain your influence." *

Such were the broad, unselfish principles on which the Duke brought to an end his formal connection with the party with which he had been so long identified—principles for which he received no credit from the leading newspapers, which represented him as clinging to power long after his own powers had failed. It is unnecessary to say that his moral influence with the peers remained, as Stanley predicted, paramount; that when the Corn Bill came before the House of Lords in May he explained to them that they had no choice in the matter; a measure

* *Apsley House MSS.*

Æт. 76. recommended by the Crown and sent up by the Commons
would not be rejected, because "without the House of
Commons and the Crown the House of Lords could do
nothing." "Privilege!" muttered some, who relished not
the introduction of the Sovereign's authority as an argument;
but Stanley had expressed no empty compliment when he

The Corn
Bill passes
the Lords.
told the Duke he was paramount, for he carried the peers
with him. "I am aware," he said in the course of his speech,
"that I address your lordships with all your prejudices
against me. . . . I never had any claim to the confidence
that your lordships have placed in me. But I will not
omit," he continued in faltering accents, "even on this night,
possibly the last on which I shall ever venture to address to
you my advice, I will not omit to counsel you as to the vote
you should give on this occasion. . . . I did think, my lords,
that the formation of a Government in which her Majesty
would have confidence was of greater importance than any
opinion of any individual upon the Corn Law or any other
law." Their lordships listened, unconvinced and sore in
spirit, many of them, but as little disposed to disobey the
order to retire from the position pronounced untenable by
their chief as any general of division to hesitate on receiving
the command to retreat from Talavera. They divided at
half-past four in the morning, and gave Ministers a majority
of forty-seven.

"God bless you, Duke!" cried one of a small crowd of
early workmen who gathered round the door of the House of
Lords on that summer morning, and the rest began to cheer.
" For Heaven's sake, people, let me get on my horse!" was
the Duke's only acknowledgment, which in any one else
would have passed for ungracious.

The Lords gave the Bill a third reading on 25th June
without a division, but on that very day burst the hurricane
which had been brewing in the House of Commons. In the
words of Benjamin Disraeli, whose rise as a politician dates
from this crisis, "Vengeance had succeeded in most breasts

to the more sanguine sentiment: the field was lost, but at Ann. 1846.
any rate there should be retribution for those who had
betrayed it." Sir Robert Peel must be turned out, and his
enemies were not squeamish about the means to be employed
for the purpose. Early in the session the Government had
introduced a Coercion Bill for Ireland, one of that long and
doleful series of temporary measures for the repression of
recurrent outbreaks of violence which it fell to successive
ministries to propose, until Lord Salisbury had the hardihood
in 1887 to place a permanent measure on the statute book.
The Whig opposition led by Lord John Russell, and the Combi-
Conservative *frondeurs* guided by Lord George Bentinck, nation
were both deeply committed to support of the Government against the Govern-
Bill, but no scruples restrained them from a change of front. ment.
Lord George advised his followers to "kick out the Bill and
her Majesty's Ministers with it," and Russell announced his
intention to go into the "No" lobby "on grounds satisfactory
to himself." It may easily be imagined how indignant was
the Duke at conduct so different from the principle he always
followed. "If I was in your position," he wrote to Peel, "I
would not allow this blackguard combination to break up
the Government. I would prefer to dissolve the Parliament,
and if your Government is to fall, it will at least fall with
honour." [*] Peel did not fancy an appeal to the country
on an Irish question, and on the same day that the Corn
Bill passed the Lords, Ministers were placed in a minority of
seventy-three on the second reading of the Coercion Bill and
resigned office.

Lord John Russell, having been commissioned to form a The Duke
Government, approached the Duke of Wellington with the declines a coalition.
view of obtaining the services and support of some of the
Peelites. The Duke told him that, although he had always
been willing to give every professional assistance to the
Government of the day, whatever had been its politics, he
would have nothing to do with a coalition of parties, because

* *Peel Letters,* iii. 353.

ÆT. 77. " such arrangements were viewed with distrust by the publick, were not creditable to the Parties, and could not be useful to any." * On the other hand, he assured Lord John, and also members of the Conservative party who sought his advice, that, so long as he held the office of Commander-in-Chief, he could not act in concert with any party opposed to the Government. Similar overtures on the part of Lord John were declined by Lord Dalhousie, Lord Lincoln, and Mr. Sidney Herbert.

### Appendix G.

*The Duke's Principles in Opposition.*

In order to throw as much light as possible upon the principles of the Duke's conduct in opposition, it may be well to give an extract from his correspondence with Lord Londonderry, the most active *frondeur* in the House of Lords at this period.

"July 7, 1846.

" . . . From the commencement of Sir Robert Peel's Gov<sup>t</sup>. until he resigned it, I have been the person charged by the Queen's command to represent in the House of Lords the conduct of the Affairs of the Queen's Government in that House. As a friend of Sir Robert Peel's, you was in constant relation with me, setting aside all other causes for the same. Sir Robert Peel's Gov<sup>t</sup>. is now broken up; and since I stated the fact to the House of Lords I have had no communication with him to enable me to form an opinion what course he proposed to take in Parliament, or in what relation I stand to the existing Administration, or what course he would wish his friends to take in either House of Parliament. And I add that if I had received such information, I should not, and indeed I could not, have acted on it myself; nor could I have endeavoured to influence the conduct of others, the friends of his Administration when in power.

* *Apsley House MSS.*

" The inclosed paper will shew you the Professional Position ANN.1840. in which I stand, and will give you the Relation of the circumstances which have placed me in it; and will define the exact political position in which I am placed.  I communicate it to you *confidentially.*

" You will see from that the position I filled heretofore.  What it may have been, and (be) the existing state of Affairs what they may, I can take but one course—that of avoiding to act in concert with any political Party in opposition to the Gov<sup>t</sup>. . . . This anomalous position is the result of my peculiar relations with the Sovereign of this Country on account of Services for Years, and the great Rewards and Favors I have received."

Of the confidential paper referred to, the following are the most important passages :—

*Memorandum on the Conservative Leadership in the House of Commons.*

" . . . Bygone circumstances have placed me in a situation which renders it impossible for me to act with a party in Parliament ; but I have always been sensible of the advantage and even necessity for the sake of Government itself of keeping together the Conservative party, and most particularly when sitting in the Queen's councils I have endeavoured to attain that object.  I stand thus at the present moment—the Queen having called upon me to give her Majesty the advantage of my professional assistance in the command of the Army, I told her Majesty that I could not become a member of her councils nor have anything to say to the political ——? under existing circumstances, but that I would serve under those who should be her Majesty's servants, and that I felt in taking that course that I ought to cease to act in concert in Parliament with any political party in opposition to the Government.  I have acted accordingly, but this course does not prevent my seeing the advantage to the publick interests, and principally to the Crown itself, of the strength and consolidation of the Conservative party in the State. . . . I am *most anxious* for Lord Stanley's success. . . . My position is certainly anomalous, and I can feel myself liable to be misunderstood. . . . But even when I was sitting in the House of Lords as leader of the Opposition against the Government of Lord Grey and Lord Melbourne, these same feelings in favour of Government *qua* Government have induced me personally to interfere to support the Government, in opposition to the party in Parliament with which I was acting, when I thought it was going too far."

## Appendix H.

### *National Defence.*

No reflection has been cast so frequently on the Duke of Wellington's public acts, none has been refuted more feebly, than that, after he took to political life, he allowed the cares of office to quench his active interest in the army and to lull his vigilance about national defence. The unprepared state of the British land forces when the long peace was broken by the outbreak of war with Russia in 1854, and the suffering and loss entailed thereby on the British army in the Crimea, have been cited as the result of actual laches on the part of him who was so long responsible as Commander-in-chief. That there had occurred a terrible degree of disorganisation— that the sword of England had been allowed to rust in its scabbard—no one will deny; and this seems a fitting place to inquire how far the Duke must be held answerable for allowing this to come about, because it was in August, 1842, that he became once more Commander-in-chief, in succession to Lord Hill, who had become exceedingly infirm.* The Duke's own inclination in resuming the command-in-chief was to leave the Cabinet, partly because of the disability of his deafness, and partly because of his unwillingness to impart anything of a party character to the administration of the army. But he yielded to the warm remonstrance of

* Lord Hill died 10th December, 1842.

Sir Robert Peel, actuated not a little by a wish to avoid all ANN. 1838. suspicion that, had he quitted the Cabinet, he had done so on account of any disapproval of its policy.*

The Duke's anxiety regarding the weakening of the national defences had been expressed long before his return to the Horse Guards in 1842. In 1827, when the Treasury was pressing for reductions in the peace establishment of the army, the Duke submitted to Lord Goderich a long memorandum which he had prepared three years before at the instance of Lord Palmerston. In this, although he expressed the opinion that steam power could never be applied to ships of war, he considered that its application to transports "would give a certainty to the movements of an expedition . . . which such expeditions have never had before, and is well deserving the consideration of the Government in the discussion of all questions of military establishment and defence."† He protested against the false economy of reductions at the expense of efficiency, and held strongly that *any* reduction must be followed by hasty augmentation.

At no time during the present century have the British land forces been at such a low ebb as during the reign of William IV., and the danger continued to weigh on the Duke's mind, although during the stormy period of Catholic Emancipation and Reform he could not get Ministers to give attention to the subject.

*The Duke of Wellington to Sir Willoughby Gordon.*

" Stratfieldsaye, 11th December, 1838.

" . . . As for my part, I have always been of opinion that nothing would enable us to settle our affairs in a short space of time, or at all (because if we don't settle them in a short space of time we shall not settle them at all), excepting to convince the World that we were in earnest in our Intentions to settle them by making a real efficient augmentation of both Army and Navy, so as to meet all difficulties and opposition as a great

---

* *Peel Letters*, ii. 537.    † *Civil Despatches*, iv. 114.

Nation ought. Instead of *dribbling* as we are, we ought to augment all the depôts in this Country and in Ireland to 500 Men each. This augmentation would give you an early Command of some Thousands. It would cost but little more than the Pay of the Men, and would be a real efficient Measure. It would be followed by no expense thereafter. It would convince friends and Enemies that we intend to be Master in Canada. I for one do not now believe that that is the Intention of all in the Cabinet. There ought to be corresponding and permanent augmentation of the Navy, which I am positively certain is not adequate in Strength to the Wants for its Service. . . .

" We should really look seriously at our Position and take Steps to make our Enemies feel that we are determined to maintain it. In this Denomination I am sorry to say that I consider the whole World. With the exception possibly of some in the Austrian Government, we have not a Friend left in the World. I ought to add to this Letter that there should be a corresponding augmentation of the dismounted Men of the Cavalry."

"27th December.

"The state of our military force is very distressing. The Government will not—they dare not—look our difficulties in the face, and provide for them. I don't believe that any Government that could be formed in these days would have the power." *

Passing on to the year 1844, Wellington is found urging Peel to deal with the defenceless state of British arsenals, and the dangers of invasion "aggravated beyond all calculation by the progress of steam navigation, its threatened application to maritime warfare, and the known preparations of our neighbour and naval State in this peculiar equipment." † He admits that all the Administrations since the peace of 1815 are to blame for the state of neglect of which he complains, and he acknowledges the difficulty of inducing Parliament to vote the necessary outlay, without laying before it a statement of the lamentable state of the case, which would be to explain

* *Apsley House MSS.*          † *Peel Letters,* iii. 199.

to foreign nations the helplessness of Great Britain against <small>Ann. 1845.</small> attack and invite their cupidity; but he adds, "we shall do no good by shutting our eyes to the danger."

Time went on; nothing or little was done, and the Duke's uneasiness increased. The attitude of France had become distinctly menacing. In 1845, on the part of the Opposition Lord Palmerston and Sir Charles Napier charged the Government with allowing the national defences to decay. Peel, in defending his colleagues, and concerned that the weakness of the nation should be published abroad, expressed himself in terms so optimist that the Duke determined he should know the truth. He therefore addressed to Sir Robert a letter which he had at first intended to send to Lord Stanley as War Minister, containing a complete scheme of defence by the land forces, including the organisation of the Militia, and requests that naval officers should be desired to explain what the movements and disposition of the fleet should be if war broke out. On the precise recommendations made it is unnecessary to dwell at this time; to show the earnestness of the warning a few passages may be cited.

"I sincerely wish that I could prevail upon you to consider calmly this great and important subject, compared with which all other interests of the country are mere trifles. All admit the great change made in the system of maritime warfare. Lord Palmerston and you call it a bridge across the Channel between France and this country. I say it is rather a multitude of bridges, from a base in France extending from Bordeaux to Dunkirk. . . . Her Majesty's dominions are in a situation for defence worse than that of the frontier in any State of Europe contiguous to France . . . every port open to attack, for the defence of which we have not one disposable soldier, and we must depend for our safety upon the operation of our fleets. . . . I put the hypothetical case of the enemy landing 25,000 men near one of our great naval arsenals, attacking, succeeding in taking, and destroying the arsenal. This hypothesis is not the representation of an impossibility, or even extravagant, considering what I have seen

done myself, having at the time superior armies in the field
opposed to me.   In this case you would not have a man. . . . If
a body of troops were landed in the neighbourhood of one of our
places, of a sufficient force to invest the place, say 25,000, then
I defy all the fleets of England to save it, without the assistance of an army in the field.   I entreat you to weigh all this
well. . . . I tell you fairly that I consider the danger so certain
and so imminent that I conceive that, if there existed an absence
of party and prejudice in our Imperial councils, that which ought
to be recommended is an alteration in the military policy of the
country. . . . It is my duty to tell you all this.   I entreat you
to investigate the subject maturely—admit nothing as true only
because I state it—and then decide whether you will incur the
risks of leaving matters as they are.   I beg you to believe that,
decide what you may, it is my wish and intention to aid and
assist the Government in anything upon which you may decide
after due examination." *

In a long reply, Peel admitted the truth of the Duke's
representations; but the financial difficulty was more immediately present in his mind than in that of the Commander-
in-Chief.

"The country is encumbered with a debt of 787 millions.
The annual interest of that debt raised by taxation amounts to
28 millions.   There has been peace in Europe for the long period
of thirty years, and but little progress has been made in the
reduction of that debt."

In the Budget for that year a million was added to the
Navy Estimates, but the army remained the same.

Next may be noted a letter to Mr. Goulburn, dated
30th January, 1846, strongly urging an increase in the
artillery, and stating that more engineer officers were absolutely necessary.   He recommends the formation of a
battalion of engineers (up to this date the pioneers of infantry
regiments had been almost the only sappers), notwithstanding

* *Peel Letters*, iii. 205.

the professional opinion of a certain admiral whom he quotes Ann. 1846. "that Gibraltar was impregnable, if the officers of engineers did not spoil it." *

On the fall of the Peel Administration in 1846 the Duke addressed to Lord John Russell, as head of the new government, a strong memorandum on the necessity for strengthening the defensive forces.† Finally, in 1847, came his famous letter to Sir John Burgoyne, which is too long to insert at length, and, besides, immediately found its way into print, much to its writer's disgust.‡ Nevertheless, of such vital and present importance is the subject to the people of these islands that some of its paragraphs deserve to be quoted once more.

"You are aware that I have for years been sensible of the alteration produced in maritime warfare and operations by the application of steam to the propelling of ships at sea. This discovery immediately exposed all parts of the coasts of those islands which a vessel could approach at all, to be approached at all times of tide, and in all seasons, by vessels so propelled, from all quarters. We are, in fact, assailable, and at least liable to insult, and to have contributions levied upon us, on all parts of our coast; that is, the coast of these (islands), including the Channel islands, which to this time, from the period of the Norman conquest, have never been successfully invaded. I have in vain endeavoured to awaken the attention of different administrations to this state of things, as well known to our neighbours (rivals in power, at least former adversaries and enemies) as it is to ourselves. . . . We hear a great deal of the spirit of the people of England, for which no man entertains higher respect than I do. But unorganised, undisciplined without systematic subordination established and well understood,

---

* *Apsley House MSS.*

† 12th August, 1846. *Apsley House MSS.*

‡ Charles Greville (2nd series, iii. 107) tells how " Pigou, a meddling zealot, who does nothing but read blue books and write letters to the *Times* and *Chronicle*," got hold of this letter and communicated it to the press, to the Duke's great indignation.

this spirit opposed to the fire of musketry and cannon, and to sabres and bayonets of disciplined troops, would only expose those animated by such spirit to confusion and destruction."

Here follows an elaborate plan for reorganising, strengthening, and disposing of the existing defensive forces, after which the Duke proceeds—

"The measure upon which I have earnestly entreated different administrations to decide, which is constitutional, and has been invariably adopted in time of peace for the last eighty years, is to raise, embody, organise and discipline the militia, of the same numbers for each of the three kingdoms, united as during the late war. This would give a mass of organised force amounting to about 150,000 men, which we might immediately set to work to discipline. This alone would enable us to establish the strength of our army. This, with an augmentation of the force of the regular army, which would not cost £400,000, would put the country on its legs in respect to personal force; and I would engage for its defence, old as I am. But as we stand now, and if it be true that the exertions of the fleet alone are not sufficient to provide for our defence, we are not safe for a week after the declaration of war.

"I am accustomed to the consideration of these questions, and have examined and reconnoitred, over and over again, the whole coast, from the North Foreland, by Dover, Folkestone, Beachyhead, Brighton, Arundel, to Selsey Bill, near Portsmouth; and I say that, excepting immediately under the fire of Dover Castle, there is not a spot on the coast on which infantry might not be thrown on shore, at any time of tide, with any wind, and in any weather, and from which such a body of infantry, so thrown on shore, would not find, within the distance of five miles, a road into the interior of the country, through the cliffs, practicable for the march of a body of troops; that in that space of coast (that is, between North Foreland and Selsey Bill,) there are not less than seven small harbours, or mouths of rivers, each without defence, of which an enemy, having landed his infantry on the coast, might take possession, and therein land his cavalry and artillery of all calibre and establish himself and his communica- Ann. 1847. tions with France. . . .

" The French army must be much altered indeed since the time at which I was better acquainted with it, if there are not now belonging to it forty *Chefs d'Etat-Majors-General* capable of sitting down and ordering the march to the coast of 40,000 men, their embarkation, with their horses and artillery, at the several French ports on the coast ; their disembarkation at named points on the English coast,—that of the artillery and cavalry in named ports or mouths of rivers, and the assembly at named points of the several columns ; and the march of each of these from stage to stage to London. Let any man examine our maps and road-books, consider the matter, and judge for himself.

"I know no mode of resistance, much less of protection, from this danger, excepting by an army in the field capable of meeting and contending with its formidable enemy, aided by all the means of fortification which experience in war can suggest.

" I shall be deemed fool-hardy in engaging for the defence of the empire with an army composed of such a force of militia. I may be so. I confess it, I should infinitely prefer, and should feel more confidence in, an army of regular troops. But I *know* that I shall not have these ; I may have others ; and if an addition is made to the existing regular army allotted for home defence of a force which will cost £400,000 a year, there would be a sufficient disciplined force in the field to enable him who should command to defend the country. . . .

" You will see from what I have written that I have contemplated the danger to which you referred. I have done so for years. I have drawn to it the attention of different administrations at different times. You will see, likewise, that I have considered of the measures of prospective security, and of the mode and cost of the attainment. I have done more. I have looked at and considered these localities in quiet detail, and have made up my mind upon the details of their defence. These are the questions to which my mind has not been unaccustomed. I have considered and provided for the defence—the successful defence—of the frontiers of many countries. . . .

" I quite concur in all your views of the danger of our position, and of the magnitude of the stake at issue. I am especially sensible of the certainty of failure if we do not, at an early moment, attend to the measures necessary for our defence, and of the disgrace, the indelible disgrace of such failure—putting out of view all the other unfortunate consequences, such as the loss of the political and social position of this country among the nations of Europe, of all its allies, in concert with, and in aid of whom, it has, in our own times, contended successfully in arms for its own honour and safety, and the independence and freedom of the world. When did any man hear of the allies of a country unable to defend itself? Views of economy of some, and I admit that the high views of national finance of others, induce them to postpone those measures absolutely necessary for mere defence and safety under existing circumstances, forgetting altogether the common practice of successful armies in modern times, imposing upon the conquered enormous pecuniary contributions, as well as other valuable and ornamental property. . . .

" I am bordering upon seventy-seven years of age, passed in honour. I hope that the Almighty may protect me from being the witness of the tragedy which I cannot persuade my contemporaries to take measures to avert.

" Believe me, ever yours sincerely,

" WELLINGTON."

Against evidence so eloquent, so convincing, how is it possible to maintain the charge that, during his political life, Wellington was indifferent to the efficiency of the army and careless about the national security? He continued through the last years of his life to press the matter on the attention of the civil government by means of letters to Lord John Russell and technical memoranda. But why, it may be asked, if the Duke's sense of the country's danger was so clear, was he so angry at the publication of his letter to Sir John Burgoyne? why was he invariably silent when national defence was discussed in Parliament? It was because, despising public opinion in regard to himself, he dreaded bringing it to bear upon the Government of the Queen. He

could not conceive anything but evil arising out of democratic interference with affairs of state, and this is most
clearly expressed in the following letter.

*The Duke of Wellington to Lady Shelley.*

"30th January, 1848.

"Upon the subject of the defences of the country, I have
formed and have given opinions to several administrations ; but
it is well known that my opinion has been that the subject would
be considered with advantage by the Government alone in the
first instance. The rules of procedure so require, and it is quite
certain that the House of Lords, of which I am a member, is *the*
place in which it would be least advantageous to suggest a discussion on such a subject. . . . It is well known that in the
course of the last session of Parliament a discussion did take
place in the House of Lords on the state of the defences of the
country. Lord Ellenborough spoke ; others spoke ; I did not
say one word ! . . . I objected to the movement on the part of
any, excepting the servants of the Crown, and positively declared
that I would not move in it. By the diligence of Lady and Miss
Burgoyne, assisted by your ladyship, the confidential letter of
the Commander-in-chief of the Army to the Chief Engineer
(Sir John Burgoyne) has been pretty generally circulated, and
has at last been published in the newspapers ! . . . Look at
what is passing all over the country in consequence of the ill-
timed and indiscreet measures adopted by the ladies—your ladyship, Lady and Miss Burgoyne among them, and the gossips of
the world, in order to bring it under discussion. I foresaw this
consequence : but I must say that my principal view in desiring
to keep the subject in its regular channel was that I knew it was
the only efficient one, and moreover the only safe one for the
public interests !" *

In the light of later days we recognise in the "ill-timed
and indiscreet measures adopted by the ladies" a real service
to the country by rousing it to a sense of peril. Half a

* *Apsley House MSS.*

century has gone by since the Duke wrote his last formal
warning; the empire has increased in extent and wealth
beyond the dreams of statesmen of those days, and the people
—that democratic power which Wellington held in such
dread—have awakened to the duty of defending the mighty
fabric. No Government could stand for ten days which
should be convicted of incurring the risks to which Great
Britain lay exposed in the 'forties. Yet the popular mood is
proverbially fickle; there may come a time, as there have
come times in the not distant past, when the nation's vigilance
shall be lulled, the martial spirit slumber. Well shall it be
then if some heedful eye retraces the lines written by one
who had such wide experience of princes and peoples; who
never exaggerated a military risk and never flinched in the
presence of peril.

# CHAPTER XII.

## LAST DAYS.

### 1848–1852.

O N 8th April, 1848, the Duke of Wellington once more found himself present at a Cabinet council. Dissociated from party and holding no political office, he attended on the invitation of the Prime Minister to advise measures for the protection of the metropolis. From no foreign quarter loomed the menace. For many years apprehension of invasion had been justified by the attitude of the French government. The first French revolution had plunged England into the mightiest war in her history; in the third French revolution, the fall of Guizot and the abdication of Louis Philippe, Palmerston read the disappearance of external danger to the United Kingdom. Not the less was there danger within the The Queen's realm. Smith O'Brien's caricature of rebellion in Chartists. Ireland, to be extinguished ingloriously among Widow Cormack's cabbages, had not yet taken shape; the centre of

Æт. 78. disturbance lay nearer the seat of Government. The Chartists had not been quenched by the repeal of the Corn Laws; they had accepted that as an instalment, but the five points of their charter were still unsatisfied; and now their ranks, swelled by the industrial depression which followed in the path of the commercial crisis of 1847, were marshalled by Feargus O'Connor, whom appearance, eloquence, and ancient lineage rendered an ideal demagogue. A mass meeting was summoned to assemble on Kennington Green on 10th April; half a million Chartists were to march thence upon Westminster, and overawe the House of Commons into accepting a monster petition said to contain 5,706,000 signatures.*

The state of public apprehension may be estimated by the expressions in a letter from a member of the Cabinet.

### *Lord Campbell to Sir George Campbell.*

"Friday night, 7th April, 1848.

" . . . The public alarm increases every hour, and many believe that by Monday evening we shall be under a Provisional Government. . . . Yesterday evening the Duke of Wellington beckoned to me to cross over to him, and he said to me : 'Lord Cammell, we shall be as quiet on Monday as we are at this hour, and it will end to the credit of the Government and the country.' But he was never famous for knowing the state of the public mind. . . . "

"Sunday night, 9th April, 1848.

" . . . This may be the last time I write to you before the Republic is established. I have no serious fears of revolution, but there may very likely be bloodshed. I have had some recompense for my anxiety in a scene I witnessed yesterday. . . . We were considering in the Cabinet how the Chartists should be

---

* The Select Committee appointed to examine this petition reduced the number of genuine signatures to 1.975,406. The names of the Queen and Prince Albert, Lord John Russell, Sir Robert Peel, Wellington himself, and other public individuals had been appended scores of times, interspersed with those of " Cheeks the Marine " and other imaginary characters.

dealt with, and when it was determined that the procession Ann. 1848. should be stopped after it had moved, we agreed that the particular place where it should be stopped was purely a military question. The Duke of Wellington was requested to come to us, which he did very readily. We had then a regular Council of War, as upon the eve of a great battle. We examined maps and returns and information of the movements of the enemy. After long deliberation, plans of attack and defence were formed to meet every contingency. The quickness, intelligence, and decision which the Duke displayed were very striking, and he inspired us all with perfect confidence. . . . It was not I alone who was struck with the consultation of yesterday. Macaulay said to me that he considered it the most interesting spectacle he had ever witnessed, and that he should remember it to his dying day."

To the Duke, then, was committed the task of stopping the The Duke's precautions. procession and defending the metropolis from the irruption of a dangerous rabble. He was hard on fourscore, yet he betrayed no signs of failure either in discretion or military instinct. Injudicious display of force might easily have precipitated a bloody riot, the tragedy of Peterloo have been reenacted on a grand scale. The London police, a force of which the Duke had first urged the creation,* numbered nearly four thousand; the Duke determined that the mob should first encounter the civil force, and that the military should only be employed if the policemen failed. Nevertheless his arrangements were as complete as if he had been preparing defence against an army of invasion. The Guards and Household cavalry were reinforced by the 17th, 62nd, and 63rd Foot, brought in from country quarters; steam-vessels were in readiness in the river and the Channel to bring other troops if need should arise; guns were placed near Westminster Bridge and neighbourhood, with strict orders that commissioned officers only were to discharge them if necessary. The Bank of England, Somerset House, the Mint, and other public

* See *ante*, p. 153.

buildings were put in a state of defence and secretly garri-
soned: the 12th Light Dragoons were billeted in Chelsea.
Yet no appearance of military preparation was allowed to
alarm the public; only the police were *en evidence*, five
hundred forming an advanced post at Kennington, and a like
number on each of the bridges of Westminster, Hungerford,
Waterloo, and Blackfriars, with reserves amounting to 1,600
on the north side of the river. So perfect were the precautions—so great the dread of the Duke's prowess—that all
ended pacifically. The meeting dissolved at the instance of
a few police-inspectors, and the monster petition was conveyed,
constitutionally but ignominiously, to Westminster in a
hackney cab.

The Duke proposes that Prince Albert should command the Army.

The dread of the growing power of the democracy, and the
menace which he discerned therein to the Monarchy and
Constitution, weighed heavily on the Duke to the end of his
days, and he attached supreme importance to the control of
the Army remaining in the hands of the Sovereign. So long
as *he* was Commander-in-chief, there was nothing to fear; he
could trust himself; but with the weight of fourscore years
on his shoulders he could not remain much longer at the post.
Accordingly on 3rd April, 1850, he laid before the Queen and
Prince Consort the project he had long cherished, namely,
that the Prince should assume the office of Commander-in-
chief. He told the Queen that so long as he (the Duke)
remained Commander-in-chief, the duties of all the offices in
his department were attended to by himself, which the Prince
Consort could not undertake, and he proposed the appointment
of a separate Chief of the Staff, uniting the offices of Adjutant-
General and Quartermaster-General. When the Prince raised
the question whether, as the Queen's Consort, he would be
acting within the Constitution in taking command of the
Army, the Duke replied that it was precisely that consideration which made him most anxious to see the Prince Commander-in-chief, " as with the daily growth of the democratic
power the executive got weaker and weaker, and that it was

of the utmost importance to the Throne and the Constitution ANN. 1850. that the command of the Army should remain in the hands of the Sovereign, and not fall into the hands of the House of Commons." He saw no security, were he gone, except in the Sovereign, or, as in the case of her Majesty, the Sovereign's Consort assuming the command. "It is a pleasure," wrote the Queen to Baron Stockmar in reference to this interview, "and a wonder to see how powerful and how clear the mind of this wonderful man is, and how loyal and kind he is to both of us. His loss, when it comes, will be a thoroughly irreparable one."

The letter in which the Prince Consort gave his reasons for declining the appointment has been published already.* They consisted in the interference which he foresaw the duties of the Command-in-chief would cause with those "most important duties connected with the welfare of the Sovereign . . . which nobody *could* perform but myself." Nobody can doubt that the Prince's decision was a wise one. On constitutional grounds, it is strange that the Duke declined to admit the objection raised by the Prince that it was undesirable to place the Sovereign or the Sovereign's Consort in such a position that it might become his duty, under certain circumstances, to direct personally operations against subjects of the Crown; on professional grounds it is still stranger that the Duke did not perceive the disadvantage to the service of placing at its head an individual without military experience in the field.

During the summer of 1850 the Duke sustained the loss of two of his few remaining friends. On 2nd July Sir Robert Death of Sir Robert Peel. Peel expired from injuries received in a fall from his horse on Constitution Hill. It has been shown that perfect harmony did not always prevail between Peel and Wellington; that there were intervals when, owing to misunderstanding, to the Duke's deafness, and to the impatience of a military spirit with the more deliberate and circuitous courses of a politician,

* Martin's *Life of the Prince Consort*, ii. 259.

all intercourse between them was interrupted. Yet there is no room to doubt that the Duke entertained profound respect and warm personal regard for Sir Robert Peel. But the Duke was not eloquent. Occasions which moved him most deeply supplied him only with words almost uncouth in their rugged plainness. Thus, in referring in Parliament to Peel's death, he was at first so much overcome that he could utter no words at all ; when they did come, they were almost grotesquely simple.

"In all the course of my acquaintance (a greater master of rhetoric would surely have said 'friendship') with Sir Robert Peel I never knew a man in whose truth and justice I had a more lively confidence, or in whom I saw a more invariable desire to promote the public service. In the whole course of my communications with him I never knew an instance in which he did not show the strongest attachment in truth ; *and I never saw in the whole course of my life the slightest reason for suspecting that he stated anything which he did not believe to be the fact.*"

Death of Mr. Arbuthnot. Higher, fuller testimony this, than could be truthfully borne to the veracity of many a statesman who has filled a large place in the world's history.

Less conspicuous than Peel's was the other figure that passed from the stage during this summer, yet one whose loss caused deeper personal sorrow to the Duke. Arbuthnot, ever since the death of his wife, had resided constantly at Apsley House, Strathfieldsaye, or Walmer. Gentle, patient, sympathetic, and inconspicuous, he was the very opposite to the Duke in all things but his love of truth. Men and women trusted him entirely ; he became a perfect magazine of state secrets and personal confidences. Wholly devoid of personal ambition, his influence with the Duke and the part he played in removing differences between the Duke, his colleagues, and his party, had a more important effect on the political history of his time than could be claimed for many more prominent personalities. When Arbuthnot died in August, 1850, he left

the Duke without a single intimate friend with whom he A.N. 1850.
could discuss, as with a contemporary, his political past.
Fitzroy Somerset was still a constant visitor at Apsley House,
and Alava had a room there as often as he chose to occupy
it; but the gallant Somerset was a soldier and indifferent to
politics and party; Alava, though a charming and cultivated
companion, was an inveterate gossip, not over scrupulous
about the way he obtained information,* than which nothing
could be more odious in the Duke's eyes.

If between the Duke and his sons, Lord Douro and Lord The Duke in private life.
Charles Wellesley, relations could never be described as other
than friendly, neither can they be considered as intimate or
confidential. The barrier of age, which no conscious diligence
avails to surmount, was heightened and hardened between
the father and his sons by the contrast of an arduous, indefatigable activity on the one part with the easy-going indolence
of well-born, well-endowed young men on the other. In
truth they had not much in common, and it was not till after
the close of the Duke's life that his elder son set to work with
praiseworthy diligence to prepare his father's civil correspondence for publication, whereby, at immense cost, he
erected his own monument, as he said himself, to the
memory of his sire. But between age and childhood there
is no such barrier, and the Duke's fondness for children, the
infinite pains he took to give them pleasure, and the love he
received from them in return, are the subject of innumerable
anecdotes, and of affectionate remembrance by those who
experienced them in early days.

Many details, also, are remembered of his old-fashioned care- The Duke as a host.
fulness as a host. When guests arrived at Strathfieldsaye or
Walmer, each one, even were he a subaltern just joined, was
shown to his bedroom by the Duke himself. The bedrooms
at Strathfieldsaye were all supplied with the same furniture,
regardless of the size of the room; hence the large ones looked
bare, while the small were somewhat inconveniently crowded.

* *Salisbury MSS.*, 1835.

The Duke had many devices for the comfort of his guests and household; he bestowed special attention to the heating apparatus, which at one time was so powerful as nearly to cook the inmates. On the breakfast table there was a teapot over a hot-water jug, the Duke's own invention, put in front of every third place, the result not infrequently being that guests unfamiliar with the arrangement used to capsize the whole affair.

His conversation. It was natural that in his later years younger men were eager to obtain information about a life so full of remarkable experience, and the Duke was exceedingly good-natured in indulging their legitimate curiosity. Lord Mahon, of whom the Duke was very fond, was one of the most industrious of these, and his notes have been given to the public in the shape of his well-known *Conversations*. The Duke, after dinner, used to sit reading the paper with a lamp on a table beside him. Lord Mahon generally contrived to get round this table, and engage him in conversation. On one occasion the ladies at Strathfieldsaye, thinking the Duke might be wearied with this pardonable importunity, arranged, as they thought without his perceiving it, a sofa and other furniture so as to bar Lord Mahon's usual access; but his lordship was not to be baffled; he managed to scale or thread the defences, and presently was deep in interrogation. That night when, as usual, the Duke was handing the ladies their bedroom candlesticks, he remarked to one of them, with a twinkle in his eye, " Your fortifications were not very effective after all ! " He had seen through the little scheme, and was much amused at the amiable enemy's determination.

His relations with women. The love-stories of men of mark have an irresistible attraction for the rest of the world, but there remains very little to tell about Wellington's after the sunset of his early romance. His passion for Catherine Pakenham, absorbing and heart-whole as it was, did not survive the strain of severance and silence; it perished with the lapse of years. A man less scrupulous—less rigid in fulfilling the obligations

FRANCES MARY, FIRST WIFE OF THE 2ND MARQUIS OF SALISBURY.
*From an Engraving of the Picture at Hatfield.*

Vol. ii. p. 445.

of duty and honour as he interpreted them—would have pronounced its *requiescat*, and no reproach could have lain against him because he bowed to the lawful opposition which had prevented his marriage. But this was a man who was never satisfied by merely fulfilling what the world exacted of him : his own conscience and sense of justice had to be at ease, be the cost what it might ; in marrying Catherine Pakenham the cost was a heavy one, but it was paid without hesitation as a just debt. Wellington's relations with other women have been the subject of endless gossip. It must be admitted that they were numerous and, with two or three notable exceptions, not of a kind on which it profits to dwell. Unlike many men who have played great parts in the world's history, Wellington never submitted his will to a woman's ; although very susceptible of the influence of beauty and wit, he treated women either as agreeable companions or as playthings. He never allowed them to control his actions, nor, with two exceptions, did he feel acute sorrow when death or other circumstances put an end to intimacy.

The two exceptions were women in whom Wellington reposed complete confidence and with whom his friendship was absolutely without reserve. With one of these—Mrs. Arbuthnot—a *liaison*, if current reports are to be credited, was the means of revealing qualities in her which far outlived the fleeting influence of her physical charms.* In the case of the other—the second Marchioness of Salisbury—no whisper of reproach was ever uttered. From first to last there existed between her and the Duke an ideally helpful friendship and *camaraderie* of common interest. Numerous references in this work to Lady Salisbury's journals and correspondence show how useful she was in smoothing away such difficulties as were created by the Duke's austere and peremptory habits of command, and illustrate the solace which his lonely spirit

* There is at Apsley House a miniature of Mrs. Arbuthnot which, it is said, the Duke constantly wore round his neck, suspended by a chain of her hair. The hair is black or dark brown.

Æt 68. derived from constant exchange of thought with one who thoroughly understood the world and his relations with it.

After the death of his duchess in 1831, it was natural that many rumours should get afloat of Wellington's intention to marry again; but only in one case does he seem to have entertained any apprehensions on the subject—that of the Hon. Mary Ann Jervis, daughter of the 2nd Viscount St. Vincent. With this young lady he certainly had a pretty strong flirtation, and the gossips made the most of it.

"The Duke," notes Lady Salisbury, "laughs extremely at the notion of his being in love with Miss Jervis. 'What is the good of being sixty-seven if one cannot speak to a young lady?' He says she is mad, but she has talent and intelligence, though with less powers of conversation than any educated person he ever saw." *

The flirtation went on for some years, and in the end assumed a serious phase. The Duke, in writing to Lady de Ros, always referred to Miss Jervis as "the Syren."

### To Lady de Ros.

"London, August 17, 1837.—I go to Walmer Castle on Saturday . . . I spoke to the Syren about coming. . . . I don't know what to do with her if you should be gone. If you should still be there, I shall be delighted to have her. . . . Walmer Castle, October 7, 1837.— . . . Between Lord Lowther and me the Syren appears on the road to get married. . . . S. S. (Stratfieldsaye), December 3, 1837.—You may tell the Syren that I have got the clock here but am sadly in want of a clockmaker. . . . December 10.— . . . It is very hard upon me to be obliged to repair my clock myself! However, it is done, and I hope to escape being loaded with shawls! . . . S. S., January 14, 1838.— . . . I am sorry to tell you the clock is broken again. The housemaid, being, I conclude, in a conspiracy to have it repaired, broke it during my absence. . . . S. S., February 11.— . . . I have had two or three notes from the Syren, but they were about a protegé of hers for the Orphan Asylum, or about the

* Salisbury MSS., 1836.

musick for the organ here, and the mode of execution, upon which Ann. 1838. subject I have five sheets of paper which poor Gerald * and Miss Walmesly are to read. . . . *S. Saye, February 25.*— . . . I have not heard from the Syren lately. I don't think it necessary to consult Buzfuz upon any letter written as yet. . . . *London, March 5.*— . . . I saw the Syren last night at Lady Salisbury's. . . . She was looking in great force, and says she is much improved in musick, and there is an organ on the tapis; but this is not so dangerous as a clock, though, by-the-by, it is at the clockmaker's. . . . *London, May 9.*— . . . I am afraid that the concert, instead of costing 19 guineas, will give us a deal of trouble. She came to town from S. S. and, contrary to my intentions and request, settled a programme with Mr. Knivett. I have been under the necessity of altering it, and she will come up in a fury, and I shall have to ask pardon. This, to be sure, is very dangerous. . . . I will let you know if the concert should produce any *extraordinary* esclandre! . . . *May 31.*—I dined with the Syren last week. It was the day of the Queen's ball, and I returned from thence to the musick; but Lady Jersey was there and talked so much that she was interrupted. I therefore came away. . . . I hope that I shall not get into any scrape to render necessary my giving a retainer to the great lawyers in such cases. . . . *August 13.*— . . . I have presented a pianoforte in exchange for the old Walmer one, which I am going to hear on Sunday evening. This will give Rogers † fresh food for jokes; but I enjoy them myself as much as I do H. B.'s caricatures. . . . *August 11.*— . . . I should like to see the Syren married to Lord Lowther or any-body excepting myself—God bless her! I cannot conceive how she came to think of me; I am old enough to be her great-grand-father. I am going to give her a crown for singing the trio in the Cenerentola (?); mind—not a coronet! Louis Philippe gave her a crown for being the best dancer in the school at Paris; I give her one for singing a trio single-handed. . . . "

In a subsequent letter the Duke expresses his dismay at the Syren having taken up her quarters in Walmer village,

---

* The Duke's nephew, rector of Strathfieldsaye, afterwards Dean of Windsor.
† Samuel Rogers the poet.

and refers to "the gossip which it creates." Finally, in 1840, Miss Jervis married Dyce Sombre, an Indian nabob, and the Duke writes to Lady de Ros greatly relieved at "the lucky coincidence of the Black Prince appearing."

It is well known from Mr. Gleig's narrative and other sources that the Duke was liberal—lavish—in bestowing money in charity. So far as he subscribed to hospitals and other well-regulated schemes, his money was bestowed to a good purpose; but in response to private applications—which were innumerable—he was not careful to satisfy himself of their genuine nature, and there can be no doubt that he allowed himself to be frequently imposed upon. Not less doubt can there be that money given in this indiscriminate way has a mischievous effect; but had the Duke been at the pains to examine into the circumstances of all his applicants, he would have had no time to devote to other affairs; he preferred to give petitioners all and sundry the benefit of every doubt.

The following anecdote, told by Stocqueler, is well authenticated, and illustrates at once the Duke's great love of children, and his thoughtfulness for their welfare. The son of Kendall, the Duke's valet, was at school near Strathfieldsaye, and was spending a day with his father at Apsley House. The Duke's bell rang; Kendall, answering it, was followed by the lad into the study.

"Whose boy is that?" asked the Duke quickly.

"Mine, your Grace," replied Kendall, "and I humbly ask your Grace's pardon for his coming into the room, not knowing your Grace was here."

"Oh! that is nothing," quoth the Duke; "but I didn't know you had a son, Kendall. Send him in and leave him with me."

So the boy—greatly trembling—was sent in to the Duke, who asked him if he knew to whom he was speaking.

"Yes, sir—your Grace, I mean."

"Oh, my little fellow," answered the Duke, "it will be

easier for you to call me 'sir.' You call your schoolmaster 'sir,' don't ye? Call me 'sir' too, if you choose. Now I wonder if you can play draughts."

"Yes, sir."

"Come on then; we'll have a game, and I'll give you two men."

Down they sat; the boy said afterwards that he really thought he was going to win the second game, but his doughty antagonist laid a trap for him, and chuckled mightily when he fell into it.

The games over, the Duke asked the boy a lot of questions in geography, and then said—

"Well, you shall dine with me to-day; but I shall not dine yet: would you like to see my pictures?" and he trotted him round the great gallery. Then the Duke took him among the statues—"important fellows" he said they were—but the boy said he preferred the pictures.

"I thought so," observed the Duke; "but tell me—which of these is most like your schoolmaster?"

Young Kendall picked out a bust without moustaches, which happened to be a likeness of the Duke himself.

"Oh! well," laughed the Duke, "that is a very good man of his sort. Come now, we'll go to dinner. I have ordered it early, as I suppose you dine early at school."

"At one o'clock, sir," said the lad.

"A very good hour," said the Duke. "I used to dine at one when I was at school."

They sat down *tête-à-tête*, the anxious father being told that the bell would ring when he was required. Having said grace, the Duke told the boy that he would give him a little of every dish, as he knew boys liked to taste all they saw. Dinner over, the lad was dismissed with the injunction—

"Be a good boy; do your duty; now you may go to your father."

About four years later the Duke was detained on the South Eastern railway for two hours, when travelling to

attend a meeting of the Privy Council. He was exceedingly
indignant, and communicated his complaint to Mr. Macgregor,
chairman of the company. Nothing more is known of the
incident, except this, that immediately afterwards young
Kendall was appointed to a clerkship in Mr. Macgregor's
bank at Liverpool, after which he was transferred to the
Ordnance Department in Ireland. The presumption is fair
that the Duke supplemented his income during the early
years of his clerkship, which is always insisted upon in a
bank, and which must have been far beyond the means of
his father to do.

The Duke's
personal
habits.

It is natural that those who apprehend the magnitude of
the work accomplished in a single lifetime, and the almost
invariable success of every enterprise undertaken therein,
should endeavour to ascertain the means by which such
results were attained. A strong will, extraordinary clearness
of decision and tenacity of purpose, a vigorous frame, abstemious
habits, keen common sense, powerful interest at the outset
—all these we recognise, but of such Wellington enjoyed
no monopoly. Goethe's prescription for becoming great
he followed also, as every great man has followed it,
unconsciously.

> " Wer grosses will muss sic zusammenraffen,
>     In der beschränkung zeigt sich erst der Meister."

But what was the secret economy which enabled him so to
use these means as to make himself for nearly half a century
the most conspicuous man in Europe? In truth, one part of
it was a habit so simple, so homely, that one runs perilously
near bathos in defining it. Arthur Wesley was born in that
rank of life the members of which usually wait to begin their
daily amusement or business till the world has been aired
and warmed for them, till carpets have been swept, morning
papers laid out, and a variety of other trivial offices per-
formed, the sum of which insensibly becomes essential to
what most of us set greatest store by—comfort. To secure

this, well-to-do people are generally content to surrender to
the majority of their fellow-creatures a start of about three
hours in each day—a sacrifice confirmed into invincible habit Early
by the accumulated sanction of generations. The world at rising.
large loses nothing by lazy people lying in bed ; idle folk out
of the way are at least out of mischief. But Wellington,
setting no store by comfort, knew that to get through his
work would take all the time he could give to it : he rose at
six every morning, thereby adding three hours to each working
day. Think what this daily increment amounted to, reckoning
from the time he went to India, for there is no evidence to
show that he practised early rising before that period. Three
hours a day for fifty-five years (allowing for leap years) amount
to 61,359 hours—2,556 days—almost exactly seven years of
wakefulness and, constituted as he was, of activity, filched
from fashion and added to his life—undoubtedly a large factor
in the volume of his life-work, even if the quality thereof be
attributed entirely to his intellectual powers. The greater
part of those wonderful despatches, much also of his private
correspondence, was penned before most of the writer's friends
had left their breakfast tables. Here is the secret of his
command of leisure for hunting in the Peninsula, for parties
and balls which he attended so regularly, for constant presence
when the House of Lords was sitting.

It may be urged that few men have strength to sustain
such long days and short nights. Perhaps so, but how many
of us have tested our powers systematically—how many have
tried resolutely to acquire the practice of compressing sleep
into six hours out of the twenty-four, recouping ourselves
at odd moments, such as Wellington's snatches of slumber
between the acts at Talavera and Salamanca or on the way-
side at Quatre-Bras? Those who should break down under
this training could never remain seventeen hours and a
half in the saddle, as Wellington did at Waterloo, his mind
all the time being filled with work of such poignant and
critical kind as few men's minds are ever applied to. Still

less could one of them face such a day's duty as Wellington discharged in the last, the eighty-third year of his
life. The anniversary meeting of the Elder Brethren of
the Trinity House fell on a very wet day. Wellington, as
Master, joined his colleagues on the Tower Hill, and went
with them to Deptford, where a carriage was in waiting to
carry him to the Trinity Almshouses. " I prefer walking,"
said the Master; and despite all remonstrance, taking a
mackintosh cape out of his pocket, trudged off at the head of
the Brethren through the streets of that comfortless borough,
a march of nearly an hour. It is the custom to present each
of the Brethren with a bouquet at the Almshouses, and the
Duke always used to give his away on leaving. The prize
was greatly coveted by the girls, who had a tradition that she
who received it was sure to be married first, and they crowded
eagerly round the Master at the end of the proceedings. The
Duke, entering into the spirit of the thing, kept them for
some time in suspense, and then, diving into the throng,
handed it to a pretty girl standing behind the others. Then
he returned to the annual banquet at the Trinity House,
observing, as he sat down, that he must get away early, as he
had to attend a juvenile party that night at Windsor Castle.
He remained at table till nearly ten, returned to Apsley
House to change his dress, and made his obeisance to the
Queen at Windsor before midnight. No mean performance,
this, for anybody, let alone an octogenarian !

On 22nd February, 1851, Lord John Russell, after the
defeat of his party in the House of Commons on Mr. Locke
King's County Franchise Bill, placed the resignation of himself and his colleagues in the hands of her Majesty, who at
once sent for Lord Stanley. He, however, being unable to
command the support of the Peelite Conservatives, in turn
advised the Queen to retain her present Minister; but, just
as the Peelites held aloof from Lord Stanley because of his
avowed policy of Protection, so they declined to support

*A long day's work.*

*The Duke's last political act.*

a Whig Cabinet pledged to a measure aimed against Papal Ann. 1852.
aggression. Lord Aberdeen, leader of the Peelites, next was sent
for, but he declined the attempt on the ground that no Ministry
could stand which should decline, as his must do, to proceed
with the Ecclesiastical Tithes Bill. Under these circumstances,
to relieve the deadlock, Lord Stanley undertook, on the 25th,
an attempt to form a Government, but by the 27th he had
realised that it was impossible, and he resigned. In this
dilemma—unprecedented since the Prince Regent's difficulties
after the assassination of Mr. Perceval in 1812—the Queen
resorted for advice to her old and well-tried servant. A
memorandum of the circumstances, drawn up by the Prince
Consort, was laid before the Duke on 1st March, ending with
this sentence—"The Queen requests the Duke of Wellington's opinion upon the problem here proposed." The Duke's
conclusion was that "the party still filling the offices, till
her Majesty's pleasure shall be declared, is the one best calculated to carry on the Government at the present moment,"
and in accordance therewith, Lord John Russell was sent
for once more, resumed office, and the *impasse* was at
an end.

Yet the Duke was destined to see one more Ministry in
office, this time a Conservative one. His reiterated warnings
and Prince Albert's wise foresight, combined with the thinly
veiled threats of invasion contained in the speeches of the
new ruler of France, Napoleon III.,* to rouse Ministers to
a sense of responsibility for the security of the country. There
were at that time not more than 24,000 regular troops in
the United Kingdom, absolutely without any reserve. The
Militia had ceased, after the peace of 1815, to exist except in
name ; Lord John Russell's Cabinet so far adopted the Duke's
advice as to devise a scheme for creating the force afresh, with
provision for fourteen days' drill in each year, the service of
each regiment to be confined to the limits of its own county.

* The French Ambassador had been recalled from the Court of St.
James.

Æт. 82.

Defeat of
the Russell
Ministry.

Both Prince Albert and the Duke of Wellington perceived that the scheme was miserably inadequate; it was a beginning, however, in the right direction, and was duly embodied in a bill. But there was a lion in the path. In the previous December Lord John Russell had been under the disagreeable necessity of conveying to Lord Palmerston the Queen's desire that he should surrender the seals of the Foreign Office, in consequence of his indiscretion in expressing approval of Louis Napoleon's *coup d'état*. Palmerston, therefore, quitted the Cabinet, and soon appeared as an enemy on the flank of his ancient colleagues. On 20th February, 1852, he persuaded the House of Commons to reject the Militia Bill by a majority of eleven votes, and the following day Ministers resigned. Lord Stanley, who had become Earl of Derby in June, 1851, on the death of his father, undertook to form a Government, which, as the Peelites still held aloof, was in a hopeless minority in the House of Commons. Except Lord Malmesbury, who took the Foreign Office, and Mr. Disraeli, who entered office for the first time as Chancellor of the Exchequer, the new Ministry was composed of men untried and unknown. It derived its distinctive name from a conversation between the Duke and the Prime Minister in the House of Lords. The Duke was eagerly inquiring of Lord Derby the names of his new colleagues, some of which he had never heard before. "Who? who?" he asked repeatedly, and the "Who-who?" Ministry was a name that stuck to the Cabinet throughout its brief existence.

The Duke
and the
Militia.

Brief as that existence was, for it survived the July elections only a few weeks, it succeeded in framing and carrying a Militia Bill which met the Duke's requirements more fully than the rejected measure, thereby laying the foundation of the existing organisation of auxiliary land forces. It was in support of this measure that the Duke of Wellington made his last speech in the House of Lords. The Militia of the United Kingdom have had to pass through a good deal of official discouragement and popular ridicule, but all practical soldiers recognise how fully the force has justified the Duke's <sub>Ann. 1852.</sub> forecast of their value.*

"Take the battle of Waterloo: look at the number of British <sub>His last speech.</sub> troops at that battle. I can tell your lordships that in that battle there were sixteen battalions of Hanoverian Militia just formed, under the command of a nobleman, late the Hanoverian Ambassador here, Count Kielmansegge, who behaved most admirably. . . . I say, my lords, that however much I admire highly disciplined troops, and most especially British disciplined troops, I tell you you must not suppose that others cannot become so too; and no doubt if you begin with the formation of militia corps under this Act of Parliament, they will in time become what their predecessors in the militia were: and if ever they do become what their predecessors in the militia were, you may rely on it they will perform all the services they may be required to perform. My lords, I recommend you to adopt this measure as the commencement of a completion of a peace establishment. It will give you a constitutional force: it may not be at first, or for some time, everything we could desire, but by degrees it will become what you want, an efficient auxiliary force to the regular army."

Brief as was the life of the Derby Ministry, it outlasted the <sub>Death of Wellington.</sub> days of him whom Disraeli aptly described as "the sovereign master of duty." On Monday, 13th September, the Duke was in excellent health and spirits, took a walk through the grounds of Walmer Castle, entered his stable and spoke to his groom about the horses. On returning to the castle he wrote a note to his niece, Lady Westmorland, telling her that he would meet her at six o'clock the following evening on her arrival at Dover. He dined in company with his son and daughter-in-law, Lord and Lady Charles Wellesley, and went to bed about ten o'clock. His servant called him next morning shortly after six, but the Duke did not rise at once as was

---

* A week later he moved for a return of the troops carried in the ill-fated *Birkenhead* transport.

his custom, and the man returned at seven. About what followed there have been printed as many conflicting accounts as there have been writers. The following is from a letter written two days later by the Hon. Mrs. Boyle to Lady de Ros:—

> "I think you may like to hear all Lady Westmorland told Henry * last night as to the last days of the Duke's life. She had given him a rendezvous at Dover the day before yesterday, and when his servant went into his room at seven, he said to him he should want the carriage to go to Dover. On the servant going again into his room soon after, he said, 'I feel very ill; send for the apothecary.' These were the last words he spoke. They think he was conscious for some time after, for he followed them with his eyes about the room, and motioned that he should like to sit in the armchair into which he was moved, and where he *remained*. Expresses were sent for doctors, but all were out of town, and M'Arthur † attended him to the last. There seems to have been no pain, and when Lady Westmorland came, just after all was over, she went into his room, and her impression was that he looked as she had often seen him, having a little sleep in his chair. The day before he appeared quite as usual, and was playing with his grandchildren the evening before."

Such was the peaceful end.

> "O motus animarum! atque o certamina tanta!
> Pulveris exigui jactus."

After a life so full of accomplishment—after a service so long and devoted—it avails not to dwell on the closing scene. Of the obsequies which followed, the departed, had he had the ordering of them, would have dispensed with the pomp; a simple grave, a prayer, a volley over the sod, such had been the Duke's parting with many a tired comrade in the field; we may rest assured that he wished no more elaborate ceremony for himself. But the nation would not forego the utmost tribute of reverence. The Queen, setting aside the

* The Duke's nephew, afterwards first Earl Cowley.
† The doctor at Walmer.

precedent of Nelson, for whom the Sovereign himself decreed Ann. 1852.
a public funeral, decreed that the Duke's remains should be
guarded until Parliament should meet in November, in order
that " such honours should not appear to emanate from the
Crown alone, and that the two Houses of Parliament should
have an opportunity, by their previous sanction, of stamping
the proposed ceremony with increased solemnity, and of
associating themselves with her Majesty in paying honour to
the memory of one whom no Englishman can name without
pride and sorrow." The Army was ordered to wear mourning in the usual way, with the addition that officers on duty
were to wear a black crape scarf over the right shoulder,
black crape over the sash, and black gloves. The funeral took
place on 18th November, all the European powers, even
France, sending their representatives—except Austria, whose
uniform had recently been insulted in London on the person
of Marshal Haiman. But Wellington was a Field-Marshal
of Austria, and although no Austrian representative accompanied the remains to their last resting-place beside those of
Nelson in St. Paul's Cathedral, a funeral parade was held
in Vienna in presence of the Emperor, and twelve batteries
surrounded the *requiescat* of the great commander.

---

Few things are more wearisome than unstinted panegyric;
yet was there never an occasion which justified the most
ample tribute of praise of a public servant and of mourning
for his loss. In all the abundance of speeches and obituary
notices at the time, perhaps nothing more felicitous can be
found than the parallel drawn by Mr. Disraeli—the leader,
since the death of Lord George Bentinck in 1848, of the
revolt against the Duke's authority in Parliament—when he
moved the vote for the funeral expenses. Recalling another
soldier-statesman, Stilicho, the great Captain and Minister
of the Emperor Honorius—"Who," he asked, " can ever
forget that classic and venerable head, white with time

Æt. 83. and radiant with glory—*Stilichonis apex, et cognita fulsit canities!*" *

Several years before, the following lines had appeared in the *Morning Post* over the signature of B. Disraeli:—

### "*To the Duke of Wellington.*

" Not only that thy puissant arm could bind
   The tyrant of a world, and, conquering fate,
   Enfranchise Europe, do I deem thee great ;
   But that in all thy actions do I find
   Exact propriety : no gusts of mind
   Fitful and wild, but that continuous state
   Of ordered impulse mariners await
   In some benignant and enriching wind,
   The breath ordained by Nature.   Thy calm mien
   Recalls old Rome, as much as thy high deed ;
   Duty thine only idol, and serene
   When all are troubled ; in the utmost need
   Prescient ; thy country's servant ever seen,
   Yet sovereign of thyself whate'er may speed."

* Claudian's allusion to Stilicho's abundant white hair.

# INDEX.

THE END.

LONDON :
PRINTED BY WILLIAM CLOWES AND SONS, LIMITED,
STAMFORD STREET AND CHARING CROSS.

www.ingramcontent.com/pod-product-compliance
Lightning Source LLC
Chambersburg PA
CBHW032022110726
47901CB00004B/1171